CORDIA'S HOPE: A STORY OF LOVE ON THE FRONTIER

FOREVER LOVE BOOK TWO

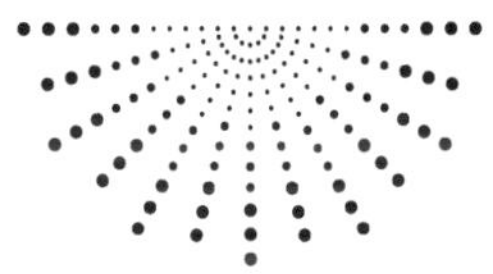

ID JOHNSON

CONTENTS

PART I

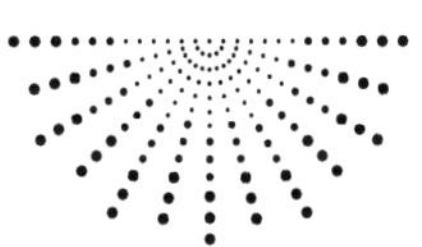

CHAPTER ONE

Hope Tucker surveyed her pupils one more time before dismissing them for the afternoon. It seemed like her class grew by a student or two every week, and at this rate, they would need a bigger schoolhouse by next fall. "Be sure to practice your letters this evening, Freddy," she said to one of the smaller students in the front row. "Take your slate home, sit by the fireplace, and practice your strokes. You'll get it in no time."

"Yes, Miss Tucker," Jimmy replied, smiling up at her with a large gap where both of his top two front teeth were missing. She patted him gently on the arm and then walked between the rows one last time. The clock showed they had two more minutes, and each child was still fast at work on their lessons, particularly the older ones in the back who would be studying for exams in just a few months. She remembered that anxious feeling; it had only been two years ago when she'd been the one brushing up on her studies in anticipation of graduating from high school, hoping to earn high enough marks to become a teacher. Now, here she was with her own class, and while she loved her work, something was missing.

She pushed those thoughts aside and cleared her throat so that she could speak loudly enough for everyone to hear. "All right, class. That is all for today. I shall see you back here bright and early in the morning."

All of the children, from the oldest to the youngest, gathered up their belongings, stopping at the cubbies and hooks along the wall to put on their coats and collect their lunch pails. Most of the older students had younger brothers and sisters, and they stopped to help them before heading out the door. None of them broke into a run until after they'd left the front porch of the building, something Hope had taught them a few months ago when the new term had started and she became the teacher of record for her hometown, Lamar, Missouri.

Grabbing a broom from the small closet across from her desk, Hope began to sweep up the day's dust and debris. There were books to straighten, shelves to dust, and the chalkboard needed erasing, but at least she didn't need to mess with the fireplace just yet. It was nearly November, and soon enough, she'd be stoking a fire in the morning and cleaning out the fireplace in the afternoon, but for now, the kids seemed warm enough with all of their bodies in one room, and she was glad to have one less duty to fulfill.

After half an hour or so of tidying up, Hope collected her own lunchbox and a stack of books before heading out the door, pulling the sweater her mother had knitted for her last fall tightly around her shoulders.

Her house was within walking distance of the school, though it was about a half-mile away. The weather was nice enough, no rain today, and too early for snow, so she took off with a pleasant smile on her face, wondering what her mother had planned for dinner.

Hope hadn't made it too far down the road when she heard the sound of a cart pulling up behind her, which wasn't unusual in a growing town, but when it slowed and came to a stop just in front of her, she turned her head to see who the driver might be, and a rush of pink filled her cheeks.

"Howdy there, Miss Hope," a familiar voice called down to her as she stopped alongside the road and looked up into the face of Jimmy Brooks. "Thought you might wanna ride home."

"Good afternoon, Jimmy," Hope replied, holding onto her books and lunch pail with both hands in front of her. "Thank you, kindly, but I think I'd rather walk. It's such a nice day out."

"Now, I can't imagine you ain't in a hurry to get home to your mama's good cooking. I'm sure you can hot foot it up the road with the best of 'em, but with ol' River here pullin' us along, you'll be home in no time." He gestured at the large brown horse at the front of the cart.

Hope continued to take him in for a second, surveying her options. She had known Jimmy since she was a baby. His mother, Susannah, was best friends with Hope's mother, Cordia, and even though Hope had lived much of her childhood out on the family farm, the two families spent many a weekend together whenever Hope's family came to town to visit her grandparents. Once her parents had come to Lamar to stay, Jimmy had attended school with her but ended up quitting before he graduated so he could help his father and brothers on their own farm. Still, he was a smart enough fellow, easy on the eyes with his dark hair and brown eyes, and Hope certainly didn't dislike him; she just wasn't sure if she felt the same way about him as he obviously felt about her.

"Well..." she began, looking at the cart and then down the road. She could practically see the turn she'd have to make to get home from here, it was so close.

Jimmy took her hesitation as opportunity. He hopped down from his seat and came around to help her up, offering his hand. "Come on, Hopey. I came all the way to town just for you."

She glanced at his hand, rough and stained from working the crops, and slipped her much smoother one into it momentarily so she could make it into the carriage without taking a spill. Jimmy held her belongings in his free hand while she pulled herself up and took a seat. He handed her books and other things to her with a smile and then dashed back around to take his seat while Hope tried not to laugh at his enthusiasm.

"How did your lessons go today?" Jimmy asked as he shook the reins, getting River to start down the road. "Them kids mindin' you all right?"

"Oh, yes. They're wonderful," Hope said, her smile growing as she thought about her pupils. "It was a lovely day. We made a lot of progress."

"That's good. I heard some of the folks at the store this mornin' talkin' about what a fine job you're doin'. Made me smile."

Hope wasn't sure how she felt about a group of people standing around in the general store talking about her. While she was glad to hear it was positive, it still made her slightly nervous. It was one thing to think about her students going home each night and telling their parents what she'd taught them, but to think those same adults would join together to discuss her, well, she wasn't sure what to think about that.

"Hope, you all right?" Jimmy asked, a tinge of concern knitting his brow together. "I meant it as a compliment, that everybody thinks the school board done good pickin' you as the new teacher."

"Oh, yes, I'm fine." She hoped her smile reassured him. "That's nice to hear."

"I know you've always wanted to be a schoolteacher, and now you are one. And a good one."

"Thank you." Hope wasn't sure what else to say. She could see the turn now; they were almost to Broadway Street. Turning left would take them to the downtown area where the new courthouse, the bank, and the general store Jimmy had mentioned all stood. The church her family attended, First Baptist, was also just a ways up the road to the left. To the right, there were lots of newer homes, all having been built after the war when so much of this part of town had been reduced to ashes. That was also the way Jimmy would turn to take her home, to the house her mother had grown up in, where Hope had lived for the last ten years while her mother helped take care of her ailing parents. Jimmy pulled the horse to the right, and Hope held in a sigh of relief that she was almost home. He was a nice enough man, but the compliments were making her uncomfortable, and Hope was hoping the conversation wouldn't turn to anything more serious.

"We finished clearin' the north field this afternoon," Jimmy said, regaining her attention.

Realizing she'd been rude not to ask about his day, Hope replied,

"Oh, that's good to hear. I bet your father's happy to have that finished."

"Yep. At this rate, we should have everything harvested before the cold weather sets in."

"Good. I'm sure we'll need it. They're sayin' it's supposed to be a rather cold winter." Hope didn't know what else to say about crops. Even though her daddy had been a farmer for years when she was younger, she'd spent most of that time inside with her mama and sister, usually with her nose in a book. She knew enough, she supposed, but she didn't consider herself a farmgirl by any stretch of the imagination, and the thought of marrying a farmer made her cringe. She'd be absolutely useless on a farm.

Jimmy pulled the cart to a halt out front of a large two-story brick home, which sat well up a small rising hill from the road. Hope gathered up her things, wondering why he was staring at her, and was just about to jump down from the seat without his hand when he said, "Can I call on you, Hope Tucker? That is… would you mind if I came around from time to time? We could go for a stroll in the park, have a picnic, somethin' like that. I know how you like your books. Maybe you could… read to me, or somethin'. What do you think?"

Hope realized that her trepidations about getting in the cart in the first place circled around the conversation she was having at that moment. In her heart, she'd known it was just a matter of time before Jimmy Brooks asked to court her, and Hope had been thinking about her answer for more time than seemed right or normal. "I, uh…" she began, not wanting to hurt his feelings, while at the same time, she knew in her heart this wasn't the best match for her, not that there was anyone else on the horizon. "I… I think, perhaps, you should speak to my daddy." There—that answer should hold for a spell. Let him take it up with her father.

Jimmy's eyes widened slightly, as if that wasn't the answer he was expecting at all, but he nodded. "I reckon that's a fair response. I ain't talked to your daddy yet. Probably should do that." He let go a soft chuckle, a mixture of embarrassment and likely admiration of her gumption. "But if'n he says yes, you'd go?"

Hope inhaled sharply. He was nothing if not persistent. "Of

course," she replied, knowing her father would say whatever she asked him to say. She just needed to speak to him before Jimmy Brooks had the chance. But then, she had a feeling her father wouldn't be too quick to supply an answer anyway; he'd want to think on it, run it by her mother. Will Tucker wasn't one for making rash decisions, especially not when it came to something important, like the hand of his eldest daughter.

Jimmy grinned so wide Hope thought she could see his back teeth. "Well, all right, then," he said, slapping his hands against his denim pants. "I'll call on Mr. Tucker directly." He leapt down off of the cart and shot around to offer his hand, which she took, and Hope sprung out of the cart as quickly as she could. "It was nice seein' you, Miss Hope."

"You, too, Mr. Brooks," she replied, not knowing what brought on the sudden formality other than nervousness. She gave him a little nod and then scurried up the drive, hoping he didn't stand there and watch her the whole time, but when Hope was near the front porch, she turned back to look, and Jimmy was still standing next to the cart. He gave a little wave, which she returned, and then she darted into the house, closing the door behind her hard enough that the jamb shook.

"Is that you, Hope?" Her mother walked in from the kitchen, wiping her hands on her apron. "Everything okay, darling? You mad at the door?"

"Sorry, Mama," Hope replied, setting her books down on a table near the stairs so she'd be sure to take them up later and crossing to kiss her mother's cheek. "I'm just a little out of sorts."

Cordia opened her arms and pulled her daughter in close, smoothing down her dark, curly hair as she did so. "You wanna talk about it?" she asked as Hope took a step back.

Looking into hazel eyes the same color as her own, Hope replied, "Jimmy Brooks gave me a ride home from school."

Her mother's eyebrows lifted. "Oh? That was nice of him."

Hope let out a sigh and walked into the kitchen where her sister sat working on her sewing in the corner, keeping her mother company while she started dinner. Faith was two years younger than Hope and had graduated high school in the spring. She was an impeccable seamstress and could sew anything. She looked up from the tiny stitches she was laying on a gown and smiled, but once she saw Hope's expression, her mood dampened. "You don't look like you had a good day at all, sister."

"Thank you for noticing." Hope set her lunch pail down on the counter, not wanting to think about refilling it just now. Maybe there'd be leftovers she could take with her the next day. From the smell of it, her mother was making something with roast in it, maybe a stew.

"I am confused," Cordia admitted, opening the lid to the pot on the fire and giving it a good stir. "You said Jimmy gave you a ride home, but I don't quite understand why you are upset about this. He's a friend of the family. We see them every Sunday at church. His mama has been my best friend since I was in pigtails."

"Your curly hair could never be tamed by pigtails," Faith commented as she picked back up on her sewing.

"True." Cordia giggled. "At any rate, I suppose I don't see why you're upset, Hope."

Pulling out a chair at the table near Faith, Hope sat down, and once her mother had finished tending the fire, she joined her daughters. In a quiet voice, Hope began to explain. "Jimmy asked if he could call on me." Her mother's mouth made an O shape, but she didn't speak. "I wasn't sure what to say, so I told him he'd need to speak to Daddy."

Faith laughed, and Hope turned her head sharply in her sister's direction. "I don't know what's so funny. Maybe if you hadn't been in love with Frankie Tyler since you were five years old, you'd understand why this is problematic."

"I'm sorry." Faith tried to rein in her merriment. "I truly wasn't laughing at you. I was only thinking of Daddy asking Jimmy a hundred and one questions about why he's good enough to date his daughter, that's all."

Cordia even chuckled at the idea, and it brought a smile to Hope's face. "Well, maybe that's why I suggested it."

"Hope, honey, I understand you wanting to spare Jimmy's feelings. He's a nice young man. But if you're not interested in courting him, all you have to do is say so. You don't owe him any explanation other than that."

Hope's eyebrows arched as she considered her mother's response. "But, Mama, isn't that rude?" she finally asked.

Folding her hands in front of her on the table, Cordia shook her head. "I'm sure that response won't be what he wants to hear, Hope, but as long as you are polite, that's all that matters. All you need to say the next time he asks is, 'No, thank you,' or if you'd like, 'I value your friendship, but I do not have any romantic inclinations toward you.' That should be sufficient."

Hope nodded, but the thought of actually saying that to someone made her stomach churn. It felt like she should at least give Jimmy the chance to prove himself to her, though she was almost certain she wouldn't ever want to be anything more than friends with the young man, and that only because their families were so close. It would make for an awkward Sunday get together if she told Jimmy she didn't want to court him, but then, it would whether she gave him a chance or not. And the longer she let things go on and get misconstrued, perhaps the more difficult it would be.

"Did any boy you didn't like ever ask you to court him, Mama?" Faith asked, laying her project aside for a moment.

Their mother's eyes went a little wide, and she cleared her throat. "I guess you could say that," she replied. "A couple of times. You must be hungry, honey. Let me get you a snack. Dinner won't be ready for another couple of hours, just in time for your daddy to get home from the bank."

Hope and Faith exchanged glances, realizing their mother was keeping something from them. Cordia went to the ice box and pulled out the milk, pouring a glass before putting the bottle back in, and then opened up the old cookie jar and pulled out a couple of oatmeal raisin cookies, sliding them on a plate and bringing them back to the table.

"Thank you," Hope said, smelling the goodness of her grandmother's recipe. She felt like a little girl again. "Mama, do you not want to talk about your suitors? Because, if you do want to talk about them, I'm sure Faith and I would like to hear."

"We would," Faith agreed. "And I would also like milk and cookies." She batted her long eyelashes at her mother, who chuckled at her youngest's antics as she got up to make a second trip to the ice box.

She set Faith's plate and glass in front of her, taking the gown her daughter had been working on and moving it away so that it wouldn't get dirty, just as she might've taken a doll away if Faith were still a small child.

Cordia let out a soft sigh and then a small smile formed across her mouth. "When I was a little girl, Grandma Jane and Grandpa Isaac were good friends with the Adams family, as they are now. We used to go out there near every Sunday for a good meal and socialization. Grandma would visit with your Great-Aunt Margaret, and Grandpa would go out to the barn with Uncle Arthur. I spent most of my time running around the pastures with the boys."

"With Zacharia and Peter?" Faith asked. "Isn't John quite a bit younger than you?"

"John wasn't even born yet, not until I was too old to be running around outside," their mother reminded them. "Sometimes Zacharia and Peter would be there, but they're younger than I am, too. No, it was mainly their older brother, Jaris, and their cousin… Carey."

Hope saw a shadow pass across her mother's face when she spoke the first name and it grew darker with mention of the second. She couldn't remember many details about Jaris Adams having only heard his name a few times associated with his service, but Carey everyone in town had heard of. He was the one who told Quantrill how best to get into Lamar, which led to the arsenal exploding and most of the town burning down. There was still a hole in the attic upstairs from a cannon ball that struck this very house. Hope knew her grandfather still suffered from a gunshot wound he'd received that awful night.

"You used to run around with Carey Adams?" Faith was just as shocked as Hope was, she could see it in her sister's face. "Why have you never mentioned this before?"

"Oh, that was a long time ago," their mother said dismissively. "And it's never come up. I didn't see the point in speaking about things that happened ages ago."

"You talk like you're as old as Grandma," Faith interjected. "Mama, what does this have to do with courting? Are you gonna tell us you were courted by Carey Adams?"

"Or Jaris Adams?" Hope said a prayer it was the celebrated

Confederate officer who had been her mother's beau and not the awful militiaman who'd betrayed his town.

"Actually, it was both of them." Cordia's voice had a far off quality to it as she spoke. "I was meant to marry Jaris, but he died in the war. It was a terrible tragedy. I had already met your father by then and had fallen in love with him. I didn't know how to tell Jaris I didn't love him like that. He was a dear friend." She paused for a moment, her eyes misty, and then turned her attention to Hope. "I know what it's like to say yes to something you don't want to agree to in order to spare someone's feelings, honey. But trust me, it can only lead to trouble."

Hope nodded, understanding her mother's point in bringing up the past now. She had a million questions, but asking them seemed like prying, and she took a swallow of her milk instead of continuing to probe.

Faith was always the one with the most gumption between the pair of them, however, so she didn't mind making their mother uncomfortable. "What about Carey? He courted you, too?"

Standing, Cordia went back across the kitchen to tend the stew and fiddle with a few other items before she returned and said, "I didn't have much of a say in that matter. He was conniving, sneaky even." She lowered her voice and added, "Your grandmother thought he was a fine catch."

Hope's eyes shot up to the ceiling, as if she might somehow see into her grandparents' room where they were both taking an afternoon nap. It was hard for her to imagine her grandmother could've ever thought Carey Adams was a catch since she wouldn't even speak his name now, but if she felt foolish for letting him talk her into courting her only child, perhaps that's why.

"What happened?" Faith asked, an excited look on her face. "Did Daddy show up and whoop 'im?"

Laughing, Cordia said, "Something like that. There was a big misunderstanding between your father and I, all due to Carey Adams stealing the letters I'd written to Will and destroying them. When Will found out the truth, well, there wasn't much Carey Adams could do."

"And then he was killed during the raid, so it doesn't matter," Faith added in. "It's too bad Jaris died, but think on what mighta happened if he hadn't. Do you think you would've married him, or would you have found a way to tell him you were in love with Daddy?"

"Oh, I would've found a way," Cordia assured her girls. "It isn't very often a love like the kind I found comes along." Now, their mother was glowing. "It would've been difficult, though, and I could've saved us both a lot of trouble if I'd just been honest with him from the beginning." Her hazel eyes focused on Hope again, and she nodded, understanding what her mother was getting at. Cordia pushed her chair out again. "I'm going to go check on your grandparents. Keep an eye on dinner, please, Hope."

"Yes, Mama." She watched her mother leave the room before finishing her last cookie and taking another drink. It had been a day of revelations.

"I always wondered what happened to that Carey Adams," Faith said, pushing her empty dishes aside and picking up her gown.

"Whose gown is that?" Hope wanted to change the subject. "That's a pretty green."

"It's Mrs. Peltzer's," Faith replied. "She's gonna wear it to her granddaughter's wedding. I just need to finish adding in a few more details."

"I'm sure she'll look lovely." Hope gathered up the dishes and carried them to the sink.

"I wonder if he was shot by his own men, if Quantrill ended him on the way out since his plans were foiled," her sister continued, but Hope wasn't ready to be pulled into her game.

"I've got some studying to do for my lessons tomorrow. I'm going to head upstairs. Keep an eye on dinner until Mama comes back?"

Faith rested the gown on her lap and looked up at her sister. The sun was coming in through the curtains, and her light brown hair had a sheen to it. While Hope was the spitting image of their mother, Faith tended to look more like the Tucker side of the family, and their father often mentioned how much she reminded him of his deceased sister, Julia, though her hair had been blonde, and Faith's was more of a caramel brown. Her eyes were the same shade of blue as their aunts, though, he said, and that fire that kept Faith fighting when most people would just step back he said also reminded him of his tenacious sister. Sometimes, Hope wished she could be more like Faith, that she could just go after her dreams without looking for a safety net.

"You should say no," Faith said, her tone even. "Jimmy Brooks isn't the one for you, sis."

"I know," Hope said with a nod, appreciating her sister's insight and her candor. "It'll be hard…"

"But like Mama said, better to break his heart now than in two or three years."

"True."

"Or marry someone you don't love. You deserve to find what Mama and Daddy have, what Frankie and I have."

Another reason to be jealous of her little sister, Hope thought. "Thank you, Faith. I'll see you at supper." She bounded out of the room, toward the stairs, before Faith could make any more case for why Hope needed to stop trying to please everyone else and put herself first for a change.

CHAPTER TWO

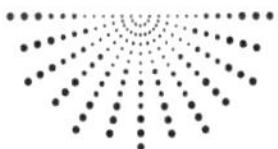

Lola Adams was tall, with strawberry-blonde hair that hung well past her waist when it was let down, which it wasn't presently, but the wind caught loose tendrils and whipped them from the bun atop her head, and Hope was careful not to walk too close to her friend for fear of getting entangled in her tresses.

"I don't quite understand what the problem is," Lola said quietly as they headed toward her carriage. Sunday meeting was over, and most everyone was headed to a nice meal with friends and family, these women included. Most Sundays, Hope's folks headed out to Aunt Margaret and Uncle Arthur's home after church, and since Lola had married their grandson, Ben, she would also be there. Lola had been Hope's best friend ever since her family moved to Lamar when she was still wearing pink bows in her hair, and if Hope felt able to confide in anyone in the world, other than her mother, Lola would be that person.

"What do you mean?" Hope asked, not sure what she'd explained so poorly that Lola didn't follow. "Jimmy wants to court me, and I am not interested in doing so."

"But... why not give him a chance?" Lola urged, stopping short of her carriage and looking past Hope for a moment to see Ben talking to his Uncle John. "How do you know you don't like 'im if you haven't given 'im a chance?"

Hope was a little surprised to hear her friend say that. She thought her advice would be similar to what her mother and sister had told her a few days ago when Jimmy had first asked if she'd like to see him. "Lola, I already know Jimmy well enough to be sure I don't have that sort of feelings for him."

"He's a good man. You could build a house out there near his folks. Then you wouldn't have to teach school anymore."

Hope's eyes widened. "Why would you say that, Lola? You know how much I love my work." Her friend had been there with her the entire time Hope was taking her exams and waiting to hear whether or not she'd scored high enough to even qualify to become a teacher. She'd been there when the superintendent of schools was considering her application and when Hope had earned the job.

"I know you do, Hope. I'm sorry. I'm not trying to be quarrelsome. It's just… you always dreamt of going to a place where students really needed a teacher. What did you call it? Unsettled territory? Wild and dangerous? I had a feeling at the time you wouldn't actually ever leave Lamar. I guess I'm just trying to say, teaching might not be exactly what you thought it was. You certainly haven't gone off into any lawless place, looking for poor wretched children to help. Which I'm thankful for." Lola reached out and touched her arm, and Hope considered snatching it away as each word burned her ears more and more. "I just think it might be time to settle down and have a family and let those dreams go."

Hope studied Lola's face for a while, not sure what to say. She'd had no idea her friend thought she'd given up on her dreams by taking the position in their hometown. "I still think about all that, Lola. I do think, someday, maybe I will go somewhere else, somewhere I can really make a difference. But these children need me, too. This might not be the lawless, wild place I spoke of when I was younger and didn't know the world so well, but these kids still need a schoolteacher."

"Yes, of course they do, Hope. And they're very blessed to have you." Her friend smiled sympathetically, and Hope wasn't sure if she was sorry for what she'd said or that she'd hurt her feelings, but she wouldn't have time to press it further as Ben had arrived and Lola would be headed out. He spoke to Hope briefly, and she forced a smile, not sure what he'd even said. "We'll see you at the farm."

With a nod, Hope backed away so Ben could turn the carriage and noted her father sitting alone in their own cart, likely waiting for the girls to all stop chatting and get in already. Hope headed over, wondering whether she wanted to confide in him at this moment or not but knowing for certain he'd find a way to make her feel better.

Will Tucker didn't say much unless something needed to be said. Hope was fairly certain he would've rather stayed out on their farm where he didn't have to see many people if the choice had been solely his, but when her grandfather had offered him a position at the bank, and her grandmother fell and broke her hip, everyone had agree that moving back to Lamar was best for the whole family. Of course, he was able to learn banking quickly and had ended up with Isaac Pike's job as bank president as soon as her grandfather was ready to retire. Now, both of her grandparents' health was poor, and they didn't leave the house even on Sundays for service. Her mother worked tirelessly to care for them, and Hope didn't feel bad about leaving the farm at all, except for on occasions like this when she saw her father so uncomfortable. Crowds were certainly not his forte.

She pulled herself up into the seat next to him. "Hope, I would've helped you up."

"It's okay, Daddy," she said, secretly glad she'd managed to sneak up on him. "You don't wanna talk to the townsfolk today?"

He chuckled and leaned back slightly against the wooden slats that made up the back of the driver's seat. "Not anymore today. Are you okay? You look troubled."

Hope scooted over, and her father put his arm around her, just as he would've done if she was still six years old and lost a doll. "I was just telling Lola about Jimmy, that's all."

"Oh, I see." He patted her shoulder but didn't say more. She had already spoken to him briefly about Jimmy's request, and Jimmy had stopped by the bank to discuss it with him, but being the diplomat he was, Will had told him he needed some time to consider the situation, and Jimmy was likely halfway across town by now. Hope hadn't even looked his direction during the service for fear he might think she had an answer for him—which she supposed she did, though she didn't want to speak it.

"Daddy, do you think I've given up on my dreams?" She blurted out the question before she could even consider how harsh it might sound spilling out of her mouth when she was still upset at Lola.

He raised an eyebrow at her, and Hope dropped her eyes to her boots, thinking he might agree with Lola's assessment. "Why would you ask that?" Will finally asked. "Who's puttin' thoughts in your head?"

"No one." She glanced back up and could tell instantly he didn't buy it. "Lola. She said I should just marry Jimmy and be a farmer's wife."

Will nodded. "And how exactly does that mean you've already given up on your dreams since you haven't done that?"

Hope spun around, putting her knee up on the seat for a second before she dropped it and took a more ladylike position, still turned to face her father. "Don't you remember, Daddy, when I used to say I was going to head out West and teach at a school where the kids really needed me? Where the parents were outlaws and saloon girls?" She lowered her voice for that last phrase, afraid some of the other church goers flocking across the yard might overhear.

He chuckled. "I remember that. Are you saying you think you aren't doing what you always intended because you are here and not out in Colorado or California or some place?"

"Or Texas…."

"Now, that's south, honey."

Hope cocked an eyebrow at him, and her father laughed. "I know that, Daddy. It's still lawless."

"I think, if you were to do that, Hope, you'd find out people are about the same wherever you go. Besides, you are making a difference here. I see it. People come in the bank all the time talking about how wonderful you are with their children, how much they're learning."

"But Daddy…." She wasn't even sure how that sentence was

supposed to end. "What if I did miss my calling because this was the comfortable, safe choice?"

Her father looked over his shoulder, and Hope realized her mother and sister were outside of the church building now, though they continued to speak with some other women, and Hope knew it could still be several minutes before they made it over to the carriage. Frankie hung back a few feet behind Faith, likely trying not to listen to women-talk but not able to give his betrothed more than few feet of space either.

"Hope, you know I've always encouraged you to do what speaks to your heart. Your mother, on the other hand.... She doesn't do so well with loved ones being away. If you were to try for a position in one of those lawless lands you speak of, you do need to talk it over with her first. I know you can handle yourself. You been shooting bottles like a deadeye since you were knee high to a grasshopper." She laughed. "But I can't imagine not having you here, and I'm not sure you understand how lonely it can be, striking out on your own and leaving everything you know behind you."

She soaked in his words, knowing he spoke from experience. He was about her age when he'd joined the Union Army and marched his way across several states, all on his own. She saw her mother laughing with Susannah, carefree, and knew she'd likely break her mother's heart if she pursued leaving Lamar. Deep inside of Hope, there was a fire still burning, telling her she needed to try or else she'd always live with regret. It had been just an ember this morning, but Lola had stoked the flame, and now, Hope felt she had more to consider than just Jimmy Brooks and his proposal.

"What was it like, Daddy?" she asked. "Being out there all alone."

He shrugged, and she thought he might not answer. She knew he didn't like to talk about the war much. "It was lonesome most times. I made friends quick. People like Frank." She nodded—Frankie's father. "But I wanted nothing more than to come back here, to your mother. To my sister. Family's the most important thing in the world, Hope. You can't forget that."

Hope stared into her father's eyes for a long moment before she nodded. The sound of her mother and sister brought her back to reality, and she remembered she was sitting in her mother's seat. "Thanks, Daddy," she said quietly, and he tilted his head down to let her know she was welcome before turning to step down from the cart so he could help her mother in. Hope jumped down, too, and as she turned her head, she saw Jimmy Brooks standing by the church. She'd thought he'd left, but he was still there, staring at her. Tears filled her eyes, and Hope had to look away. Maybe he was just one man, maybe there were others in town she hadn't thought about, but Hope realized if she wanted a love like her parents', she'd have to look elsewhere. She climbed into the back seat of the cart and listened to her sister tell Frankie she'd see him later, her heart longing for something like that more than she'd even considered before Jimmy Brooks had asked the question that led to a thousand others.

CHAPTER THREE

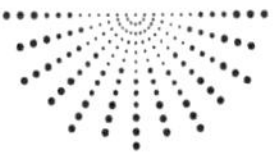

In all of the years she'd been coming to the Adams Farm, Hope had never walked the grounds. The furthest she could ever remember going was to the barn out back to visit the horses. Knowing her mother used to run through the pastures, past them to the woods, to a little pond, made her curious as to what may lie out there in the pleasant countryside. So after the meal was over, and she'd helped clear the dishes, she decided to take a little stroll.

She hadn't made it too far before she heard her name shouted from the distance. Without turning back, she knew it was Faith, so she slowed her step and waited as her sister rushed to catch up to her. "Where are you going?" She was out of breath by the time she caught up, and Hope almost laughed as she pressed a hand to her side and tried to control her breathing.

"Perhaps you need to get out of the house more," she said, poking fun at her younger sibling.

"Perhaps I would if I could sew and walk at the same time," Faith shot back. "What are you doing?"

With a shrug, Hope replied, "I just realized I hadn't actually explored the farm much. Mama said she used to run around here as a child. I thought it might be interesting to take a little walk. You wanna come?"

"Yes, of course," Faith replied, breathing easier now. They took off at a leisurely pace, headed in no particular direction, and soon found themselves walking through an overgrown orchard.

"I wonder why this place hasn't been taken care of," Hope said as they wandered through apple and pear trees with last year's fruit still scattered around the ground.

"Maybe Uncle Arthur can't take care of all of it anymore," Faith replied. "All of his sons have married and gone off, as you know, and the grandsons have their own responsibilities."

One of those grandsons, Lola's husband, had his own farm now. Maybe that's why Lola wanted her to become a farmer's wife, so they'd have something in common, though Hope remembered a time when Lola had also wanted to teach school. Her marks were good enough, but she chose to marry Ben and stay in Lamar after graduation, and since Hope was the only teacher the town needed for now, she'd settled out at the farm, not too far down the road from the Adams Farm.

"He could've just parceled it up," Hope thought aloud.

"Maybe no one wanted it."

They walked a little farther, and up ahead, they saw a stone fence, nearly waist high, that squared off a small area about thirty feet by thirty feet. The grass on the outside of the space was overgrown, but inside, it looked like it was well taken care of, and as they drew closer, Hope realized what she was looking at. "It's a cemetery."

"A family plot," Faith agreed. "Maybe we shouldn't go in."

"Why not? Clearly someone does. It's well tended." She stepped through a small opening in the stone, careful where she tread. There were only five or six markers, but there was room for more, and she wondered if Great-Aunt Margaret and Great-Uncle Arthur would be buried here someday.

"Baby boy Adams," Faith read, her voice filled with sadness. "I didn't know Aunt Margaret lost a child." It was sad, Hope agreed, but not uncommon. Poor baby didn't even have a name, and the dates showed he hadn't lived a day.

Something else caught her attention. "Look!" Hope said, peering past the first row. "Look at the large one, with the muskets at the top." They carefully stepped around the child's marker. "Jaris Adams." Hope turned and looked at her sister, whose eyes were wide.

"He's the one Mama was supposed to marry," Faith remembered. "Look. He died at Wilson's Creek. It says Confederate officer."

"Wasn't Daddy at Wilson's Creek?" Hope turned to look at her sister, puzzled.

"Oh, can you imagine fighting against your own cousin?"

Hope shook her head. "I think there's a lot they're not telling us." Her eyes drifted again to another headstone near Jaris Adams's final resting place. "Julia Tucker." She moved a few steps over. "Aunt Julia. Your namesake."

Faith grabbed ahold of her arm. Her name, Faith Julia, was for the girl who lay beneath the ground here. "Daddy loved her so much."

They stood and looked at Julia's grave for a few more minutes before moving on. What Hope saw next stunned her. "Carey Adams is buried here?"

"Why would they allow him in the family plot after what he did?" Faith asked, her voice taking on a tone of outrage.

"I don't know." Her eyes flickered down the tombstone. It was small and only had his name and dates on it, but she was certain by the year 1864 that this was the same man who had betrayed their town to Quantrill.

"Carey was still part of the family."

They both turned at the sound of their mother's voice. She was standing on the other side of the low stone wall but stepped through as she continued. "Aunt Margaret insisted, and I could hardly protest, even though what that man did was pure evil."

The girls exchanged glances, realizing their mother wasn't just speaking about the town now. "Mama," Faith began, carefully crossing back to where her mother stood. "Can you tell us the rest of the story? I feel like you started to the other day, but there's more, isn't there?"

"Was Daddy there when Jaris died?" Hope asked, remembering what the tombstone had said about Wilson's Creek."

"He was at the battle, honey, but he didn't see him that day. Your father was wounded badly at Wilson's Creek, and he almost died as well."

Hope looked at Faith, and their eyes met. How many times when she was little had Hope traced the scars on her father's shoulder, his collarbone? She'd asked what happened, but he never seemed to want to talk about it. Hope had met lots of people who'd lived through the war, many vets, people who had defended their homes against Quantrill, and she knew most of them would rather not speak of those days, but she felt like she needed to know her parents story because it was a part of who she was.

"Mama, tell us," Faith said, her voice quiet as if speaking too loudly would wake the dead. "Tell us about Jaris, and Julia—and Carey. We want to know."

Cordia drew in a deep breath through her nose and nodded. "But not here." Silently, she walked out of the little cemetery and over to some trees. She kept walking until she'd reached a pond, and Hope imagined this was the one she used to run to whenever Jaris and Carey were chasing her. Finding a shady spot beneath a tree, Cordia fanned out her skirts and lowered herself to the ground, her daughters doing the same. And then, she began to tell them a story of the ones she'd loved, and the ones she'd lost, during the war.

"I was engaged to Jaris, as I mentioned, but it was here, at this farm, the day after your Uncle Nolan was killed, that I met your father. I had seen him a few times when we were much younger, but I didn't remember him. I was out fetching water with Susannah when he and Julia rode up, and I remember thinking he was the most handsome man I'd ever laid eyes on."

"But you were engaged," Faith reminded her.

"I know. It was a dilemma. And your father being your father, it wasn't as if I could just saunter over and have a discussion with him." They all giggled. "It took some coaxing. And a spilled cup of water at a sending off party. But once I had him alone, there was no doubt in my mind he was the one for me."

Hope wasn't quite sure what a spilled cup of water would have to do with anything, but she couldn't help smile at her mother as her face radiated the sort of love Hope had only dreamt of. "Did he kiss you that night? Even though you were engaged to Jaris?"

"No," Cordia said quickly. "I kissed him."

Both girls gasped, and Cordia's laugh rang out around them. "Mama!" Faith admonished.

"I know, I know. It was very… bold of me. But I knew what I wanted, and I wasn't willing to just sit back and let others dictate my life."

"But then, how did you end up engaged to Carey Adams then?" Faith asked.

"You're getting ahead of the story, Faithy," their mother replied. She picked up where she'd left off, at the sending off celebration, told them about how she'd ridden to Springfield after Wilson's Creek to find their father and Jaris, with her beloved servant Frieda, God rest her soul, and how she'd found Will in a church—alive but wounded. Jaris hadn't been so lucky, and she'd brought his remains back with her.

She went on to tell about letter writing for many years, and how she'd visited Julia almost every day when she was well. "No one knew about our promise to each other," she explained. "Except Julia. She figured it out." She went on to tell about how Carey had asked for her hand, and her mother was so overjoyed, she'd somehow found herself engaged to the tyrant without ever having said yes. "Your Aunt Margaret let your daddy know, and he thought I'd done something awful, that I was just toying with his emotions."

"Why would she do that?" Faith asked, wrinkling her nose.

"She didn't know about my engagement to your father, of course," Cordia explained, absently twirling the ring on her finger. "She thought she was sharing good news."

"Was Daddy mad?" Hope asked, wondering how this repaired itself.

"He was devastated." Their mother still sounded upset about the situation, even though it had happened over two decades earlier. "He came home from the war and didn't even tell me. I discovered he was here when I came to visit Aunt Margaret."

"Did he yell at you?" Faith asked.

"Yes, something like that," Cordia admitted, and Hope couldn't imagine her father yelling at anyone, let alone her mother. "And then I went straight to Carey's house and threw his ring at him, even though I will admit I was frightened of him."

"Did he hurt you?" Hope was practically holding her breath, despite knowing the eventual outcome.

"Not right then, but later that night, he snuck into our house and tried to hurt me. If your father hadn't come over to bring me the coat I'd left here, who knows what might've happened to me."

"That's terrifying, Mama," Faith said, covering her mouth.

"In our very kitchen, your father rescued me from Carey Adams. And then that man went and told the law your father had kidnapped me, had a whole search party out looking for us. But I left with your father, you see, because I was afraid of Carey. I left a note for Grandpa in a secret location."

"Where at?" Hope wanted to know.

Laughing, her mother said, "The cookie jar, of course. We went off and got married, and then Julia got awful sick, so Uncle Arthur came to get us."

"How did he know where you were?" Faith asked.

"He was one of the only ones who knew where the family farm was."

Hope realized she meant the farm they'd grown up on, and she remembered another little cemetery like the one they'd stumbled on that day, one where she'd visited the graves of her Uncle Nolan and her paternal grandparents.

"We came back to town, and Julia passed away that night."

"Daddy must've been heartbroken." Faith had a tear in her eye as she spoke.

"He was. So much so, he insisted I go to my parents' house while he stayed here with her. He didn't want me to see him all choked up like that. But you see, that was the night of Quantrill's raid, and Carey Adams and his men showed up at the house that evening, so Grandpa and I had to defend it. And then your daddy rode in and took care of most of Carey's men, driving the rest of them away."

"You mean he shot them?" Hope asked, wondering just how many men her father might've killed in his life, something he would never talk about.

"I do," Cordia confirmed. "And then we helped the townsfolk clean up and start over. We eventually went back to the farm, where we raised you two little angels until we needed to come back here to help Grandma and Grandpa. After Frieda passed away, they needed someone, and I didn't see any sense in hiring someone when I was capable of doing it myself. Besides, I missed them. Family is very important to both your father and I."

The girls soaked in the story, and Hope reflected on just how much her parents must've loved each other to go through all of that. "But Mama, you didn't exactly say what happened to Carey Adams. No one in town seems to know, but I think maybe you do."

"That's not something we care to talk about, Hopey. You have to remember, Carey was your Uncle Arthur's nephew, same as your daddy is Aunt Margaret's nephew, and those were some dark times. Lots of families had lines right down the middle, some for the Union, and some for the Rebs."

Hope nodded, but she had a feeling her mother had answered her question without doing so directly. She swallowed hard, wondering if her father might be willing to tell her a little bit more since she'd put the pieces together for the most part already.

"You and Daddy sure did have a one in a million kind of love, didn't you?" Faith asked, her eyes still teary.

"We did. We still do." Their mother's face was glowing, and Hope felt a tinge of envy. She doubted she'd ever have her entire face light up at the mention of a man the way her mother's face was glowing now.

"That's how I feel about Frankie," Faith said, swiping at her eyes with the back of her hand. "Even though we haven't had to fight for each other, or go through a war, or nothin' like that. I think we could survive it, though. Like you and Daddy did."

"Be thankful you haven't had to, honey." Cordia leaned over and wiped a stray tear from her youngest daughter's eyes. "Men like your father and Frankie's father fought so that your generation wouldn't have to. People like Jaris gave their lives for what they believed in, even if we didn't quite see eye to eye."

"Was Jaris for slavery then, Mama?" Hope asked, just curious. Being a border state, there were lots of folks in Missouri who were. But the Adams family had never had slaves on their farm.

"No, he was fighting for states' rights. He didn't think it was right for the federal government to interfere with the laws of each state," Cordia explained.

"And was Daddy fighting to free the slaves?" Faith asked, her tears all dried up now.

"Partially. But mostly, your father entered the war because of the guerilla forces that were sweeping through here at the time. He wanted to do something to combat them. I guess he figured if the Confederacy fell, they'd have to quit their marauding as well."

"It must've been difficult for you to have someone on each side of the war that you loved." Hope gave her mother a small smile.

"It was, but I wasn't alone. There were lots of families torn apart." She let out a loud sigh and brushed a stray strand of curly, dark hair off of her cheek. "I pray nothing like that ever happens to our country again. It was a horrible time."

"Things aren't much better now in some parts," Faith reminded them. "There's still marauders; they're just not flying a flag."

Hope thought about her discussion earlier with her father. What Faith said was true. There were lawless parts of the country for sure, and she'd wanted to go there. Part of her still did. Her mother had defended her home against intruders, a rifle in her hand. Could she do the same thing? Her father was a dead-eye and had taught both of his girls to shoot as soon as they were big enough to hold a gun. She'd never even shot an animal before, though, and couldn't imagine taking a person's life, but maybe if the circumstances called for it....

"We don't have to worry about any of that around here," Cordia said with a dismissive smile. "Now, we need to be heading home soon. Grandma and Grandpa will be missing us."

They'd stopped by home to make sure her grandparents had everything they needed before heading out to the farm, but Hope agreed they didn't need to be left home alone for too long. Grandma had trouble walking anymore, and Grandpa's shoulder gave him fits from where he'd been shot over twenty years ago. Cordia didn't like to leave them home alone for more than a couple of hours.

The three of them came to their feet, stretching their backs, and Hope looked around one last time, wondering if she'd ever meander out here again. It had been interesting to see the cemetery. She wondered what may have happened if Jaris Adams had lived. Would her mother have given in and married him instead of her father? Or if she married Will Tucker anyway, would it have caused such a rift in her family that Aunt Margaret would never speak to her nephew again?

As they walked back toward the house, Faith said, "Someday, you'll need to tell us about Julia."

"Yes, someday I will. She was a lovely young lady."

"Why didn't you name Hope after her then?" Faith asked.

"Because Hope was born just about the time Frieda got sick, and I promised her I'd name a baby after her. She'd done so much for me. She went with me that day, when I went to Springfield to see about your father and Jaris. Without Frieda, I'm not sure I would've made it." She rested a hand on each of her daughter's shoulders.

Hope had never been fond of her middle name. It always reminded her of a little old lady, but the more she learned about her mother's caretaker, the more proudly she could call herself Hope Frieda Tucker. She just wondered if she'd ever accomplish anything worthy of having a baby named after her.

CHAPTER FOUR

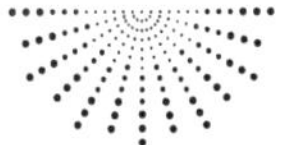

A brisk fall breeze blew against the door of the schoolhouse as the last student left for the day, and Hope looked around at the leaves that she'd need to sweep up before she left for the weekend. She'd also have to make sure the fire was good and doused so that the wooden building didn't end up a pile of ashes. Otherwise, the room was fairly neat, and she hoped to be on her way home in a half-hour or so. She needed a break after the last three weeks. It seemed like the colder the weather got outside, the less capable of getting their work done the students became, as if their minds were starting to freeze up. But today, she'd had a breakthrough with one of her toughest students, and he finally seemed to be getting his multiplication, so that was something she could smile about on the walk home.

Grabbing the broom out of the closet, Hope set about sweeping up the debris of the day, and her mind wandered back to thoughts of what it might be like if this wasn't a schoolhouse in the middle of a well-established little town in Missouri but one out west, maybe in Montana or California. Would she hear shots fired outside of her classroom windows all hours of the day? Would she be able to walk home alone, or would she need an escort? The thought of being out where the world was expanding and anything was a possibility was exciting, but at the same time, she thought about her mother's good cooking and the safety of her grandparents' solid, two-story brick home and knew it would be a hard trade to make, especially if the position didn't come with her own home, which she'd heard a lot of them out there in the new settlements didn't.

"You're fantasizing again, Hope Tucker," she muttered to herself, brushing the last bits of dirt and leaves into the dustpan and carrying it over to the trash bin. It wasn't nearly full so there was no reason to take it out that afternoon. She put the fire out, straightened a few more items around the room and then bundled up tightly against a cold October wind and headed out the door with just her lunch pail. No schoolwork for her this weekend—she was taking a few days off.

She hadn't made it far when she saw Jimmy Brooks coming up the other side of the road. He had on a thick coat and his hat was pulled down low over his ears, like he was just as cold as she was. It had been weeks since she'd spoken to him, and even at a distance she could see the pathetic look in his eyes, as if she'd broken his heart. It had never been her intention to do so, but her mother's words hit home with her. Why would she want to give him the impression she might be interested in marrying him when that wasn't even a possibility?

He pulled his wagon to a halt across from her, and Hope found a smile. "Good afternoon, Jimmy," she called, gazing up at him. "You in town to visit the general store again?"

"No, miss," he replied, not smiling at all; he looked pathetic, staring down at her. "I stopped by the bank to speak to your daddy."

Hope raised an eyebrow. "You did?"

"Yes, miss." She wondered why he was suddenly being so formal. "Might I give you a ride home?"

She tipped her head and took him in, suspicious. Hope knew her father wouldn't have promised him anything, but she may as well hear Jimmy out. "All right." She was still uncertain but could see no harm in it.

Jimmy leapt down and helped her into the other side of the wagon seat, and River whinnied, reminding them it was much colder out than it should've been for mid-October. Hope settled to the far side of the seat, leaving just enough space so as not to fall out and waited for Jimmy to come back around to the driver's seat.

He climbed up and gave the reins a quick jerk. Since he'd been headed the opposite direction of her house, they'd have to take a little longer route, and Hope found herself going back the way she'd just come. They sat in silence, and she felt more uncomfortable by the moment.

Once he'd turned and headed the right way, Jimmy cleared his throat. "Your daddy said the same thing he did last time, that it was up to you. Now, I figured the way you been avoidin' me, I had my answer already, that you ain't interested in courtin' me, Hope Tucker. But I wanted to make sure that's right, cause I ain't about to just give up on you."

Hope felt her stomach tighten as it had the last time he mentioned the possibility of the two of them spending more time together, and she shifted her gaze from the side of his face to the road in front of him. She remembered what her mother had said, but part of her thought it might be easier to just say yes, to go on a few dates with him, and then, maybe he'd see for himself that they were not a good match.

But then, there was the possibility he might think they were, and then what would she do? He turned his head to look at her; she could feel the weight of his brown eyes on the side of her face, and Hope knew she'd have to speak. "Listen, Jimmy, I guess I've always just thought of you more as a friend than… anything else."

"But we could be more, Hope. You don't know unless you give me a try."

It seemed like a legitimate argument, but she didn't think she needed to date him to know it just wouldn't work out. "Jimmy…."

"You got someone else in mind, Hope?"

She turned to look at him, her eyes wide. "No, of course not." Why was she being so defensive? Couldn't she have someone else in mind if she wanted to? She didn't owe him any explanations. The fact of the matter was, she couldn't even think of another person who might be the "someone else."

"It ain't Henry Morris, is it? Because I hear he's sweet on Fanny Winters."

"No." Even the thought of loud Henry Morris, with his big belly that shook when he laughed, made her nauseated. "It isn't anyone else, Jimmy. I told you. I just think we're better off as friends."

River turned the corner so they were headed down the street that went to her house, and she wished she could tell the horse to walk faster. "You know, Hope, there ain't a lot of single fellows left in this one horse town. Me and Henry and Nelson Smith, Seth Donahue, that's about it. Everyone else is either an old man or a young kid."

Hope stared at him, not sure what he was trying to say but letting him speak.

"You ain't gonna find another fellow better 'an me 'round these parts." Jimmy pulled the wagon to a stop in front of her house, looking at her as if he expected a response to his bold statement.

"Are you implying that if I don't marry you, I'll die an old maid?" she asked, not quite able to believe what she'd heard.

"Well, unless you plan to marry one of those other fellows I named…."

"And how do you know that I'm not madly in love with a gentleman from one of the neighboring towns, Jimmy Brooks?" Her dander was up now. "What if I'm courting someone from Nevada, or Jasper, or Golden City?"

"Are you?" he asked, eyebrows up near his hat brim.

"It's not your business!" Hope spewed, standing and getting ready to jump down from the wagon. "I told you, I don't want to court you, Jimmy Brooks, and if you feel the need to present yourself as the only viable option for an old bitty like me, well, then so be it…."

"Hope, that's not what I meant…."

"I assure you, the man I'm meant to marry is out there somewhere, and I won't settle for just anyone because it's convenient. Now, if you'll excuse me…."

"Hope!" He reached for her, but Hope was already gone, leaping down into the grass next to the road and taking off for her front door as fast as her feet could carry her. "Hope! I didn't mean to upset you."

"Go away, Jimmy!" she shouted without turning back. She didn't hear the sound of the wagon taking off as she reached the porch, but he wasn't chasing after her either, and Hope opened the door thinking she'd slam it behind her like she had the last time Jimmy Brooks had given her a ride home, but since that had alarmed her mother, she shut it quietly and then took off for the stairs and her room before she had to answer any questions from anyone.

Hope tossed herself down on her bed, thankful Faith was downstairs so she wouldn't come barging in, and hot, angry tears wet her pillowcase. Who was Jimmy Brooks to tell her she was out of options? That she was going to die an old maid if she didn't marry him? Her distress turned to anger, and she flipped over so that she was looking at the ceiling. What if he was right, and he was the best option she had available? Everyone else she'd gone to school with was married, and even her younger sister was engaged. Hope grabbed a pillow and shoved it over her face, wondering how this had become her life. While she was happy to be teaching school, she knew there was something more out there for her, and she'd been too frightened to take the opportunity to go searching for it. If she died here, all alone, it would be her own doing.

A knock at the door had her sitting up, and she assumed when she said, "Come in," it would be her mother, but it wasn't. The concerned face of her grandmother, Jane, poked in the crack in the door. "Grandma, come in." Hope spun so that her legs were hanging off the edge of the bed so that her grandmother would have a place to sit down. She shuffled in and had a seat, taking a few deep breaths as she did so, as if the short walk from her room down the hall had been too much.

"I heard you come in, and you sounded upset. What's troubling you, honey?"

Hope wiped the tears from her cheeks and tried to put into words what she was feeling, which was more complicated than she expected. Finally, she said, "I guess I just wonder if I'm doing what I'm meant to do, that's all."

Her grandmother raised a gray eyebrow behind her spectacles. "I thought you enjoyed your work at the school."

"I do, Grandma. It's just… I always thought I'd go off somewhere, that my life would be an adventure, more like Daddy's I guess."

"Your father had adventures out of necessity, Hope, not because he wanted to. He hasn't left southwest Missouri for the last twenty years, and I think he's just fine with that."

Hope let out a sigh. "I know, Grandma Jane. That's not what I meant. I guess I'm trying to say I thought I'd do something more important with my life, that the students I taught would be in dire need of a schoolteacher, that I could reach them when they're young, children of the lawless, and raise 'em up right." Her grandmother chuckled, and Hope supposed everything just wasn't coming out right. "I sound ridiculous, don't I?"

"No, honey, but you do remind me of someone else I know. And it isn't your daddy."

With her eyes wide, Hope stared at her grandmother's face, trying to figure out who she was talking about. Having no idea, she asked, "Who do you mean?"

"There was a time when another young lady slept under this roof, and sometimes I'd wake up in the middle of the night and wonder if she was still here. Couple of times she wasn't." Hope realized she was talking about her mother, and her mouth dropped open. "Don't think that this adventurous spirit of yours comes solely from the Tucker side of the family. I'm afraid your mother had a bit of a wanderlust, too, Hope."

Shaking her head, Hope said, "I never would've imagined."

"Went to Springfield to see about your daddy without our permission." She glanced over her shoulder at the window. "Pretty sure she snuck out to meet him a time or two. She was engaged for over a year, and I had no idea. Your mama knows what she wants, and she fights for it, honey. You get that from her."

The idea of her mother doing anything remotely dangerous was difficult to accept, but she did remember Mama saying that it was Frieda who went with her to Springfield. She'd just assumed her grandfather had also been there, but apparently not. Several questions sprung to mind about the adventures her mother might've had, but now wasn't the time to ask them. Instead, Hope asked, "Have you ever felt that way, Grandma? Like maybe there's more out there?"

Jane gave a small chuckle and posed another question. "Do you know how I met your grandfather?"

"No, I don't think anyone has ever told us," Hope admitted, shaking her head.

The chuckle turned into a laugh. "Your mama doesn't even know the full story. I'll tell you, but you've gotta keep it to yourself, you hear?"

"Of course, Grandma," Hope replied, sure she'd promise anything to hear the story that made her grandmother chuckle so mischievously.

"I answered an ad in the newspaper."

Hope stared at the wrinkled, smiling face before her for a long moment before the pieces began to come together. "Wait—you were a mail order bride?"

Jane's laughing increased. "I surely was. Came to Missouri from Ohio. My parents had fits over the whole thing, but I knew I needed to go. There was just something else out here for me, and I'm so glad I did. Marrying your grandfather was the best decision I ever did make in all of my sixty-five years."

"But Grandma, why did Grandpa have to send away for a bride? He's educated, handsome, well-to-do."

"He surely is," she nodded. "But there weren't many ladies out in these parts those days, and he was so busy starting up the bank, he didn't have time to do much courtin'. So, his sister persuaded him to write an advertisement, and he did. We wrote each other a spell, a few months, and he seemed like a nice enough man. We exchanged pictures, and I almost thought he must've borrowed a picture from a good lookin' friend a his because, like you said, I couldn't understand why he wouldn't have a dozen young ladies fallin' all over him. But when I stepped off the train and saw his handsome face, I knew I'd done the right thing. Not just because he was a sight for sore eyes either, but because he's a good man."

"So you think this spirit inside of me came from you?"

"Maybe so. Maybe from your great-grandparents. Your grandfather's folks came across the ocean from England before he was born. There's just no tellin', honey, but you come by it naturally."

Hope thought over her grandmother's stories for a few moments. She'd never heard her sister mention leaving Lamar, but then, she had Frankie. Maybe she didn't get stung by the same bug as Hope. "Grandma, if I ever did think about looking for a position somewhere else, out west, or down in Texas, don't you think it would break Mama's heart? Would it break yours?"

"Honey, I would miss you so much." Her grandmother's small hand rested on Hope's knee. "I would think on you every day and write you letters every chance I got. I'm sure your mama would feel the same way, but if you think there might be something else out there for you, who are we to stand in your way? The world can be a cruel, dangerous place. Lamar was unsettled and fierce back when I first came here, and my mama worried I'd be killed the first day when I stepped down from the train. But the world shifts and changes. And it takes good people to make that happen. Maybe you'll go out there and find there's nothing for you and be back directly. Maybe you'll be the ember that starts the world ablaze for good. I can't rightly say. But if you've got a whisper of a dream in your heart, that ain't gonna settle down. And it sure ain't something Jimmy Brooks can quiet."

Once again, Hope's eyebrows shot up. "How do you know about Jimmy?"

"I gotta window in my bedroom looks right out on the road, don't I?" She giggled again, and Hope was glad to see her so happy. It was rare, what with all of the pain her grandmother had been in recently.

"Do you think Grandpa would agree with you?"

"I do. But it don't matter. You just need to do what's right for you Hope Frieda Tucker. The rest of us will handle ourselves."

Hope stretched over and wrapped her arms around her grandmother's neck and kissed her on the cheek. She still had no idea if she should take a chance and leave Lamar behind, but at least she knew her grandparents would be supportive, and that was something else. And, should her mother decide to stand in her way, she had plenty of ammunition now to remind her that she once had a vagabond heart as well. "I love you, Grandma Jane," she said, looking into a pair of the wisest eyes she'd ever seen.

"I love you, too, my sweet Hope. Don't you ever forget it either." Grandma Jane patted her on the knee again, and Hope stood to help her up. She made her way slowly to the bedroom door, and Hope heard her shuffle on down the hall before she leaned back against her pillows again. She had a lot of thinking to do, and while it wouldn't be an easy decision, she knew in her heart she'd have to at least give it a try. If there was a school out there that needed her, then that's where she would go, even if it meant leaving everyone she loved behind.

CHAPTER FIVE

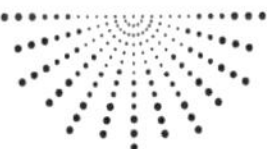

Autumn turned to winter, and Hope let her grandmother's words ruminate inside of her heart, though she took little action. It would be difficult to leave her students in the middle of the school year, even at semester break, so she'd decided to wait until the spring, and if she was still feeling as if she needed to get out into the world and spread her wings, she'd start looking for an opportunity elsewhere that would start in the fall. Though it would be difficult to leave her family behind, she began to think if she never tried, she'd spend the rest of her life wondering what might've been.

A time or two, the chance to discuss the situation with her mother arose, and she'd made a few hints that maybe she wouldn't stay in Lamar for the rest of her life, but Cordia hadn't taken the bait, so they'd let the conversation lay in front of them. She could tell, though, that her mother knew she had something on her mind. If the free-spirited young lady Grandma Jane had described still lived inside of her mother somewhere, surly it wouldn't be so hard to tell her when the time came.

Hope had patched things up with Lola pretty quickly. There just weren't enough friends in her life to let something silly keep her from her best one. While she'd tried to avoid the topics of going away and courting ever since their disagreement in the churchyard, Hope had made a comment or two to let her friend know she was considering leaving town someday. Lola was mostly quiet on that topic. And on the subject of Jimmy Brooks, who continued to stare at Hope at church but otherwise avoided her.

A few weeks before Christmas, Hope sat in the church pew listening to the sermon and marveling at the Christmas decorations adorning the stage. Two large tree stood behind Pastor Vincent, one on either side. Glass baubles, handmade popcorn strings, and lots of other ornaments made by the women of the church decorated the tall cedars, their aroma making the sanctuary even more welcoming than usual. Strands of garland hung around each of the windows and above the stage, decorated with crimson, velvet bows that offset nicely against the deep green. Pastor Vincent spoke of how Christ had left his home and went out into the world to preach the gospel, compelling others to do the same. He reminded the congregation, "At this time of year when we imagine Him a small, helpless babe, let us not forget how capable He became."

Hope shifted to look at her mother next to her, but Cordia was enthralled in the message, and Hope couldn't even catch her eye. Her father's arm was wrapped around her mother's shoulders. But as Hope returned her attention to the pastor, she felt Will's fingers on her shoulder. She glanced over, seeing he hadn't removed his focus from the short, balding man before them either, but he'd seen that she needed an affirmation, so he'd given it to her. Hope wished she could reach over and place her hand on top of her father's to let him know how much it meant to her, but then, she supposed, he already knew.

When the sermon was over, they rose to sing "Silent Night" as an altar call. Hope's mouth was moving, but she wasn't feeling the words, only going through the motions, as her mind wandered away again. Would Jesus wait until the end of the school year? She had no idea, but maybe it wasn't too early to start looking after all.

The song ended and everyone began gathering up their belongings, bundling up in hats, coats, gloves, and scarfs to fight against the brisk December wind. It had been snowing all night and quite a bit of the white, fluffy substance had accumulated on the roads and grass. Hope imagined living somewhere warm, where she didn't have to trudge through slush to reach her destination, but the idea was almost too hard to grasp.

"Hope!" a voice called out behind her, and she knew it was Lola. She turned and waited for her friend to reach her, stepping out of the aisle so that others could get by. "I'm glad I caught you. I should hate to try to stand outside and talk to you in this miserable weather."

"It's beautiful, just not pleasant to walk through," Hope replied with a smile. "How are you?"

"I'm well, thank you. I trust you had a good week? Are the children getting excited for Christmas?"

"Oh, yes. They are ready to take a few days off right now." Hope giggled, thinking about how excited the children had been when her father had helped her bring in a little Christmas tree earlier in the week. They were even allowed to make ornaments once they'd finished with their work.

"I'm sure they're bursting at the seams." Lola smiled, but Hope could tell she had something else on her mind. "Listen, I don't want to bring up a sore subject, but I got a Christmas card from my aunt who lives in Texas. I'm not sure if you remember her. Nita? She visited once a few years ago."

"Of course, I remember her," Hope replied with a nod. "Her husband's name is Bradford, isn't it?"

"Yes, that's them. They have two sons a bit older than us. Anyway, my aunt mentioned in her card that it's too bad I'm hitched because they are looking for a schoolteacher in her hometown, McKinney, Texas. I'm not sure if she was just mentioning it in passing, or if she is really part of the search committee. My aunt likes to be involved in the politicking of the town as much as she can, which gives my uncle fits. Anyway, I thought… if you were still thinkin' on going somewhere else maybe…."

Hope was already shaking her head no, though she had no reason why. Perhaps it was the thought of actually packing up and leaving town, but she didn't think that was quite it—it was more like the fear of rejection bubbling up inside of her. What if she went chasing this dream, and it didn't work out. "Lola, thank you, but I'm not sure…."

"All right. Well, I just thought I'd mention it. They'd be looking for someone before school let out for the summer anyhow. Probably sooner rather than later. Of course, after the new year, I'd suppose."

"Your aunt said a lot in her card about something you wouldn't be interested in," Hope noted, straightening her hat. She was beginning to overheat a little, wearing all of that in the church building.

"Well, she also wrote my mother a letter," Lola explained, "just talking about life in general. Some of that information came from the letter. Anyway, if you're not interested, I can't say as though I blame you. Moving all the way to Texas, by yourself, would be frightening. And I'd hate to see you go."

"Oh, it's not that," Hope assured her friend before she'd even finished her statement. "It's not that I'm frightened. And of course, I'd miss you, too. And my family. But it's not that."

"It isn't?" Lola asked, glancing around. Hope saw Lola's husband across the room speaking to Frankie—and Jimmy. "What is it then?"

Hope had no good answer for that. How could she admit she was afraid she'd chase a dream and wind up falling off a cliff? "Well, it's just… I'd hate to leave my students without a teacher before the end of the year. The older ones will be studying for their exams about then."

"That's true. It would be difficult. Of course, if they had trouble finding a full-time teacher to replace you, I could stand in for a bit. Just to, you know, help with the transition."

Hope cocked her head to the side. "Is that what this is about, Lola?" she asked, trying to keep her voice down but suddenly feeling as if she'd been betrayed. "Are you hoping I take another position so that you can have mine?"

Lola's face went pale. "Hope Tucker, you aren't actually accusing me of something so low, are you? You think I'd rather have your job than my best friend? Well I never!" Lola slid her way out of the pew and took off toward the back of the church, her nose in the air as if she'd been personally wronged, and Hope stared after her, not sure what she should do. While she did feel sorry for accusing Lola of such a thing, it wouldn't surprise her if it was the truth. Lola had always been a bit selfish. Didn't it sound like something Lola would come up with, a scheme to get rid of Hope so that she could become the temporary teacher of record and then take over the position?

"Hope, are you ready to go?" her father said right behind her, and Hope jumped, not even knowing he was there. "Sorry," he muttered. "Are you okay?"

She assumed he must've missed the conversation she'd just had with Lola, the storming off, at least. Turning around, she found a smile and stuck it on her face. "I'm fine, Daddy, thank you. Yes, I'm ready to go."

He nodded but his eyes narrowed slightly, as if he wasn't quite sure he believed her. Hope slid out the end of the pew and took her father's arm, seeing the rest of the family waiting at the back of the church. They headed out into the snow, but Hope felt overheated by emotions and thought perhaps the kiss of winter on her cheek might do her some good. She had plenty to think about now, and as upset as she was with Lola, Hope couldn't help but think perhaps there was more to this position in Texas than she'd allowed herself to consider.

A FEW DAYS WENT BY, and Hope continued to carry the weight of her argument with Lola around on her sleeve, as well as thoughts of whether or not she should further investigate the teaching job in Texas. She hadn't mentioned either to her parents or her sister, though she had an idea Faith knew something was up simply because Lola's husband was friends with Frankie, and she wouldn't put it past any of them to mention how accusatory Hope had been. Despite the cold weather, Hope found herself putting her coat on and wandering out to the back yard where her father was chopping wood, deciding perhaps it was time to unburden herself a bit.

The sun was down, so Hope took a lantern out to hold while Will chopped. She knew he could do it just fine by himself, but she thought it might give her an opportunity to talk to him, and it seemed like her only motivation was to be helpful. He already had a pile started by the time she made it over, though, and she wondered which would give out first, the remaining logs or her resolve to ask his advice.

"Hope, honey, you don't have to do that," her father said as he positioned the next block of wood to be dissected. "It's cold out here."

"I know, Daddy. I just thought maybe you could use a little light and some company. I'm sorry I didn't think to come and the chopping this earlier, when the sun was still up."

"Don't worry on that," he replied. "I just can't hardly get home before the sun's set these days."

She wasn't sure if he meant these days as in busy ones at the bank or the shorter winter daylight hours but decided it didn't matter. She listened to the rhythm of the ax for a few minutes before finally saying, "Daddy, can I ask you a question?"

"I believe you just did," he replied with a little twinkle in his eye that had her giggling. "What is it, Hope?"

Inhaling the brisk December air, she considered her words. She'd been thinking about the topic for so long, she had so many sentences floating around in her head for how to start, she didn't know which was best. Finally, she just said, "Lola's aunt wrote her that she's looking for a teacher, in their hometown. I mean, her aunt's hometown. In Texas."

Will said nothing for a moment, only picked up another large piece of wood and set it on the stump to be chopped. He took a few swings before asking, "And you wanna go?"

"I don't know," Hope admitted. "I think part of me does. Or wants to learn more, anyway. Part of me is mad at Lola over the whole thing."

He raised his eyes and stared at her for a moment. "Why is that?"

Hope felt silly even speaking it aloud, but she admitted, "I think she just wants me to take this job so that she can have mine."

"Oh." The ax connected with the wood a few more times before he said, "I guess that does make sense."

"It does?" Hope asked, startled to hear her father say such a thing. She nearly dropped the lantern.

"Yes. Her pa came into the bank around the time you got your position and made a few remarks about how he thought Lola was sure to get the teaching job. Said he thought the superintendent discriminated because she was getting married and you… weren't courting anyone."

Hope's mouth dropped open and then she closed it again, thinking over what her father had said before she finally replied, "Well, that's ridiculous. I know some towns don't like to hire married schoolteachers, but that didn't have anything to do with it. My marks were higher than hers. I am friendlier, more personable…."

"Hope, honey, you don't have to defend yourself to me. I set him straight. But it does make sense to me that Lola would want to apply for your position if you were to go elsewhere."

Tears came to her eyes as she thought about her best friend trying to get rid of her just to claim her role as schoolteacher. Hope felt foolish for having trusted Lola, but she also felt silly for not trusting her gut all week long when she tried to tell herself that Lola would never do that. She lowered the lantern, momentarily distracted, and when her father cleared his throat, she put her arm back up, wishing she could just go back to her room now that she had her answer, though she wouldn't abandon him when she'd volunteered to help.

The chopped wood pile continued to grow, and Hope stood in silence, listening to the comforting thunk of the ax. Once her father was done, she continued to hold the lantern while he stacked the fresh wood into the pile and gathered some to take in. "You know, Hope, if you're interested in this position in Texas, I wouldn't let Lola's scheming interfere with that. The two are not necessarily related."

"How do you mean?" she asked as he proceeded to make his way toward the back porch, arms loaded with wood. She went ahead to get the door.

"I mean… if you think you want to find out more about her aunt's hometown school, then do it. Don't let the fact that she wants your job dictate what you decide to do. Are you interested in it?"

Hope held the door, and Will made his way through the kitchen to the living room where the largest fireplace was and where they kept most of the extra wood. She closed up the back door tight and followed him, glad her mother wasn't anywhere to be seen. She wasn't ready to have this conversation with her.

"I'm not sure," Hope admitted, setting the lantern on a side table and sitting down in a chair near the fireplace before she even took her coat off. She watched as her father stacked the wood and then pulled off his gloves. "Lola said they'd want someone who could start right away, and I don't think I could do that."

"Maybe they'd be willing to wait until the fall for the right candidate." He walked across the room to hang his work coat by the door, and Hope decided she should take off her snow gear.

"I guess that's possible," she replied, pulling her own gloves off and shoving them into the pockets of her coat. "But I'd hate to bother them if I'm not what they're looking for."

"How will you know if you don't ask?" Her father sat down on the hearth just in front of her. Hope imagined what he'd looked like twenty-two years ago when he'd married her mother and thought he must've been even more handsome then. He was a special man, and she felt so blessed to be his daughter, to have him to confide in. She knew he'd never steer her wrong.

"I suppose I wouldn't. But… what about Mama?"

"Your mama? That lady up those stairs? The one who eloped when she was nineteen?"

Hope raised an eyebrow. "I am finding out all kinds of things about Mama I never knew."

Will laughed. "Listen, Hopey, don't you worry about your mother. She won't be thrilled, but she'll come around. I can't imagine not seeing you every day either, but you're an adult now. You've got your own life to live, your own adventures to chase. If you feel like you want to investigate this school, see if it's a good fit for you, then you do it. We'll support you. If it seems like something you wanna try, then do it. You don't like it, you come back here."

"But by then, my job will be filled," Hope reminded him.

"Then you'll find a new one."

"But there's only one school."

"Hope, if you can't find the right school, then we'll build it."

She cocked her head to the side, confused at first, but then she realized what he was saying. If you don't like your circumstances, make new ones. Don't limit yourself by your present situation. "All right, Daddy. I'll look into it."

He gave her a small smile and patted her knee, and Hope could see he was pained, as if he would've rather told her to just stay home forever. "Do you need me to figure out who to contact? Or do you wanna ask Lola for the address?"

That was a good question. It would've been much easier for her to just let her father figure out an address, but Hope couldn't just go on about her business without speaking to Lola about it. She needed to apologize to her friend, even if she'd been right, not because Lola needed to forgive her but because Hope would feel better when she did so. "I'll talk to Lola."

"That's my girl," he said, standing, his hand still on her knee. He kissed her on the forehead and headed out of the room.

He was in the doorway that led to the dining room when she called, "Daddy?" Will turned to look at her. "Thank you."

Will smiled at her. "We'll always do whatever we can to help you, Hope." He headed into the kitchen, and Hope leaned back in the chair, wondering exactly what she would say to Lola, and what she'd write in her query letter. She had a lot of important conversations ahead of her, and the thought of them made her stomach churn, but then, there was another sensation as well, one of adventure, of new experiences—of hope, and that was something she could embrace.

CHAPTER SIX

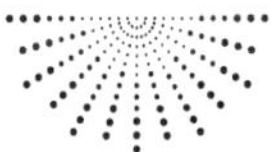

Saturday morning, Hope woke up resolved to go speak to Lola. The snow and cold weather, along with the early sunset, had kept her from venturing out into the countryside during the work week, but now that she had a day off, it was time to go deal with at least one of the two items she'd spent most every night worrying over well past the time she needed to go to sleep. Even if she didn't end up going to Texas, at least she'd right the situation with her friend. Maybe then she'd get some rest.

The sun had made an appearance the day before, melting all of the snow, leaving rivulets of water that had refrozen the night before and were already beginning to melt again now that the sun had risen. Hope decided not to take the carriage through the slush and muddy roads. Instead, she saddled her horse, Pixie, and set on her way, bundled against the chill but happy to feel the sun on her face as she rode.

Lola and Ben only lived about three miles out of town. Their farm was near Aunt Margaret and Uncle Arthur's land, though it was much smaller. Ben's father had bought a parcel across from his parents' and divided large sections of it out for his sons. Ben was the only one old enough to move out of the family house, since his younger brothers were only fifteen and twelve, but Ben was a good man and worked the land diligently. Hope had to admit she was a little jealous that Lola had made a life for herself out here, fairly independent from either one of their families. Perhaps it was silly of her to think Lola would still want her position in town. It would be rough, going back and forth every day, getting there before the sun came up and heading home while the sun was going down. While it would be nice to rely on her friend during a transition if Hope couldn't wait to leave until the school year was over, she began to realize she was being silly deciding Lola was only thinking of herself when she'd suggested Hope look into the new school in Texas, despite the fact that Lola had wanted her position years ago when they'd finished their own schooling.

Pixie was named appropriately as she was a small white mare with a lustrous coat, and she stepped around the mud and potholes as best she could, trying to stay clean. Hope often teased her horse that she was a dainty lady, but she appreciated having her own ride just the same and thought she would certainly miss the old girl if she did move away. It's not as if she could take her on a train, though images of sitting next to a horse in a train car were a good way to fill her time as she made the trip to Lola's. She hoped her friend would be home, and she wouldn't be interrupting anything. She was sure she wouldn't be expected.

Tying the horse to the hitching post, Hope chose her footing carefully. Ice, mud, puddles of water, and even a bit of brown grass dotted the path, so she tried to stick to the grass as much as she could as she made her way to the porch. With a deep breath, she gave a hearty knock on the door and then waited.

Lola came to the door quickly, and when she pulled it open, her eyes widened and her mouth hung open a moment before she said, "Oh? Hope! I wasn't expecting you."

"I know. I came by to apologize. And to bring you this." She handed over a loaf of pumpkin bread she'd made the night before. A pie might've been a better a gesture but much harder to transport in the conditions.

"Oh, Hope, you didn't have to do that," Lola said, taking the gift.

"Won't you come in?" She held the door open and stepped out of the way, and Hope gratefully stepped into the warm farmhouse.

It wasn't large, just a small living room and kitchen on the bottom floor with a staircase that led to two quaint bedrooms upstairs, but Hope was proud of her friend for having her own place. She'd been there when all the neighbors came to help Ben build the house, and she'd been to the barn raising, too. At the time, Hope had let her mind wander to what it might be like to have that sort of a celebration for herself and some nameless, faceless man, but she'd let that particular dream fade away, thinking she didn't want to be a farmer's wife anyway. Sometimes she still wondered about the man, though, if he even existed.

Lola led her into the kitchen where Ben was sitting at the breakfast table sipping a cup of coffee. "Good morning, Hope," he said, his tone giving away that he was surprised to see her, too. "What brings you by?"

"Good morning, Ben. I hope I'm not intruding. I just brought over a loaf of pumpkin bread, and I was hoping to have a chance to talk to Lola for a few minutes." She held short of exclaiming she felt the need to apologize, but she was certain he knew everything that had transpired; Lola wasn't exactly the sort to keep her feelings tucked in.

"Well, it sure is nice to see you," he said, rising from the table. "You're not intruding at all. But I have some animals to tend to." He walked across the room and pecked the cheek of his wife, who was slicing the pumpkin bread, and then headed to the back door where his coat and hat were. He grabbed them both and stepped out onto the back porch to put them on, and Hope felt as if she'd run him out of his own kitchen.

"Ben's got a lot of work to do today," Lola explained, coming to the table with the bread. "Do you want some coffee?"

"That would be lovely," Hope replied, shrugging out of her own coat and hanging it on the hook next to where Ben's had been. She'd been here enough times to know it was just fine to act as if she were home, though Lola seemed slightly more formal than normal, likely because of the circumstances.

Lola poured two mugs of coffee, bringing them over, along with a spoon, and Hope helped herself to the cream and sugar still on the table from breakfast. The beginning phrases of several apologies were swirling around in her head, but actually choosing one was problematic. Hope sat stirring her drink for far too long before setting her spoon aside and saying quietly, "I apologize for what I said at church." She took a sip of the coffee, finding it cooler than she preferred but a good distraction. "It wasn't fair of me, and I'm sorry I hurt your feelings."

Silence hung between them for a few moments as Lola also concentrated on her beverage before she raised her nose in the air and said, "I accept your apology. I never intended to give you the indication I'd want your position full-time. It's a long trip into town for us."

"I know," Hope said, her head still down. "I realize that now."

"While I certainly wouldn't mind making it for a few months while they try to find another full-time schoolteacher, I can't imagine leaving the farm every single day. I have duties here, too, you know. It's not just Ben that minds this place."

Hope raised her eyes to look at her friend. "I'm sure it is hard work, Lola. I apologize for being so rude the other day."

"When I applied for that position, we hadn't moved out here yet, you know that. I wasn't even married. I'm not even sure if they'd allow a married woman the full-time position. I think the superintendent is a bit more of a free-thinker than some, but you know they prefer someone without her own family, someone who has as much time as necessary to devote to the students."

Thinking of herself as someone without a family stung a little bit, particularly when her family was so wonderful, but she knew what her friend was saying. "Yes, some places have stricter requirements than others, it's true. I would think Mr. Cartwright would choose the best candidate regardless of marital status, but it's possible he would prefer an unmarried woman as well."

Lola's eyes enlarged. "I think it's evident he did. Whether that's changed now, I can't say."

Feeling a tightening in her abdomen that alerted that they were on the verge of another disagreement, Hope asked, "What do you mean?"

"Nothing, only that my pa heard that the only reason Mr.

Cartwright gave you the position the first time was because you were not promised to anyone, and Ben and I already had a date set, that's all."

Hope took a deep breath, deciding to choose her words carefully. Lola certainly had a way of making her upset, but she hated actually fighting with her friend. "I think we were both well-qualified for the position, Lola."

That answer seemed to satisfy her friend who took a bite of the pumpkin bread. "Mmm!" Lola finished chewing, mostly, before saying, "This is really good, Hope."

"Thank you. It's my grandmother's recipe." She smiled and took a little nibble herself, though she really wasn't hungry. The anxiety of having to apologize, as well as the rest of the conversation she still needed to have, made her stomach restrict. Hope dusted her hands off and cleared her throat. "I've been thinking about the position in Texas you mentioned, the one in your aunt's hometown. Do you happen to know if it is still available?"

It seemed to take forever for Lola to finish chewing, and Hope waited, staring at her friend's face, looking for any sort of an indication that the position hadn't been filled, but when Lola finally finished, she only said, "I haven't the foggiest. Aunt Nita only mentioned it in passing, as a project of her own. It wasn't as if she thought I'd actually know someone who might want to move there and take the job."

"Oh," Hope replied quietly. That made sense. For some reason, she'd thought perhaps her aunt would keep her appraised of the situation.

Before Hope could say more, Lola asked, "Why? Are you thinking of putting your name in? Hope, it's far away. You know how long it will take for you to get down there? Do you really want to spend all that time on a train? And once you get there, what if it's awful? My aunt says it's still a lawless place there, you know? I'm sure she'd do her best to look after you, but she's a busy woman. You might get there and truly hate it and end up coming back here, and by then, your position would be filled. Then what would you do? I'm just not sure it's a good idea, Hope, that's all." Lola stopped then, shaking her head, and finishing the last bite of her pumpkin bread.

"I've told myself all of that a hundred times," Hope began, her voice even. "But how will I know if I don't try? I feel like, I've got a burning inside of me, Lola, an urge to go out there into the world and see what it's like. Lamar's a fine place to live, but I'm not sure it's where I want to spend the rest of my life."

Lola was quiet, taking her in, and Hope adjusted her gaze out the window so she wasn't staring at her friend. The snow had melted everywhere except for under the trees, though she was sure there'd be more soon. With Christmas a week away, the worst weather was still in front of them. She wondered how much snow they got in that part of Texas, if the summer heat was deplorable, if it rained regularly or only certain times of the year.

"Are you gonna eat that?" Lola asked, breaking Hope out of her thoughts. She slid the bread across the table, and Lola tore off the corner, shoving it in her mouth, still thinking. She swallowed before she asked, "Does this have to do with Jimmy Brooks?"

Hope's eyes widened. "Jimmy? What? No! Why would you ask that?"

Lola shrugged. "I don't know. It's just... you know him and Ben are friends. He's been by a few times. Said he'd asked to court you more than once, and you keep sayin' no."

"I already told you that," Hope reminded her friend. It wasn't as if Lola wasn't aware of the situation.

"No, I know. It's only... to hear his side of it. It makes me think... maybe you should give him a chance, Hope. If you're afraid you might end up an old maid if you don't leave here, maybe you don't have to. Jimmy's a nice enough feller. He's sort of handsome in a certain way. He'd take good care of you."

"Lola, I don't want someone to take care of me," Hope replied. "I want to continue to teach. I want to help children. There's nothing particularly wrong with Jimmy. I just don't... have feelings for him."

"Sometimes feelings come later."

"Lola, please don't take this the wrong way as I don't mean it to be offensive at all, but I have lived on a farm before, most of my growing up years, and I just don't take to it as some people do. There's nothing at all wrong with it. You know my daddy's people are all farmers. I am kin to Ben's folks, who are all farmers. It's just not for me."

Lola looked as if she wanted to be offended, but the way Hope had worded it made it difficult to poke holes through her statement. "Maybe not Jimmy then. There are a few other fellers. Henry, maybe?" Hope wrinkled her nose. "Or Nelson. Seth?"

"Stop!" Hope implored, though she kept her voice low. "I'm aware of the eligible bachelors in town, Lola. No, it's not about that. It isn't about me not being able to find a husband. It's about me not wanting one, not right now anyhow. I want to go out into the world and make something of myself, something important."

"And you think teaching school in McKinney, Texas, will fulfill that yearning inside of you?" Lola looked skeptical, and it was irritating to Hope.

"I don't know," she admitted. "But I would be willing to find out, I think. If the position and responsibilities are suitable."

"You mean if the pay is enough?" Lola finished the second slice of pumpkin bread.

"Well, of course I have to consider the wages if I'm to be taking care of myself," Hope countered, not that she didn't have plenty of money saved up from her current station. Living at home with her parents and grandparents allowed her to save more money than being out on her own would've. "But there are other considerations as well. Accommodations, specific duties, all of those sorts of things."

"What if they want you to start right away? Would you be able to leave your students?"

Hope thought about her class and how hard they'd been working lately, especially the little ones. "It would be very difficult, that's for certain. But if you were to take over for me, I'm sure it would be all right. Those kids know and respect you. You're certainly capable." That last part she wasn't sure of. For all of the talk earlier about it being a neck-and-neck contest for the teaching job, Hope knew her marks had always been better than Lola's. She was also more patient and had been studying on best practices in teaching even before she had her own school. Lola hadn't and was likely out of practice. But she would certainly do for a few months while the superintendent looked for a more seasoned teacher.

Lola stood, taking the plates and coffee cups over to the washbasin. "I can give you my aunt's information as well as the telegraph number that's closest by. I'm pretty sure it's at the post office."

"That would be lovely," Hope replied, wishing there was a telephone connection from Missouri to Texas, but seeing as though there were only a handful of phones in all of Lamar, she didn't see that being the case any time soon.

Lola went into the living room, and Hope followed her. She opened a desk drawer and moved a few papers around until she found what she was looking for. "Here it is," she said before taking out a pencil and a scrap of paper and writing the information down for Hope. "Now, it usually takes a week or two for my aunt to get any mail from us, and then to hear back is something else."

"Right." Hope took the paper, made sure she could read it, and then placed it in her pocket. "Thank you, Lola. I appreciate it."

A worried look took over her friend's normally carefree face. "Do you really think you might go?" she asked, stepping forward and putting both hands on Hope's shoulders. "Oh, I just can't imagine what it would be like around here without you."

Hope gave her friend a sympathetic smile. "I'm not sure what I'll do, Lola. But all I can do at this point is try." She leaned in and hugged her, thinking if she did go to Texas, she would miss Lola, but she'd also hope to make some other friends, possibly better friends, as she and this woman had certainly grown apart over the years.

"Just be careful, Hope. It's a big world out there," Lola said, leaning up and looking Hope in the eye. "And it's just not the same as you might think, not having your daddy or anyone to protect you."

"I know," Hope replied, understanding that Lola spoke out of concern, not because she was trying to get her dander up again. Hope knew it wouldn't be easy to leave everyone she loved behind, but she was compelled to toss her name into the hat and see what happened. She hugged Lola one more time and then went to fetch her coat, thinking she might wanna hurry and leave before they broke into another argument. If she really was going, she wanted to do so on good terms.

As Hope rode away, she wondered if she'd ever visit Lola's house again. She turned and looked over her shoulder at the small dwelling in the middle of such vast emptiness. Surely she would return here soon enough. It wasn't as if she'd be asked to get on a train right away. Shaking her head, Hope turned back around, leaving Lola and her world behind her.

CHAPTER SEVEN

Agonizing over correspondence to both Lola's aunt and the telegram she would send took up most of the rest of the weekend, and with just three days of school that week before Christmas Eve and Christmas Day, Hope decided to take her time and make sure the messages said exactly what she intended them to before she sent them. It seemed like the most intelligent way to go about sending a missive.

That, and she also didn't want to say anything to her mother yet. It wasn't that she didn't think Cordia would understand, but she thought it would be difficult for her mother to hear, that she might try to talk her out of it. Every night since she'd visited Lola, Hope had lain awake in her bed, thinking about the possibilities, the adventures that might lay before her. To have her mother snuff her dreams out before they'd even had a chance to take flight was a fear that kept Hope's intentions secreted away from the one person who might tell her she couldn't do go forward with her plan.

Her father had been helpful, reading over her letter and intended telegram for her and suggesting a word here or there. Her grandmother had nothing to add, only wished her luck, and by the time Christmas Eve was upon them, Hope was fairly certain she knew exactly what she'd say. Her plan was to mail the letter the day after Christmas and send the telegram a few days after that, so that perhaps they'd arrive about the same time.

She was just putting the finishing touches on her hair when her sister knocked on her bedroom door. Her head was already poking through before Hope could even beckon her in, and she couldn't help but make a face at Faith. "Why do you knock if you're coming in anyway?"

"Why do you bother to shut the door if you're not going to lock it?"

Hope didn't think her sister's question made much sense, but she didn't want to argue. She turned to face her. "Can I help you?"

"Yes. I have a question for you. I've noticed you've been spending a lot of time in here, writing. So… I had a sneak around. Are you planning to go to Texas?"

Hope's eyes widened in fury. "A sneak around? You've been going through my papers?"

Faith shrugged as if it was no big deal. "Just answer my question."

"And why do you think it's okay for you to come into my room at all, let alone to go through my things while I'm not here?"

"Because—if you're planning on going somewhere, I deserve to know!" Her sister folded her arms and gave her a stern look, but Hope could see beyond anger, there was also fear. Her sister didn't want her to leave.

"Faith, I am thinking of applying for a teaching position in Texas, northeast Texas, so not so horribly far away. That's all."

"And does Mother know this?"

"No, but Daddy does. So does Grandma—and I'm sure she's told Grandpa because she can't keep anything from him."

Faith pursed her lips together and her shoulders relaxed slightly. "How did you hear of it?"

"From Lola," Hope replied. "Her aunt let her know about the opening."

"Lola?" Faith repeated, a bit of amusement suddenly filling her pretty face. "You do realize she will be at the party we are leaving for directly, don't you?"

Of course, Hope knew that Lola would be at the mayor's Christmas party. Nearly the whole town would turn out. "Yes, of course. Why do you ask?"

Faith began to chuckle. "Don't you think you best tell Mama before Lola does?"

Hope's eyebrows drew together as she considered her sister's words. "Surely… she wouldn't…."

The chuckle turned into a loud laugh as Faith headed for the door, and Hope was no longer concerned with her evil younger sister's feelings about her leaving. "Fine. If you trust Lola Adams not to say anything…."

"Oh, you! Faith Julia!"

"Me?" Faith asked, turning back to face her sister. "What did I do? Only gave you the opportunity to speak to Mama before Lola stole it away from you, that's all."

"You think it's all a lark, don't you?" Hope shouted, not realizing they were not alone now.

"Speak to me about what?" Cordia asked, coming out of her bedroom, one earring in her ear, the other in her hand. "What are you two fussing about?"

Hope looked from her sister to her mother, realizing now was the time. If she was going to tell her Mama herself, it would have to be before the Christmas Eve party. Perhaps Faith had done her a favor after all, though she didn't have to be so mean about it.

"Mama, I need to tell you something," Hope began, her voice low. "I… I think I might… try for a school teaching position… in Texas."

Cordia's already alabaster skin went even whiter as she studied her oldest daughter. "Texas?" she repeated.

"Yes—but not deep Texas. Just the northwest part. Near Dallas. Nearer to here than Dallas." All of the words she'd considered when explaining the situation to her mother over the last few days seemed to jumble together.

Before Cordia could say anything, Grandpa Isaac came out of his bedroom, dressed for the party, a large grin on his face. "Isn't it wonderful?" he asked, clapping his hands together. "Our little granddaughter going out into the world to make something of herself. She has that adventurous spirit in her, Cordie, same as you did. Same as your mother."

Hope wasn't sure if she should run over and give her grandfather a hug for his support, or run to her mother and apologize for not having told her sooner. Cordia turned her head and looked at her father and then her eyes fell back to Hope. She cleared her throat. "We must hurry or else we will be late for the party." She flashed her daughter a tight-lipped smile and then headed back into her bedroom.

She stared after her mother for a while before turning to Grandpa Isaac. "Thank you," she said, taking a few steps over toward him. "You already knew, though, didn't you?"

"Course I did. Your grandma can't keep a secret to save her life." He chuckled, and Hope straightened his bowtie a bit. He looked so handsome, and she was glad he was feeling well enough to attend the get-together at least for a bit. "I'm proud of you, Hopey. What you're trying to do won't be easy, but it will be rewarding."

A blush came to her cheeks as she considered his words. "Grandpa, I'm not doing anything extraordinary. Besides, I'm not even sure I'll be granted the position...."

"You will," he said, as if he could see the future. "And you'll change lives, Hope Tucker. I just know it. You're a fine young woman, just like your mother and her mother before her, and you're going to go down to Texas and tame those little cowboys and cowgirls and make scholars out of 'em."

Picturing herself lassoing children dressed in boots and spurs, hats and chaps, made her giggle, and Hope leaned in and wrapped her arms around her grandfather. "Thank you, Grandpa," she said again, and this time she really meant it. If there'd been any doubt in her mind whether or not she should contact the good people of McKinney, Texas, that all faded away. Whether or not her grandfather was a soothsayer remained to be seen, but she had to try. Hopefully, her mother would give her blessing as well, but if the sounds of sobbing coming from the bedroom across the hall were any indication, Cordia wasn't ready to let her little birdy fly free.

CHRISTMAS CAME AND WENT, as did New Years. Hope had sent the letter and telegram as intended, and every day that the post office was open, she went and checked to see if she had anything back from Nita Howard only to return empty handed. Likewise, every evening, she'd wait by the front door for her daddy to return from work to see if he'd received a telegram, and each night she went to bed disappointed.

Hope had just about given up when January turned to February, and she still hadn't heard anything at all. Her grandparents recommended she send another letter; perhaps the first one had gotten lost in the post. While Hope considered it, she'd been sure to mention her letter in the telegram, which she was sure had gone through, and since she hadn't received an answer to that inquiry either, she thought it might seem a little desperate to write another correspondence.

She'd taken to walking straight from the school to the post office, and even though it was out of the way and took a bit longer, it was a good way to clear her head. The students in her class were doing so well, she didn't worry about most of them anymore, with the exception of little Freddy. But he was young, and he'd get it. If she were to leave, she wanted all of her students to be well-prepared for the coming school year, in case they didn't have a competent replacement handy, and she felt they had managed to make at least a year's progress already and it wasn't even spring yet.

The looming courthouse building was visible before she reached the square, and each time she looked at it, memories of the stories she'd heard about the night Quantrill raided the town and burned down the original structure filled her mind. Her folks had been involved in stopping that deadly invasion, maybe more so than she even imagined. It was a wonder to think the same woman who had shot a rifle at marauders that night was afraid to let her move to Texas to teach children.

Cordia hadn't spoken a word about it ever since Hope had first mentioned her intentions on Christmas Eve. She seemed to be waiting to see if there was anything to worry about. Faith wondered aloud to Hope from time to time that perhaps correspondence had come and their mother had "misplaced it" but having heard the story about how Carey Adams had claimed her own mail, there was little doubt in

Hope's mind that Cordia would never do such a thing. Still, as the days wore on, she wondered what her mother might do if a letter did arrive for her before Hope could get to the post office. And what would she say if she finally had to face the possibility of Hope leaving?

There were other schools, after all. Other positions. She'd been checking the newspaper regularly for them and had noted a couple that seemed promising. One was out in Utah, the other all the way in California. That would be much farther than Texas, and she wouldn't know anyone at all. At least, if she went to McKinney, she'd know of Lola's aunt. She'd have a family member of a friend to help her get settled. Hope had determined to put off looking at any other openings until she heard back from McKinney, but as the days accumulated with no word, she wasn't sure if she should try another place or give up altogether.

She'd reached the town square and looked across to the other side only to see Jimmy Brooks loading up his wagon at the feed store. He hadn't spoken to her at all since Christmas Eve when she'd declined to dance with him. At the time, she hadn't meant to be rude or unfair; she'd been looking out for his feelings. But he didn't seem to see it that way, and he looked away now, as if he didn't recognize her. Hope hated to have sore feelings between them, but she didn't know what else to do.

The post office door resounded with a clank of the bell, and she tried to keep her voice cheery as she greeted Mr. Green, the attendant. "Good afternoon, sir. No letters today?"

Mr. Green was a middle-aged man who'd been running the post office for about ten or fifteen years. He was always friendly, and every time he told Hope he had nothing for her, he offered a sympathetic smile. But today his smile looked different. "Miss Hope Tucker. Just the gal I've been wantin' to see." He gave a short chuckle and then pulled out an envelope and slid it across the counter to her.

Hope stared at it for a few seconds, unable to believe it was real. But not only was the envelope addressed to her, she could see by the return address that it was from Nita Howard. "Thank you, Mr. Green," she muttered, picking the letter up and staring at it in fascination. Part of her wanted to tear it open right then and there, but if it was bad news, she'd just as soon read it in her own home. And if it was good news, well, she wasn't exactly sure what that would mean either. Could she really move to Texas?

She took off out the door, not even paying attention to where she was headed, and was halfway home before she even took her eyes away from the envelope. Realizing she probably looked silly to anyone passing by, she tucked it into her pocket and increased her speed even more, thankful she'd managed to navigate around puddles and other obstacles while she hadn't been looking where she was going.

Flinging the door open, she dropped the rest of the items she'd brought home from school on the table by the stairs and then flew up to her room, certain the amount of noise she was making would draw an audience, but she might at least have the opportunity to scan the letter before the rest of her family came to see what all the commotion was about.

Hope used her teeth to pull off her gloves and sank down on the bed. She slipped her finger underneath the fold of the envelope, carefully tearing the seal, and unfolded the single sheet of paper. The handwriting was neat and formal, and as she read, she held her breath.

Dear Miss Tucker,

I hope this letter finds you well. I am writing to you on behalf of the school board of the town of McKinney, Texas, and the school board president, Mr. Gabriel Stewart. We received your letter regarding the schoolteacher position and are impressed with your qualifications. We have received other letters of interest but feel of those who have applied, your experience puts you above the others, so we would like to offer you the position.

Before you accept, please be aware that this area is mostly unsettled. While I feel it is safe, I am sure it is not like anything you are used to, having visited Lamar, Missouri, myself on occasion. The position pays $6 per month with no pay in the summer months when school is out of session. As of now, there is no residence for the schoolteacher, so you are invited to stay with my husband and I. Room and board will be provided to you for as long as you live here. The *town is looking into constructing a small cottage on the school grounds. If this structure is completed, you may live there at no cost to you, though you will be required to provide your own meals at that time. The school board insists you remain unmarried for as long as you are in employment as the school-teacher. We uphold Godly values in our town, and I am glad to know you attend church with my niece Lola and are a strict Southern Baptist, as am I. We expect you to refrain from any behavior which could be categorized as sinful in any capacity, including drinking alcohol, swearing, or being seen unaccompanied with an unwed young man in public. It is important that the children of our town are able to see you as a good role model and that you uphold good Christian morals and values.*

Currently, there are approximately twenty-six students between the ages of six and seventeen who would make up your class. Most of them have received very little schooling. Very few can read or write or do their sums, though their mothers have worked with them at various levels at home. The schoolhouse was just completed in the fall and is spacious enough for all of the current students plus a few more. We are in need of supplies but would like to hear from you as to exactly what is necessary before the school board approves any purchases.

If all of this sounds agreeable to you, please let us know that you accept the position. We would like for you to start as soon as possible but no later than March 1st. If you are unable to make it to McKinney before then, please do not accept the position. As mentioned, we do have other candidates.

Sincerely,

Nita Howard, School Board Secretary, McKinney, Texas

Hope finished reading and looked up to see her mother and Faith standing in the doorway. Without comment, she stretched out her arm, handing the letter to Cordia. She took it and read the whole thing through before handing it to Faith and moving to sit next to her daughter on the bed.

They said nothing for a full minute or two before Cordia noted, "That salary is greater than a dollar a month more than what you make now."

"And you'd have free room and board, at least for a while. That sounds nice." Faith managed a small smile and then took a seat on the stool in front of Hope's vanity.

"Yes, that's true," Hope noted. "Mrs. Howard seems… pleasant."

"Very matter-of-fact but nice. Her brother is the same way, isn't he?" Faith asked, meaning Lola's father.

"I'd say so," Cordia nodded. "And Sam's nice enough, once you get to know him."

"Did Lola say anything about her cousins? Do they still live at home?" Faith wanted to know.

"I'm not sure." Hope looked at the letter, which Faith still held in her hand, and seeing her gaze, her sister handed it over. "It would be awfully hard to leave my current students." The thought of not seeing them finish made her stomach tighten, but she knew they were ready. These children, the ones in McKinney, sounded like they were in desperate need of a good teacher, and while these other candidates might be able to help them, if the school board chose her, it must be for a reason.

"Why don't you think on it, and when your father gets home, we can discuss it as a family?" Cordia reached over and patted her daughter's hand, but she could see the sadness in her mother's eyes as she considered not having her little girl at home anymore.

"That's a good idea," Hope replied. "Thank you." She didn't know what else to say, so she said nothing more, and after a moment, her mother and sister got up and walked out the bedroom door, leaving her alone with the letter.

Hope read it a few more times and then imagined what it would be like to tell the superintendent she'd accepted another job. It would be hard, but she thought he'd understand, particularly if Hope suggested Lola as a temporary replacement. There was a girl in her class now, Becky, who was doing quite well and might even score high enough on her exams to take over the schoolteacher position in the fall if the superintendent thought it was a good fit.

Her eyes flittered around her room, and she imagined packing her belongings and heading to Texas. How would she ever decide what to take and what to leave behind? What would it be like to live in another family's home, not knowing anyone? Would she feel comfortable taking her meals with a couple she didn't know? What about their sons? Would they be there? She remembered meeting Lola's cousins when she was younger, and they seemed nice enough, though a bit rambunctious. Hadn't she said they'd both moved out recently? Hope couldn't remember how old they were either. What if one of them was handsome, and she fell in love with him? Would she have to give up her teaching position?

Realizing she was getting ahead of herself, she laid back on her pillow and set the letter aside. She needed to make sure she was considering this change for the right reasons. Did she want to be a schoolteacher in Texas to help the students, to follow her own dreams of making the world a better place, or was she running away from Jimmy Brooks? While Hope was fairly settled her reasons were mostly the first two, she'd be lying to herself if she didn't at least admit that part of it was the latter. When she looked at her parents' story, it was certainly the adventure that sparked her enthusiasm, but for them, it had also been about love, about finding themselves but also coming together. Hope wouldn't exactly describe herself as a romantic, but she knew that those feelings of passion and desire that had brought her folks together were woven into her soul as well.

The letter had said she couldn't be married and work as the schoolteacher in McKinney, however, so she needed to keep that in mind. If she moved there and met some handsome gentleman, she may find herself choosing between becoming his wife and keeping her employment, which wasn't at all fair, but it needed to be considered. Even the thought of falling in love had her shaking her head. If she hadn't been able to find someone in the last twenty years, she had no idea why she thought she'd find him in Texas.

The sound of the front door opening announced that her father was home. Hope took a few deep breaths, thinking it would be nice if her grandparents felt well enough to come down for supper so that they could all discuss the situation together. Ultimately, she would be the one to decide, but it would be helpful if the rest of her family weighed in since she valued their opinions so much.

She sat up, taking the letter and slipping it into her pocket, thinking her daddy would most definitely want to study it before he gave any sort of recommendation. She definitely trusted his judgment and knew he wouldn't let emotion sway him the way her mother and sister would.

Hope headed for the stairs, glad to have the letter in her pocket. At least she knew now, and they did want her. Now it was only a question of whether or not she wanted them, and that decision might just end up being the most difficult one she'd ever made in her life.

PART II

CHAPTER EIGHT

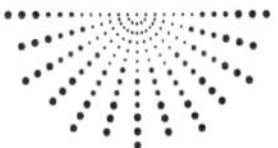

Hope Tucker stepped off of the train and made a sweep of the platform. Very few passengers were disembarking here. Most would go on to Dallas or Fort Worth. She had her carry-on bag over her shoulder and watched as the porters pulled out her two large trunks. Even they must've thought she'd overpacked as they groaned beneath their weight, and they had to have seen all kinds of folks come and go.

She thanked them and slipped them a few coins as her father had suggested. Then, she found herself standing in a lonely train station as the locomotive passed away. The engineer blew the horn, and it sounded like the most solemn noise she'd ever heard in her life.

It was the end of February, which meant she'd arrived only a few days before the deadline, just before she was meant to take over the school. Her previous superintendent had insisted she stay as long as possible and help Lola transition into her role. He hadn't been happy at all with her decision, but by the time Hope announced her intentions, she had decided it was the best one for her and for the students waiting for her. With her family's support, she'd loaded up, and now here she was, glancing around, looking for Mr. Howard and wondering where in the world he might be.

She checked her telegram again. The receipt said she'd told him she'd be arriving on the 2:00 train, and his response was that he'd see her there. Perhaps there had been a delay of some sort. She was sure she was at the right station as the depot was clearly labeled, McKinney, Texas. There was a bench and a ticket window where a little old man stood fiddling with papers and otherwise looking bored. The only other passengers who had gotten off here were long gone, so Hope found herself standing all alone thinking perhaps she'd made an awful mistake and should just purchase a ticket home on the next train heading north.

"Can I help you, darling?" the little old man finally asked, just when Hope thought she might actually start to cry, very uncharacteristic of her. "You waitin' on someone?"

"Yes, sir," she replied, setting her bag down by her trunks and crossing over. "Mr. Bradford Howard was supposed to meet me here."

"Oh, you must be the new schoolteacher." He gave her a grin and adjusted his spectacles. "Well you seem awfully pretty to be a teacher."

Not sure what to think of that, Hope only replied, "Thank you." She didn't know what a schoolteacher was expected to look like or why they couldn't be pretty. "Do you think Mr. Howard will be by directly?"

"Now, that I cannot say. You see, the town's just over that rise in the ground there. Don't take too long to get there, and Mr. Howard is usually punctual. We go to the same church, you see." She nodded, again not sure she followed. "He mighta gotten busy, though. He runs the town's only feed store. Used to farm, but sold most of it off. Except the parcels he kept for his son. Big cattle rancher come in and bought lots of acres. The town's a growin' perty fast, but then so's the whole state...."

The man continued to prattle on for several minutes, and while Hope did her best to pay attention, she wasn't familiar enough with the area to build any context for his words. She imagined he was the sort of man who might talk to just about anyone, and presently, she was a captive audience since she had no way of leaving.

"Miss? Are you the schoolteacher?"

The sound of a male voice behind her made Hope jump. She spun around to find a tall, broad shouldered fellow in a cowboy hat, dressed as if he'd just left a ranch. He looked a little impatient, standing with his hands pushed deep into his pockets. His eyes were familiar, the same shape and light green color as Lola's, she believed, and though she could only see a bit of his hair, it seemed to be a similar light shade.

"I am," she finally managed to get out. "I'm Hope Tucker."

He nodded. "Brady Howard. Nice to meet you, miss. My pa asked me to come fetch you. All this yours?"

Hope looked at her trunks and the bag she'd just set next to them. "It is. Perhaps we need…."

He muttered a curse word, and Hope wondered if his mother knew he wasn't exactly living up to her standards of displaying a character of high Christian morals and values. "Looks real heavy, miss," he added.

"I'm sure it is. Would you like for me to help you?"

He made a rumbling sound deep in his throat, as if she couldn't be of any help at all and said, "I'll manage."

She'd seen two porters struggle to lift her trunks off of the train. She couldn't imagine anyone could carry them by himself, especially not all the way to the wagon, which she saw parked some ways off. But before she could protest, Brady Howard lifted her first trunk all by himself and staggered his way toward the wagon, making it over halfway there before he set it down and rubbed his back.

Thinking she may as well help a bit if she could, Hope grabbed ahold of the strap on the other trunk, deciding she'd drag it to the edge of the platform. It was so heavy, it hardly moved at all, even when she gave it all the effort she had in her. Seeing as though she would just embarrass herself if he saw her trying, she decided to leave it alone and picked up her carry-on bag instead, walking toward the wagon. She'd nearly left the platform before she realized she hadn't said goodbye to the teller. "Have a nice day!" she called, and he waved, though she imagined he'd find something else to say if she stood there long enough.

Brady had her trunk to the back of the wagon now but was struggling to lift it high enough to slide it inside. Hope rushed over, thinking she could at least give it the extra oomph to get it over the lip of the wagon, but by the time she got there, he'd gotten it up. "Did you pack everything you own?" he muttered but didn't wait for a response before heading back to get the other trunk.

Hope didn't bother to follow him, not even with her eyes, though she imagined he was having even more trouble this time. He had to be tired from the first effort, and she thought the second trunk was likely the heaviest. Her mother had done a good job of packing most of her gowns and shoes into that one. She climbed up into the wagon seat, averting her eyes the best she could and trying to take in the Texas landscape.

It seemed to take a good half-hour for Brady to haul the second trunk over, and while he was lifting it into the back, it fell on his toe, causing him to blurt that curse word again. Hope covered her mouth, trying to look shocked, though she honestly wanted to laugh. Served him right for being so dismissive of her help. Once he had it up, he slid it to the back with a violent push and then came around to climb into the driver's seat.

"Thank you." Hope was still unwilling to look at him, though she tried to act friendly. There was something about Lola's cousin she didn't exactly like. He had a look about him, as if he thought he was pretty important. She also didn't like to be dismissed.

Brady said nothing, only jerked the reins, and the horses backed up before straightening out and heading toward town. A few houses came into view first, followed by what appeared to be a main street area off in the distance. Her eyes followed the dirt road up to a large building that towered over everything else in the vicinity. Even at this distance, she could see it sprawled across the center of town. The architecture reminded her of drawings she'd seen of France. "What in the world is that?" she asked, gawking at the structure.

"The courthouse?" Brady asked, his tone letting her know he thought it a silly question. "Ain't you heard of the Collin County Courthouse? It's the tallest building north of San Antonio."

Hope turned her face to look at him, absently wondering what in San Antonio was taller. "It's quite a sight," she replied.

Brady shrugged as if the courthouse was old news. "That's my folks' feed store over yonder." He pointed across the square. "Post office over here. And the schoolhouse is just down that road there."

He turned the wagon, and Hope fought the urge to swivel her head around so that she could continue to stare at the large structure. Instead, she gazed at the buildings on the other side of the street. There was a bank, a five-and-dime, and what appeared to be a saloon, though she thought that probably wasn't the case from what Mrs. Howard had said. Hope had gotten the impression the town was full of teetotalling, Bible-thumping Baptists.

Just a few blocks away from the square, Brady pulled the wagon to a stop in front of a large two-story home. He jumped out and went around back but didn't stop to get her trunks. Not sure what she should do, Hope turned her body so that she could see him as he headed up the walkway. "You need help getting down?" he yelled to her. "I figured if you could get up, you could get down. You ain't a kitten in a tree are you?"

"Are we here then?" Hope asked. She set her bag down near her boots and climbed down from the wagon before he changed his mind and decided she needed help. Once her feet were on the ground, she turned and grabbed her bag.

"Yep. This is my folks' house." He was far ahead of her, but she let him go, choosing to stand back by the road for a moment and look at the dwelling. The structure was painted a grayish blue color with a wide porch and wide windows. Hope had no idea what architectural style it might be, but she liked it.

The front door opened and an older woman stepped out, wiping her hands on a tea towel. Hope studied her for a second. She did look a little unfriendly. She was wearing a dark purple dress with no frills at all, buttoned up to her chin. Her slate gray hair was pulled up on top of her head in a tight bun, and she peered at Hope over the top of her spectacles. "Well, come on in!" she hollered. "Ain't no sense in standing in the front yard."

Swallowing hard, Hope headed for the porch, wondering what she'd gotten herself into. Was everyone in this town so straightforward? "Mrs. Howard?" Hope asked as she stepped up on the porch. She looked more familiar now, and Hope remembered being at Lola's house once when she visited and thinking she didn't look any friendlier than. "I'm Hope Tucker. It's lovely to meet you." She stretched her hand out and forced a smile.

Nita Howard looked at her hand suspiciously before giving it a quick shake. "Nice to meet you, too. Come on in. That all you brought with you?"

"Hell, no it ain't all she brought with her," Brady said from just inside the front door.

"Watch your language, Son," Nita scolded. "Where is it, then? Ain't you gonna fetch it?"

"It weighs more than you, Ma. I figure you can let Doc come carry it up the stairs later when he ain't busy tendin' to every scrape and bump in town."

Confused, Hope looked back at her belongings in the wagon, thinking someone might just abscond with the entire cart. "Perhaps I could empty them and carry my things up the stairs that way?"

"Oh, don't be ridiculous," Nita laughed. "Brady will carry them in for you in a few minutes. Just give him a moment." In a quieter voice, she whispered, "He's not nearly as terrible as he seems."

The kindness in the older woman's voice made Hope think perhaps she was not as terrible as she seemed at first either. "All right," Hope acquiesced. "Your home is lovely." She looked around and noticed the furnishings weren't so different from what her folks had in their home, though some of the pieces looked more worn, as if they'd traveled a great distance to get here, which she imagined some had. She was standing in a small foyer between what appeared to be a parlor and a dining room. Ahead of her, she could see the kitchen, and the stairs were just behind Mrs. Howard. While the house was not nearly as stately as her grandparents' home, it was large enough, and Hope thought she might feel welcome here, so long as Mrs. Howard remained kind—and Brady remained absent.

"Thank you," Mrs. Howard said, ushering her toward the kitchen. "I bet you're ravished after such a long trip. Why don't you set your bag down by the stairs, and I'll fix you some vittles?"

Hope wondered if the woman was under the impression she hadn't eaten or drank anything the whole time she was on the train but supposed that couldn't be the case. She really wasn't hungry, but she found herself saying, "Yes, ma'am. Thank you," and following Mrs. Howard into the kitchen.

There was a round table in the kitchen, and Mrs. Howard pulled out a chair for Hope, which she took. The room was small, but there was an ice box as well as a fireplace for cooking and a washbasin, though it didn't look like they had a pump here. Glancing out the back window, Hope could see a well. At least it was close by.

After a few minutes of scurrying around, Mrs. Howard passed Hope a glass of milk, a piece of salted meat, and a roll. "Hope that's okay. We'll have something better for dinner."

"It's just fine, thank you," Hope replied, not sure what to think of the meat. She had no utensils, so she picked it up and took a bite. It was tough and salty, but otherwise good.

"You like it? We get jerky from one of the local ranchers. Purty good, ain't it?"

Hope wasn't quite sure how to answer that. She didn't want to be impolite. "It's… unique." She smiled, hoping not to sound offensive.

Mrs. Howard raised an eyebrow at her, like she wasn't quite sure what that meant. She did a few more quick chores around the kitchen while Hope drank the fresh milk, which was very good, and had a bite of the roll that was also tasty. Then, Mrs. Howard pulled out the chair across from her and had a seat.

"Now, you should probably know teachin' here ain't gonna be the same as the school yer used to. I'm one of the most educated women in this here town, and I don't speak proper or nothin' at all like that. My letter mighta been deceivin', but I had some help with it."

Hope cleared her throat, planning to choose her words carefully. "You sound educated to me." It did seem as if Mrs. Howard was a better writer than a speaker, though, considering how formal her letter sounded compared to how she was speaking now, she wondered how much help she'd gotten and from whom. Hope had eaten most of the jerky and pulled off another piece of the roll, wondering if she was supposed to eat all of it. "But I know this will be different."

"I taught both of my sons how to read and write, how to do math. Brady, well, he don't care much for book learnin'. He started workin' at the ranch outside of town when he was about fourteen. That was enough schoolin' for him. Nicholas, on the other hand, he always loved to read. Out-learned me when he was about twelve. Then, we had to turn to borrowin' books from the libraries down in Dallas and San Antone by correspondence. He went back east to study medicine, and now he's the town doctor. I'm so proud of that boy, I can't rightly tell you. But that ain't for most around here. I think you'll find most of your students are more like Brady, wishin' to get outside and do somethin' rather than sittin' in a schoolhouse listen to lectures all day."

"I completely understand," Hope nodded, thinking it must be Nicholas who helped with the letter. "There will be many students who are needed at home, especially during the fall and spring. I know that. And there will be many who will miss regularly because of that. But I hope to give them the best education possible while they are in my classroom and to inspire others in the town to understand the necessities of getting a solid education. I'm certain your help with the latter, especially, will be most beneficial. If the other women in town could come to have the understanding you do, I'm certain we can be successful. Perhaps we will have many more doctors and lawyers come from this part of Texas."

The smile on Nita's face was most generous, but before she could speak, laughter from the adjoining room jarred both of them, and Hope heard Brady mutter, "That's the dumbest thing I ever heard," before the front door slammed.

Shaking her head, Mrs. Howard said, "You'll have to excuse my oldest. Just because he don't understand the importance of a good education don't mean others won't, though I reckon there are more who think like Brady than don't round these parts."

Hope wasn't sure what to say to that, so she decided not to respond at all. Instead, she asked, "Do you think I should go lend him a hand? Is he moving my trunks?"

"I reckon that's what he's doing, but I don't think you should bother tryin' to help. He's liable to send you back in anyhow. He won't want no help from a lady."

It was hard to be offended when she realized the mother knew the son pretty well. "I am gracious that you're allowing me to stay in your home. It would've been a more difficult choice if I'd had to stay with strangers. At least, we've met before. And Lola speaks of your family often."

"Lola is a good gal. I wish we lived closer to my brother's family, but my husband has always wanted to live in what he considered untamed country. I wonder if he'll wanna get up and move the more settled this part of Texas becomes. But for now, I suppose it's wild enough. You do have to watch yerself a little now. From time to time, we'll get some lawless folk wandering in here. For the most part, people are friendly enough, don't want to harm nobody. But you jest never know what you might run into."

Hope let that sink in, taking another swallow of her milk before saying, "I noticed the saloon on the town square."

"That's right. It's owned by the sheriff, fellow by the name of Bill Roan. You'll wanna stay on his good side. There's a couple more saloons elsewhere in town. Sometimes we get a whole slew of cattle hands, ranchers, in all at once, wantin' to get themselves a little tipsy and play cards. Some of yer students 'ill also be the offspring of the town's other unmentionables." She raised her eyebrows and tipped her forehead in Hope's direction, like she was hoping her guest would catch her drift.

Racking her brain to figure out what Mrs. Howard was getting at did Hope little good. She had a few extra moments to think on it as Brady worked her first trunk through the door, cursing and smashing into things, mostly the floor.

"Don't mind him," the embarrassed mother said. "He'll get it up the stairs in one piece."

"I sure hope that's the heavy one," Hope muttered, though she had a feeling it was the smaller of the two. "What other unmentionables are you speaking of?"

"You know—entertainers." Hope was still drawing a blank. "*Women* entertainers." Her eyebrows knit together, but Hope was still completely clueless. Mrs. Howard leaned forward. "Prostitutes, honey."

"Oh. Oh!" Of course, Hope knew what that word meant, but she'd never imagined she might actually see a woman of ill repute, especially not at a conference with a student's parent. "I didn't realize…."

"I hate it for our town, but there ain't much anyone can do. Anywhere you have so many men and not enough women to marry 'em all, well, they're gonna move in. There's a red light district. Small —just a house or two. It's awful, and I'm working with the mayor and the city council to try to move 'em out. Maybe you can help with that."

Hope nodded, though she had no idea how she could be of any help. "I do hope most of them will send their children to the school."

"I'm sure they will. Someone to look after their kids for free? Why not?"

Thinking of herself as a nanny didn't sit well with Hope, but listening to Brady drag her trunk up the stairs was even more unsettling, and she decided just to put the whole idea of what may be going on at night out of her mind. "The school is fairly close by, isn't it? So I may walk to and from the building during daylight hours without fearing for my safety?"

"Oh, it's about three-quarters of a mile across town, not too far. Most days, Mr. Howard can likely give you a ride part of the way when he heads to the store. He don't like to walk, especially in inclement weather. And it's almost the rainy season. We got two rainy seasons. Spring and fall. Then, winter ain't so cold most of the time compared to what you're used to. It's the summer that's dreadful hot."

"I have no doubt." Hope knew enough about the Texas climate that she had counted on hot summers. "Will I have to pass by the red light district you spoke of to get back here?"

"No, not exactly. It's about two blocks away from the street you'd likely use. It's a few blocks behind the saloon that sits on the square. Gotta be close enough for them men folk to stumble over when they's good and drunk."

Hope had never actually even tasted any alcohol. Being a Southern Baptist, it was frowned upon, and since her mama didn't drink spirits, she'd always just abstained herself. She'd seen a few drunk men at get-togethers, and her own daddy had been known to drink a bit, though never past what was proper. Imagining a bunch of drunk men stumbling out of a saloon to head to a brothel made her head feel as if Brady was pounding into it with her trunk instead of the stairs.

"Sounds like he's got that one up into the hall," Nita said with a smile. "You finished with your food, honey?"

"Oh, yes, thank you," Hope replied, sliding her plate away. Nita took it without questioning her lack of appetite and disposed of the scraps in what looked like a slop box and the rinsed the plate. "Is there anything I can do to help?"

"No, thank you. I can run the place just fine. One more mouth to feed won't be too much of an inconvenience when I'm used to cookin' for two growin' boys. Now, sometimes Brady comes over for dinner." They heard his boots on the stairs and then as he passed through the front room, still cursing under his breath. "Doc hires out most of his cookin' and cleanin' but he comes over some days. We call him Doc because we're so proud of him."

"I'm sure you are," Hope said with a broad smile. She could imagine how it might feel to have a child who accomplished so much and couldn't blame the mother for being so pleased with everything her child had accomplished.

Brady had made it to the front door now, and by the commotion, Hope could tell he had the larger trunk this time. She prayed it would fit through the narrow passage, and when she heard a scraping sound and then what sounded like quick steps backward, followed by a thunk, she figured that meant he had it in. His success did not keep him from letting go several swear words.

"Brady didn't quite take after his folks when it comes to church going and fittin' into polite society. But he's a good man. Hard worker. Strong as an ox."

"Clearly," Hope replied, meaning the latter. She had no idea if the rest of what Mrs. Howard said was true. "When do you think I might be able to see the school? Classes are to start on Monday, aren't they? That's just a few days away."

"I reckon you can go see it as soon as you're settled. I can have Brady drive you over, or you can wait till tomorrow, and maybe Bradford will have time to take you, though he's been awful busy at the store these days."

"I don't want to be any trouble," Hope replied with a small smile. The idea of going anywhere else with Brady was anything but inviting. "Perhaps I can just walk over."

"I suppose you could if yer good at directions." The mistress of the house gave a small shrug. "Why don't you head upstairs and get settled? Sounds like Brady's got yer things in yer room."

It did sound as if Brady was done. There was a floor jarring bang and the slamming of a door to accentuate his completion, followed by the shouting of an elderly woman to cut down on all that racket. Hope wondered what had taken the person she assumed must be his grandmother so long to shout. Or maybe she had been yelling the whole time, and it was only now that he was finished that they could hear.

"I think that's a fine idea," Hope replied, thinking maybe she could tarry long enough for Brady to clear out. She stood, pushing in her chair, and took her glass to the washbasin, intending to wash it out herself.

"I've got it, honey," Mrs. Howard assured her. "Now yer room'll be the third door on the right."

"The third door on the right?" Hope repeated with a nod. She was sure she could find that. While directions weren't necessarily her strongest suit, she could handle counting to three and knew her right from left, obviously. Perhaps she should just visit the school on her own.

Brady was coming down the stairs as she entered the living room. She walked slowly, hoping to avoid as much interaction as possible. He stopped at the foot of the stairs, though, as if waiting on her, so she was inclined to speak. "Thank you, kindly, Mr. Howard."

"I am inclined to hope you stay on as schoolteacher, Miss Tucker, because if you ever decide to move back home, I am sure as hell not gonna be the one to load you up." He gave a shake of his head and then headed out the door, leaving Hope staring after him with her mouth agape, not sure how to respond.

Of course, she couldn't blame him for being annoyed with her. It had sounded like a lot of work. Her mother had loaded those trunks for her, and she didn't even think her daddy had moved them down the stairs by himself, not that he couldn't, but her mother had invited a few friends over to help since her father was getting on in years, and Cordia hadn't wanted to risk any sort of injury. Even the porters at the train station had struggled, and there'd been two of them. She headed up the stairs, thinking about how silly it was to even consider going home at this point. She was living out her dream, and though there'd been some obstacles, she was determined to see things through.

At the top of the stairs, she saw a thin form in a white nightgown waiting for her. "Good afternoon," she said in a cautious voice, not sure what to think of the woman standing before her. She was fairly certain this was Mr. Howard's mother because she thought Lola's grandmother still lived in Kentucky or wherever it was they'd originally come from. It was hard to say just by looking though; the woman's face was so wrinkled and hidden behind her spectacles and grimace. Hope couldn't tell if she looked like Nita Howard or not.

"You the new schoolteacher?" The voice trembled, and Hope couldn't tell if there was disdain in it or just curiosity.

"Yes, ma'am," she said with a friendly smile. "I'm Hope Tucker. Pleased to meet you." She offered her hand, and the woman looked at it like she thought it might be dirty or hold a weapon.

Without taking her hand, the woman looked her up and down. "We need a schoolteacher. All them kids out there is a bunch of hoodlums." She turned and headed back down the hallway in a shuffle step, and Hope put her hand down. At the end of the hall, she stopped and turned back. "I sure hope you ain't loud."

"No, ma'am," Hope assured her, still standing in the same spot at the top of the stairs.

"Good. I need my rest. I'm sixty-seven years old." She opened the door and went inside, closing it behind her, and Hope thought she looked a lot older than that but would've never said a word. With a deep breath, she walked as carefully as she could across the hallway floor to the third door on the right, which just happened to be directly across the hall from the old woman's room.

She thought the house looked deceptively small from the outside; she never would've guessed there'd be so many rooms up here, but when she opened the door, she got an idea why that might be. The room she stood in couldn't have been larger than ten by eight. It held her two trunks—and her bag, which Brady must've brought up on a separate, more discrete trip—a small bed that she thought she'd just barely fit on, a dresser with a mirror, and the smallest armoire she'd ever seen. Next to the bed was a small night stand, and when Hope opened the cabinet, she was not at all surprised to see it housed a chamber pot. She hadn't noticed an outhouse but was fairly certain if she'd looked hard enough out the back door, she would've found one.

Taking a good look around, Hope suddenly felt overwhelmed. She sat on the bed and held her head in her hands for a few moments. What she really needed was a long soak in a tub of hot water, but she didn't know if that was even a possibility and didn't want to inconvenience her hosts to ask, at least not presently. She lay back on the bed, noticing that at least the quilt was soft, and tried not to let the faded beige wallpaper bother her. This room was a far cry from what she was used to, and she thought for a few moments about the beautiful, ornate, pink and white wallpaper with the tiny flowers and the beautiful pink bedspread she'd left behind. She imagined all of her things in her room, as she'd left them, other than the items she'd brought along, which were not all of her personal items as Brady had assumed. Would her mother leave them just so, and for how long?

Thinking of her mother made her homesick, and a single tear slid down Hope's cheek. She couldn't dwell too much on her folks or else she'd be on the next train back to Missouri, even if that meant leaving all that she'd brought behind since Brady had already warned her he'd be unlikely to take it back down the stairs for her. She did think she should probably send a telegram to her parents and let them know she's arrived. She knew there was a machine in town because she'd sent one to Mrs. Howard before, and they had corresponded a bit that way while Hope was planning her trip. It was still a mystery why Mrs. Howard sounded so educated in writing but when she spoke, she sounded more like what Hope would've expected from these parts. Did her doctor son always help her? Perhaps she had grown accustomed to speaking like those she lived with and didn't give it another thought in her own home.

There was a small clock on the wall, and Hope could see that it was a quarter past three. She wondered if she could walk to the post office and send the message before it closed. They had passed the building on the way in, and it was only a half a mile down the road from what she could tell. Surely, that would be plenty of time.

Hope stood, wiping her cheek on the back of her hand, and went over to the mirror. Her hair was still mostly pinned in place, and her dress, which was a clean one she'd put on that morning on the train, looked presentable. She decided she may as well walk into town and start getting used to her new home. Her parents would want to know she was safe and that she had arrived at the Howards' without incident.

Digging into her bag, she found her purse and dug out enough money to send the telegram. She had brought a decent amount of funds with her and didn't want to carry it all through town when she hadn't any idea what sort of people she might run into at this juncture. Her father had recommended she open a bank account as soon as she had the chance, and that's what she intended to do, but for now, she'd only carry what she needed and trust the rest would be safe here.

Quietly, Hope opened the door, thinking she shouldn't disturb her neighbor. The sound of snoring alerted her that the elderly woman was asleep, and the last thing she wanted to do was wake her with the noise of her traveling boots on the wooden floor or stairs. Thoughts of having to walk that gently for the next year or so made Hope cringe, but she supposed there were worst ways to live.

Once she reached the first floor, she heard Mrs. Howard in the kitchen and was surprised when she heard Brady's voice responding to his mother's, though they were too far away for her to understand what they were saying.

Hope walked in loudly enough for them to hear her coming and change their conversation if necessary. "Pardon the interruption," she said from the doorway, "but I was just thinking I'd walk into town and send my folks a telegram to let them know I made it here safely."

"I'm sure they'd appreciate that," Mrs. Howard replied. "Brady's headed that way. He can give you a ride."

Brady's eyes almost popped out of his head. "Ma, I'm going to the feed store."

"Which is near the post office."

"It's fine. I can walk."

"No, I'll give you a ride," Brady said reluctantly, his eyes now narrowed.

"I really don't want to be any trouble." Hope wasn't any more excited about getting into the wagon with Brady than he seemed to be about being her escort again.

"Don't be ridiculous," Nita insisted. "It's just a few blocks. It certainly won't hurt you none." She gave her son a look that meant business.

"I said I'd take her." Brady headed right toward Hope without even saying goodbye to his mother, and she had to dodge out of his way to avoid a collision.

"Thank you," Hope said to Mrs. Howard who only nodded, her arms crossed. She hurried after Brady, but with his long legs, he was halfway across the yard before Hope even reached the porch. She paused for a while, looking after him, thinking to herself, if this was what McKinney, Texas, was going to be like, she was in for a long school year.

CHAPTER NINE

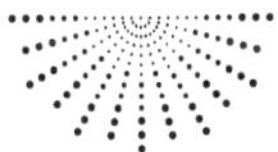

Brady didn't pause to help Hope into the seat of the wagon, but then, she'd already shown him she could handle that herself. Still, his manners were starting to wear on her, and once she was settled, she said, "You can just take me as far as your ma can see if you'd like, and then let me down."

He jerked the reins and circled the wagon around so that it was facing the right direction without replying. "It's not that I mind," he said, his voice displaying only a small bit of remorse. "It's that my ma seems to think I can spend all day catering to whatever she wants, whatever you need."

"Oh." Hope hadn't considered there were other things he should be doing. "Do you need to get to work?"

"I need to get back to my place, but… it don't matter now. The days all but done."

"Maybe I could help. I used to live on a farm when I was younger." Hope wanted to do something to make up for the time he'd lost. She understood farming was a full-time occupation.

He scoffed. "No offense, Miss Tucker, but I can hardly see you out in a field like a farmhand."

She gave him a sharp look but imagined he was probably right.

When she was younger, she used to help her daddy feed the animals and do some of the lighter work, but nothing too taxing, and she knew Brady was strong enough to handle most of those jobs himself, but she wondered if there was nothing at all she could do to repay him for his inconvenience. Hope chose not to argue and turned her head to look where they were going rather than continue to gape at him.

They were headed back the way they came, which made perfect sense because they'd come past the post office where she thought the telegram machine was located. There was a bustle of activity centered around the square, mostly men going in and out of establishments, though Hope did see a few women and children as well, and she wondered if any of them would be her students. The saloon doors were closed tight, a sign, she hoped, that they didn't open until later. She'd just as soon be home safe in the Howards' home before anyone started publicly drinking.

"Most everyone around here's purty friendly," Brady said as they made their way up one side of the square. There were a few wagons and carts in front of them, so he slowed down to make way. "There's a few to stay away from. You'll know most of 'em when you see 'em. Mostly the kind that are drunk before noon. Like old Oscar there." He gestured at a man stumbling down the sidewalk on the inside of the square, near the courthouse.

"Good heavens," Hope muttered, watching him stop to lean on a streetlamp pole. "He looks a mess." The man was older and probably no stronger than she was, but that didn't mean she'd want to encounter him if she could steer clear.

"That he is," Brady agreed. "You'll wanna stay away from any of the transients, too. The cattle and farm hands who are just passing through. Sometimes they can be a little lawless. Sheriff Roan knows how to keep 'em in check for the most part, though."

Hope wasn't sure what to say, so she said nothing. She had yet to see the jail but imagined it must be a large building if so many desperate men passed through town.

"There's a telegraph in the bank and one in the post office. This one'll be faster." They pulled to a stop in front of the bank, and Hope prepared herself to get down from the wagon seat, imagining Brady would just wait for her there, but before she could alight, he made a deep sound in his throat, and Hope paused, wondering what was the matter.

His eyes were fixated on a man coming out of the building. Hope followed the path of his stare to see what looked like an ordinary man wearing dark trousers, a brown vest over his white shirt, and a hat similar to the one everyone else was wearing. She couldn't see much of his face through the brim of the hat, but when he removed it to say good afternoon to an elderly woman coming up the sidewalk, she caught a glimpse of dark blonde hair and blue eyes. If he noticed Brady's penetrating glare, he didn't turn to address it, and a few seconds later, he was on his way down the walkway.

"What is it?" Hope finally asked, once Brady seemed to relax a little.

The large man shook his head, running his hands down his pantlegs like his palms were suddenly sweaty. "Probably nothing," Brady finally replied. "But you know how I told you you could most often tell who to steer clear of?"

"Yes." There was a questioning lilt to her voice Hope hadn't intended, but it was there just the same.

"Well, not every wolf looks like one. That there's Judah Lawless, and he's aptly named. I'd suggest you leave that feller alone. Might be hard cause he may be helpin' out with his sister's kids. They live so far outta town, if'n she decides to bring 'em to school, you may catch wind of 'im again. Stay clear." There was a precision in Brady's eyes that made a shiver run down Hope's spine, but she got the message.

The only problem was, the man looked innocent enough. He wasn't nearly as broad shouldered or tall as Brady, though she thought he looked to be in fine shape and tall enough. He certainly wasn't an intimidating brute. "I understand," she said with a nod of her head, hoping to pacify him a bit, or at least give credence to what he was saying, but curiosity got the better of her, and she asked, "Would you mind telling me why?"

A crooked smile spread across Brady's face, as if he was certain she'd ask before the question even entered her mind. "Because his last name is properly fittin'," Brady replied. "Got two dead wives before the age of thirty. I'd say there's something to that."

"Two dead wives?" Hope repeated, her hands flying to cover her mouth. "He… killed them?"

Brady shrugged. "Says he didn't, a' course, but then, who would say they did? They ain't lived here too awful long, him and his sister and her husband. Two kids. Boy and a girl. They bought land out west of town. Built themselves a big old house. Fancy house, too. Heard he was a builder or something up in New York City for a spell, before they moved here from Kansas. Not sure on any of it. His brother-in-law's a nice enough guy. Paul Pembroke. Who could be scared of a guy named Paul Pembroke?" Brady chuckled, but Hope wasn't sure why it was funny. "At any rate, I suggest you stay away from 'im. He seems nice enough, but generally speakin' there's truth behind most rumors, least in my experience. Now, you wanna go on in and send yer message? I'll wait for you here."

Hope glanced down the walkway and decided Judah Lawless was long gone, so she went ahead and climbed down from the wagon. Almost immediately, she felt like dozens of pairs of eyes were on her, despite the fact that there were not that many people present, and she wondered why she felt that way. Deciding it must be because she was new in town and everyone would be curious about her, she tried putting her shoulders back and her chin up and headed into the bank, a place she should feel comfortable in considering her father and grandfather spent so much of their time in such an institution.

When Hope pushed through the door, she was greeted by what she expected to see. Polished marble floor, intricately carved wooden beams, and two teller stations. The place looked similar to the bank she visited frequently to bring a meal to her father or check in on him when he had to work late. She glimpsed two older gentlemen behind the counter, and although it did seem slightly odd to her that there were thick iron bars between them and the rest of the bank, she thought that must be because there was a higher chance of a robbery here than in Lamar where she'd never seen such a thing before.

She approached the counter, intending to ask directions for how to send a telegram when she overheard a conversation between a pair of women standing near the door. She glanced over to see they looked to be slightly older than her, and while she didn't mean to hear anything they said, she caught a few words that made the hair on the back of her neck stand up.

"Such a shame God wasted good looks on a killer like him," the first one said.

"Yes, and he's so polite, too. Maybe that's how he lures them in," replied the second one. She turned her head and noticed Hope staring, raising an eyebrow at her under her dark blue flowered bonnet.

Remembering herself, Hope forced a small smile and then hurried on to the counter. It seemed evident to her that Brady wasn't the only one who'd heard the stories about Judah Lawless.

"Can I help you, miss?" the teller asked, stepping up to speak to Hope between the bars.

"Yes, I'm new in town, and I'd like to send a telegram to my parents to let them know I've arrived safely."

Before the man could even respond, the other teller, a slightly larger man with a friendly smile, came over and proclaimed, "Why you must be the new schoolteacher!"

Hope felt a rush of color to her cheeks. "Yes, that's right." She wondered how in the world he'd surmised that so quickly.

That brought over the two women and a third Hope hadn't noticed before, and in a few seconds, she felt overwhelmed by all the welcoming statements and handshaking. While she was glad to be appreciated, having so much attention on her made her anxious, and she wished she could just melt back out the door and disappear.

"Now, what is it you wanna say?" the first teller, a man she'd learned was named Harry Garner, asked, a pencil in his hand.

"Just that I've made it to McKinney and all is well. That I'll write them a letter soon." She thought that would have to do since she certainly wouldn't try to describe the Howards' home or Brady's girth in a telegram.

Mr. Garner jotted her message down on an official form, and Hope gave him the information he needed so that he could send it to her father at the bank. She hoped he'd still be there in time to receive it.

As the teller stepped away to send the message, the women she'd heard speaking at the door continued to chatter. "My daughter will be coming to school," said the one in the blue hat. "Her name is Elsie. You'll just love her. She's so clever."

Hope smiled, excited to learn about one of her students. "I'm looking forward to it."

"My son Robert will also be in your class, but his sister isn't old enough yet. She's only four," the other woman, a brunette with a pointy nose stated. "You'll get her soon enough, though, assuming you stay." They all laughed, as if there was a chance Hope might run away, and while her laughter was fake, the idea that she might need to get back on that train wasn't far from her mind.

The third woman was much quieter, but she said, "I don't have children yet, but when I do, I'll feel much better knowing they've got such a pretty teacher to learn from."

"Why, thank you," Hope said with another smile. She had no idea what being pretty and teaching school had to do with each other, but she knew the woman was trying to pay her a compliment, so she accepted.

"All right, Miss Tucker, the message has been sent," Mr. Garner said, coming back to the window.

"Wonderful. How much do I owe you?" Hope dug into her pocket for her money.

"Oh, no charge, not today," Mr. Garner replied, causing Hope to look up at him in confusion. "We're so happy to have you in town, t'would be a shame to charge you to let yer parents know you're here."

"That's Harry Garner for you," the blue hat woman laughed. "One of the most generous man in town."

Harry's cheeks turned red. "Now, don't you go tellin' folks that. They'll all expect free telegrams. And free money, too!"

That caused another roar of laughter, and Hope found herself swept up in the wave again, even though she didn't think it was all that funny. Still, these people had been kind and welcoming, and she appreciated it.

"Thank you kindly, Mr. Garner." She did find a genuine smile for the older man and thought he reminded her a little of the teller at her father's bank who was always so kind.

"Don't mention it, Miss Tucker. Hope to see you soon."

Hope gave him a wave, thinking she should come back in a few days and open an account here. She would need some place to keep her money safe, both the amount she'd brought with her and the money she'd be earning soon, but she didn't want to trouble Mr. Garner with it now, especially not with so many people standing around. What she really wanted to do was climb back into the wagon and insist that Brady take her back to his mother's house so she could go lie down in the small bed she'd just inherited. Either that or back to the train station.

"It was lovely to meet all of you," Hope said as she headed for the door, the women seeming to hang on her as she went.

"We are looking forward to seeing you at church Sunday," one of the women said.

"Yes, please say you'll be there," added another.

"Oh, yes, of course, assuming you mean Mrs. Howard's church?" Hope replied, glad to be outside in the sunshine where at least she could breathe.

"Yes, the very same. First Baptist," blue hat nodded, her lips pursed together.

"I'll be there." Hope managed one more smile and then headed for Brady's waiting wagon. He looked perturbed, as usual, and she imagined he'd wondered what in the world was taking her so long, but she felt she'd completed her errand as quickly as possible under the circumstances, and clearly he could see she'd been ambushed.

The women continued to call after her as Hope looked both ways and crossed the road to the wagon. She was up and in the seat, waving at them while they still chattered on.

"Well, I was gonna ask you what in blazes took so long, but now I know," Brady said, pulling the reins so that the wagon started moving in the opposite direction of the way they'd come.

"Who are those women?" Hope asked, still smiling as she spoke through her teeth.

Brady chortled. "The one in the blue is Mrs. Davinia Murphy. Her husband owns the bakery, and the other is Mrs. Helen Stamine. Her husband owns the five-and-dime, and both of them have too much free time on their hands and love to hear the sounds of their own voices. You'll get to know 'em pretty well if you stick around."

Hope didn't like the doubt she heard in his voice, but she didn't bother to say anything about it. "And what about the other one, the soft-spoken lady in the pink?"

"Oh, that was Celia Jones. Nice woman. Maybe has a screw loose."

"What do you mean?" Hope asked as they made their way past the feed store. She peered inside, wondering if she'd catch a glimpse of Bradford Howard, but she couldn't see through the glare of the sun reflecting off of the glass.

"Celia will tell you all about her true love, Donald Petrie, even calls him her husband from time to time. Ain't no one ever met Donald Petrie, though. She insists he's off fighting the Mexicans, but… if he exists, it might only be in her imagination." Brady raised an eyebrow, and Hope had to pull her eyes off of him, thinking of how pathetic Celia sounded. Had she invented Donald in her mind?

"Who takes care of her?" Hope asked, realizing now that Brady must be taking her to the school.

"She lives with her folks. Real nice people. Her daddy owns the grocery store. So everyone's nice to Celia. But, clearly, she ain't right in the head."

"And what do her folks say about Donald?"

"They patronize her, tell her he'll be home soon enough. Behind closed doors, they've admitted they ain't sure where she got this feller, but it's obvious there ain't no such person."

Hope's stomach fell, thinking of poor Celia. She'd seemed awfully kind in the bank, and she didn't look to be too much older than Hope. It was a shame to think there was something wrong with her. "Has she been to see your brother, the doctor?"

"Nah. He couldn't help her anyhow. He don't treat wanderin' minds. I heard her folks took her to some fancy brain doctor in San Antone, but I guess they ain't helped her none. I'm sure she'd be locked up in one of them institutions if she were livin' in New England or some place, but round here, we just tolerate her."

Hope supposed that was better than the alternative, but she didn't say anything else. This was sure shaping up to be a strange place. In front of her, she saw a building that had to be the schoolhouse. It was longer than the one she was used to teaching in, and the outer walls were white, not red, but there was a large bell hanging over top of it, and she couldn't imagine it was anything else.

There was plenty of land around the building, despite still being close to a few houses, and Hope could imagine the kids running around, playing here during recess. If only there were some swings or a teeter totter like they were putting in at some of the schools back East. She did see two outhouses and a well in back.

"Well, this is it. What do you think?" Brady pulled up close to the front entrance, and Hope couldn't contain her smile.

"It's lovely. Would it be possible for me to go inside?"

Brady let out a loud sigh like she was taking up his valuable time, but he nodded, and she didn't need to be told twice. She jumped down and headed for the door.

Inside, there were rows of mismatched benches and tables. Some of them looked like they'd belonged in another schoolhouse at the turn of the century. Others looked like they'd just been made. The smell of chalk and freshly cut wood filled her lungs, and Hope felt as if she were home.

A quick glance around left her with several questions, however. There were shelves, but no books. Rows of chalk lined the front blackboard, but there were no slates, not enough erasers. She opened the drawers to her desk and found them empty. While the building itself looked large enough, with plenty of storage, and a nice fireplace, there were still supplies and other items she would need. With a deep breath, she headed back outside.

Brady was standing next to the door, his arms folded, and she imagined he was not the person she needed to talk to. "Can you tell me where the school board president lives?" she asked, hoping her voice sounded chipper and not panicked or ungrateful.

"Mr. Stewart? He lives two houses down, but he's likely still at the bank."

"The bank?" Hope asked, confused.

"Yes. He's the acting superintendent of schools, as well as the school board president, but he's also the president of the bank."

Wishing she'd known that while she was at the bank, Hope could only mutter, "Oh." She folded her arms as well and leaned back against the building, wondering what she should do.

"Is something wrong?"

"Well, it's just... there are supplies I will need, and since school starts on Monday—in just a few days—I was hoping to see if I could get them before class started, that's all." Perhaps she could speak with Mr. Stewart the next day.

"I see," Brady commented, more kindness and understanding in the statement than Hope would've expected. "Maybe my ma knows something about it. She can probably help you with that."

Hope's eyes widened. "Yes, of course. I'm sure that Mrs. Howard will know how important the proper supplies are. Thank you, Brady."

"Shall we head home then?"

"Yes, let's do." Hope was still nervous, but she headed for the wagon with optimism in her heart. If Mrs. Howard couldn't help her, perhaps she could at least point her in the right direction. Surely, Mr. Stewart wouldn't go to all the trouble to hire a schoolteacher but not give her the proper supplies she needed to be successful.

"Now, when you walk home of a' afternoon, I think you should go this way," Brady said, taking a different road than the one they'd come down. "This'll steer you away from the square."

"Is the square dangerous?" Hope asked, thinking all she'd seen that was a threat was the saloon, if she didn't count the man who may have murdered his wives—but he was liable to be anywhere.

"Nah, but if there's trouble, that's likely where it'll be. Or over behind the saloon in the red light district." She knew what he was talking about. "The church is up there on the corner."

He pointed to a red brick building, which was substantially larger than what Hope would've expected. But then the mammoth sized courthouse should've been a clue that everything was bigger in Texas. "It's lovely." She couldn't think of any other way to describe it and a sudden weariness settled around her. A nap was sounding like a wonderful idea.

"My girl's father is the preacher."

Hope turned her head quickly to look at Brady, confusion washing over her once again. "Your girl?" she repeated, not sure who he was talking about. "What do you mean?"

A blush filled his cheeks as Brady explained. "My girl—my betrothed. Anna. Her father's the preacher at the church. Name's Jeb Wilcox. You'll like 'im just fine. Nice man."

Hope continued to stare. "I had no idea you had a girl." She was glad for him and relieved. The last thing in the world she needed was for Brady Howard to take a liking to her.

He shrugged, and she could see he was embarrassed for some reason. "Anna's a mighty fine woman. Round here, we ain't got too many ladies to choose from, so I claimed stakes to her a long time ago, when we was in Sunday school together."

A smile slipped across Hope's face as she saw a tender side to Brady, something she would've never imagined a few hours ago when he was cursing at her trunks. "And are you going to get married?"

"We are. Anna wants to wait until Christmastime, though. Says she's always wanted a December weddin', and that's fine with me. I ain't in no hurry."

Now that, Hope thought was odd. "What do you mean?"

He let out a sigh and shifted in his seat. "Nothin'. It's only… Anna ain't the same girl as she was when I first started courtin' her, that's all. She's purty enough, it's just... I'm hopin' she'll be more like herself before we get married. She… she says she is who she is, and she ain't changin' for nobody. And I can live with that, I suppose. It's just…." He stopped talking, and Hope wasn't sure what in the world he might be getting at. Was she crazy like Celia? Or was it something else? "I guess you'll see when you meet her."

Hope's forehead was crinkled so tightly, she imagined it looked as if she only had one eyebrow, but she decided not to prod. Brady had been helpful to her, if not particularly nice, and there was no reason to press him if he didn't want to talk about it. "She seems like a nice girl. I hope we can be friends."

"I am fairly certain you will be," Brady replied, and once again, Hope found herself lost. "That is, she is a nice girl. And yer a nice girl. So maybe you will be." He gave Hope a small smile, but she thought she saw something else in his eyes, and she prayed that Brady Howard wasn't starting to think she was nice in more ways than just her disposition.

The Howards' home came into view in front of them, and Hope noticed a carriage tied up outside, a brown horse with a nice sheen to it standing near the hitching post. Before she could inquire as to who might be visiting, Brady muttered, "Great. Now he shows up—after the trunks are upstairs." No further explanation was needed, and Hope realized she was about to meet the other Howard son. Hopefully, this one would be a little less rough around the edges, although Brady Howard wasn't quite as tough as he seemed. Otherwise, she imagined mentioning his girl probably wouldn't have brought a blush to his cheeks. If she was lucky, Nicholas Howard would be his opposite. And in a perfect world he would also be betrothed because if there was anything in the world Hope didn't need at the moment it was a man developing feelings for her. That might be enough to put her right back on the first train out of Texas.

CHAPTER TEN

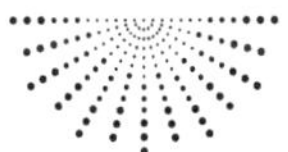

Nicholas Howard looked nothing like his brother. He was slender, though Hope got the impression there was strength in his arms when he shook her hand. Without his hat, he was only an inch or two taller than her, and he had a friendly smile, the sort that put a person at ease almost immediately.

Hope found a gentleness in his nature from the moment he asked how her trip was. Seated on the settee in Mrs. Howard's parlor, Doc, as the rest of the family called him, across from her in a chair, Hope found herself prattling on for quite some time about the train ride, and he listened and asked questions. She felt instantly comfortable and confided in him more than she had ever done so with a complete stranger.

Mrs. Howard brought them tea and settled on the other side of the room in a chair next to the window where she could better see to do her embroidery while Brady had simply dropped her at the side of the road and left. Hope got the impression the two brothers were not particularly close.

"I feel as if I've been talking for ages," Hope said after giving a full description of her trip. "Tell me about your practice."

Doc smoothed back his light brown hair and gave a humble shrug.

"There's not too much to tell, I suppose. I treat every sort of ailment you can imagine, from whooping cough to broken bones. Bein' the only doctor for some twenty miles keeps me busy."

"I can imagine. It sounds quite interesting to me." Hope smiled and took a sip of her tea. "Are you on-call all hours of the day and night?"

"I'm afraid so," Doc admitted. "It makes having a personal life difficult."

"He even got called out to deliver a baby on Christmas Eve," Nita mentioned, glancing up from her stitching.

"Is that so?" Hope couldn't imagine having to leave her family in the middle of a holiday, but in an emergency, he would be the only one who could help.

"Yes, but it was all worth it when that tiny baby boy cried for the first time. It reminded me of Jesus' birth."

"I can imagine such an experience would be rather spiritual." Hope stifled a yawn. As much as she enjoyed speaking to this Mr. Howard, she found her eyes heavy.

Nita took note. "Supper will be ready shortly. Do you think you can stay awake long enough to eat, or would you rather go lie down?"

"Oh, I'm sure I can manage...."

"Forgive me," Doc said, leaning forward in his seat. "I didn't think about how exhausted you must be from the train ride. And here I am asking you a hundred and one questions."

"No, it's fine," Hope assured him. "It would be silly for me to try to lie down when supper is almost ready."

"Mr. Howard should be home momentarily. I think he's been working longer these past few days." Mrs. Howard leaned forward so she could see out the window, and Hope turned as well, but there was no sign of him.

Looking at the road reminded Hope of her trip to the school with Brady. "Mrs. Howard, I forgot to mention, when Brady took me to the school, I noticed there were no books, not enough chalk, and no slates for the children. Are those items we will have available to us? It will make it much more difficult to teach without them."

Mrs. Howard's forehead puckered. "I'm not rightly sure," she said, brushing loose hair back into her bun. "I reckon we oughtta check with Mr. Stewart."

"Yes, that's what I was thinking. It's just… having never met the man, I wasn't sure how to approach him."

"We could go by the bank tomorrow and speak to him," Nita suggested. "That way you can check to see if you have any news from your parents as well."

"Good idea." Hope felt slightly relieved. Knowing that Mrs. Howard would be with her, and that she was such an advocate for the school, made her feel much better about facing a gentlemen she did not know.

"If you'd like to stop by my office while you're downtown, I'd be happy to give you a tour," Doc offered. "It's not much, but it's near the pharmacy. I still make house calls, but I prefer to have one place where people can find me." His smile was friendly and warm, and Hope noticed a tinge of pink in his cheeks, as if asking her to visit the office really meant something else entirely. She thought the idea of having his own office was revolutionary and wondered why other doctors didn't run their practices that way.

"I think that would be lovely," Hope said, fighting a blush in her own cheeks. Mrs. Howard made a small noise in the back of her throat, and Hope's head turned immediately in her direction to see a smile creeping across the woman's lips.

Before she could question what the look might be for, the front door flew open, and Nita shot out of her seat and into the adjoining foyer.

Startled, Hope leaned back on the settee, her hand clutched at her throat.

"That's just my pa," Nicholas said, rising. "He always seems to feel the need to make a grand entrance."

Feeling a little silly, Hope said, "Oh, yes, of course."

The doctor offered her his hand, and she took it. He pulled her up to standing, and then released her, but the warmth from his touch lingered even after they walked into the parlor. It was a sensation Hope wasn't used to, but she found it pleasant. She also thought his cologne was nice. The scent of pine and spice mixed together, masking the faint scent of a chemical she didn't recognize, though she thought it had to be medicinal.

Mr. Howard was tall and wide, much like Brady only larger. He had a loud laugh that echoed around the foyer, but since Hope wasn't sure what was so funny, she stood smiling in the doorway.

"And then, I told them if they wanted to feed horse food to their cattle, that was none of my concern," he continued, making his wife burst into a fit of laughter. Mr. Howard paused mid-story, his eyes having fallen on Hope. "Ah, the schoolteacher. How are you Miss Tucker?" He stepped around his wife and offered his hand, which Hope took. "I'm so sorry I wasn't able to pick you up at the train station myself. I trust Brady was on time?"

Seeing no point in notifying his parents that Brady had been a few minutes late, Hope replied, "Yes, Brady was most helpful. It's a pleasure to meet you, Mr. Howard. Thank you so much for allowing me to stay in your home."

"The pleasure is all ours." There was a twinkle in Mr. Howard's eye that Hope couldn't quite place, but she felt welcome just the same. "I see you've met Doc as well."

Nicholas had moved out of the way as Bradford crossed the oak floor to shake Hope's hand, and he only offered her a small smile now.

"Yes. We've had the most wonderful conversation. I forgot to mention that my mother trained as a nurse during the war." She looked at Doc as she spoke and he nodded with interest. "I have always been fascinated by medicine, though I don't know much about it."

"Yet another reason for you to come by the office tomorrow." Doc smiled at her, and Hope found herself returning the gesture.

"Well, I am half-starved!" Mr. Howard proclaimed, his hands on his bulging belly.

"We should head on into the kitchen," Nita replied, leading the way. "The cornbread should've browned by now."

Hope started to move in that direction, following Mr. Bradford, but Doc stepped directly in her path, as if he were headed out the door, and they sidestepped each other several times before he said, "I'll stay still. You go."

Giggling, Hope proceeded past him. "Aren't you staying for supper?"

"Not tonight," Doc replied. "I have some reports to write up and a few other matters to attend to."

Disappointed, Hope only managed a small, "Oh."

"But I do hope you'll stop by tomorrow, Hope." Noticing he'd said her name twice, he gave a small chuckle and turned a shade of pink again.

"I definitely hope to." Most of the time saying her name in any other context was bothersome to her, but when he laughed at her attempt at humor, Hope couldn't help but laugh as well.

"Have a good evening." Doc stepped backward toward the door.

"You as well." Giving a small wave, Hope headed on to the kitchen as Doc shouted his goodbyes to his parents who answered in turn.

The scent of freshly made cornbread wafted through the air, mingling with beans and ham, and Hope found herself placing a hand over her stomach to keep it from growling. Despite her earlier snack, she was famished, and everything smelled delightful. "Can I help with anything?" she asked upon entering the kitchen.

"Nope, all ready to go," Mrs. Howard said, setting a final pot down in the middle of the round dining table. Hope thought it was nice and quaint to sit in the nook in the kitchen, rather than the formal dining room, and she imagined they mostly used the larger room for get-togethers. Mr. Howard did take up a bit more than his fair share of the table, but there was plenty of room, plenty of food, and plenty of friendly faces. Hope felt like perhaps she would get along just fine in McKinney, Texas, so long as her students had the supplies they needed, and she intended to take care of that the next day. After that, perhaps she'd have a few minutes to spend with a certain handsome doctor. Thoughts of boarding the next train back to Missouri began to dissipate as Mr. Howard launched into another anecdote, and Hope was thankful she'd decided to take a chance on this new adventure.

CHAPTER ELEVEN

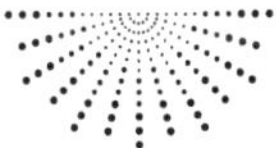

The first night in her new bed was uncomfortable to say the least, and Hope woke up with a crick in her neck. She wasn't sure if it was the size of the mattress or just the being away from home, but other than the sleeping arrangement itself, the rest of the stay was pleasant. She'd had a lovely time getting to know the Howard family. Even Brady, who she had decided wasn't as gruff and fierce as he seemed, was an interesting addition to her circle, and when Hope hopped out of her bed with the sun the next morning, she was ready to face the day.

Downstairs, Mrs. Howard was just finishing up breakfast, and Hope wondered what time she must've risen in order to have bacon, eggs, and biscuits ready at such an early hour. As if reading her mind, Nita smiled and said, "My mother-in-law tends to rise early. She expects her oatmeal by five."

Hope's eyebrows perked up, but she didn't know what to say, so she didn't respond. "Do you need any help?"

"No, dear, thank you," Mrs. Howard replied, sliding a full plate of breakfast across the table to the seat where Hope had eaten supper the night before. "Why don't you go ahead and start, and I'll go check on Mr. Howard."

Hope felt a little awkward eating without the rest of the family, but the sizzling bacon made her mouth water, and she went ahead and had a seat while Mrs. Howard headed back upstairs. Though she missed the easy conversation of the evening before, it was relaxing to sit and look out the window at the back garden while she ate all alone with just the chirping birds to keep her company.

She decided Mr. Howard must be hard to rouse in the morning because she was nearly done with her entire breakfast by the time she heard creaking floorboards above her. She'd already rinsed her plate and set about sweeping up the kitchen floor before Mrs. Howard reappeared. Hope imagined her husband was still getting dressed.

"Oh, honey, you don't have to do that," Nita said, gesturing at the broom.

"It's the least I could do," Hope replied. "All of you have been so kind to me. I feel like I'm taking advantage, not helping out in anyway."

"You just concentrate on learnin' them kids," Mrs. Howard replied, though she didn't take the broom. She went over to the stove and fixed herself a plate, taking it to the table and digging in while Hope finished sweeping and did a few more household chores.

When Mr. Howard finally made his appearance, Mrs. Howard jumped up to fix his plate. "I sure hope this is still warm," she muttered.

He stretched and took his seat at the table. "You say that every morning, darlin', and every morning it's wonderful."

"Yes, well, one of us needs to get up earlier…"

"Or the other needs to get up later." He laughed, and Hope imagined they must say the same thing to each other every morning. "Now, Miss Tucker, what are you doin'? Don't you know you are a guest in our home?"

With a sheepish grin, Hope stopped wiping the counters for a moment and said, "Yes, Mr. Howard, I know that. It's just not in my nature to keep from helping out."

"Well, maybe once you get started at school you'll feel different," Mrs. Howard said, setting a huge platter full of breakfast items in front of her husband.

"Maybe so," Hope conceded. She may well be exhausted after a couple of days of teaching children who had never been to school before. She finished tidying up and then wondered what to do with herself.

"The bank won't be open for another couple of hours, so if you have some things to do in yer room, I can holler atcha when it's time to go," Nita said.

The idea of going back to the small room and sitting on that uncomfortable bed wasn't too inviting. She'd penned a letter to her folks the evening before and it already had a stamp on it. "Actually, I think I'll walk down to the post office and mail a letter. It has a drop box, doesn't it?"

"Sure does," Mr. Howard answered her.

"All right. Do you want me to just meet you up there in a spell or do you wanna come back here?" Nita asked, pulling out a chair and sitting next to her husband as he finished his breakfast.

Hope considered her options, and seeing as though the saloon was closed this time of day, she could see no harm in taking a little stroll around the square while she waited for the bank to open. "I can meet you at the bank."

"Alrighty. Opens at nine." Nita gave her a smile and then turned her attention to her husband.

On her way up the stairs to grab her letter, Hope checked the time and saw that it wasn't quite seven. She'd have plenty of time to wander around town, maybe a bit too much time, but then she had nothing else to do. She slipped the letter into the pocket of her skirt and checked her hair, pressing a few pins into place, before she grabbed her best sun bonnet and slipped it on. The yellow flowers would match the same shade in her dress.

Since she was going to the bank anyway, Hope decided to go ahead and open an account. She pulled out most of the money she'd brought with her, all but a few coins and bills she might need for incidentals, and placed it in her other skirt pocket. She hoped it would be as easy to open an account here as it was in Lamar, but then, she did have a few connections at the Barton County State Bank.

Hope took one more look around the small room and decided there was nothing else that needed to be done here, so she headed down the stairs, glad to be out of her cramped quarters.

In the foyer, she heard Mr. Howard's raucous laughter and paused to enjoy it for a moment. *Living with him must be entertaining,* she thought, and she wondered why it was Brady looked so much like his father but didn't have his disposition at all.

Thinking of Brady made his brother come to mind. She pulled open the door and stepped out into the fresh morning air, noticing the dew on the grass, and thought about how nice Doc was. Even though she'd just had one conversation with him, she felt like she'd known him for ages. He was intelligent, educated, polite, and not at all bad to look at.

Hope went on her way to the town square thinking about the rules she'd agreed to regarding her own marriage, and then she almost laughed aloud at her own silliness. She certainly was jumping ahead of herself. For all she knew, Nicholas was engaged to be married, the same as Brady. How long had it taken the other brother to mention Anna? No, it was more than a little foolish for Hope to start thinking about her future somehow being connected to Nicholas Howard.

The sound of children's laughter hit her ears, and she looked around to see a little girl and a slightly taller boy playing in the back of one of the houses. They looked to be school-aged, and she wondered if they would be in her class. The girl caught her staring, and Hope gave a little wave. The young girl waved back, her smile showing several missing teeth. Hope was certain she'd remember her face if she saw her again, and since school started in just a few days, she thought maybe the little one would remember her, too.

The enormous courthouse building came into view as Hope approached the square. There were already some wagons and carriages passing through, some bustle behind the buildings as merchants prepared for the day. She wondered if Mr. Howard's days were long because he didn't arrive as early as these other people. Passing by some of the shops, she noticed that many of them opened at 8:00. She thought perhaps the bank was the only building that opened later.

Situated on the corner across from the bank, which was on the opposite side of the street, the post office would have been an impressive building if it weren't overshadowed by the courthouse. An older gentleman approached the steps that led up to the door and the drop box as Hope stood and stared at the grand architecture. "Mornin', miss," he said, giving her a nod.

"Good morning." She smiled, glad that her first encounter on the street had been a pleasant one.

"You gotta letter?"

"Yes, I do." She patted her pocket.

"Well, I can take it fer ya. I'm the postmaster. Name's Dale Twinston, but people call me Twinny."

"It's very nice to meet you, Twinny." He bowed his head, and she nodded. "I'm Hope Tucker, the new schoolteacher."

"Well, I'll be!" he shouted, leaning back and putting his hands on his hips. "It's real nice to meet you, Miss Tucker. My grandbabies'll be in yer class. Joshua and Nancy Twinston. Their ma's been learnin' 'em at home these past few years, but they's real excited to have a real teacher. They'll be extra excited to see she's young and perty." He giggled a little with the last statement, and Hope felt her face flush.

"Why, thank you, Twinny," she said, not sure what else to say. "The letter has a stamp and everything." She pulled it out of her pocket.

"I'll make sure it goes out today." He took the letter and glanced down at it. "Missouri, huh? Far off from here."

"It is," she agreed. "But I have no doubt McKinney will feel like home to me real soon."

"It's a nice place," Twinny agreed. "Most folks is real nice, and you can be sure we's excited to have you here. Just... there's a few you gotta be leery of, that's all. I'm sure you'll scout 'em out right quick." He chuckled, and she smiled at him, even though she wasn't quite sure how it was she was supposed to know who he was referring to.

"Thank you, Twinny." It seemed as if there wasn't much else to say, and even though Twinny was nice, Hope was curious to see the rest of the shops on the square. "It was lovely to meet you."

"You, too, Miss Tucker." He gave a little wave and then headed up the stairs, her letter in his hand, and Hope said a little prayer that it would actually make it into the outgoing mail. At least it wasn't anything too horribly important.

She continued to explore the square for the next couple of hours. Before the shops opened, she found a spot on a bench and watched the people driving by and the shop owners preparing for the day. Once the doors began to switch their signs to open, she weaved her way through several of them, taking in all that McKinney had to offer. There was a bakery that made divine pastries; after she'd eaten the first one, she'd purchased and pocketed a second. The dress shop had all sorts of lovely fabric, some with patterns she'd never seen before. She was astounded to know a small town in Texas could have such a selection, but the owner, a sweet older woman by the name of Carlotta, explained that she was able to procure much of her wares from New Orleans and that her husband made a special trip every few months. The prices reflected her trouble, and Hope wondered how in the world she managed to sell such finery to the folks she'd met so far, but then, Carlotta mentioned she had clientele come from all over, including Dallas and San Antone.

When Hope spotted a bookstore on the corner across from the feed store, her eyes nearly bulged out of her head. She flew the last few steps and pulled open the door so quickly, she almost ran into a man exiting.

"Pardon me," he said, lurching out of the way.

Hope froze, her hand still on the door, a lump forming in her throat. At first, all she noticed were crystal blue eyes, and that alone would've been enough to set her heart palpitating, but then she realized she recognized the face. It was him—the man Brady had warned her about. Judah Lawless. She stammered, unable to speak, and continued to stare at him.

Judah lowered the book he'd been staring at before they'd nearly collided. "You okay, miss?" His eyebrows knit together in concern, and Hope couldn't help but think he was the most handsome man she'd ever seen. His jaw was square, his nose perfectly proportioned, and his hair was a light caramel color. For a second, she forgot all about his two poor dead wives and imagined herself strolling through the park on his arm while he read Shakespeare to her. "Miss?"

"Oh, uh, yes. I'm fine." Hope took a deep breath, wanting to kick herself. "It's just... I'm new here, and I had no idea there was a bookstore."

One corner of his upper lip pulled up sharply so that he was grinning at her impishly. "I see. Well, I'm sorry to disappoint you, but it's actually a library."

Hope's eyes widened. "Even better!"

The sound of his laughter was melodic, and Hope found herself staring once again. "Mr. Canton's a good fellow. He'll hook you up with whatever you like to read." He gestured at a short, balding man who was gawking at them from between two rows of bookshelves. The older man gave a little wave, and Hope's free hand shot up in recognition. "Just don't get lost in there."

Hope giggled, her eyes tracing over all the shelves of books. "I think I could. I never imagined...." There was a library in Lamar, and it was one of Hope's favorite places to visit when she was a little girl. But she never would've dreamed there would be a library here. Even though it wasn't that large and probably held only a fraction of the books she'd had to choose from back home, she couldn't wipe the smile from her face.

"I best be going. I need to get this book back to my niece before she has a conniption. It was nice to meet you, Miss...?"

"Tucker. Hope Tucker." She propped the door with her boot and offered her hand, though as he reached out to shake it, Brady's words danced through her mind, and Hope felt a zing of electricity when Judah's hand touched hers. This man was dangerous, despite the fact that he was holding a copy of a children's primer in his other hand and had the sort of smile that made a girl weak in the knees.

"Hope Tucker. The new schoolteacher." It wasn't a question. He continued to hold her hand a bit too long before releasing it. "I'm Judah. Nice to meet you."

"You, too," she said, noticing he didn't bother to mention his last name. "Will your niece be in my class?"

"She will," he nodded. "Ginny Pembroke. My nephew, George, will be there, too. They are so excited I don't know how my sister will contain them for the next few days."

"I'm looking forward to meeting them." Hope imagined two children that looked similar to Judah bouncing around a farmhouse, eagerly awaiting the start of school.

"They'll be happy just to know I've met you, and you really do exist." He laughed again, that musical sound sending a flutter through Hope's heart. "Take care, Miss Tucker."

"You, too."

He stepped aside, and she fought the urge to follow him with her eyes. Instead, she took a deep breath and walked into the library. Mr. Canton was running a cloth along the top of the shelves, and Hope thought she saw a bit of an amused expression in his eyes as he turned to her. "Good mornin'. It's nice to meet you. We're lucky to have you in these parts."

"Why, thank you," Hope replied, not even sure where to begin. There were no labels on any of the shelves, so it was difficult to tell where the children's books might be, or where the ones she might want to read herself were located. "How long has the library been open?"

"Not long," Mr. Canton replied, lifting the cloth and shifting it back and forth between his hands. "I figured if we was going to have a schoolteacher, we should have a library. So… as soon as they started building the school last summer, I started bringing in the books."

"I see." Hope's eyes flickered over some of the volumes close by. She recognized many of the titles and authors. Swift, Dickens, Twain. Some were newer while others were well-loved. She even saw a copy of her mother's favorite book, *Pride and Prejudice*. "I wonder, do you happen to know why there are no books at the school?"

Mr. Canton made a low rumble in his throat and looked away. "I'm afraid you'll need to talk to Mr. Stewart about that decision," he replied, and Hope got the feeling that procuring a student library might be a little more difficult than she'd initially imagined.

"Why is that?" Her fingers traced the spines of some of the books as she inhaled the intoxicating smell of old pages and binding glue.

"He's the one who made that determination." Mr. Canton began to walk away from her, back toward a desk with several volumes stacked atop it. She imagined these were new additions.

Since he clearly wasn't able or willing to help her understand Mr.

Stewart's thinking, Hope decided to change her line of questioning. "Are there many people who come to check out books? Do they bring their children?"

"Honestly," Mr. Canton said, letting out a sigh, "I'm afraid it isn't as popular as I had hoped. Because I also have another business to run, the library is only open in the morning on Monday, Wednesday, and Friday, and then only for a few hours. Most people don't have extra time to read. They're too busy tending their farms or raising their children."

"That's too bad," Hope thought aloud. "Perhaps if the library were open on a Saturday, more people could come."

"Perhaps." Mr. Canton shrugged his shoulders, and Hope could see that this was a problem he'd been dealing with for some time. "I'm not sure how much longer I'll be able to manage. I was relying on donations to procure the books, that and my own money. Funds have sort of dried up."

Hope nodded in understanding. If people weren't borrowing the books, there'd be no one to support the library itself. "Perhaps now that I'm here, I can encourage parents to check out books for their children, maybe give a little extra if they can. I'm hoping to speak to Mr. Stewart soon about obtaining books for the school. Maybe I can mention the library then as well. With his support…."

Mr. Canton cut her off with a shake of his head. "The superintendent is for learning, but he is very careful about what he expects students to read. He would say everyone has a copy of the Bible—let them read that."

"The Bible?" Hope echoed. "Why, that's one of the most difficult books to read. How would a child learn to read by studying a book written with words that we no longer use, like thee and thou?"

"You're preachin' to the choir, miss," Canton replied. "If you can get an answer for that, please let me know."

Hope let out a sigh of frustration but realized Mr. Canton could be an ally to her. They both needed support from the school board and the rest of the community. "Do you mind if I borrow a book?"

"No, please do," he said with a smile, likely happy to have moved to another subject.

Hope began to explore the aisles of books, not really sure what she was looking for. She still had over a half an hour before she had to meet Mrs. Howard, but she kept one eye on the cuckoo clock on the wall to make sure she didn't get lost in the pages. Eventually, she settled on a well-loved copy of *A Tale of Two Cities* and brought it over to Mr. Canton so he could make note.

"Dickens. One of my favorite authors. Have you read this one?"

"I have." She smiled, thinking about the last time she'd flipped through these pages, sitting by the hearth while her mother embroidered. She'd read it aloud to her mother and sister, and Faith had gushed about how noble Lucie was. Thinking of her family made Hope long for home, and she had to push those memories aside.

"Did you bring any books with you?" Mr. Canton asked, handing over the volume.

"Only a few. I brought some I thought the children might like—*Gulliver's Travels. Little Women. Frankenstein.*"

"Oh, yes, all good ones. We have some other volumes of Louisa May Alcott if you ever care to borrow them." He gestured to a shelf Hope hadn't made it to, and she made a mental note. She was very fond of Miss Alcott's writing style and especially loved *Little Women* because of its mention of the war; it reminded her of her parents.

"I will have to choose one next time." Hope smiled, tucking the book under her arm. "Thank you very much, Mr. Canton. It was lovely to meet you."

"You, too, Miss Tucker. As I said, we are very lucky to have you in our little town. I hope you'll be happy here." He pressed his lips together, the ends turning up in a partial smile. His eyes widened slightly, as if he wanted to say something else but wasn't sure, so Hope continued to stare at him expectantly. "You... you should know, not everything you hear in these parts is true. Give folks a chance." He gave a solid nod, as if that was all he intended to say about that, and then moved away from her.

Hope's forehead crinkled. She wasn't quite sure what he was trying to say, but she thanked him one more time and then moved toward the door. Whatever might he be talking about?

The square was definitely busier now than it had been when she'd stepped inside the library, and standing on the walkway with the door in her hand, she remembered her encounter with Judah Lawless. A chill went up her spine. He didn't at all seem like the sort of man who could kill another person, particularly not his own wives. But then, Hope had heard tell of plenty of men who were nice enough to your face, and the next thing you know, they were shooting up a saloon, robbing a bank, or stealing horses. She had no reason to think Judah Lawless was a bad person, but surely the townsfolk knew him better than she did.

She let go of the door and tried to push the thoughts aside. Moving to McKinney had been about teaching the children and nothing more. What she thought about Judah Lawless had nothing to do with anything. With only a few minutes to spare, she hurried to the other side of the square where the bank was located, hoping to see Nita on the way.

It was a bright day, and Hope pulled her bonnet down a bit to block the sun. With only one side of the square left to traverse, she saw a familiar figure coming from the other direction and couldn't help but smile. Nita's straight back and slender figure were easy to pick out despite there being plenty of other folks going about their daily routine and entering and exiting the shops.

Once she was certain Nita could see her, Hope gave a little wave, and Nita waved back. Picking up her pace, Hope soon joined her outside of the establishment. "How has your morning been?" she asked, glad to see another friendly face.

"Fair to middlin'," Nita replied. "What's that under your arm?"

"Oh, I found the library." She held the book up for Nita to see. "I was so excited to find out the town has one. Mr. Canton is a wonderful fellow."

Nita nodded, but there was something about her expression that wasn't quite as pleased as Hope had imagined. "Well, come on, now. Let's go speak to Mr. Stewart before he gets too busy."

Curious as to why Mrs. Howard wasn't as excited as she was about the books, but unwilling to upset her hostess, Hope simply followed her up the steps. A few other people were headed inside as well, and

Hope was glad to see that the doors were open, even though it had just turned nine.

Inside, Hope recognized the same teller, Mr. Garner, who had helped her send her message the day before. He waved her over, and Hope waited for him to finish with an older gentleman dressed in dirty trousers and a wide-brimmed cowboy hat before she stepped to the window.

"Mornin' Miss Tucker. I got a telegram for you!" he said, pulling it off of a stack. "Came in a few minutes after you left yesterday."

Hope's enthusiasm bubbled to the surface as she took the paper. "Thank you! My daddy works at a bank, so I'm sure he was able to send his response quickly." She longed to read it right then, but they had other business to take care of. "I would like to open an account while I'm here."

"And we would like to speak to Mr. Stewart when he has a few minutes," Nita added from over Hope's shoulder.

"Good mornin' Mrs. Howard," Mr. Garner replied. "Mr. Stewart's awful busy this morning. But I'll let him know. Now, Miss Tucker, I'll need a bit of information to start your account."

It didn't take long for Hope to provide the necessary information so that she could start her account. She handed over the money she'd brought with her and watched as the teller counted it and made note. "That's a nice little sum to start your independent living off with," he said with a smile.

Hope was glad Mrs. Howard had wandered over to speak to a friend so she wasn't keeping careful count of how much Hope had to her name. "My family has been generous to let me live at home while I've been teaching in Missouri," she explained.

He didn't make any other comment, only wrote out a deposit slip and gave her the information about her account. He collected the money, likely going to put it in the vault, and said, "I'll go let Mr. Stewart know you'd like to speak to him."

Hope thanked him and then turned back to see if Mrs. Howard was ready. She was still carrying on an animated conversation, now with two other women, and Hope wondered if the bank was the place people came to discuss the town's news. Hope took the opportunity to read the telegram from her parents. It was brief, stating only that they were glad she'd arrived safely and would write letters soon enough. While she was disappointed it didn't say more, she realized it was hard to send too much in a telegram.

A few moments later, Mr. Garner returned, and Hope looked at him expectantly. "Mr. Stewart said he'll be out to meet you directly."

"Thank you." Hope stepped aside so that another person could speak to the teller and walked to a bulletin board on the wall. There were plenty of pictures of criminals wanted for bank robbery, and she thought it a little odd to have it posted here. Wouldn't it frighten the tellers to constantly be reminded that they could be held up at any moment?

"I like the tellers to know what they look like," a gruff voice said behind her, and Hope turned to see a large man with a dark mustache which curled up at the ends. He was dressed nicely in a suit but smelled of bacon grease, and Hope had trouble deciding how all of those contradictions worked together. "You must be Miss Tucker."

She offered her hand. "Yes, I am. Pleased to meet you. Mr. Stewart?"

He nodded, a grin spreading across his wide face. "Who else?" He laughed, and Hope was puzzled as to whether or not he was laughing at her or if he was simply trying to lighten the mood. "Glad to see you made it to our little town safely."

Hope could've thought of many words to describe McKinney, but "little" really wasn't one of them. She didn't comment. "Yes, thank you. I arrived yesterday. Mr. Brady Howard took me over to see the school. It's a fine building." She thought it best to start with the positive. Her eyes wandered over to Nita who was still talking and hadn't seemed to notice that Mr. Stewart was present.

"It is, isn't it? Many a fine man contributed to the building of that schoolhouse. We hope it will be large enough to house our growing population for several years to come."

"The schoolhouse is certainly large enough. And I believe there are enough desks. The blackboard was a great size." She tried to think if there was anything else she could comment about but couldn't think of anything else without sounding ridiculous—one didn't compliment the outhouses, after all. "I did notice there were not any slates."

"Slates?" he asked, running his hand across his chin. "Wouldn't the children bring those?"

"Do they have them?" she countered. "I would think most students wouldn't have their own slates. I am used to there being a certain number of supplies provided by the school district."

Mr. Stewart's face puckered slightly. "There's plenty of chalk. I think the students could bring their own slates. They can order them from the five-and-dime."

Hope drew in a breath through her nose. "Might we be able to purchase five or ten to have on hand, just in case some students aren't able to get them? They certainly won't have them before Monday."

"Well, I can't provide them before Monday either," he countered.

"Yes, I realize that, sir. I only think… it would be helpful if we could order some. And then there's the situation with the books."

"Books? What books?" he asked. Now, his hand tugged at his waistline, slipping in and out from his belt, and Hope could tell he was growing agitated.

"Yes, sir, that's just it. There aren't any. I will need primers—a curriculum—as well as some volumes for the children to practice their reading."

Mr. Stewart was already shaking his head before she finished speaking. "Miss Tucker, we hired you to teach because we were under the impression you knew how to do all of that. Haven't you already taught dozens of children how to read? Can't you rely on your own knowledge?"

"Mr. Stewart, being able to teach and having the resources one needs are separate issues. Yes, of course, I can teach. But I require certain materials in order to be able to do so."

"Miss Tucker, I'm not sure what the environment is like where you come from, but here, people are very cautious about what they read. I'm sure every family that attends school will own a Bible. You can teach them to read from that, rather than the drivel you may find in a library." He gestured at the book under her arm, and Hope pulled it out so that he could see.

"This?" she asked. "Charles Dickens? I wouldn't read this particular book to students, but certainly you can see the merit in such works as *Oliver Twist*? Or *David Copperfield*?"

Mr. Stewart ran a hand through his thin hair and took a step back. "Miss Tucker, I'm afraid we have no budget for books. But I will appropriate enough funds to get you a few slates. I will send the request over to the store later this morning. That will have to do. I'm afraid you will have to make do with what the town can provide for you."

She could tell the conversation was over, and Mr. Stewart took a few steps backward. Frustrated, Hope took a deep breath. "Thank you for the slates," she said, each word measured. This argument wasn't over yet.

With a nod, Mr. Stewart headed for his office. It was then that Nita realized he'd even made his appearance, and she ran after him. Hope was far enough away that she couldn't hear what they were saying, but she imagined it wasn't pleasant from the gestures each of them was making. She had wished Nita was with her while she spoke to him, but now, seeing how upset he seemed to be, she was glad to be spared from the conversation.

The chatter from the other women had been a constant such that Hope hadn't even noticed it until it abruptly stopped. Her head swiveled to see what had brought them to silence, and a familiar figure caught her attention. Judah tipped his hat to the women, and they all scrambled toward the door, as if he had an infectious disease.

He didn't seem to notice, or he didn't care. His eyes were on Mr. Stewart and Nita as he crossed to stand next to Hope. "I'm guessin' you met Mr. Stewart?"

In light of the other women's desperation to stay away from this man, Hope wasn't sure what to say. Perhaps she should also shoot for the door. But there was nothing threatening about him as he stood next to her, smelling like a spring day and hard work mixed with horses and leather. It was an intriguing aroma, not at all offensive, and she fought the urge to step closer to him and take a deep breath. "I have," she managed to say.

He shook his head. "Good luck gettin' anything you don't already have. 'Fraid you have no idea what you've gotten yourself into, Miss Tucker."

"What does that mean?" she asked, cocking her head to the side, puzzled.

Judah wore a look of amusement, as if her confusion was humorous. "Only that there are some folks around here who would label any book that isn't the Holy Bible devil's work. That's all."

"Oh, is that all? Well, if that's the case, it'll be simple to teach their children how to read and write." She shook her head, beginning to see he was right.

He chuckled, and her head spun so that she was facing him again. "Somethin' tells me you'll manage." He stepped away with a tip of his hat, leaving Hope wondering what in the world that comment was supposed to mean. She didn't ask, though. Nita was headed to her now, her eyes larger than saucers, and Hope imagined she was angry as a hornet about whatever it was Mr. Stewart had told her.

"Miss Tucker!" she admonished, taking Hope by the arm and dragging her toward the door, and Hope suddenly realized the expression had less to do with Mr. Stewart and more to do with Mr. Lawless.

Mrs. Howard was spry for her age, and Hope found herself fumbling down the stairs, her boots crossing and nearly tripping her as she struggled to keep up. They were a ways down the walkway before Nita stopped. "Do you have any idea who you were just speaking with?"

Unsure how to answer, Hope only stared with her mouth open. Nita had released her arm, but it stung where the woman's grasp had dug into her skin. "I... yes. I guess. Brady said something about him yesterday. I ran into him at the library...."

"That man is a murderer!" Nita replied through clenched teeth. "You must absolutely stay away from him!"

Shocked at the urgency in her hostess's voice, Hope had to look away. Her eyes wandered to the saloon, and she wondered how many other men might take up residence in there each evening but then go home to their families and even show up at church on a Sunday morning. "He didn't even say anything, not really," Hope assured her. "He only asked if I'd met Mr. Stewart." She didn't see that it was necessary to tell Mrs. Howard anything else about either conversation she'd had with Judah Lawless.

"Well, you best mind what Brady told you. My son knows about townsfolk."

Hope wanted to know if Brady frequented the saloon to find out that information or if he'd procured it by some other measures, but she kept her mouth shut. Had Brady been the one to convince his mother that Judah was so awful, or was it someone else?

"Now, Mr. Stewart said he would order the slates, which is wonderful. But he's not so keen on gettin' any books for the school. He said you can teach from the Bible."

Hope's eyes narrowed. "You know I can't actually do that, don't you? I need materials. Curriculum."

"Yes, yes, I know. But we won't be getting any funds from him. There might be other ways. We'll have to think on it."

Drawing in a deep breath through her nose, Hope decided there wasn't much else to say about it at the moment. Mr. Stewart seemed like a powerful man whose priorities were quite different than Hope's despite the fact that they were both involved in education. She'd just have to think of some other way to get the books and other things she needed in order to best serve her students.

"I'm headed back to the house," Nita said, her eyes flickering to the bank. "You going to visit Doc?"

Hope had forgotten all about her promise to go by Nicholas's office. Only when she'd walked past it earlier in the day had it even crossed her mind. "Yes, I told him I would."

"All right. I will see you back at the house." She took a step closer. "Stay away from that man, Miss Tucker. He's trouble."

She knew who Nita meant. Hope nodded, thinking the chances of running into the same man three times in the same day were slim anyway—especially since he'd said he was going back to his homestead over an hour ago.

Nita's eyes narrowed, telling Hope she meant business, and she stepped around the schoolteacher to head back to her house.

Hope took another deep breath and fought the urge to run her hands down her face. This day had not turned out like she expected at all. The library was a wonderful find, but the fact that Mr. Stewart was an unreasonable, pompous man was something else. And the fact that she kept running into a handsome stranger who might just be a murderer wasn't helpful.

She glanced back toward the bank, thinking Judah would appear at any moment and decided not to linger. With a quick glance around, she reminded herself of where she needed to go to reach Doc's office and headed that way without looking back, even when she heard the door open and felt the weight of blue eyes on the back of her head.

CHAPTER TWELVE

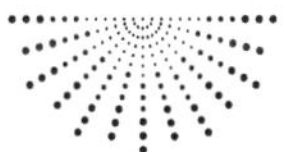

Nicholas's office was busy. Hope had no idea what to expect having never visited an office for medicine before. She pushed open the door to find a woman comforting a crying child, an older man cradling his arm, and a woman with a bulging belly all sitting in chairs while someone in the back of the space shouted as if he was being tortured. Part of her wanted to back right out the door, but a friendly smile from a woman behind a desk caught her eye, and Hope knew she couldn't leave.

"You must be Miss Tucker!" the middle-aged woman with jet black hair and sun kissed skin proclaimed. Hope thought her accent sounded peculiar, like perhaps she was from much further south. "It's lovely to meet you. I'm Lluvia, Dr. Howard's nurse." She offered a slender hand, and Hope took it.

"Yes, I am Miss Tucker. It's nice to meet you as well." She glanced around the waiting room and thought she should come back some other time. "I don't want to inconvenience Doc, though. He seems awfully busy."

"Oh, it's always like this. He's with a patient right now. A little boy fell out of a tree, hurt his leg. I just came up to fetch some more bandages. I'll let him know you're here if you'd like to have a seat."

Hope glanced around, not sure where she should sit. It seemed as if the little girl who was crying might have a fever, so she decided to sit on the other side of the room, nearer the pregnant woman. At least that wasn't catching.

The child couldn't have been more than three, and she sobbed into her mother's apron. Her cheeks were red with fever, and Hope prayed it wasn't anything too serious. She looked at the old man who was staring at the wall across from him, almost completely still, but the woman next to her was rubbing her stomach, humming a quiet song.

Hope turned to take her in, wondering why she might be there. She didn't appear to be in any distress and her disposition implied she wasn't in any pain. "How far along are you?" she asked in a quiet voice.

"Well, Doc says it could be any day now," the woman said with a broad smile. "I'm a little anxious, but I'm sure we'll be just fine. Doc ain't never lost a baby or a mother."

"Really?" Hope thought that sounded impressive, though she had no idea how many babies he'd birthed either. "What brought you in?"

"He wants to check and make sure everything's all right. It's what he calls prenatal checkups. He likes to see me every month or so. Now that my baby's comin' soon, he wants to see me even more often. Wants to make sure everythin' looks right. This is my first baby, so I'm nervous. But knowing I have a good physician is reassurin'."

Hope had never heard of such a thing, but it sounded like a good idea. If there was something wrong, would Doc be able to detect it in time to save the mother or the child? Was that why he had never lost either?

The shouting from the back room finally stopped, and Hope could hear Nicholas's voice, though he was so far away she couldn't make out what he was saying. Still, the tenor of it was soothing, and she could see why so many folks spoke so highly of him.

A few moments later, a man stepped out from the back, carrying a boy who looked to be eight or nine, and Hope assumed that would be one of her students—as soon as he was well enough to come to school. Her eyes followed him out the door as she tried to commit his face to memory, so she didn't even realize Doc was there until she heard his voice beside her. "How are you today, Miss Tucker?"

She startled, and then looked over at him, trying to keep the color out of her face, but he looked a bit rosy himself. "Just fine, thank you. I didn't mean to bother you when you're so busy."

"Oh, it's all right. Sorry I alarmed you." He gave her a sheepish grin, and Hope waved it away like it was nothing. "I'm always busy, particularly this time of morning. But if you'll let me tend to Mr. Sullivan's arm right quick, get little Sally here some elixir for her fever, and do a quick check on Mrs. Talbot, I should be good for a few minutes, then I can show you around."

"How do you know no one else will come in?" Hope asked.

The doctor shrugged. "They might, but they can wait a few minutes, 'less they're bleedin' heavily."

Hope had nothing else she needed to get to, other than the book she had sitting in her lap, and she could read it here just as well as at home in her tiny room. "All right then." She smiled, and he grinned back at her like she'd just given him the best news he'd ever heard.

"Mr. Sullivan, let's have a look," he said, helping the elderly gentleman to his feet and leading him to the back.

The room was silent, except for the soft hum of Mrs. Talbot soothing her baby, so Hope could hear Nicholas speaking to his patient in the examination room, but she didn't want to eavesdrop, and it was difficult to distinguish the words. She decided to open her book. By the time Doc was finished seeing the last of the three patients, another had come in, an older woman who wanted him to look at a bunion on her foot. The nurse said it might be a few minutes, and she settled into the chair Mr. Sullivan had vacated and took out some knitting.

"Well, that's the last one," Nicholas proclaimed as Mrs. Talbot walked out the door. "Would you like to come on back now." Hope gestured at the old woman, too caught up in her work to notice. Doc mouthed back, "She can wait."

Deciding he knew best, Hope rose and followed him to the back room. "This is where the excitement happens," he said, gesturing at the patient table and the cabinets full of supplies. "I can do all sorts of procedures here."

"I'll say," Hope replied. "I've seen you work plenty of miracles this morning. What about the woman who is out there now? Will she have to wait long?"

"That's Mrs. Murry. She comes in every day for me to look at her foot. It's the same every morning—nothing wrong with it except a small bunion. I've explained I'd have to do surgery to really help her, but she doesn't want that, so she just comes in every day for me to put a salve and a fresh bandage on it."

"I see," Hope said with a shake of her head. "She must not have much to do at home if she can come in every day."

"Well, her husband passed last year, and she's moved in with her daughter, so I don't think she does. I reckon the quiet of my office is more conducive to her knitting than a house full of small children."

"That does make sense," Hope replied. She looked around the room and saw all sorts of bottles of medicine, salves, and ingredients for poultices. Some of them she recognized from her mother's collection, but others were foreign to her. "Where do you order your supplies from?"

"All over the world," he replied, crossing over to a cabinet. "This herb is from China, and it's known to work wonders on a sore back." He put the canister on the shelf and reached for another. "This one is from India. I haven't used it much, but it's for blisters and boils. And this one came all the way from the distant land of Mexico."

Hope couldn't help but laugh. His serious expression didn't match the exaggeration of his words at all. "My, it must take forever to get all the way to Texas. Does it come by boat?"

"No, all imports to Texas must come by winged horses." Again his expression was completely serious, and she found herself laughing again.

The tour of the back room only took a few minutes, but it was evident Doc was enthusiastic about his work and all of the specialized medicine and supplies he had procured. He even showed her where he kept his jars of oddities—which Hope declined to inspect too carefully for fear her stomach might not be able to handle it.

"Well, I do appreciate you taking time out of your day to give me a tour," Hope finally said, once she was certain she'd seen all that there was to see. "But I've heard your door a few times since I've come back, and I'm sure you have a few waiting customers."

"Yes, I'm afraid I do." She couldn't tell if he was content with that statement or bothered, but he did manage to smile at her. "Thank you for stopping by."

"It truly was a fascinating exploration into the methods of modern medicine." She hoped she didn't sound unreasonably satisfied with her declaration.

Walking toward the hallway, Doc said, "My mother has invited me over for dinner tonight. I plan to be there, assuming there are no emergencies."

"Oh? And what if someone comes calling, and you're not home?" She seemed to recall that had been his reasoning for not staying the night before. She asked out of mere curiosity and not at all to be accusatory.

He led her down the hallway. "I'll leave a note on my front door." Doc shrugged, like it was something he did often. "My house is only a quarter mile from my folks. Hopefully, if anyone needs me, it will be someone who can read and knows where they live."

"You could put their address," Hope added thoughtfully.

"I could, but most people don't know the streets around here by their names. They only know them by landmarks."

"Really?" They were back in the waiting room now, and there were four patients waiting to see the doctor.

"Yes, that's the way it's always been around here. Take a right at the big oak tree. Turn left at Sumner's pond, that sort of thing."

Hope understood; she'd seen a bit of that back home as well. "Perhaps you could draw a map."

"Yes—X marks the spot or something." Doc chuckled, and Hope had an image of him as a pirate pop into her mind. While he would make a dashing sea captain, she couldn't envision him as a seafaring buccaneer. He was too honest for that.

Doc pulled the door open. "I'll see you soon, Miss Tucker."

"Have a good day, Dr. Howard," she replied, stepping out into the late morning sunshine and giving a brief wave to his nurse over his shoulder. She returned her attention to Doc to see his eyes lingering on her through the glass as he shut the door, and heat rose in her cheeks. While his friendliness seemed innocent enough, there was something in the way he looked at her that reminded Hope of Jimmy Brooks. Only, when Nicholas Howard looked at her that way, she liked it.

CHAPTER THIRTEEN

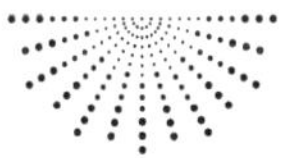

Monday morning came at last. It seemed like the weekend had worn on for more than twenty-four hours each day. Even though Hope had been busy, preparing her lessons, exploring the town more, and getting to know the folks at church, she had felt as if time were dragging on and that the first day of school would never arrive.

She was up before the sun, taking care of her morning toiletry needs, and dressed in her nicest teaching outfit—a white shirtwaist and black skirt. Her daddy said it was a nice mix of strictness and encouragement, the black and white representing the good and evil of the world. She laughed when he'd said it, but she thought it must've stuck in her mind because she wore it often. She'd also donned her most comfortable pair of ankle boots and put her hair up tightly so it would be out of her way. Today was an important day. After all, the first impression these children and their parents received of their new teacher would set the tone for the rest of the school year and potentially many more years to come.

Nita was up already when Hope came down to the kitchen. She was preparing oatmeal for her mother-in-law, her eyes still bleary with sleep. "Well, don't you look nice," Mrs. Howard said before yawning loudly. "Them kids sure will be happy to have such a perty teacher."

"Well, thank you," Hope replied, not bothering to say being pretty had nothing to do with it, but she knew a compliment when she heard it. "Would you mind if I made myself a quick breakfast before I head out?"

"No, a'course not, but if you wait a minute, I'll be happy to do it fer you. Just gotta take this up to Ma."

"It's okay. I don't mind," Hope insisted, taking up a pan. As soon as Nita was done with the oatmeal, she stepped into her place and went about scrambling a few eggs and frying up a few pieces of bacon. There was plenty left for Nita to cook for Mr. Howard, and she was certain he would eat a good helping of it.

Nita had returned by the time Hope sat down at the table, and she used the same frying pan to start on Mr. Howard's breakfast. Hope wondered if he wouldn't have to get up earlier than usual if he were to eat it warm. The sun wasn't even up yet.

"You must be excited," the older woman remarked. "Bet'cha can't wait to meet the rest of your students."

"I am," Hope agreed. "I've already met about half of them, I think, between church yesterday and my walk around town. But I am eager to meet the others and see what sort of skills they already have."

Mrs. Howard chuckled in her throat. "I'm sorry to disappoint you, honey, but they ain't likely to have many at all."

Hope didn't think that was true. The children she'd already met seemed intelligent enough for the most part. Surely, if their parents had been working with them at all, they would at least know the basics, such as the alphabet, maybe even how to read a few easily recognizable words, like the, am, my, me, etc. She was optimistic. "I suppose we'll find out shortly," she said with a smile as she scooped up the last bite of eggs.

"What will you do about lunch?"

"Oh, my lunchbox!" Hope had left it upstairs. She'd been so excited, she hadn't even thought about packing a lunch. Taking her plate to the washbasin, she began to rinse it off, but Mrs. Howard nudged her out of the way, and Hope ran back upstairs to fetch her trusty lunchbox.

When she returned, Mrs. Howard was wrapping wax paper around what appeared to be a ham and cheese sandwich on homemade sliced bread. "I've got apples and a few cookies, if that will do?"

"Mrs. Howard, that's so nice of you!" Hope exclaimed, feeling right at home. Many times, if she was excited or in a hurry, her mother would make her lunch for her. "Thank you so much!"

"It's nothing, honey." Mrs. Howard wrapped the cookies up as well, and Hope placed the items inside her lunchbox. She took out her thermos and filled it with water from the pump outside, thinking it should stay cool for most of the day. She hadn't noticed if there was a pump at the school, but she had seen a well, so that should do, assuming they'd thought to rig up a bucket. The idea that the children might fall in the well crossed her mind, but she assumed most of them had grown up with the structures and knew better than to act foolishly around them.

"Is there anything else?" Nita asked as Hope came back indoors, bringing her out of her own head.

Hope looked around, thinking about her typical day at school. She had no books to take with her, and there would be none waiting for her either. She wished she had the supplies Mr. Stewart had promised, but she'd just have to make do. She did have a few notes she'd made for herself folded and tucked inside the pocket of her skirt. "I can't think of anything."

"All right. I'm sorry Mr. Howard isn't up to give you a ride on your first day, but he's more of a night owl than a morning person."

Hope had gathered that already. "It's fine. The morning air will do me good."

Nita nodded, and then, resting the spatula she'd been using to cook breakfast on the counter near the hearth, she wrapped her arms around Hope. "Good luck today, honey. Those kids sure are fortunate to have you."

The gesture caught her off guard, but Hope was pleasantly surprised that the woman she'd thought looked so stern just a few days ago had already proven she had a gentle side. "Thank you, Mrs.

Howard." Hope hugged her back and then collected her lunchbox. With a deep breath, she set off out the door.

The warmth of pink and orange sunbeams kept the morning chill away as Hope started her walk, glad to have enough time that there was no need to hurry. Back in Lamar, her morning trip to work had always been a time to clear her head and prepare for the day. She was constantly thinking about her students—she assumed all teachers did—but on her morning stroll, she finalized decisions, put together last minute preparations, and thought about how she should order her day. This morning, everything would be a bit chaotic at first as she met the students and parents and made sure the children were aware of her expectations. She imagined most of them had never had any formal schooling at all, and many of them would likely have difficulty sitting still for so many hours at a time. Planning frequent short breaks to run about the yard should help with that. Hopefully, the parents would be supportive, and most of them would come in to meet her on this first day. If the students understood that the parents supported her, hopefully, they would mind and follow the rules. Hope had high expectations for behavior in her classroom, and students who followed them were rewarded with more free time and more choices.

A few wagons and carts passed by as she made her way down the last street, and off in the distance, she could hear hammers and shouting as men worked to put up a new house. The town was growing, and before long, there might even be need for another school. Hope wondered what part she would play in all of it.

The school looked shiny and new from a distance. It was evident the men who had built it went to great lengths to make it as welcoming as possible. It was a symbol for the whole town; McKinney was making progress. Learning was important. Citizens here could afford to invest in their children's future by allowing them to leave the farms and homesteads to brighten their minds.

Hope arrived at the school an hour before any of the children were expected. She went about her morning routine, sweeping up the floor, dusting off the desks, and opening the window. There was no need for a fire, even though it was slightly cooler outside than she'd expected. Still, she imagined the rest of spring before summer break would be hot in Texas, and she doubted she'd have need to test the fireplace until next fall, likely October or even November.

Once she was certain the classroom was in order, she went to the chalkboard, and with a deep breath, wrote her name in perfect cursive. She wondered how many of the students would actually be able to read it. Hopefully, at least a few. She then wrote three rules she wanted her class to know right from the beginning. One of the first things she would do is go over the expectations she had for her classroom.

It was still early. There weren't enough items in the classroom to take up too much of her time, but before she had a chance to wonder what she might do with her extra few minutes, she heard voices coming from the front of the school and looked out the window. A little girl dressed in a long beige dress and a boy a half-head shorter than her came up the steps holding hands. Hope hurried out the door and around the corner to the formal entrance of the school. "Good morning," she said. "Are you my first students?"

"Yes, ma'am," the little girl said. When she opened her mouth, Hope spotted several missing teeth and thought she had to be six or seven at the oldest. She didn't say more, only looked at her shoes, and Hope thought they must both be nervous. She wondered if the little boy was even old enough to attend.

"I'm Miss Tucker. Did your parents not accompany you this morning?"

"No, ma'am," the girl replied, not lifting her eyes.

"Pa's in the field," the boy explained. "Ma's gotta tend the baby."

"I see. And what is your name?"

"Hank," he said proudly. "This is my sister, Sally."

"Well, Hank and Sally, it is very nice to meet you," Hope said giving them both a reassuring nod. "And how old are you, Hank?"

"I'm six. Sally is eight."

"Really?" Hope was shocked to hear that. He was so small, and his sister didn't look like she could possibly be ready for third grade. "It is so very nice to have both of you in my class. Please, come in. You may sit together for now, but later I will be separating children into groups based on age. Don't worry. We're all in the same room." She noticed Sally carried a small bundle, and she hoped that was their noontime meal, though it didn't look large enough to feed two children. She made a note to bring more food the next day, in case some of the children didn't have a proper meal.

The children sat on the first row, their feet not even reaching the floor, and Hope wondered if they were malnourished and that's why they seemed so small. She didn't have too much time to interact with them before she heard a wagon pull up outside and glanced out the window to see the next students were accompanied by their parents. Down the road, she saw several other carriages and thought it must be about time to ring the bell.

"I'm going to go greet our classmates. The two of you may wait here." Hope gave the siblings another smile and headed back out to the front steps. Before long, she was caught in a whirlwind of handshaking and introductions. Most of the parents let her know how thankful they were that she'd arrived. They all seemed very supportive, though others showed it a little differently by threatening to box their children's ears if they didn't behave.

The children also seemed to understand school was a place to come and learn, and rather than running around the schoolyard as Hope had feared they might, all but a few went right in and took a seat in the classroom, carrying their lunches, a couple with books or a slate, and only two had to be chased down by their parents and made to go inside.

She recognized several children from church, as well as the pair she'd seen playing in their yard and some she'd seen on her jaunts around town. Only a few appeared unaccompanied. One was a small boy with blond hair who said nothing, only stomped his way inside and took a seat in the back of the classroom. Hope was worrying over him when she heard the clearing of a voice, and an "Excuse me, Miss Tucker," coming from waist-height. She turned and looked down to see a little girl with brown braids, one on either side of her pretty little head, which was hidden slightly behind a pair of spectacles. The child stood with her hand extended, and Hope couldn't help but smile at her.

"Yes?" the schoolteacher asked, shaking her hand. "How do you do?"

"I'm well, thank you. I'm Virginia Pembroke, and this is my brother, George. Everyone calls me Ginny. It's very nice to meet you."

Hope wasn't quite sure what to say as she released the girl's hand and turned to George. Her formality was unexpected, especially considering she couldn't be more than ten. Hope shook George's hand. "It's a pleasure to meet you both."

"Miss Tucker," an adult voice said from behind the children, and Hope raised her head to see a woman who looked very much like Ginny, though without the glasses, and her hair was hidden beneath her bonnet. She rested her hands on Ginny's shoulders. "We are so thankful to have you here. I'm Caroline Pembroke, Ginny and George's mother." Hope shook her hand as well. "When we heard the children would finally be able to get a formal education, my husband Paul and I were so excited. I've done my best to teach them at home, but I'm not nearly as experienced as you are."

Hope was still listening, but at the mention of her husband, she looked over Caroline's shoulder, expecting the form she'd noticed but not yet acknowledged to be the man she spoke of. When it wasn't, she had to hold back a gasp. No wonder these names sounded familiar. She tuned back in to hear Caroline say, "Paul's working the fields this morning, so my brother, Judah, brought us in. The two of you have met, haven't you?"

Her tongue seemed unmalleable all of a sudden, like no words could come out of her mouth no matter how hard she tried to speak, so Hope only nodded, and Judah filled in for her, "It's nice to see you again, Miss Tucker."

He reached for her hand, and hers shot out instinctively, but her mouth still wasn't working, and the tingling sensation that shot up her arm at the contact with his rough fingertips didn't serve to loosen her tongue any at all. She realized avoiding his eyes might be helpful so she returned her gaze to Mrs. Pembroke, and suddenly she was able to create coherent sentences again. "It's delightful to meet all of you. I'm excited to have Ginny and George in my class."

Caroline let out a little sigh, as if she had been worried Hope was dumbstruck. "As I said, we are happy to make your acquaintance as well. We live a ways out of town, so one of us will likely be dropping the kids off of a morning, weather permitting. Sometimes our road gets mudded in."

"I understand." Hope smiled down at Ginny, thinking she'd do anything she could to get to school.

"I won't want to miss," the child said, reading her mind.

"I'm sure you won't. Why don't you and George go on in and take a seat?" Hope glanced around to see a few more families waiting to meet her, but all of them were standing a good ten or fifteen feet back, which she thought was odd. Before, she'd hardly been able to take introductions one family at a time because they'd been so crowded together. But then, she realized why that might be. The other parents held their children close, and a few of them were whispering to each other.

"What time is the dismissal bell?" Caroline asked, not seeming to notice or care what the folks behind her were doing.

"Two o'clock," Hope replied. "Will the children walk home?"

"No, I'll come get 'em. It's just too far," Caroline replied. Hope wasn't used to the idea that parents would drop off and pick up their children. Even her students who lived a great distance tended to walk to school in Lamar, but then, she wondered if the fact that the other adults seemed frightened of this particular family had anything to do with the decision.

"All right then," Hope said, thinking she would need to rush the process a bit if she was going to have a chance to greet the others and get her day started on time. She hadn't even bothered to ring the bell since it appeared as if all of her children must be there. Mrs. Howard had said there would be around twenty-six, and Hope thought there were already that many, if not more.

"Thank you kindly, Miss Tucker," Caroline said as she looked lovingly through the window at her children who were sitting together near the back, close to the little blond boy who'd made it evident school was not his favorite.

Judah tipped his hat at her but didn't say anything else, and Hope forced her eyes away from him and on to the next family. Even when she heard him signal his horse to pull their carriage away, she fought the urge to look.

"If I'da known them folks was comin', I mighta decided to keep Saul at home," the woman before her was saying, and Hope had to keep her mind from wandering off.

"Oh, no. I'm so glad Saul is here," she assured the redheaded woman who had a scowl on her face. Her husband, a portly man who smelled of whisky, looked even less friendly. "This is a school. We will focus on learning reading and math and not worry about... anything else." What she said and what she wanted to say were two different things—we would not be chastising other classmates based on rumors that had not been verified. But her smile was tight, and the parents seemed to catch her meaning.

"Be good, Saul," the mother said with a sharp pat to his head, and then she and her potentially inebriated husband stepped away, and Hope wondered how someone who would show up at a schoolhouse smelling like a saloon could point fingers.

She met the last two families and watched as another little girl, maybe Ginny's age, skipped up the steps, a large smile on her face. She was unaccompanied, and by now, Hope was beginning to prefer it that way. The last little boy was making his way into the school room when she looked up to see Mr. Stewart sauntering over. Remembering the bank opened later and he lived nearby, she wasn't too surprised to see him on foot. He was dressed to the nines, as if he were going to a grand affair and not just the first day of school. Hope put on her most pleasant smile. "Good morning, Mr. Stewart."

"Well, Miss Tucker, it's nice to see you. I'm surprised to see you standing outside. Shouldn't school have started ten minutes ago?" He glanced at a pocket watch and then reinserted it inside of his jacket.

"Yes, well, it is the first day. Many of the parents wanted to meet me. Don't worry. We'll make up for it."

"I didn't hear the bell sound this morning."

"No, I decided there was no need to ring it. Students started arriving before the fifteen-till bell, and then they just kept coming. So... since everyone is here, I didn't bother."

"Well, let's just give it a try anyhow. What do you say?" Mr. Stewart didn't wait for her input and walked over to the rope that hung by the door, untying it and giving it a good pull. The bell pealed twice, and then Mr. Stewart retied the rope. "There. The townsfolks will be happy to hear the sound."

Hope hadn't considered the people in town might be waiting to hear the bell toll, but it did make sense. A lot of people had worked hard to make the school a reality. "Thank you, Mr. Stewart."

He tipped his hat and headed back across the schoolyard, shouting, "Have a nice day," over his shoulder.

"Oh, Mr. Stewart, I did want to thank you again for ordering the slates. When do you think we can expect them?"

He stopped in his tracks and turned back to face her. "I'm not sure, if I'm honest. It will take some time."

Something about the way he made the statement brought to mind he may not have even ordered them yet. "Well, I do hope it isn't too long. The children do need them."

"And they need a teacher, so best get to it," he replied with a no-nonsense nod, and Hope took a deep breath, biting back her response that she knew exactly what she was doing.

Inside, the children were much quieter than she'd expected. A few of them looked terrified, while others had tears in their eyes. Hope wondered what they may have heard about attending school. She took a deep breath and sat on the corner of her desk. "Good morning, class."

Most of the students only looked at her, having no idea what to say, but Ginny Pembroke answered enthusiastically, "Good morning, Miss Tucker."

"Good!" Hope said, her smile becoming more genuine. "That's precisely how you should answer. Now, let's try that again. Good morning, class."

Not quite in unison, and not at all as cheerfully as Ginny had been on her own, the class replied, "Good morning, Miss Tucker."

Hope congratulated them anyway. "Well done! I knew as soon as I walked in the door this was going to be the brightest class I've ever had. Now, let's get to know each other a little bit, shall we?"

Hope spent most of the morning learning the children's names, ages, and skill levels. While many of the older ones did know the basics of reading, some of them didn't even know their alphabet. And the little ones were mostly all beginners, with the exception of George who could've read her initial primer, if she'd had that book available to give to him. All of the children were agreeable for the most part, except Steven, the blond boy who protested everything, including where he was to sit and that he may go to the outhouse as long as he came back directly. He was going to be a tough cookie, Hope knew that much from the start.

The morning went by quickly, and Hope was tired out herself by the time she released the children to the schoolyard for lunch and recess. She heard Steven mumble, "Thank the Lord," but didn't get on to him. Clearly, he was not used to sitting still for this long, and she was hopeful he'd get some energy out in the sunshine.

She took her own lunch with her and sat on the front stoop, watching as most of the children scarfed down what they'd brought while others decided to play first. She decided to give them a few minutes, and then, if their rumbling bellies didn't remind them it was eat first and then play, she'd shout a reminder.

Most of the children appeared to have enough to eat, though she was worried when Sally unwrapped what didn't look like enough for one child, let alone two. But some of the others had brought extra and gladly shared. She noticed Ginny take a few extra apple slices over to Hank and thought about what a blessing that child was going to be. She could tell already that Ginny was an exceptional child, and Hope imagined her doing great things one day.

After lunch and recess, the children had trouble settling back into their seats, and Hope noticed immediately that Steven was not with them. "Did anyone see where he went?" she asked.

"He run off," an older boy, Thomas, replied. "I can go get 'im, if you want."

Hope sighed. She didn't have time to chase him, and neither did Thomas. "Do you happen to know where he lives?"

"I do," Sally said, raising her hand after she spoke. They'd need to work on that. "He lives down the street from us. With his granny."

"I see," Hope said, beginning to put the picture together. "And does Steven have parents?"

"His folks live way out, past the outlaw's house," another child, Emily, explained.

Hope heard a gasp from the other side of the room and immediately realized what Emily was referring to. "Emily, sweetheart, be mindful of your words, please."

Emily's forehead crinkled, as if she had no idea what Miss Tucker was getting at. "I mean, her house," she said, pointing at Ginny, making the situation ten times worse.

Ginny didn't gasp the second time, but she turned her face away. George seemed confused but said nothing.

"Emily, dear, that would be the Pembroke home, or the Pembroke Farm. Ginny's last name is Pembroke. Her father is a farmer. No one there is an outlaw."

"But my mama said..." another boy, Jeffrey, began from the back of the classroom.

Hope cut him off. "Who here knows Sheriff Roan?" she asked. Almost every hand went up. "Good. Now, who thinks Sheriff Roan is a responsible lawman who does his job right?" Again, hands went up. "Very good. Now, if we trust the sheriff and know he will do whatever he can to keep our town safe, how can we think there are outlaws taking up residence on the outskirts of town? Now, that doesn't make a whole lotta sense, does it?"

"But my mama said..." Jeffrey began again.

"Listen, boys and girls. What parents and other adults say outside of our school has nothing to do with what goes on inside of these four walls. Here, we will treat each other with kindness and fairness. While I appreciate your efforts to enlighten me as to where Steven's parents live, let's be mindful of the way we speak about each other. All right?"

"Yes, Miss Tucker," the class answered, and Hope was glad to see that Ginny was looking at her again. She had a feeling a few parents may want to speak to her about the way she chose to handle the situation, but she would be happy to address it with them if the topic came up. So long as there wasn't a refusal by the other families to send their children to school where the Pembrokes attended, she wouldn't count this as a problem just yet. And Steven was another issue. She had a feeling there wouldn't be much she could do to get him to stay at school, but she'd have to go visit his granny once the day was over.

She pushed all of those thoughts aside and focused on arithmetic, the next subject she needed to teach. Of course, she'd have to assess what prior knowledge her students had of the subject before she could begin any sort of lessons, and that took much of the afternoon because without any slates, the children had to come to the board. By the time she'd established most of her students were able to count and some could do simple sums, it was time to go home.

"All right, boys and girls," Hope said, sitting back on the corner of her desk. "Our first day together is almost over. I want to thank all of you for your hard work today. Your behavior today was exceptional, and I hope that you will continue to put your studies first while you are at school. Now, there are no assignments for home tonight." She couldn't have made any with no books or slates even if she'd wanted to. "I suggest you get plenty of rest tonight, and be back here in the morning by the second bell. Please be careful exiting the building."

The children stood and walked out in line, though some of them seemed in a hurry and wanted to push. Hope shouted out a reminder about lunch pails that got a few to come back, but soon enough, all of the children were either headed down the lane on their way home or making a beeline for waiting carriages. There were not many who wouldn't walk home. Hope looked out the window to watch them disperse, satisfied smiles on their faces.

Ginny and George did not take off running like the other children did. Instead, they took their time walking to the wagon where their mother waited. Ginny glanced over her shoulder several times at the schoolhouse, and Hope waved at her, but she wondered what was wrong. Surely, the girl wasn't still thinking about Emily's and Jeffrey's comments. She wondered if any of the children would go home and report what she'd said. There was a possibility she would have a few irate parents awaiting her arrival in the morning. Hopefully, she'd made her meaning clear, and the children would respect her enough not to go home and infuriate their parents. But even if they were angered, she would deal with it. There was no reason Ginny and George shouldn't feel welcome in the schoolhouse. They had every bit as much of a right to be there as the others. If she had to stand up to parents in their defense, she would do so.

Thinking of Ginny and George's plight caused her to think of Judah, and Hope let out a sigh. How could it be that someone so friendly had such an awful reputation? He certainly didn't look like the sort of person who would murder his wives... not even one of them, let alone two. She wondered what the true story was and if she'd ever know his side of it. It crossed her mind that Ginny might know, but she couldn't imagine sitting down with the young lady and asking her details about such a heinous affair.

Hope shook her head and set about righting the schoolhouse. She'd wiped down the desks and the chalkboard and was almost finished with the floor when she heard another carriage outside. It was an unexpected sound since all the children were long gone, and part of her feared someone had already decided to come and protest her standing up for the Pembroke children, but when she saw Nicholas hop down from the seat, a smile warmed her face. He saw her through the window and waved. Hope returned the gesture and then turned away, hoping he didn't notice her smooth her hair back or the fact that her cheeks felt as if they were on fire.

Grabbing her lunch pail, Hope headed for the door, certain everything was as ready for the next day's lessons as could be expected. He met her on the porch. "Dr. Howard! It's so nice to see you. What brings you away from your patients in the middle of the day?"

Nicholas shoved his hands into his trouser pockets and gave a slight shrug. "I wasn't busy, so I decided to come and offer you a ride home. I hope your first day went well."

"What a lovely gesture." Normally, Hope enjoyed her strolls home. It gave her time to reflect, much like the walk to school in the morning. But today, she was exhausted from a long day, and her head was beginning to ache slightly. "I would gladly accompany you, sir."

A grin lit up his face as he offered his arm, but then Hope wondered if this would count as appearing in public unchaperoned by a single male. "I can manage," she said, still smiling, though she hoped she wouldn't offend him. Nicholas nodded but followed her around to the far side of the carriage and watched carefully as she boosted herself up. While she seriously doubted anyone would question her riding along with the son of the couple whose home she was staying in, she didn't necessarily want anyone to misread what they might observe either. And, if Mrs. Howard was concerned about her own sons, would she have allowed Brady to take her to the bank or pick her up at the station? She didn't bother to remind herself that Brady was betrothed, and as far as she knew Nicholas was not.

Which begged the question. Once he was settled in his seat and had the horses turned around, she thought she might ask him, but the question caught in her throat. Easing into it would be better. "How was your day?" she asked.

"I thought I should ask you the same. Mine was fair. A sprained wrist and a few colds is about all. I did some house calls, saw some of the older folks around town. That's about all. How was yours? Do you have a good class?"

Hope's immediate response was a resounding yes, and then she remembered Steven. She'd meant to find out where his granny lived but only had a general idea. There was a good chance Nicholas would know, but she decided she'd give Steven another opportunity to come back to school in the morning before she went too far out of her way to track him down.

"It was wonderful," she finally said. "More students than I expected, and no supplies. But the children all listened and followed directions well. I hope that part stays. There are some that know very little and some that know a bit more. It will be challenging, but I hope to have them on their way to reading by the end of the year. And then there was one in particular who stood out. Now, that little girl has a wonderful chance of becoming a star pupil and perhaps even a teacher, or a doctor, or a lawyer, whatever she would like to be one day."

Nicholas's eyebrows perked up, and she could tell he appreciated the fact that Hope had a true scholar since he was so fond of learning himself. "Now, that sounds promising. Which child is it? I'm sure I know her."

"It's actually the little Pembroke girl, Ginny." Hope used a cautious tone and watched his face for a reaction. She wasn't surprised to see he was a little stunned. "She's remarkably bright. I only hope the other children don't tease her and her little brother George, who also shows great promise."

"I see," Doc said quietly, and then he seemed to reason over his next statement carefully. "I don't think the other children have had many opportunities to get to know them. They don't come in for church for one. Nor do they seem to have many friends. I could imagine there are lots of reasons for that. They live far out of town. They haven't lived here that long...."

"And everyone thinks their uncle is a murderer?" Hope filled in the rest of the sentence before Doc had to. It came out more sarcastic than she had intended, as if she didn't believe it herself, and maybe she didn't. Maybe she was of the camp that people should have to prove themselves to be bad before she would cease to give them the benefit of the doubt.

"Well, yes. There's that. I take it Brady has mentioned it to you, then?"

"How did you know it was Brady?"

Nicholas smirked. "Let's just say the first time Anna, his fiancée, first laid eyes on Judah Lawless, her eyeballs nearly came unattached. I was just thankful I wouldn't have to do surgery. Brady, on the other hand, was infuriated."

Hope covered her mouth to stifle a giggle. She hadn't met Anna yet because she'd not been feeling well the day before and missed church. It was just as well; Hope had met so many other people she couldn't possibly remember them all. "I can see why that might be upsetting to Brady."

"Yes, but one could hardly blame poor Anna." Hope raised an eyebrow, wondering what Nicholas was implying, and he shook his head. "That is... all of the ladies acted similarly. At first. Then, Paul Pembroke got drunk one night in the saloon, and well, they don't look at him like that no more."

Hope nodded. It was a similar story to the one Brady had told her, though he'd left out the part about his girl gawking at Mr. Lawless. "And do you think it's true? That is... could someone truly get away with killing two wives and never do any sort of time in jail?"

"Honestly, Miss Hope, I haven't the foggiest. I guess it's possible, but my take on the whole thing is, why not stay away, just in case? The children is another story. They seem like they have a chance to be something real special from what you've said. But if you don't have to interact with Judah Lawless, why would you? He didn't come by today did he?"

Hope felt her cheeks flare up again, and Nicholas read the answer before she could speak. "I mostly spoke to his sister, Caroline. She seems nice enough."

"Caroline is always polite whenever I interact with her," Nicholas agreed. "Course, I don't see her much... anymore."

"It seems a shame. They got along just fine until Paul opened his mouth. I wonder how different it might be for those poor children if he hadn't."

"Now, that I certainly can't say," Nicholas replied, turning the corner toward his folks' home. "But so long as you aren't ever alone in his presence, I should think you'll fair just fine. Besides, those eyes is deceivin', Miss Tucker. I've seen him work 'em, even on my own Lluvia. Don't trust him." He looked her right in the eye with that last phrase, and Hope felt her stomach churn. Had Judah been attempting to charm her for the sake of his niece and nephew?

"As for the children," Nicholas continued, "I think they should fair all right. Most youngin's in these parts aren't lookin' to start a fight. So long as you remind 'em that they're at school to learn and not there to socialize, I can't imagine it'd be too much of a problem."

Hope wanted to believe that would be the case. She had always been very good at inspiring her students to behave while in class and treat each other with respect. She always took the approach that she wasn't just teaching them how to read and write but how to be productive citizens as well.

They pulled to a stop in front of the Howards' home, and Nicholas motioned for her to wait. He jumped down and scurried around to offer his hand, and once again, Hope found herself taken aback. Nicholas certainly was more polite than most. She couldn't remember Jimmy Brooks ever making such a fuss over her.

She took his hand and marveled at how smooth his skin was. Not a callous at all from what she could feel. So different than the rough hand she'd shaken earlier that day. But she tried not to compare; there was really no point. Nicholas likely hadn't done much labor, what with his studies and practice. Once Hope's feet were on the ground, she meant to pull her hand away, but it lingered in his, either of its own accord or because he didn't release it quite as quickly as he should've.

Hope swung her lunch pail back and forth as she made her way up the walk next to Nicholas. He opened the door for her, and she thanked him. "That you home so soon, Miss Hope?" Nita called, stepping through the dining room. "Oh, Nicholas. I wasn't expecting you, Son." Her face lit up as she came over to kiss him on the cheek. Then, she turned to Hope. "How was your first day?"

"Busy," Hope replied, feeling an exhaustion that only the first day of school could bring. "But otherwise, good."

"How many students showed up?"

"Twenty-seven," Hope replied. "But Steven left while we were eating outside."

"That's more than we expected!" Nita exclaimed. "Steven Hawker is a little troublemaker. I'm sure his granny will send him back tomorrow. You should box his ears."

Hope had never laid a hand on any of her students and didn't intend to start. But she would have a discussion with Steven, assuming he did return the next day. Stifling a yawn, she said, "If you don't mind, I think I'll go rest for a bit and then come down and help with the cooking."

"You go right ahead and rest, dear. But don't you worry about helping me. I'd be cookin' whether you was here or not." She patted Hope on the shoulder.

Relieved that she could take her time in her room, small and plain as it was, Hope turned to Doc. "Thanks so much for the ride home."

"You betcha," he replied, and she thought it sounded slightly awkward but kept her giggle inside.

She made her way up the staircase, trying to decide whether she should take a little nap or write a letter to her folks. She wanted to tell them how the first day had gone, but she wasn't sure she had the energy for it.

Hope had made it almost to her door when she heard Nita say in a hushed voice that still managed to carry up the stairs, "You do realize it is in her contract that she can't do no courtin' don't you, Son."

"I know that, Mother," Nicholas answered. Hope paused, wondering if he might say more. When a few long seconds went by with no more, she decided he must be finished and quietly opened her door, but then she thought she heard him ask, "Any chance you can get that changed?"

The only response she heard from Nita before her footsteps pounded out of the room was, "No."

CHAPTER FOURTEEN

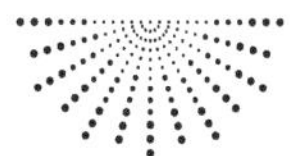

"Now class, who can tell me who the second president of the United States was?" Hope asked, standing in front of her class with a history book she'd checked out from the library, not that she needed it for that particular question. It had been two weeks and there was no update on the slates, nor had she made any progress on getting books from Mr. Stewart. Luckily, she'd worked a deal with Robert Canton that the students could walk to the library once a week and each check out a book. She'd also borrowed several for them to have in the classroom and would exchange them every week or so. Without slates, teaching was still a challenge, but the good behavior had stayed in place, for the most part, and the children all seemed eager to learn.

Only one child raised her hand, and of course it was Ginny. Hope was reluctant to call on her again because she wanted the other students to have a chance to answer, but it seemed none of them knew much about social studies, so she nodded for her star pupil to answer the question. "John Adams," she said, her voice not at all implying that she thought she was smarter than the other students.

"Very good," Hope replied. She turned her back to write the answer on the blackboard and heard snickering from the back of the room. Turning back to face the class, she saw Elsie Jones trying to hide a laugh and Peggy Cline had a smirk on her face.

These two were the oldest girls in the class at fourteen and fifteen. They could've studied for their exams this spring if they'd wanted to or been ready, but Hope wasn't recommending it. They were both smart enough to get by and could read fairly well, but she needed another school year with both of them to get the girls ready to graduate. Now, she was alarmed at their behavior. This wasn't the first time she'd caught the two giggling over something, and by the expression on Ginny's face, she'd overheard them this time.

"Would you care to share with the whole class, Peggy?" Hope asked, giving her sharpest teacher look.

"No, Miss Tucker. It's nothing," Peggy replied, her eyes downcast now that she'd been called out.

"Then I suggest you mind your words." She glanced over at Ginny and thought she saw tears in her eyes. Hope debated calling Peggy outside to tell her what she'd said but thought it might be best to let it go at this point and possibly address it later. The last thing she wanted was to embarrass Ginny or bring the attention of the entire class to the situation. With one more warning look, she turned back to the blackboard.

"Now, we've already discussed George Washington and his presidency. Today, we will learn about John Adams, and tomorrow we will move on to our third president, also a very important man, so I suggest a few of you go home and ask your parents his name." She turned back to look at her students. "I know that many of you are capable of learning this information so that you are able to answer my questions, so please, don't be timid."

Using the history book as a reference, she began to explain the key points of John Adams's presidency, thinking she may want to shift the schedule around the next day so that social studies wasn't so late in the school day. The children were tired, and many stifled yawns as she talked about a time in history that wasn't exactly exciting to almost anyone. She wished she could skip ahead and talk about the war between the states. That was something the children would want to hear about. Every one of them knew someone who'd fought for either the North or the South, and Hope loved to tell her students about the battles her daddy had fought in. But she doubted they'd make it that far in social studies this year. She'd have to save it for the fall term.

Once she'd given them an overview, Hope asked some questions for the students to ponder and soon had an energetic discussion going about Abigail Adams's call for her husband to consider giving women more rights, such as the power to vote. Most of the boys in class gave plenty of reasons why they thought that was ridiculous, while the girls, even Peggy and Elsie who usually had nothing positive to contribute unless it was pulled from their teeth, were adamant that women should have the same rights as men. Hope was proud of herself for breathing life into what may have otherwise been a forgettable lesson, though she was disappointed that Ginny said nothing.

A glance at the clock told her it was time to send the students home for the day. "All right, boys and girls. Who can tell me your assignment for tomorrow?" She was met with blank stares and tried not to sigh in frustration. Ginny didn't raise her hand either, though Hope was certain she knew the answer. Surprisingly enough, the lone, dirt-caked hand that slowly raised came from the second row, one of the younger students.

"Yes, Steven?"

"You said to ask our folks about the third president. Is that what you mean, Miss Tucker?"

"Yes, Steven. Very good." She tried not to make a show of how proud she was that the little boy, the one she'd spent weeks coaxing into staying long enough to hear her lessons on math and social studies, was not only in his seat this time of day, but had answered a question. "Please don't forget. Now, you may gather your things and walk quietly out to the play yard, and I will see you in the morning."

There was a bit of low murmuring as some of the older students made sure their younger siblings had their lunch pails and library books, but for the most part, the children were quiet until they reached the yard, and then there was plenty of laughter as they skipped home or the few that had rides headed toward their waiting carriages. Ginny and George took their time and were the last ones to leave. This was generally the case, and Hope had wondered about it for a while. Today, she decided to ask.

"Ginny, is everything all right? I see your carriage waiting out there for you. Is there a reason why it seems to take you and George a little longer to get your things together?"

The girl had her back to Hope, but she could see her shoulders rise and fall, as if she was contemplating exactly what to say. Without turning around, she finally said, "Everything is fine, Miss Tucker. We just like to take our time." She turned then, a smile on her face that seemed etched. "Everyone is always in such a rush."

Hope nodded but didn't know if she should trust that response. Perhaps she should start walking the children out for a few days to see if there was something she was overlooking. "All right. It looks like your mother is waiting."

"It's not Mama today," George said, seeming less worried than his sister as he swung his lunch pail over his shoulder. "She's bakin' pies."

Another glance out the window told her he was right—about it not being their mama, anyway. The way the seat was situated, she couldn't see the driver until he hopped down, probably wondering where his niece and nephew were. Hope drew in a ragged breath, and saw Ginny's forehead crinkle questioningly. Hope had no explanation, not that she could share with the child, anyway, but she imagined Ginny was used to people reacting to the sight of her uncle. She wanted Ginny to know it wasn't fear that had caused her throat to catch, though she could hardly explain what it was. The sight of Judah's frame enhanced by the mid-afternoon sun, the way the streaks of light highlighted the blond in his caramel hair when he adjusted his hat, the purely masculine essence that ebbed off of him with each step he took in her direction made Hope's stomach clench in a way she'd not felt before. No, she certainly couldn't share that with the wide-eyed girl standing before her.

"I'll walk you out," she said with what she hoped was an encouraging smile. Ginny nodded, clutching her book and lunch kit, and headed out behind George who was already down the porch steps before the ladies reached the door.

"Uncle Judah!" George said, launching himself the last few feet into his uncle's waiting arms. "We learned about John Adams today and how he didn't want women to be right!"

"You did?" Judah looked puzzled, and Hope could only shake her head. Perhaps her lesson wasn't as clear for the younger students.

Judah gave his nephew a squeeze before setting him on the wagon seat, messing up his hair, and then turning back to face her. Hope thought she saw his eyes shift down the length of her and back up, and it made her slightly uncomfortable, but not in the way it might if this were Jimmy Brooks taking her in. Instead, it made her heartbeat increase and her palms sweaty. "Miss Tucker, it's nice to see you." Hope's answer was caught in her throat, so she said nothing, and he turned his attention to Ginny. "You have a good day, Gins?"

"Yes, Uncle Judah." Once again, Ginny's smile wasn't true, and he could sense it as well but didn't question her, and Ginny climbed up to sit by her brother while Hope fought herself on the topic of whether or not to voice her concerns.

It ended up not being her decision. Judah glanced over his shoulder at the kids as he walked toward her. In a quiet voice, he asked, "Did something happen?"

Hope opened her mouth and a guttural squawk came out that was a mix between a stammer and a groan. She shook her head, closed her mouth, and took a few steps backward. Though he looked slightly amused now instead of wholeheartedly concerned, he followed her. Hope drew in a deep breath and tried again. "I think... some of the other girls are being a little unkind. I'm not sure. I haven't actually overheard them say anything, only caught a few giggles I feel may be at Ginny's expense."

All humor was gone from his face as he turned and looked back at the wagon. Both children had their library books open and didn't seem troubled that their teacher and uncle were talking. Judah pulled his hat off and ran his hand through his hair, sighed, and replaced it. "I was afraid of something like this."

Hope swallowed hard, not sure what else she should say, if anything. He had his hands on his hips and was staring at the ground, as if he was also debating what to say to her. Hope decided to give him a moment and kept her mouth shut.

"There are some rumors about me." He glanced up, meeting her eyes. Hope held perfectly still, not showing her hand yet. Her heart was racing. He had no way of knowing for sure what she'd heard, though he had to suspect it was something. "Most of them aren't true. But that don't matter, now does it?"

"Most of them?" The question was out before Hope could censor it. She closed her eyes for a second, trying to decide if she could find a way to take the nosy question back, but when she opened them again, Judah was smiling at her. "I apologize, Mr. Lawless. It's not my business. I only meant.... I want to do whatever I can to help Ginny. She shows so much promise. I think she could do quite a lot with that brilliant mind of hers. I'd hate to think the words of some silly girls who are likely more concerned with finding a husband than getting a good education might make Ginny feel poorly about herself. It doesn't seem to affect George at all. Perhaps he hasn't been targeted, or perhaps he's too young to understand, but I want to do what I can to help Ginny."

"I greatly appreciate that, Miss Tucker." He looked relieved, as if he might've thought she was frightened of him or that she might believe all of the rumors. She wondered what he meant by "most of them," but she could hardly ask again at the moment. It was impossible to think that the man in front of her could've taken anyone's life, unless he was defending his family. But to kill his wife? Twice? She couldn't see it. Nicholas's words rang through her mind. *"Those eyes is decevin'."*

"Both of them are wonderful children." Hope glanced over his shoulder to see Ginny helping George with a word he didn't know. "You and your sister, and her husband, should be proud."

"I have very little to do with any of that, but thank you. I shall pass your kind words on to Caroline. She's busy bakin' pies for the barn raisin' Saturday, so she sent me to fetch the children."

Hope had heard mention of a barn going up somewhere west of town, but the name of the family wasn't familiar to her. "Are you...." She caught herself being nosy again but then remembered that she'd heard he was a carpenter. Of course, that could've been one of the rumors that wasn't true.

"Am I... what?" He looked amused again, like there were at least a dozen words she could've been meaning to finish that sentence with.

"Are you a carpenter?" She decided that was the safest way to ask the question, and then, she couldn't help but laugh at herself. "I mean... is that one of the rumors that is true?"

"Why? Do you need a new table or chair?"

Hope thought about the too-small bed in her room at the Howards' and how she had nothing to write on. She assumed he was teasing. "No, it's not that. I just thought a barn raising might need a carpenter, that's all."

"I am not a carpenter," he said, his grin growing with each word. "But I am going to the barn raising." He took a step backward, like he was done talking about himself. "You should consider going yourself, Miss Tucker. The Coys don't have any kids yet, but they might someday."

"Oh, well, I can hardly just show up somewhere I'm uninvited," she stammered. "I wouldn't even know how to get there."

"Come on over and help Caroline load up her pies Saturday morning. They'll be happy to have you, especially if you know how to bake something that isn't pie." He was headed for the wagon now, turning and talking every few steps.

Hope laughed but quickly covered her mouth. "I don't know where you live either."

"All right. I'll send Caroline to fetch you. Most of the women folk won't get there until around ten. By then, we should have a good portion of the frame up."

"But...."

"Have a nice evening, Miss Tucker." He climbed into the wagon seat in one fluid motion, leaving Hope staring after him with her mouth hanging open, unsure of what had just happened. She stood in the schoolyard for a long moment, watching as the wagon moved down the road.

Eventually, Hope closed her mouth and went back into the school, going about her chores while puzzling over Judah Lawless. What would Mrs. Howard say if Caroline Pembroke pulled up outside of their home Saturday morning, the day after tomorrow, expecting to take her to a barn raising that no one else in the household was asked to attend? Or would they be headed there, too? Was it possible that the

Coys and the Howards knew each other, and Nita just hadn't mentioned it?

She doubted that was the case. Maybe she could get away with telling Mrs. Howard that a parent had asked her to go without telling her who it was. That didn't sound right either. Hope placed the broom in the closet, closing the door and leaning back against it. She didn't like the idea of keeping secrets, not from the Howards or anyone else. But it seemed that everyone in town thought Judah Lawless was bad news, and they'd lumped his family in alongside him, regardless of the fact that his niece was a wonderful young woman with lots of promise.

Glad to have a long walk home to ponder the situation, Hope gathered up her belongings and shut the schoolhouse door behind her. For a moment, she contemplated whether or not she should swing by the bank and check with Mr. Stewart about the slates, but then she remembered the saloon was close to the other establishment, and she thought it might be open by now. Chances were she could make it to the bank without being harassed, but she'd had enough confrontation for one day and decided she'd just wait until the next time Doc came by to give her a ride and ask him to drive her there first. He had already taken her home four times out of the nine days she'd had class, and said he would do so as often as his schedule permitted.

The March breeze was in full force as she made her way along the dirt road that led across town, back to the Howards' place, which was beginning to feel more and more like home. After the conversation she'd accidentally overheard between Doc and his mother, she didn't quite look at him the same way. She'd thought he might be developing feelings for her, and there were times when she thought maybe she might be reciprocating. Doc was a good looking fellow. He was kind and intelligent. He certainly knew how to help others. At the same time, the spark between them just didn't seem as bright as she'd always imagined it would be when she met the man she'd marry. Of course, the fact that she was not in a situation where she could even entertain a man's request to court her might've had something to do with it. If she didn't have her contract to worry about, and Doc asked her to go for a romantic ride through the park, or to have a picnic, or some other getaway, just the two of them, she thought she might say yes. Did that mean she was interested in Doc romantically?

It was times like this when Hope wished her mother was nearby. She'd written plenty of letters already, mentioning family members and her students. She had told her mother about the interesting doctor, leaving out that he was boyishly handsome. Her mother had written back, saying she'd sent several letters, too, though Hope had only received two. She thought that was pretty decent for only having lived in Texas a couple of weeks.

But it wasn't the same. And she could hardly send a telegram to her mother asking if she thought she should attend a barn raising for a couple she'd never met. There were other questions she longed to ask her mother, though. Questions about rumors and what constituted a bad person. Could it be everyone else in town was wrong, and Judah Lawless was simply misunderstood? Even if that was the case, was there anything she could do about it? If her contract didn't allow her to court Doc Howard, it certainly wouldn't allow her to be seen in public with Judah Lawless. In fact, she thought the best way to get fired and run out of town was to be seen anywhere with Judah Lawless.

Yet, she was pondering attending a barn raising as his guest, along with his sister. It seemed like a silly idea. She'd been to a few barn raisings, and if the ones in Texas were similar to the ones she'd attended in Missouri, after the barn was up, there'd be dancing. Hope loved to dance, but she was fairly certain she wouldn't be allowed to. Would it be inappropriate to ask Mrs. Howard if taking a turn on the dance floor with a nice gentleman would go against the promises she'd made when she signed her contract? Even if Nita said it was permissible, that gentlemen could certainly never be Judah.

The sound of Nita humming from the kitchen reached her ears when she entered the house. Upstairs, she heard the elder Mrs. Howard snoring. Not wanting to disturb either of the women, she closed the door quietly and crept up the stairs to put away her lunch pail and the few books she'd been taking back and forth with her. Her mother's most recent letter sat on the nightstand, and Hope read through it again before deciding to send another response. She took out a sheet of paper and a fountain pen and picked up one of the larger books from her stack to use as a table as she balanced the paper on top of it on her lap. Maybe she should've asked Judah if he could make her a table after all.

Dear Mama,

I hope this letter finds all of you well. This is my sixth letter since arriving, so that you can keep track of how many you have received. It is Thursday, and we had an interesting discussion this afternoon in social studies about Abigail Adams and her request of her husband that he give women more rights, which sparked the discussion as to whether or not women should be allowed to vote. It really was interesting, and I am so proud that my students were able to articulate their convictions so well, even if I did not always agree with what was said, particularly by some of the boys.

Nicholas, Mrs. Howard's youngest son, continues to be a good friend to me. He has come by after school several times to give me a ride home when his schedule allows for it. Being the town physician keeps him quite busy. Any discussions I have with him regarding medicine make me think of you. I do not pretend to have any real knowledge but find that I learn something new every time I have a chance to speak with him.

Today after school, I walked out with two of my students. Ginny, the girl I've mentioned before, and her brother George, are both quite bright. I am concerned about Ginny, though. There are rumors about her family, particularly her uncle, and I think the other children may be teasing her. It is all too heartbreaking to think about. Ginny holds such promise, and I would hate to have the other children repeating what they've heard adults say in a way that hurts her dear heart. I spoke to her uncle about it this afternoon and hope that this proves helpful. Perhaps I should speak to her mother as well. I've been invited, by the uncle, to a barn raising on Saturday. He said he would send his sister by to collect me. I have not decided whether or not I should attend as I do not know the family whose barn is being raised, but I may go just so that I will have the opportunity to speak to Mrs. Pembroke about the situation with her child. I do think that Mrs. Howard will disapprove of my attending, however, since she seems to think the rumors are true and that I should be careful around the uncle. Do not worry, Mama. I shall not put myself in any compromising situations.

I have written to Lola to inquire about how my former students are progressing, but I have not received a letter from her yet. If you hear anything about any of them, at church, or around town, please let me know. I do hope this decision was for the best. Every day that I am here, it seems a little more like home. Yet, I do miss all of you terribly. I know you said I would. I hope it will get easier to abide as time passes.

We still have no slates, but I have managed to work out an arrangement with the town librarian so that we can at least borrow books. As I have mentioned before, I was so surprised to hear this town had a library. I will certainly be volunteering to help Mr. Canton run it, once I have more free time and have settled into my employment a little more. Without him, I fear the work ahead of me would be even more difficult.

I must go now. I should speak to Mrs. Howard about the barn raising. Oh, that you were here so I could hear your words of advice. I am sure they would be perfect. Tell Daddy, Faith, Grandma, and Grandpa I love them.

All my love,

Hope

SHE LAID the letter aside so that the ink would have a chance to dry and addressed the envelope before taking another glance around her room and deciding it was time to head downstairs. Part of her hoped the opportunity to discuss the barn raising would present itself while the rest hoped she wouldn't have a chance to mention it until Caroline arrived. Then, she'd either go or tell the sweet woman that she wasn't able to, depending upon Mrs. Howard's countenance.

Hope was quiet in the hallway, thinking she shouldn't disturb her neighbor who was still snoring. The stairs creaked a little, but not enough to interrupt the cadence of the senior Mrs. Howard's breathing. She was glad because sometimes the older woman would shout at her if she was too loud in the hall, even though Hope thought she was being relatively quiet.

Mrs. Howard was chopping vegetables and dropping them into a kettle hung over the fire, and the savory scent of roast filled Hope's lungs. It had been a long time since she'd had a good stew, and her stomach rumbled to announce she was ready for supper already.

"Well, I didn't even hear you come in," Mrs. Howard said, looking away from the carrot she was chopping. "How was your day?"

"Good," Hope said with a genuine smile, thinking back to some of her triumphs of the day. Steven hadn't left during lunch, which marked progress. The older kids had had a good discussion about President and Mrs. Adams, though she needed to clarify some things for the younger students, apparently, and Ginny had done remarkably well on her math assessment. The latter was no surprise, but it still made Hope happy. "How has your day been?"

"Oh, 'bout the same as always. I did go check on your slates this morning."

"You did?" Hope was glad to hear it and relieved she hadn't wasted a trip into town. "What did you find out?"

"Mr. Stamine, the shop owner, said he'd ordered 'em, but it'll be a few weeks before they get here. He didn't seem all that concerned, though. I let him know it was urgent, and he assured me he'd do all he could to get 'em in quick as possible. So... I guess we'll see."

Hope didn't like the sound of it. For a moment, she wondered how close this Mr. Stamine and Mr. Stewart were. Maybe neither one of them wanted her to have slates for her class. The whole thing was becoming ridiculous. How was she supposed to teach without them?

"Mr. Canton is a workin' on getting' some of them primers you said you needed, too. Maybe we'll have more luck with 'im."

"Did you stop by the library, too?" Hope asked. She absolutely loved the library and couldn't believe Mrs. Howard didn't visit there regularly, but she insisted she didn't have as much time for reading as she would like. Hope knew that was likely true since she had her mother-in-law to care for, and she was fairly certain Brady still brought his clothes by to be cleaned every week. She also regularly made enough food for both of her sons for supper, though Brady hadn't visited since the first night Hope arrived. She had a feeling he didn't much care for her. Or maybe that was just his disposition.

"I did. I decided to take your advice and find a few minutes in my day to read. You know, I always loved reading as a girl, but since the boys came along, I ain't had five minutes to myself. But I deserve that, so I'm gonna make it happen." Nita's smile lit up the room, and Hope was glad she'd had a positive effect on the woman who'd been taking such good care of her.

"Is there anything I can do to help you with supper?"

"Oh, no, dear. I'm just dropping these last vegetables into the pot."

"All right then." Hope looked around but couldn't see anything that needed to be done. She contemplated going back upstairs to get her book. It was a nice day outside; maybe she could sit out there and read. But then, she imagined now was as good a time as any to ask about the barn raising. She just wasn't sure how to broach the subject. She let out a breath and realized she was fiddling with the corner of the counter so she folded her hands in front of her.

"Somethin' on your mind, dear?" Nita asked, scooping the last of the vegetables up and dropping them into the pot.

"No," Hope said before she could even consider the fact that Mrs. Howard had given her an opening. But the other woman wasn't fooled. She wiped her knife off, picked up her cutting board, and took them both to the washbasin before taking off her apron and setting it aside. Then she turned and slowly looked at Hope with an expectant look upon her face. "Maybe."

Nita gave a little chuckle. "What is it, dear? Did something happen at school today?"

"No, nothing in particular," Hope replied, trying to pick her words carefully. "It's only—do you know the Coy family? I think they live pretty far out of town."

Pursing her lips together, Nita seemed to consider where Hope might be going with her question. "Yes, I know the Coys. They's kin to the Wilcoxes, Anna's folks."

"They are?" Hope asked. She still hadn't met Brady's fiancée but hoped to soon.

"Yes. Melissa Coy is Anna's first cousin. So we know of 'em."

There was something about the way Mrs. Howard spoke that made Hope think there was a falling out of sorts or something that made the Coys less than desirable. "Well, apparently, they're having a barn raising on Saturday, and I've been asked to go—not by the Coys. I've never met them. But...." She had to choose her words with care now. She didn't want to lie, but she could hardly tell Nita the truth either.

"Caroline Pembroke can pick me up Saturday morning, if I'd like to go."

Mrs. Howard cocked her head to the side and studied Hope so intently, the schoolteacher had to look away. She couldn't tell if it was the mention of Caroline's name that had Nita's dander up or something else, so she waited, trying to seem nonchalant. Finally, Nita asked, "Do you think that's a good idea, Miss Tucker? Cavortin' with Carline Pembroke?"

Hope wasn't exactly sure how to answer that question without sounding rude to her hostess. She thought for a moment before she said, "I don't guess she's done anything wrong, has she? I mean, she seems nice enough. Her children are excellent students and very well mannered. I suppose my mama would ask what would Jesus do, and I can't imagine he'd stay clear of someone because of what her brother is rumored to have done."

"Rumored to have done?"

Hope bit her lip. Had she been so close to making a case for herself and then ruined it with the last phrase? She tried to keep her voice calm and even, not at all like she was questioning the logic of Mrs. Howard's opinion. "Is there evidence that Mr. Lawless killed his wives, or is it all speculation?"

"Well, considerin' his sister is married to the man who did all the talking, and he seemed to think there was guilt the law never discovered, I guess that's gotta serve some purpose. Listen, Miss Hope, you're a grown woman, and I ain't yer mama. You know what your contract says. If you'd like to go to a barn raisin' with a woman whose known to have a man livin' with her kids whose had two wives die under mysterious circumstances, then that's your choice, my dear. But what I will remind you of is that you are not allowed to be seen in public with an unwed man for any purpose that might be considered courtin'. Now, I don't think Doc given you a ride back and forth to the schoolhouse would fit that description. But at that barn raisin' there's bound to be some dancin' and carryin' on. You best be careful about that."

Despite her words, it was clear to Hope that Mrs. Howard did not approve of her attending the barn raising with Mrs. Pembroke. Maybe she didn't like the idea of Hope going with anyone at all, but definitely not Judah's sister. But she was certainly right on one count; Mrs. Howard was not her mother. "Are you saying that dancing with a gentleman in public would be a violation of my contract?" Hope asked, still keeping her voice even.

"I am saying I think Mr. Stewart may consider it so, and if you like your appointment, and I think you do, I wouldn't be willing to take the chance if I were you."

Hope nodded, clear on the point now. "I think I'll go up to my room for a spell," she said, trying not to show her emotions. "If you need me to do anything before supper, please let me know."

"Of course." Mrs. Howard's smile was tight, and Hope imagined she likely had a few more disapproving comments to make if she was willing to listen. But she understood now. If she went to the barn raising at all, she had better not do any dancing. While it seemed like a small sacrifice for the opportunity she'd dreamt of for so many years, this was the first time the rules of her contract seemed confining, and like a woman with a corset drawn too tight, Hope was beginning to have trouble breathing. She could only hope she'd get to the barn raising and realize there was no one she cared to dance with, but something told her that would not be the case.

She crept up the stairs almost laughing at herself. Why would it matter if she couldn't dance with Judah Lawless when she could be chastised for even speaking to the man? And then, why would she want to dance with him when everyone else believed he'd done the unspeakable? Despite Doc's warning, however, when she looked into his eyes, she didn't see a man capable of killing, but she did see one capable of much more than anyone was giving him credit for.

CHAPTER FIFTEEN

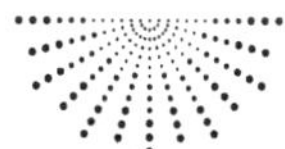

Caroline Pembroke pulled her wagon to a halt right in front of the Howard place at just past 9:30 Saturday morning. Hope watched from the window, thinking it was best not to wait for Caroline to come inside. While neither of her hosts had forbidden her to go, she was under the impression they'd just as soon she didn't. And yet, here she was, three loaves of pumpkin bread in a basket over her arm. She'd had to use canned pumpkin, which wasn't nearly as good as the real thing, but she remembered what Judah had said about bringing something that wasn't pie and thought this was the best she could do.

"Good mornin'!" Caroline hollered, waving from behind the reins. "How are you today, Miss Tucker?"

Hope waved back as she approached. She couldn't help but smile at the friendly face. Caroline looked so much like Ginny—or rather the other way around. Same large, inquisitive brown eyes and light brown hair, same bright smile. "I'm well, thank you kindly. How are you, Mrs. Pembroke?"

"Oh, please, it's Caroline, I insist."

"Then, please call me Hope." She set her basket down on the seat, and Caroline pulled it over so Hope could hoist herself up. "Sure is a nice day, isn't it?"

"It is. Thank goodness for it, too. After the rain we had yesterday, I wasn't sure."

The ground was still a little damp from yesterday's showers, but one thing Hope noticed about this part of Texas was that the sun would dry up any sort of precipitation pretty quickly. Caroline gave the horses a tap with the reins and they took off. "Where are the children?"

"They went on ahead with their pa and uncle this morning," Caroline explained. "Men wanted to get to it, tryin' to get it all done today. Besides, it's easier work in the morning before it gets too hot."

"I suppose that makes perfect sense."

"When we raised our barn last fall, it was August and intolerable hot. At least when our house went up it was early spring." Caroline's bonnet covered most of her face but occasionally she turned to look at Hope as she spoke. "I reckon there'll be less hands for this even than there was for ours."

"Oh? Why is that?" Hope asked, naturally curious.

Caroline didn't answer for a moment, and Hope wondered if she'd hit a sore spot. The mother cleared her throat and said, "Back when we first moved here, things was different. Now, ain't many folk who care to be around us. Not sure what you've heard. Anyhow, the Coys is different. And we've got plenty of friends from church who'll be out there helpin', too."

"Church?" Hope had been under the impression the Pembrokes didn't attend church.

Laughing, Caroline said, "What, you thought just because we no longer attend First Baptist we don't go?"

"No, it's not that," Hope insisted. "I mean, I realize there are other churches in town. It's only...."

"Someone mentioned that we don't attend?"

Hope wasn't actually sure how she had been under the impression that the family didn't attend anywhere. "What sort of church do you go to?"

"One for devil worshippers." Caroline turned and looked at her, hardly able to keep a straight face, and Hope watched in amusement, waiting for her to say she was joking. She had to be. "It's just a little country church. No real denomination, I suppose."

"I see you and your brother have a similar sense of humor," Hope muttered, shaking her head.

That made Caroline laugh as well. "You would not be the first person to say that. I'm sorry, Miss Tucker—Hope. I didn't mean to offend you. It's only... sometimes you gotta make light of things or else you may end up never seeing the humor in anything."

Hope considered her words and remembered thinking Judah did have an awfully optimistic countenance considering the circumstances. "I wasn't offended," Hope assured her. "Do you like it? The church that is?"

"Oh, yes. It's a friendly place. There's the Coys and us and a couple other families. A few children. None of the others come in for school, though. It's too far. Ginny has a good friend, Liza, who's the preacher's daughter. She was torn between going out with her pa early to visit with Liza and comin' into town with me to pick you up. She is quite fond of you."

Hope couldn't help but smile. "Ginny is wonderful. She's brilliant, you know. And such a good sister. You should be proud of both of your children. George is learning a lot as well."

"I am," Caroline assured her. "I was nervous sending them to school. I wasn't sure how they'd fit in or if they'd even learn anything under the circumstances, but you've inspired Ginny. She says she wants to be a schoolteacher when she grows up, just like you."

Hope felt a blush coming on. "That's so sweet of her. I think Ginny could be whatever she'd like. She has all the potential in the world."

They were out of town a little ways now, and Hope felt slightly relieved that they hadn't seen anyone she knew. While she would hold her head up high should anyone question her decision to accompany Mrs. Pembroke, she also wanted to avoid confrontation if she could. As her grandmother always said, "There's enough trouble in the world to stumble into. Ain't no sense a'lookin' for it."

They rode along in silence for a few moments before Carline noted, "This road right up here leads to our property. You just go down this lane about two miles and our house is the first one on the left, in case you ever need to know."

"Good to know," Hope replied, staring down the road as they passed. A particularly unique apple tree stood off in the distance, one she thought she might remember. She couldn't imagine why she might need to know that, but it was conversation at least. Deciding to keep the dialogue flowing, she asked, "Do you like it here? You haven't lived here long, have you?"

Caroline answered the second question first. "We moved down a little over a year and a half ago. Paul couldn't decide whether he wanted cattle or cotton." She shook her head but smiled, like she was used to putting up with her husband's antics. "So he is tryin' to do both. We liked it a lot at first. But then...." Her voice trailed off, and her countenance changed completely. Shaking her head back and forth, she said, "I know you've heard the rumors. You can't step foot in McKinney and not have someone tellin' you about the scandalous Judah Lawless and his family of miscreants."

Hope almost chuckled; it just sounded so ridiculous when she put it like that. "I have heard a few things, though I don't take to rumors much. I prefer to judge a person by the character they show me, not by what others presume to know about them."

Caroline turned to look at her and smiled. "I had a feelin' you must or else you wouldn't be here." She turned back to face the road. "At any rate, things changed all of a sudden, and we no longer felt welcome in town. Oh, sure, it's not so bad that I can't run by the five-and-dime or the feed store. I've never had nobody harass me directly. And Judah acts like no one has ever said a word to him. Maybe they haven't. But they talk behind his back, behind my back. Paul won't come to town no more. That's why you've never met 'im. If he needs somethin' for the farm, Judah'll go get it for him. "

That seemed a little strange to Hope. After all, it wasn't Paul who had been accused of murder. "I'm sure it's none of my business, but why is it that Paul won't come to town?"

Caroline pressed her lips together, her eyes moving around a bit as she pondered whether or not to answer the question. "He felt guilty, I guess." She let out a loud sigh, and Hope wished she hadn't asked if it made her uncomfortable to talk about it. "I ain't sure what you know exactly...."

"Very little. As I said, I prefer to avoid rumors when I can."

"I won't tell Judah's story 'cause it ain't my place. But I will tell you, Judah was married to Paul's sister, Sylvia. She passed away—about three years ago. Paul ain't moved past it. None of us has, but he especially gets upset whenever he drinks."

The deep breath Hope drew in at the mention that Judah's most recently deceased wife was actually Paul's sister was silent, and she was glad for it. "That's tragic. I'm so sorry. Were the two of you close?"

"Oh, yes. Sylvia was my best friend. Had been for years. And her death was... awful. Anyhow, Paul blames himself for puttin' us in this position. We'd all agreed not to mention her to anyone. But one night, on the third anniversary of her passin' he went to town and drank a little too much. He said some things, things he regrets. Though he swears he didn't say what the town folks decided to hear. At any rate, that was the end of the friendliness between us and the rest of the citizens of McKinney, save for a few who, like yourself, ain't so judgmental."

Mr. Canton came to mind. He seemed to believe Judah was innocent. She wondered who else Caroline might be talking about—certainly not the Howards or those ladies in the bank. Even the kind teller had seemed apprehensive when Judah walked in. "It must be difficult living that way," Hope said, her voice soft. "Do you ever think of going somewhere else?"

"No, I haven't," Caroline answered quickly. "Judah built me the house of my dreams when we moved here. I know it was because he felt sorry for my loss. Like I said, Sylvia was a dear friend to me. Obviously, it couldn't replace her, but it meant a lot to me that he was willing to go to so much trouble to give me such a nice place. So even though folks aren't too friendly any more, we can handle it. We stay clear as much as we can, and then we have our little community out here that accepts us just fine. I only... worry about the children." She shifted the reins so that she only had them by one hand and raised her other hand to the brim of her bonnet, as if it wasn't quite wide enough to block the sun from her eyes. "Judah told me about your concerns yesterday."

"I am concerned. I don't think George has any idea that some of the other children are being unkind, but it seems to be wearing on Ginny. The problem is, I never actually hear it. And she doesn't report it, so it's hard for me to address. Other than pullin' the other girls aside and tellin' them to quit—which I don't think Ginny would like either—I'm not sure what to do."

"Children can be so cruel," Caroline murmured. She turned the wagon down another dirt lane. This one looked more like a well-traveled pair of wagon ruts than an actual road, and in the distance, Hope could hear hammering. She took a deep breath, realizing she'd likely be seeing Judah soon. Her stomach twisted at the idea, which was unsettling. How could someone be both delightful and dangerous at the same time, and why was she even thinking of him when she had been warned by so many to stay away for more reasons than she could count?

"I will do my best to prevent the teasing from happening in the future," Hope assured the worried mother. "I will also remind Ginny that her armor is thicker than their arrows."

Caroline turned her head and smiled at Hope. "What a lovely way to put it."

There were a few other wagons pulled up near a small farmhouse. The sound of hammering grew louder, as did the shouts of children and laughter. Hope could see George running around the yard with another boy as Caroline pulled the wagon in next to a similar cart. She took her basket and climbed down only to be enveloped by his little arms. "Miss Tucker! You came!"

Laughing, Hope bent down to hug him back, grateful he felt so comfortable with her already. "I did! You look like you're having fun!"

"I am. This is my friend Tom. He caught a frog over by the pond!"

Hope turned to see Tom had a large bull frog in his grubby hands. "Oh, my! That is some croaker you've got there, Tom."

"George, honey, don't get Miss Tucker's nice dress all muddy." Caroline's scold was still loving.

"It's fine," Hope assured her, looking down to see George had left a few stray pieces of grass on the front of her dark blue dress, but other than that it was clean. She'd worn it because the yellow flowers in the print seemed bright and cheerful, and she thought it would make a good dress for such an occasion, but looking around at some of the other ladies in the distance, she thought she might be overdressed. Caroline was wearing a white shirtwaist and a simple green skirt but looked lovely. Most of the other women were dressed similarly. There were only a dozen or so of them, but they were laughing as they set about preparing dinner for the menfolk.

There was a fire going well away from the long row of tables set together behind the house, and over it a pig was roasting. It was a huge beast of a creature, but Hope imagined there'd have to be plenty of sides to feed a dozen famished men. She hoped her little contribution would be enough.

Caroline had one large basket over each arm, the scent of pie wafting from them. Hope's stomach rumbled despite the large breakfast she'd fixed herself. It seemed like there would be plenty of pie if nothing else.

"Caroline! You're here!" a tall woman with long red hair proclaimed, walking over with her arms open. "It's so nice to see you!" She managed to hug Caroline without disrupting the baskets and then insisted on taking one. Then, turning to Hope she said, "You must be Miss Tucker. I'm Melissa Coy. It's so nice to meet you."

"Please, call me Hope." Melissa embraced her as well, as if they were long lost friends, and Hope felt very welcomed at her home.

"Come on over! We were just setting up the tables. I'll introduce you to everyone, Hope."

There were about a half a dozen other women standing near the tables, the others up near the house or out in the yard. They spreading table cloths or discussing where to set the food items in the baskets. Hope could hear them talking about what needed to stay inside until it was closer to time to eat and what they could go ahead and set out. "As soon as Delia gets here, we'll have another table," an older woman with graying hair said before they seemed to notice they had company.

"Caroline!" one of the women shouted. "It's nice to see you. And is this the schoolteacher? Miss Tucker?"

"Hope, please," she said, loud enough for everyone to hear so that maybe she wouldn't have to keep saying it.

"It's lovely to meet you. I'm Evelynn Driggs. Welcome, welcome!"

"Evelynn is pastor Maxwell's wife," Caroline explained, setting her basket down near a row of others. She reached for Hope's, which she handed off, and she set that down, too, as Hope shook Evelynn's hand.

"We are so excited to have you," the pastor's wife said, patting her hand. "Welcome to Texas."

"Thank you, kindly. Everyone has been very nice so far."

Melissa stepped over. "This is Rita Koontz." Hope shook hands with the older woman who'd had her back to her. "And this is Beth Holloway and her sister Tabitha."

"How do you do?" Hope said to the sisters who were polite and waved but didn't come around the tables that stood between them.

"And this is my cousin Anna. Have the two of you met?" Melissa said, gesturing to the other woman who was standing near the end of the row of tables.

Hope was confused at first as she studied the woman. She was quite pretty with blonde hair and blue eyes, though she was a bit curvy. For some reason, she felt as if she should know who she was.

"We haven't met yet." Anna's smile seemed forced. "It's nice to finally meet you, though. Brady has mentioned you a few times. How do you like living with his folks?"

It suddenly dawned on her who this woman was—Brady's fiancée. She remembered now that Mrs. Howard had mentioned Anna and Melissa were cousins. But then, she hadn't expected to see her here. Brady had spoken so viciously about Judah, it was a wonder he could stand to be on the same premises. Hope's head swiveled to the area of the yard where the sound of hammering was coming from. There he was—Brady's large form would've been difficult to miss even amidst what appeared to be nearly two dozen other men. He wasn't paying her any mind, though. But as Hope returned her attention to Anna, her eyes flickered past Judah's familiar face. He had noticed her. Hope's breath caught in her throat.

Somehow she managed to push past the barrier. "It is so nice to finally meet you, Anna. Brady told me all about you. You're just as pretty as he mentioned."

Anna laughed. "Now, I know you're just bein' polite."

"No, he did say so," Hope insisted, wondering why she would say such a thing. The other women looked uncomfortable and continued with whatever tasks they'd been working on before Hope came over. Anna waved her off, like her statement didn't matter, but Hope distinctly remembered Brady's comment about his fiancée. He had said she was "purty" enough and that she was nice. Though she did remember some other comment—something about her not being the same as she had been when they'd first met or something like that.

Hope spotted Ginny across the yard, sitting underneath a tree with another little girl, a book open on each of their laps. "Would you mind if I went and said hello to Ginny before I help?" she asked Caroline, thinking she'd meet the other ladies later.

"Please do," the mother replied. "She'll be so happy to see you."

Hope crossed the yard, getting to within a few feet before Ginny hopped up with excitement. Opening her arms, Hope leaned down and wrapped her up. "How are you?"

"Miss Tucker! You came! I'm so excited to see you!"

She couldn't help but laugh at the enthusiasm. "I'm so happy to see you, Ginny. And this is your friend Liza?" The other girl, with dark hair and a smile with a gap in the middle top, nodded. Hope was glad she remembered her name. She'd learned so many all of a sudden, it was difficult to keep everyone straight. "It's lovely to meet you, Liza."

Liza smiled, but didn't answer, and Hope assumed she must just be shy.

"We are reading *Little Women,*" Ginny explained. "Can you read with us for a few minutes?"

Hope glanced back over to the table and saw the women were greeting a few newcomers. She wasn't too excited about meeting anyone else right now. "Certainly," she said, smoothing out her skirt and sitting down with the girls. "But just for a few minutes." She didn't want to be an impolite guest either.

After a chapter, Hope decided it was time to go rejoin the other women. The other table had arrived so she helped set it up, spreading out white tablecloths that made the disjointed tables seem more like one massive piece of furniture. The plates didn't all match, many of them likely brought from other women who had come to help, but no one cared, and Hope helped set those out, too.

Hope noticed some tension between Melissa and Anna as the women went about getting everything ready for the hungry men. Everyone else was friendly and welcoming, and both ladies were nice enough to the rest of the women, but whenever they spoke to each other, there was certainly something there. Hope imagined it had something to do with Melissa and her husband being friendly toward the Pembrokes, or more specifically, Judah, but she couldn't make that assertion, and she certainly couldn't ask. Despite the strain between the families, Hope felt a part of the group and could see herself fitting in just fine with these ladies if future plans ever called for her to rejoin them.

There was a slight breeze, and it threatened to blow the napkins off of the table, so Hope and Anna set about tucking them underneath plates. Shouting from the jobsite caught her attention, and Hope looked over her shoulder, certain that the booming voice she heard belonged to Brady.

"He sure is loud, ain't he?" Anna said with a small smile on her face. "I think he'd rather be workin' on his own farm today."

Hope glanced over her shoulder, wondering why they were here, then. It looked like Brady and Judah might be having an argument, though Brady was gesturing wildly with each statement he made, and Judah was standing calmly, seeming to listen rationally. Hope wondered where the foreman was. Didn't every barn raising have a dedicated foreman?

"He likes you, you know?"

Hope turned back to Anna, unsure of who she meant. "What's that?"

"Brady. He might've been all gruff the other day when he had to help you from the train station. But he's fond of you."

"Oh." Of course she meant Brady. Who else could she have meant? "I have a feelin' he's mostly bark and no bite, but he did speak highly of you."

Once again, Anna let out a chuckle, like there was some sort of joke Hope wasn't privy to. "Miss Tucker..."

"Hope."

"Right, Hope." Anna tucked the last napkin in and stood up taller. "Look over there and see how many men there are." Hope turned and faced the barn again. There were at least twenty, probably more she couldn't see. She shifted back around to face Anna. "And how many women are there?"

"Not nearly as many."

"Right," she said again. "And most of these women are married. So... Brady got this idea in his head when he was a little boy, 'bout George's age, I reckon, that he wasn't gonna be the one with no wife."

Hope remembered Brady had said something to her about that. "You don't think he...." She wasn't sure how to finish that sentence.

"It ain't like he don't love me. I'm sure he does. But it ain't like some of the others. Like Melissa and her husband Horace."

Glancing back over her shoulder, Hope wondered if most of the other men were unwed. She had noticed a disproportionate amount of single men around town, but she imagined that was just because their wives were home. Thinking that the West was mostly populated by single men was one thing. But McKinney hadn't turned out to be the outlaw-ridden town she'd expected, so why would that aspect be the same?

"Listen, honey, you're a beautiful woman," Anna said, stepping in close where only Hope could hear. "There's plenty of menfolk over there who'd like to take you for a twirl on the dance floor once that barn's up. I just hope my Brady ain't one of 'em."

Both of Hope's eyebrows shot up. "I assure you, I have no interest in Mr. Howard."

"I know you don't. That don't mean he ain't got no interest in you. Don't worry—I ain't angry at you over bein' purtier than me or havin' a more attractive figure. I'm just tellin' you to be careful, miss schoolteacher." Anna pursed her lips together and strode away, leaving Hope with more questions than answers.

"You all right, Hope?" Caroline's voice called Hope back to the table.

"I'm fine, thank you." She wasn't quite sure it was true, nor did she think the warning was just about Brady Howard and the number of single men for that matter. Hadn't Doc mentioned Anna had made it known she thought Judah Lawless was good looking before she found out his past—or at least the rumors about him? Was that yet another warning about her students' uncle?

"The upper beams'll be goin' up in a moment," Caroline said, placing her hand gently on Hope's shoulder. "We'll all wanna watch that."

Hope had seen it before but always marveled at how it was done, the way the men worked together to hoist the framework of the roof. She never envied the poor men who had to go to the top and join everything together, make sure everything was flush and perfectly joined. At least this barn didn't appear to be too horribly tall. She'd heard of people falling to their deaths or to great injury and silently wished Doc was there with them in case someone was injured.

"Don't worry, they'll be fine," Caroline assured her as if she could read her mind.

"They gotta good supervisor," Melissa added with a laugh, also patting Hope on the arm, and then both of the ladies walked away giggling, leaving Hope to wonder what that meant and what she should be doing to help.

She didn't get too far into the deciding process when there were shouts that the final beams for the roof were being lifted into place. She imagined there'd been just as much excitement earlier when the men had used poles and ropes to get the walls upright, but she'd missed all of that. Now, the children and women all walked closer to the barn together to watch the large support beam that ran across the top of the barn for the structure of the roof to be lifted into place.

It was hard work, especially since there weren't as many men as Hope was used to seeing. But they all worked together to hoist it up, and then she realized who was waiting for it at the top, poised on a beam so high in the sky, she might not have recognized him if it weren't for the way the sun glinted off the shock of caramel brown hair poking out from beneath his hat. And then she heard him give a direction and was certain Judah was in charge of this operation.

The sun was beating down already, and all of the men were covered in sweat. She could see the grimaces on their faces as they struggled to overcome gravity, but with one final heave, the beam was raised, and Judah was able to work one end into place. He balanced on a plank of wood narrower than his feet were wide and made his way to the other end of the barn, making sure that one fell into place as well and then pulled a hammer and large nails out of his belt to fasten it into place. Everyone cheered as one end was secured and then after careful trapeze work, so was the other.

"That would've been much easier if there were more men," Caroline muttered under her breath.

"It's done now," another woman—Rita, Hope remembered—said patting her on the arm. "Come on. They'll be wanting to stop to eat soon."

"You think?" Caroline asked. "Judah will keep 'em workin' as long as he can." They both chuckled like there was a history to that statement.

Hope turned to walk away with the other ladies, fighting the urge to turn and look at Judah one more time. She was acting like a silly schoolgirl, gawking at him all the time. The number of reasons why she should just avoid him at all costs was higher than she could even begin to count.

"Anna! Water!" Brady's booming voice reverberated around her, and Hope did turn, then, seeing Anna pick up two empty buckets, each with a ladle in it. She'd seen other women carrying them back and forth earlier but hadn't taken a turn because she didn't want to speak to either of the men she knew or any of the ones she didn't.

Anna was mumbling as she walked past Hope. "Do you need some help?"

"Nah, I got it." Her disposition suggested she didn't appreciate the way Brady spoke to her, and Hope couldn't blame her. Anna passed her, headed at an angle to the house, but then someone at the table called her over, and she set the buckets down, hurrying over to help another woman with something in one of the baskets, which Hope couldn't see.

By the time Hope got to the table, Anna was involved in another activity, and Hope imagined she might've forgotten the men were waiting for a drink. She glanced at the buckets and then back at the barn. The frame was so impressive, standing there against an azure sky. Hardly a cloud dotted the horizon, but the sun was bright and harsh, even for an early spring day.

"Should I fill the buckets?" Hope asked no one in particular. The other women were busy unpacking baskets, setting dishes down the center of the table. She cleared her throat and asked again, "Should I fetch the water?"

Evelynn, the pastor's wife, called over her shoulder, "Yes, dear. That would be lovely of you. Pump's a little hard to find." She gestured in a vague direction toward the far side of the house.

Hope figured she could manage to find the pump. She was certain it must look like every other pump she'd ever seen, though once she had buckets in hand and began to look for it, she noticed Melissa had plenty of flowers growing in the beds around her house that might obscure it. She wandered around the corner and took in the pond. It looked cool and inviting and she thought it was too bad those poor men couldn't take a dunk really quickly as relief from the scorching sun.

She turned the corner to see if perhaps the pump was on the back side of the house, closer to the well, and promptly dropped both buckets with a clatter. Her mouth gaped open as she took in the sight of Judah Lawless shirtless with rivulets of water running down his well sculpted chest past the muscles of his abdomen, wetting the waistband of his tan trousers, which were belted just below his navel. Hope's eyes wandered of their own accord farther than they should have and then back up again to blue eyes wide with the degree of shock Hope felt at stumbling upon such a vision. And yet, despite her gasp and the fact that she realized she'd intruded on a private moment, she could not look away.

"I apologize, Miss Tucker," Judah, said, sliding his light blue shirt back over his head. It clung to his wet torso, and he wiggled his shoulders to loosen it as he refastened the top three buttons. "It is intolerably hot up there."

With the heat rolling through her own flesh, she imagined she knew the feeling. She felt like her cheeks were aflame, and there was a tightness in her stomach like she'd never experienced before. He was fully dressed now, his shirt tucked in, and his hat, which had been resting atop the pump, was back on his head, but Hope thought it might take the rest of her life to get the image of Judah's bare chest out of her mind.

"Hope? Are you all right?" His expression was a mixture of true concern and that amusement she often saw play across his face whenever they interacted.

"Water." Her tongue had finally loosened enough for her to speak. She looked down by her boots and saw the two upset buckets, their ladles in and out, but mostly out, and gathered them up. "I was meant to fetch water."

"Well, bring them on over, and I'll help you," he said, priming the pump.

Hope did as instructed, still trying to gather her wits. She placed the first bucket under the spigot, and Judah filled it with cool water from the well. "You know, you walked right past another pump?"

She had been studying the liquid as it filled the metal bucket but glanced up now and caught his eyes. "No, I looked over there." She turned and gestured back the way she'd come, praying that she'd find a way to speak coherently again soon.

"It's hidden in Melissa's rose bushes," he explained, switching out the full bucket for the other one. She meant to move it out of the way, and their fingers grazed each other sending a wave of sparks up Hope's arm.

"I guess I walked right past it then." She realized as soon as the sentence was out of her mouth that was precisely what he'd just said and felt silly again.

Judah laughed, and she was suddenly jarred back to the moment. If it had been anyone else, she might've playfully smacked him on the arm, but she couldn't do that. Touching him was dangerous for more reasons than she was willing to admit.

"You havin' a good time?" he asked, topping off the last bucket.

"Yes, everyone is so nice." She thought back to her conversation with Anna and decided to omit it. "Melissa is lovely. So is Evelynn."

"These are some fine folks," he agreed, and she thought she heard a tinge of sadness in his voice, perhaps because not everyone had been so kind.

"How'd you learn to do that?" she asked, nodding in the direction of the barn. "You sure you're not a carpenter?"

"I'm sure," he said, leaning on the pump casually. She imagined she might have more difficulty talking to someone who'd just seen her half-naked, but it didn't seem to bother him nearly as much as it did her.

"You just raised a lot of barns?" He didn't seem particularly forthcoming with information.

Snickering, he said. "Something like that."

"Fine. Don't tell me anything." Hope bent to pick up the buckets, trying on the pouty look she'd seen some of her friends try when they wanted something from a man.

He let out a sigh, and she knew she'd won. "I was an architect, Hope. Still am, I guess. Here, I'll take them back with me."

She handed him one bucket but kept the other, glad to have his help since they were heavier than she'd expected. "An architect? Really?"

"Yep. Though I haven't used my skills for much more than barns since we finished Caroline's house. You gonna give me that bucket?"

"Nope," she replied, beginning to walk toward the barn. "I can't hardly keep talking to you if I hand you the bucket and leave."

His eyebrows arched, but then he smiled. "You ain't worried about that?"

She ignored the question. "What type of buildings did you erect?"

"Mostly the ones made outta wood." He was teasing her again, and she fought the urge to strike him in the arm while her eyes narrowed. "All sorts. Mostly town squares. A few standalone structures. Post offices. Courthouses."

"Like the massive one on the square?"

"Nothin' that elaborate."

"Why did you stop?" They were nearly halfway there now and she slowed her steps even though she knew the men were likely anxious for the water they carried.

"Not too much goin' on here, and this is where Paul and Caroline wanted to settle. I came with 'im to build Caroline's house. Then, I guess I got a little caught up with the children and decided to stay. For now."

There was more information in those few sentences than she could discern at the moment, so she decided to think on it later and ask another question. "Y'all came from Kansas? Where abouts did y'all live before that? New York City?"

The sound of his laughter reminded her of music, the way it had the first time she'd heard it. "You been listen to the town folk, Miss Tucker?"

"Nah, just Brady Howard."

"Well, he is not a fan of mine if you haven't heard."

"I heard him bellowin' earlier. I think he's more of a rooster than a fox."

"That's true. The idea that we used to live in New York is yet another mixed up notion strung together from pieces of misinformation as a result of too much alcohol on the part of my dear brother-in-law." He pointed up to one of the higher beams where a man who looked like an older version of George was hammering a nail into a supporting truss.

Hope knew that must be Paul, and while she'd hoped to meet him, at least she had an idea of who he was now. "So not New York City?"

"No. Manhattan. Kansas."

A peal of laughter rang out of Hope's mouth which caught Brady's attention. He was on the ground, and now that he saw she had water, his tree-trunk legs were carrying him in her direction quickly. "Thank you for your help, Mr. Lawless."

Judah nodded and handed his bucket over to a waiting man who looked to be a little older than both of them but didn't say anything else as Brady bounded over and grabbed her bucket, splashing cold water upon her dress. He took the ladle out and gulped it down, repeating the process twice before Hope decided to just back away.

But he wasn't finished with her. Stepping forward, he asked, "What are you doin'?"

Hope froze, her forehead crinkling. She took a step back in Brady's direction. Another man took the bucket from Brady. "What are you talkin' about?" she asked, her head tipped to the side.

Brady stormed at her, causing Hope to shrink back slightly, though she held her ground. "Do you not remember what I told you the day I picked you up from the station? Did you forget you got yerself a purty specific teachin' contract, Miss Tucker?"

Hope's dander was up now. "I was just fetchin' the water because Anna got busy, Mr. Howard," she said, no longer a shrinking violet. "I didn't forget anything. Mr. Lawless happened to be at the pump and volunteered to help." Her eyes flickered past the rampaging bull standing in front of her, and saw Judah hadn't gone too far. If she needed him, he'd be there, but she had enough of her mama in her not to need him, not yet anyway.

Brady seemed sufficiently warned to mind his own business but needed to have the final say. "Just remember my folks has done a lot fer you. My mama'd be awful upset if it turns out the only reason you come here is because you's huntin' a man." He turned and walked away, leaving Hope staring after him, her eyes bulging.

Judah was concerned. She could see it in his eyes, even though he didn't take a step toward her. She managed a smile, hoping to assure him she was okay. He didn't seem to quite believe her, but he didn't come over, and Hope turned and walked back toward the other women, fuming.

She understood now. At first she'd thought Brady and Anna were there because Melissa was Anna's cousin, that even though their relationships seemed strained, family helped family out when it was needed. But she knew now that wasn't the case at all. Brady'd been forced to come to keep an eye on her. Nita had likely talked him into it after she'd told her hostess she'd decided to come. Whether or not it had anything to do with Judah or Nita just wanted to make sure she didn't break her contract didn't matter to Hope. She was a trustworthy woman, not a child who needed to be looked after. Part of her wanted to march right over to Anna and give her a piece of her mind.

But Anna wasn't the culprit here. If anything, she was a victim. She likely didn't want to be there either. By the time she reached the other women, Hope had calmed down some. Melissa was talking to

Evelynn, the two of them laughing about something, but Hope still felt to blame for the fact that the woman had unwanted guests at her barn raising. If Hope wasn't there, Anna and Brady wouldn't be either.

"That Brady sure is a strong feller," Rita said, sneaking up to Hope's shoulder. "It's a good thing he decided to come." She turned and looked at the shorter woman. "I know he's a bit loud and don't always think before he speaks, but he's got his good points to. And Anna ain't seen her cousin in a long spell. It's nice they had this chance to be reminded of the friendship they used to have."

Hope nodded, realizing what Rita was saying. Maybe it was Hope's fault the couple had come, but there were positives to them being there. At the moment, though, Hope was thinking maybe she was the one who should've stayed home, in her too small room, with her not enough furniture. If she just did exactly what everyone expected her to do, stayed in line, focused on her students, used the materials she was given and stopped asking for more, perhaps everyone else would be happy. Hope would be miserable, though, and she wasn't sure she could handle such an existence, even if it did mean she'd keep her position indefinitely. What good could she do as a teacher if she wasn't a happy individual?

Deciding there was nothing she could do at the moment, she pitched in and helped finish off the final work that needed to be done before the ladies could demand the men lay down their hammers and come on over to eat. One thing was certain, she'd sit as far away from Judah as possible. Regardless of whatever else she decided to do, it did seem like a sensible decision to avoid the man with the secret past, even if every word spoken about him was untrue. He seemed like a surefire way to get herself into a mess of trouble, the kind that would end her career and leave her packing her bags, headed back to Missouri a failure having let down all of her students. And those children already meant too much to her for her to let that happen.

CHAPTER SIXTEEN

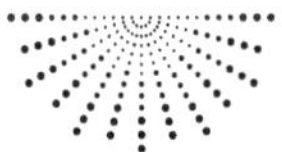

Fiddle music reverberated off of the freshly assembled barn walls. The hand organ, flute, a guitar, and a steel drum accented the melody as one of the men who'd worked so hard all day sat on an upturned barrel, playing his heart out on the beautiful instrument. Hope sat on a bale of hay, watching, her toes tapping, keeping time with her hand on her thigh as the others took turns on the dance floor, celebrating the finished barn.

How she wanted to leap up and join them! Ever since she'd been a little girl, she'd loved to dance. Her father used to pick her up and twirl her around in his arms, sometimes in their very own parlor while her mother hummed a tune. A rush of memories flooded Hope's mind, and she was overwhelmed with homesickness. Dwelling on that now would cause her to cry, so she didn't let the images linger. Instead, she turned her attention to Ginny and Tom, George's friend, who didn't even come to her chin, but she was schooling him on proper hand position as he attempted to lead her across the floor. Hope giggled and caught Caroline's eye.

Not for the first time, one of the single men sauntered over to her. "You sure you don't wanna dance?" he asked. "Ain't no one here on the school board."

Hope smiled up at him. It wasn't the first time she'd explained the situation to him. "No, thank you," she said. Apparently, her explanation for why she couldn't join him, or any of the others who had asked, wasn't clear enough. "I'm all right."

"You know, your contract says you can't be seen with any single men, but what about an old married one?" The man who came to rest next to her on the bale of hay had been identified earlier as Homer Coy, Horace's dad. His wife hadn't come because she was feeling poorly. So far, he'd danced with his daughter-in-law and Caroline, who'd had a lovely time trying out some of the older dances from his day, and Hope imagined it would be a lot of fun to take a spin herself, but her head was shaking before her mouth started speaking.

"I do appreciate the offer, Mr. Coy, but I think I'd rather just sit and watch."

"Too bad," he said, patting his leg. "Purty girl like you oughtta be able to cut a rug with whoever she wants." He stayed next to her, his foot keeping the beat, and Hope silently agreed with him.

The other man had moved on, much to Hope's relief, and her eyes traced back over all of the singles standing around talking. There really weren't enough women to go around. All the rest of the gals were married except for a couple of distant cousins of Evelynn's who'd shown up after the barn was up. They took turns with the other men so no one was left out, but Hope was getting a whole new perspective on the situation. She imagined there were plenty of unwed women back in McKinney who simply weren't part of this group. Her understanding was that these people all lived fairly far out of town, but most of them likely wouldn't fit in with the crowd from town anyway since they seemed to think Judah and his family were acceptable human beings that shouldn't be chastised for simply existing.

Brady and Anna had done a few turns on the dance floor before there had been some sort of tiff between them, and Anna had stormed out, Brady on her heels. Whether or not they'd actually left was beyond Hope. She wasn't too surprised to see it. Brady had a way of choosing words that infuriated whomever he was speaking to, particularly women.

Caroline was dancing with Judah now, and Hope tried not to

watch, though it was difficult. She'd managed to avoid him ever since Brady's interference earlier in the day. Both times they'd gathered around the table, she'd sat down at the far end near the children, and he'd stayed nearer the barn with the other men who had no families with them. When he'd danced with Ginny earlier in the evening, her eyes had held fast to the pair, Ginny's giggling ringing over the sound of the musicians as he spun her faster than necessary and then bowed to her like she was a princess when the song was over.

He hadn't been among those who'd come and asked her to dance, and she was glad for it, because she would've been too tempted to say yes. Even now, it was difficult to keep her eyes off of him. He had a grace about him, the way he moved across the floor with his sister in his arms like she was light as air and they were dancing on a cloud. Part of her wanted to assume her thoughts were muddled by their encounter earlier, that seeing him bare chested had messed with her propriety, but in her heart Hope knew better. All those years of yearning for someone to get a reaction out of her, to feel something for someone, and she was beginning to understand at last what it was that had made her mama risk everything to reach out to her daddy when she was already betrothed to someone else.

The song ended, and another melody filled the night. It was a familiar tune, one she'd heard her daddy sing to her mama a thousand times. Though no one sang the lyrics, she knew them all by heart, hearing echoes of her daddy's voice in her head as she followed along. When they reached the part that mentioned "raven black hair," the shade of her mother's and her own, Hope remembered how he'd always reach over and pluck a curl from each of his girls, letting it spring back before he continued. Overcome with emotion, Hope got up and headed for the door, thinking she'd catch her breath outside where it wasn't so stuffy and there were no eyes to see the tear slipping down her cheek.

The music followed her away from the barn, so she kept walking until she found herself in a thick copse of trees and then in a wooded area. The moon was bright in the sky and the heat of the day had sizzled away, leaving a refreshing breeze. She wiped her tear with her fingertips and leaned back against the trunk of a stately pine whose branches began at least a half a foot above her head. The scent of nature was calming, but the music was still discernible.

I woke from my dreaming
My idols of clay
My visions of love
Have all faded away.

She took a few deep breaths, hoping to calm her spirit. She'd expected to miss her family, but this was almost unbearable, and to think there was no one to comfort her, no shoulder to cry on, made it even more intolerable.

When the song was over, the little band picked up the tempo and played something unfamiliar to her, which was a relief since the last thing she wanted was to dwell on sad love songs from her parents' time during the war. She had just about decided she could handle going back in when she heard a cautious footstep and pressed herself up against the trunk of the tree, praying she hadn't managed to get herself into any trouble. Just because she'd felt safe so far didn't mean she wouldn't encounter any men with questionable morals.

Judah stepped into a beam of moonlight, and Hope felt her heart seize up for a moment, unsure whether she should be relieved that it was him and not an actual murderer or if she should take off running before he could infiltrate her fragile heart any more. "Are you all right, Miss Tucker?" he asked, his voice soft in the night air. "I saw you light out of there. That song remind you of some long lost love?"

He had worked his way under the canopy of branches now, but even through their filter she could still see concern in his eyes. "I'm fine, thank you. Not a lover but my daddy. He used to sing it when I was a girl."

"I see."

A small chuckle escaped her lips. "You must think I'm awful silly takin' off over something like that."

"Why would you say that?" He moved even closer, though there were still a few feet between them. "Memories can be powerful, especially when they creep up on us."

From the way he spoke, she sensed he wasn't just talking about her own memories. He adjusted his hat so that it was further back on his head and she could fully see his face now. She could've described him many ways, but looking into those eyes, she was certain he was no killer, regardless of what Doc and the others may have to say. "Why are you out here?" she asked, not sure what she was hoping to hear.

"I saw you take off, wanted to make sure you were okay."

Hope let that settle into her chest for a moment, not sure how to respond. She ran a hand through some loose curls and spread them back to where the rest of her tresses were gathered on the top of her head, trying to avoid thoughts of this man without his shirt on from earlier. "If I had my own cart, I'd probably head back home... back to the Howards' home, anyhow."

He glanced back toward the barn. "I'm sure Caroline'd give ya a ride whenever you want. I'd take you myself, but I know that's against yer rules, though I guess it's okay for someone like Brady or Doc Howard."

Had he been keeping tabs on who she'd been riding around with? "Well, Brady's engaged, so he's not a single man. And Doc... I'm not sure on that one. I asked Nita if it was okay, and she sorta just laughed at me." She held in the conversation she'd heard when Doc had asked if the rules of her contract could be changed.

Judah didn't appear to be dwelling on her statement anyway as he studied the ground between his boots. "I guess if they wanna get real technical, I ain't single either."

She stared at him for a moment, not quite understanding before she realized he meant there was a difference between being a bachelor and being a man who'd been made a widower twice, at least that's what she assumed. She'd never heard him mention either of his wives, and since the rumors had been wrong on so many other counts, she thought perhaps she shouldn't take anything for granted. Was there a chance he was still married and had just left his wife in Kansas for some reason? "I don't mean to pry, Mr. Lawless, but, I heard you lost your wife. Two of 'em, in fact. Do you mind telling me if that part of the rumors is true?"

He looked up at her, and she could see in his eyes that the answer was yes before he gave a short nod. Hope felt like an intruder for having asked and gazed past him, through the trees at the lights coming from the barn. What if someone came out here and caught them speaking? Would she be released from her employment?

The song shifted to something slow and haunting, similar to the melody that had sent her running, but she didn't know this one. "I'd ask you to dance, but I think that would be dangerous," Judah said, his voice as gentle as the breeze that stirred her hair. "For both of us."

"Why is that?" Hope couldn't stop the question before it came out of her mouth, and she found herself leaning toward him as well. "Why would it be dangerous for you?"

He made a noise that sounded like a cross between a snicker and a yelp. "Because... I've determined to never, ever get involved with another woman again for as long as I live." He was looking directly into her eyes now, and Hope felt a stirring in her chest as her heart caught and tried to restart again. "You seem like the kinda woman that could make me forget that vow, Hope Tucker. And that ain't safe for no one."

The ability to think rationally had fled her mind, and despite all the warnings, all the things she had to lose, Hope stepped forward, closing the gap between them and pressed her lips to his. He didn't jerk back in surprise as she would've imagined, not that she'd spent much time thinking at all, but instead his hand slipped around the back of her waist, pulling her closer, and Hope melted into him, the feel of his soft lips on hers assuring her nothing in the world could ever be wrong again.

But it was only for a moment, and then the realization of what she'd done hit her like a stone in the stomach. Hope pulled away, and he let her go. "I'm so sorry," she muttered, taking off between the trees, careful not to tangle her hair in the branches or misstep and stumble and fall. She needed to get away, back to reality, before it was too late.

She ran almost all the way back to the barn, not even glancing over her shoulder to see if Judah was following. She knew he wasn't—she would've heard his footsteps if he was. Once she felt as if she'd put enough distance between herself and temptation, she paused to catch her breath and knew her lungs were burning for reasons other than the short sprint. He'd taken her breath away, and she'd let him. Hope smoothed her hair back and ran her hands down the length of her gown before slowly proceeding back to the barn. A quick glance around let her know if she'd been missed at all, no one would say anything. Caroline and Paul were taking a turn on the dance floor now, but Hope desperately wished she could run all the way back to McKinney, or maybe Missouri. Instead, she took a seat on her hay bale, praying it would all be over soon.

When Judah came back in, it was through another door, and no one seemed to think anything of that either. She couldn't look at him, not while he was looking at her anyway, so she avoided his gaze. Once the song ended, she followed his boots over to his sister and the next thing she knew, Caroline was approaching, asking if she was ready to call it a night. It had been his work, she was certain. And she knew he would've said something generic, such as, "Look at Hope sittin' over there all pathetic by herself. Maybe you should take her back to her prison at the Howards' house," only not that harsh. But suddenly that's how she felt—caged.

She took Caroline up on her offer and followed her out the barn door, along with George and Ginny who needed to get to bed so they could be up for church the next morning. Hope fought the urge to look over her shoulder as she went, but she was certain blue eyes followed her into the night.

CHAPTER SEVENTEEN

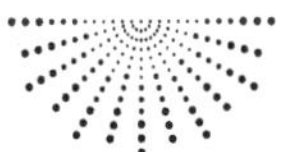

Hope intended to do everything within her power to avoid Judah Lawless, not because she thought he was a murderer, but because he held the sort of danger within him that could hurt her in ways she had yet to experience. He'd made his position very clear, and she could hardly blame him. After having already lost two wives, why in the world would he ever want to get married again? He'd left no doubt—he didn't. And she loved being a schoolteacher; every day the students grew on her a little more. With less than a month to go before the students took the summer off, she was already thinking about next year. Despite missing her family, she knew this is where she wanted to be, with these students, in this community. McKinney may have been wrong about Judah, but there was a lot to love in the thriving community, and Hope intended to make it her home.

Staying away from Judah proved easier than she would've thought considering she felt drawn to him. But since he lived so far away and they didn't attend the same church, the only times she ever saw him were when he came to pick up his niece and nephew, and then he never got out of the wagon and parked further down the lane than he had previously. He knew she wanted to avoid him and respected that decision. She imagined he wanted to avoid her, too. After all, she hadn't been very ladylike at the barn raising—spying on him shirtless and then kissing him like some sort of woman with loose morals. The fact that her own mother had told her a similar story about kissing her father made it seem more respectable, though she was aware the circumstances were much different for her parents. Her father had been leaving for war, after all.

Ginny was still having a few issues with the other girls, but Hope mentioned them to her mother whenever she came to pick the children up. She also addressed it with the other girls, hoping that would make it stop. It didn't; they just made it even more covert. Hope knew enough not to mention it to their parents.

Life at the Howards' was uncomfortable, and she missed her family more than she expected to after having been gone for so long. Letters came and went between them almost every day, but it wasn't the same. And living in the cramped quarters was doing a number on her as well. But Mr. and Mrs. Howard were kind and courteous, and Hope didn't want to question the possibility of the little house being built on the school grounds because she didn't want to hurt their feelings. Still, when she had a chance to daydream, her mind wandered to what it would be like to have her own place, where she could be herself and not have to worry about waking the elderly or stepping on Mrs. Howard's toes when their ways of doing things weren't quite the same. Since she still hadn't received the slates she needed, she doubted there was any chance of construction starting on the home any time soon and tried to put it out of her mind.

One early May afternoon, she'd finished cleaning up the classroom and was headed out when Doc's wagon pulled up out front. She smiled and gathered her things. While she was aware his feelings for her were different than the way she felt about him, he was a good friend, respectable and easy to talk to. The contract assured her he wouldn't do anything to make her feel uncomfortable, other than stare at her and blush sometimes if she sat too close on the wagon bench.

"Howdy there," he called as she stepped out onto the porch. "I think I've got just enough time to run you home before I head over to the Talbot's place. Shirleen ain't been able to make it in this week. I think she might be havin' that baby at any moment."

"My goodness! Is it time already?" Hope asked, excitement bubbling up inside of her for the woman she'd met the first time she stopped by Doc's office. "Are you sure you shouldn't head on over there right now?"

"She hasn't sent anyone to fetch me yet, so I think it's okay. I just have a feelin' based on the last examination I did. It can't be long."

"All right then," Hope said, hopping up into the wagon like it was her own. She had considered getting herself a little pony and trap but wasn't sure if the Howards would let her keep it in the small carriage house. "Actually, I have a favor to ask," Hope said, clearing her throat. "I was thinking I should head uptown and speak to Mr. Stamine about those slates. It's been a few weeks since I checked with him, and he seems to be givin' me the run around."

"I cannot imagine Joe Stamine givin' anyone the run around," Doc said, but the twinkle in his eye told her he was pulling her leg. "Yes'm, Miss Tucker. Let's head thataway," Doc said with a nod, and he pulled the horse around.

It was a hot afternoon, and Hope had it on good authority it would only be getting hotter. They weren't deep in the heart of Texas; it wasn't all that far to Oklahoma from here. But the longtime residents said she could expect scorching heat from May until September and then lots of rain and a mild winter. She was looking forward to less snow and sleet, but the idea of living through months of temperatures even higher than the suffocating she was experiencing in May did not sound inviting.

There weren't too many other folks on the square when they arrived, but Hope did see one familiar face. As soon as the wagon passed Doc's office, Lluvia came running out, flagging him down. "Sal Masters fell and broke her hip!" she shouted. "She's in the back room! Her husband just went lookin' for you!"

Doc was clearly alarmed. "I'll be right there!" he called.

"I'll take the reins," Hope assured him, knowing where he parked, and he nodded his thanks before jumping down out of the wagon and running to his waiting assistant. She changed course, headed to his preferred spot, and hitched the horse and wagon securely before proceeding to his office herself. She doubted there was anything she could do to help, but a broken hip sounded serious.

When she opened the door, she could hear the older woman crying in the back room, and Doc was telling Lluvia what medicine to give her to calm her down. A younger woman stood in the hall, wringing her hands, and Hope imagined this must be her daughter. She didn't seem to notice Hope standing there, and she didn't say anything because she suddenly felt like an intruder. A moment later, she heard Nicholas say, "There you go, Sal. Take some deep breaths, and that'll help with the pain." She didn't know for sure what he'd given her but imagined it might've been morphine or heroin.

Deciding there wasn't much she could do, Hope backed out the door. It might've been stifling hot, but at least no one was screaming here. She looked across the square toward the general store and decided she'd go ahead and pay Mr. Stamine a visit. Never would she have imagined it would've been so difficult to get two dozen slates for her students, but every time she went in there, he gave her some other excuse as to why they had yet to be delivered. At this rate, it would be next fall before they arrived—if she was lucky.

There was only one other customer inside when Hope pushed through the door. The scent of assorted candy wafted through the air, and she imagined all the chocolate would soon be in a pool on the floor. Her students were lucky to have so many choices. Between here, the pharmacy, and the grocer, there had to be two dozen different kinds of sweets available. There were all kinds of interesting wares in the five-and-dime, and Hope could've gotten distracted by anything related at all to school, so she kept her eyes focused and headed straight to the counter.

Mr. Stamine was speaking to a woman Hope recognized from church, though she couldn't recall her name. The conversation had to do with their grown children, and Hope realized at least two minutes into the conversation that Mr. Stamine was avoiding her. She heard the door open and close a few times behind her, only turning her head when she heard a child's voice, but the little boy was too young to be her student. He held his mother's hand and didn't stray to the toy trucks he was pointing at. Hope turned back around and cleared her voice.

"Well, I best be headed home," the woman finally said, giving Hope a smile, even though the teacher had a feeling the look of annoyance in her eyes was a more fitting reaction to her butting in.

"All right, Mrs. Harris. Have a good evening!" Mr. Stamine called, looking past Hope at his other customers, looking for an escape.

She wouldn't give it to him. "Good afternoon, Mr. Stamine. Any word?"

"Ah, Miss Tucker! How are you today? I bet your students kept you busy. You must be tired."

"I am, Mr. Stamine, thank you. I am headed home right now. I just wanted to know if you'd heard anything about the slates. I need them, you know."

"I know, Miss Tucker. I remember you saying so. Often. I'm sorry, I don't have any update for you."

Hope was frustrated, not only at their lack of progress but the fact that he was clearly putting her off. "But Mr. Stamine, surely you can send a telegram and inquire about their location. It's been months."

"This is Texas, Miss Tucker. It takes forever for anything to get here."

"Then how come the primers Mr. Canton requested arrived within a month? You don't seem to have any trouble receiving any of your other items."

"Miss Tucker, calm down," Mr. Stamine said, raising his hands up in front of him. He took a deep breath, and Hope noticed a shift in his expression as he glanced over her shoulder. She was fuming now, not appreciating being told to calm down and didn't glance behind her. "They'll get here when they get here."

She pressed her lips together, folding her arms around the books she carried, her lunch pail still in her hand. "Did you even order them?" she asked.

"Yes, of course," he said too quickly. "I ordered them just like Mr. Stewart asked me to."

"Did he ask you to?"

"Why in the world would you think otherwise?" Mr. Stamine stammered. There was something about the look in his beady eyes that made her think he wasn't being honest.

"Fine, Mr. Stamine. I hope you're truly doing everything you can to get me those slates because there are lots of students waiting for them. I cannot teach to the best of my ability without them. We are talking about the future of our community, you know?"

"Yes, yes, Miss Tucker, I understand," Mr. Stamine replied, waving her away. "I'll check on them again for you."

Hope glared at him, deciding he must be finished, and she didn't know what else to say. She turned around in a huff and almost collided with Judah, not even realizing he'd been standing behind her. No wonder Mr. Stamine's eyes kept twitching. She looked up at him, surprised, but still angry at Mr. Stamine and the town he represented. "Pardon me, Mr. Lawless," she said, glancing back over her shoulder and daring Mr. Stamine to say anything about her addressing the town outlaw.

"Are you all right, Miss Tucker?" Judah asked, his eyes also flickering between her face and the store keep.

"I'm fine, thank you. Just frustrated. Have a nice evening." She stepped around him and proceeded outside. Since she no longer had a ride home, she headed out on foot toward the Howards' place, thinking the walk might be good for her anyway. It wouldn't hurt for her to walk off some of the aggression she was feeling after her discussion with Mr. Stamine.

She hadn't even made it past the next shop door when she heard Judah shouting her name. Part of her wanted to ignore him and keep walking, knowing it wouldn't be good for either of them to be seen speaking to each other on the square. But he'd stayed away from her for over two months, so she figured there must be some reason he was hollering for her now. She stopped and slowly turned to face him, just as he caught up to her.

"Tell me about the slates," he said, his head cocked to the side. "You're teaching without any?"

"Yes," she replied, sighing with frustration. "Mr. Stewart was supposed to order them when I first arrived, but something tells me this is all just a ruse to appease me. I didn't have any books either. Still don't have enough. Mr. Canton has been a godsend in getting me what he can. The children need slates." She pushed back a loose curl that threatened to catch in her mouth and placed her hands on her hips the best she could with her belongings still in her grasp. "No one seems to care what the children need."

His face was blank for a moment, and Hope felt a little foolish for going on about something no one else could possibly understand without ever having taught school. Slowly, Judah nodded his head, and she felt a little less like a crazy woman having a conniption fit in the middle of the walkway. "What else do you need?"

A laugh escaped her lips, and she threw her hand up to cover it, almost slamming herself in the mouth with her lunch pail. Once she'd recovered, she said, "I need a lot of things, Mr. Lawless. The children need a lot of things. A swing would be wonderful. A slide. Maybe something to climb on. They need a break from their learning so that their minds can be free. New information from out east shows playgrounds aid learning. Now, all they can do is run around the yard and chase each other." She folded her arms, frustration turning into sadness. It wasn't fair that her students didn't have a proper playground.

Once again, he nodded. "What else? What do you need, Hope?"

"What do I need?" Her eyes flickered lower than they should have, to the top button of his shirt which wasn't fastened and exposed just the hint of flesh below his neck. Thoughts of that day in March when she'd wandered behind the Coy house to see his sculpted, bare chest made a flush come to her cheeks, and she reminded herself he was asking about the school—not about her personally.

"Yes, Hope. What else do you need at the school? What do you need in order to do your job? For that matter, what do you need to make yourself comfortable here?"

If he noticed her response, he didn't let on. Did he really want to know what she needed? Could she even say? "I need... I just need the items for the students, that's all. Thank you for asking." Hope spun around and headed back down the sidewalk, thinking there was no reason to say anything more. It wasn't as if Judah could make the items materialize anyway. Why had he bothered to ask? Why had she given him an answer?

She didn't expect to feel his hand gripping the crook of her elbow and gently turning her back to face him. Her eyes flashed around them to see who might be watching, and there were a few pairs of eyes following with interest, no one she recognized, but it didn't matter. "Hope, there's something else you're not telling me. What is it?"

"No, there's not," she replied, glad he let go of her so she didn't have to rudely yank her arm away. The feel of him wasn't offensive in the least, which told her it was all for the better he'd released her. "I don't need anything else, Judah. Thank you."

He cocked his head to the side and studied her, and Hope noted she'd seen George do the same thing every day in class. "You were supposed to have a house, weren't you?"

Her mouth fell open as she pondered who would've told him that. "It was mentioned...."

Judah nodded. "Anything else?"

Exasperated, Hope giggled. "Yes, I would like an express train that can get me to and from my folks' house in a few hours' time—at worst. Or a winged chariot. The entire library at Alexandria would be nice. And while you're at it, one of those fancy Parisian hats with the long feather. In blue. It's my favorite color." She narrowed her eyes wondering what in the world had gotten into her. He brought out a side of her she'd never encountered before, but in a way, she liked it. It was sort of fun to let her hair down.

A crooked grin spread across his handsome face as he contemplated her wish list. "What, no flyin' elephants?"

"If you can manage. I'll take one in pink." Hope turned on her heel, thinking he likely wouldn't follow her after that, but she'd only gone a few steps before she turned back around. Having reflected on her own words, she said, "Thank you for asking, Mr. Lawless. It was nice to be heard." She spun back around and headed toward the Howards', wishing he'd offer to give her a ride but knowing he wouldn't because she'd have to decline, which would lead to wishing she'd accepted his offer later when she was in her too-small bed reminding herself that Judah Lawless was hazardous in more ways than she could name.

CHAPTER EIGHTEEN

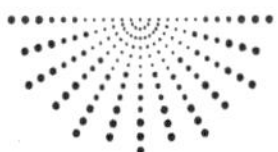

The following Monday morning, a full three days from her encounter with Mr. Stamine and her discussion with Mr. Lawless, Hope walked into the schoolyard to see a fully erected swing set, a slide, and an elaborate climbing gym the likes of which she'd only ever seen in photographs. She could hardly believe her eyes. She was still marveling at it when Mr. Stewart stepped around the climbing apparatus, a scowl on his face. "Miss Tucker!" he barked, and she wiped the smile off her face.

"Mr. Stewart, good morning."

"What is the meaning of this?" he asked, gawking at the new playground equipment. "Did you order this?"

"No. I mean... not exactly. I may have mentioned to a parent or two that I thought the children needed more play equipment. It's important to their learning, Mr. Stewart. Without proper play, they cannot pay as much attention to their lessons."

"Miss Tucker, children come here to learn, not to cavort outside and have fun...."

"While I wholeheartedly agree, sir, that learning should be our number one priority, I believe you will see an increase in the children's assessment scores if you allow it to stay. Give me until the end of the school year to show you, and if you're not convinced by their end of year exams, then you can have it hauled away."

Mr. Stewart folded his arms across his stout chest and took in the petite woman in front of him for a moment. "Very well, Miss Tucker. You have three weeks. I've seen the children's scores recently, you know? While they were better than I expected considering where they started out, the last thing I want is for parents to think their children cannot learn at our public school." He started to walk away but stopped and came back. "And if one parent complains that their child is spending too much time playing...."

"I understand, sir," she said with a nod, hardly able to contain her excitement. She watched him exit the schoolyard before she let her smile loose again. The children would be so excited. It's too bad she couldn't give them an extra few minutes during school to play—but she wouldn't stop them once the day was over. She ran her hand along the frame of the swing set, wondering how in the world this had all been put together so quickly. There were chains on the three swings and the seats looked to be leather. It was all finely crafted despite the fact that she'd just dreamt it up three days ago.

But then, she imagined the same people who had put this together had also managed to put an entire barn together in a third of the time.

How in the world could she possibly thank Judah for doing all of this? The simple answer was she couldn't. He had taken her rant and made it a reality far beyond what she had even imagined. Of course, she reminded herself, he had done it for the children, his niece and nephew included, and not for her. But still, she couldn't help but think that the person who went to all of this trouble for someone he hardly knew must've been the kind of husband a woman dreams about, not a nightmare in the least.

It was hard to walk away from the lovely playground equipment, but she had a bit of work to do inside before her students arrived, so she pushed through the schoolhouse door. Her eyes fell on two stacks of slates situated neatly on her desk, along with a sizable box marked "chalk," and another large white object that appeared to be a hat box with a folded piece of paper on top. Once again, she couldn't believe her eyes. She picked up one of the slates and examined it. She could tell they were handmade, but they were of a high quality, and there was no doubt her children would be able to utilize them. The classroom already had enough chalk to last her for the rest of the school year, but he wouldn't have known that, and the fact that he'd somehow managed to get that for her, too, only proved his thoughtfulness.

Setting the slate aside, she opened the white box and found a fancy hat, the sort one would wear around the streets of Paris. It was mostly blue and green, with a bit of purple, like a peacock, with one long blue feather out the top. Hope covered her mouth with her free hand as a giggle escaped her lips. She tried it on and wished she had a mirror so she could see herself. It only took her a moment to remember the fancy shop on the square she'd visited when she first arrived and she assumed it must've come from there. She tucked it back into the box, hoping it hadn't cost too much because she couldn't imagine where she'd ever wear it. She was delighted, though. Putting the lid back on the box, she was reminded that she should be careful what she wished for. With a sigh, she picked up the note and read:

Dear Miss Tucker,

I'm sorry to report I could not find enough iron to build a railroad track for your special train but am working on it. Likewise, the Egyptians did not wish to part with their library. Give me some time on the other items. Hope these help. Great teachers deserve the tools they need in order to teach.

JL

She read the note over twice before holding it to her chest for a moment and thinking of him sitting at a desk or a table, probably one he carved himself out of twigs and tree branches, writing these words just for her. Hope slipped the note into her pocket, suddenly realizing she was in much deeper water than she'd ever imagined, and while she knew how to swim, she felt there was an undertow, dragging her down to depths previously unfathomable.

The children absolutely loved the playground, and Hope promised them they could have an extra few minutes to play after lunch if they did well on their assignments that morning. After school, those who walked home went back outside to play for quite some time before they scurried to their houses, liable to be in trouble for being late. Hope was packing up her items to take home, including the hat she'd have to smuggle upstairs when Nicholas's wagon pulled in and her plan to be sneaky went out the window.

His mouth was wide as he looked around. Hope decided she may as well go on out and meet him, so she took her regular items and the large hat box and headed for the door. "Good afternoon, Doc."

"Well, I'll be, Miss Tucker. How'd this happen overnight?"

"I'm not quite sure," Hope admitted, "but I have a feeling most of it was constructed off-site."

"It sure is a marvel. I bet the kids like it. I've heard of a few places like this back East, but I ain't never heard of anyone buildin' something for youngsters in a place like this"

"They do like it." Hope realized she was ahead of her time—that most teachers didn't realize how important play was for the children, but her school in Lamar had had a rope swing and a four-square box painted on the walkway, and the children loved it. That was nothing compared to this, she realized, but she thought it would make an impact on their ability to learn. Hope gave Nicholas a half-smile, waiting for the next question, assuming she'd have to figure out a way to answer truthfully without having a lot of explaining to do.

"Who do you think is responsible?"

There it was. "I'm not exactly sure. I've been saying that the children needed more play equipment since I arrived. I guess one of the parents finally took it to heart." She pressed her lips together and hoped that would be enough.

Nicholas looked around at the play equipment one more time before he asked, "Whatcha got there?"

Trying to pretend as if she didn't know what he was referring to, Hope looked at the objects in her hands before saying, "Oh, one of the students brought me a gift."

"Which one?"

"One of the girls. It was a nice gesture. Now, if you're ready, Mr. Howard, I would appreciate a lift to your folks' house, assuming that's why you've come." She kept her smile pleasant, praying he'd let it go, but he still looked suspicious.

Nicholas nodded and she followed him to the wagon. She set the hatbox inside in order to climb up, and Nicholas helped her by lifting her at the waist, though she really didn't need it. When he went around and climbed up in the seat, he was still eyeing the box. "What's it look like?"

Hope let out a long breath. "It's sort of fancy," she replied, waving her hand. "I can't even imagine where I'd wear it."

"A fancy hat? From one of our children? Where would they have gotten the money for that?"

"I honestly don't know. Maybe it belonged to her mother."

Doc didn't seem to buy that either, but he turned the horses around and headed toward the road without further comment, and Hope prayed that the uncomfortable situation was over.

But it wasn't. About halfway to his parents' house, Nicholas cleared his throat. "Did you know there's a school board election coming up this fall? Mr. Stewart is up for re-election, and I've heard that Mr. Canton is considering running against him. I considered throwing my own name in the hat." He looked down at the box. "But I wasn't sure what you'd think about that."

Hope was confused at first. While it seemed like a wonderful idea to have someone like Mr. Canton who genuinely seemed to care about the students as the school board president, she had no idea why Nicholas might think she'd have an opinion as to whether or not he decided to run. "What do you mean?"

"I mean... if I were to run, of course, I'd want to help you in any way I could, but mostly, I'd just want to make sure there were some changes to your contract." His face was turning a bright red, and Hope had a feeling it had nothing to do with the May afternoon sun.

"What sort of changes?" she asked, a lump forming in her throat. She wasn't sure she wanted to hear the answer.

Nicholas took a deep breath. "I just think... maybe you should be allowed to court, that's all. There are plenty of bachelors in town who would agree with me. I could run on that platform alone and be sure to win the election." He chuckled nervously, and suddenly, Hope understood what he was getting at. She had to avert her eyes.

Over the last couple of months, she'd spent a lot of time getting to know the doctor and was very fond of him. He was intelligent and kind, and he wasn't at all unpleasant to look at. But now that she'd had a feeling of what true sparks felt like, now that she'd had a bit more experience with longing and sleepless nights, she was sure that Nicholas Howard was not the man she'd want to be with, even if someone did come along and change her contract. And since the only man she'd even considered had been pretty clear on the fact that he wasn't taking another wife, the contract was actually her saving grace at the moment. The way Nicholas described it, the second the document was amended, she'd have gentlemen callers lined up from here to the Mexican border.

Undeterred by her expression, he continued. "Anyhow, Miss Tucker, I just think... well, I mean... you're a beautiful, intelligent gal, and it'd be a shame if you weren't allowed to court anybody just on the account of your teaching contract. My understanding is that a lot of school districts are doing away with them sorta rules."

Hope cleared her throat, glad he had yet to make it too personal. He hadn't declared his love for her or said he was hoping to court her himself, not yet anyhow. "While I do think any steps toward giving women more rights are positive, Doc, I'm not sure how I feel about amending my contract. Being so new to the area, I haven't had the opportunity to meet many men, except for my students' fathers, and I'm sort of happy for it since it has allowed me to focus on my students." She hoped he'd understand what she was getting at without her having to say more.

Nicholas looked a little hurt. "But you've gotten to know me."

"Yes, and I'm very happy to have you as such a good friend." She turned to look at him then, praying that she hadn't hurt his feelings, but she saw his expression shift and realized he was intelligent enough to put the pieces of the puzzle together.

"I see," Doc said, turning the horse so that the wagon was headed up his parents' street. He didn't say anything else, and Hope felt awful. He'd done so much to help her, and he really was a wonderful person. It was just too bad the tingles she'd initially felt when she'd been around him had been snuffed out, replaced by something so powerfully strong she couldn't even contain it, let alone pretend to understand it.

When he pulled the wagon to a stop, Hope quickly thanked him and then jumped down before he even had a chance to come around to help. She pulled her belongings along with her and rushed up the front steps.

"What in the world is that?" Nita inquired as she opened the front door, a large smile on her face.

Hope didn't tarry. "Just a gift from a student." She brushed past and headed right up the stairs, leaving Nita to inquire of her son what had taken place. Nicholas could tell her whatever he liked, but Hope needed to be out of their presence for a while. She hoped Doc wouldn't stay for dinner. Something told her this was the last time he'd give her a ride home.

In her room, she set the hatbox on a shelf in the tiny closet and then took a seat on the edge of the bed. She could hear Doc and Nita were talking, though she had no idea what they were saying. Neither of them sounded particularly happy. Hope ran her hands up her face and then smoothed her hair back. It was days like this when she wished her mother was close by.

After the barn raising, Hope had been tempted to write her mother a letter and tell her everything about Judah—including spying him at the pump and how she'd actually kissed him before she ran away at the dance. It all sounded so ridiculous, though, and Hope couldn't believe she'd done either of those things, let alone putting it down on paper where anyone might discover it. She couldn't believe Judah had even spoken to her again after that last one, but he'd gone to so much trouble to get her everything she needed for the school, and he said he wasn't done yet, though she couldn't imagine he could do anything further. It wasn't as if he could actually build the railroad she'd pined for. He wouldn't be able to start construction on her little cabin either. There was no way Mr. Stewart would allow him to do that, and if he tried to build it without permission, it would be taken down. So... she was certain his gifts were done with now. But they had been enough—more than enough.

Hope could only assume he'd gone to so much trouble because of his niece and nephew. He'd mentioned only staying around these parts because of them, so it would make sense that he'd want them to have playground equipment if that's what their teacher said they needed, and of course he'd realize how important the slates were. She could dismiss most of his gifts that way—but not the hat. Why in the world had he gotten her the ridiculous Parisian hat she'd joked about?

She hadn't even tried it on now that she'd be able to see herself in a mirror. She'd been in such a hurry to hide it the thought hadn't occurred to her. But now that the voices downstairs had faded some, she went over and pulled the box back down and brought it over to her dresser. Carefully, she removed the hat, laughing quietly about how beautiful and completely ridiculous it was. She put it on and had a look at herself in the mirror. For a moment, she pretended she was a fancy French woman without a care in the world. It would be lovely to think of herself living in Paris, her husband a famous architect. They'd have several children, and she'd have a nanny to help and to clean up after them while she read them books and taught them how to sing. It would be a lovely, carefree life, and her husband would be so fond of her, he'd bring her a new hat with a different colored feather every Friday afternoon, along with a dozen long stemmed roses.

"You have lost your mind," Hope muttered, taking the hat off and putting it back in the box. She thought of poor Celia waiting for her man to arrive back from the Mexican war and wondered if she might end up like that, walking around town muttering about how someday her outlaw betrothed would claim her hand. Shaking her head, she put the hatbox back in the closet and quietly shut the door, listening for any noise from Mrs. Howard's room. She heard nothing and thought perhaps she'd managed to move around her room without disturbing the other woman, though there had been instances in the past when the woman would seem to be asleep only to shout at her in an angry voice out of nowhere.

Hope sat back down on the bed, not sure what to do next. She should probably return the hat. Why in the world...? But then, she couldn't do that without speaking to Judah, and she would have to borrow a horse or cart just to travel all the way out to his house. Ginny and George hadn't seemed to know anything about the gifts being from their uncle, so it wasn't as if she could tell Ginny she wished to speak to him. And Caroline may or may not know. No, she should keep it. She wanted to keep it. If she had nothing else from him, at least she could always save that hat and remember the misunderstood soul who was so charming she'd lost herself completely in his eyes one night beneath a silvery moon.

But she didn't want to have a fond memory of Judah Lawless in the form of a hat. She wanted him—and every day that passed by, she knew it would always be that way. What if Nicholas did change the contract, and then she'd be free to be seen in public with Judah? Then, maybe if he spent enough time with her, she'd be able to convince him that whatever had happened in his past couldn't possibly happen again.

The fact that she had no idea what had happened to Sylvia and his other wife didn't seem to make any difference to her, even though logically she told herself it should. What if he really had killed them? She didn't think that was possible, but she wanted to hear the story from his own lips.

Thinking of his lips was dangerous. She dropped backward onto her pillow, remembering what those lips had felt like when she'd pressed hers to them. How many times had she dreamt of them since that night, over two months ago?

Hope was in a heap of trouble, and she knew it. Part of her thought it might be best to leave and go back to Missouri before she dug herself in too deep. But she realized it was already too late for that. And Judah's gifts just made it worse. Something told her the situation was bound to get far more troublesome before it got better, if it ever did, and she had no idea how she could possibly get through it without a single friend or family member to lend a shoulder to cry on. And now she'd lost one of the few friends she'd made in Nicholas.

Closing her eyes, Hope thought about what her mama would do in this situation, and she realized she could never do what her mother would do. Cordia would've demanded the truth from Judah and then made him see he had nothing to worry about, that they'd be happy together. Hope had a lot of her mother in her, but not enough for any of that. She took a deep breath and decided the only action she could take was to continue doing what she had been doing—nothing. As long as she could keep avoiding him, she couldn't dig herself in any deeper, and while it hadn't been easy, it had to be better than trying to force something that could never be.

She'd decided on that course of action and started to drift off to sleep when it occurred to her that if this could never be, then why in the world did she have a Parisian hat in her closet?

CHAPTER NINETEEN

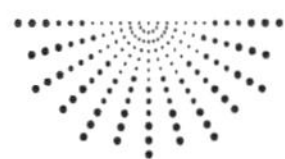

Saying goodbye to her students for the summer was difficult, but by the middle of June, Hope had gotten into a new routine and was keeping herself busy volunteering at the library and working with some of the other ladies from church on charitable programs. She also spent a good deal of time doing campaign work for Mr. Canton, who had decided to run for school board president, not on the same platform as Nicholas would've, but on the premise that students needed more books and other supplies than what Mr. Stewart was willing to provide. Mr. Stewart argued that the budget was tight, and he'd had to be selective while Mr. Canton argued that any community that could build such a grand courthouse had enough funds to provide books for their students. While the election itself was a long way off, Hope thought Mr. Canton had a good chance at winning.

Some days, she'd go down to the playground and watch her students play. Of course, it was only those who lived nearby who had the opportunity, and then any child who was expected to be helping out in the fields or around the house during the summer couldn't stay for long if they came at all. She saw some of them at the library as well. Caroline brought George and Ginny in at least once a week, and Hope was always happy to see them. She didn't see Judah, though, not once, not since she'd run into him at the five-and-dime, regardless of how often she stuck her head out of the library door during her shifts.

She'd considered taking a trip back to Missouri for a week or two. It likely would've done her good to see her family. Then, she'd have a chance to tell her mama and daddy everything that had transpired. But Hope was afraid if she headed home, she'd never come back, so instead, she planned to go back to Lamar during the two week break she'd have over Christmas. It was the best way for her to focus on what was happening in Texas, particularly since Lola had written to let her know that she was with child and there'd be no one to teach the children that fall unless the school board found a replacement for her. The idea of going back to her old school was too tempting for Hope to put herself in a situation where Mr. Cartwright, the superintendent, had a chance to try to talk her into staying.

Now that she knew her students, she could spend more time planning lessons for them. She didn't have much space in the cramped bedroom at the Howard's house, so Mr. Canton had allowed her to use one of his offices, and she spent time in there even when he was out in the library himself. It was good for her to have a place to think about her lessons so close to the books she could borrow to help drive her points across.

One afternoon in late July, she wandered out of her space to pull a book off of the shelf and overheard Mr. Canton speaking quietly to Mr. Jones, Celia's father. She didn't know the man well, only that he owned the grocery, and every time she saw him, he'd smile at her. When she bumped into Celia, Hope was always kind and even sat with her at church sometimes, so she assumed he was appreciative of her efforts.

When they noticed her, they shifted slightly, and Hope got the impression whatever they were discussing had something to do with her. She grabbed the book she'd wanted and headed back into the room, leaving the door slightly ajar so that she might be able to accidentally overhear the discussion.

Her sleuthiness worked. "I'll speak to Stewart," Mr. Jones was saying. "He's got to realize he's fighting an uphill battle at this point. If he won't take advantage of this generous offer, he'll be shooting himself in the foot."

"I'd appreciate it if you'd reach out to him. He's certainly more likely to find the offer favorable if you're the one who presents it. I am willing to let Mr. Stewart take full credit so long as it gets done."

Mr. Jones sighed loud enough for Hope to hear him and said, "I'll keep you posted."

She had no idea what in the world they might be talking about, but the fact that it involved a generous offer to Mr. Stewart made her wonder if Mr. Canton wasn't considering dropping out of the race. She hoped not. So many people had been working very hard to get him elected. She got the impression that's not what the conversation was about, but she could hardly ask, so she didn't. Instead, she tried to put it out of her mind and concentrate on building a lesson on the Revolutionary War that would be both engaging and memorable.

It wasn't for several more weeks that Hope finally got an idea of what it might be that the two gentlemen were discussing. School was set to start in just two weeks, and she'd gone to the playground to see if any of her students were there when she noticed the beginnings of a structure behind the school. She'd stared in wonder for a few moments, not sure exactly what she was looking at, but then it all came together. Somehow, Mr. Canton and Mr. Jones must've arranged for her little cabin to be built while giving Mr. Stewart full credit. How or why, she didn't know, but rather than spending time on the playground, she decided to head to the bank to discuss the matter with Mr. Stewart.

She hadn't made her work on Mr. Canton's campaign public because, at the moment, Mr. Stewart still had control over her contract and could end it at any time for any reason, so she'd tried to appear neutral, despite all the hours she'd spent making posters and helping Mr. Canton write speeches to present at local churches and events. Hope had an idea that Mr. Stewart was suspicious, however, so she tried to avoid him whenever possible. She was headed up the bank steps when she saw the father of one of her students coming down.

Deputy Neil Forester worked for Sheriff Roan—at his day job, not in the saloon—and he always had a polite word for Hope. His daughter, Jessica, would be starting the third grade in a few weeks. "Howdy do, Miss Tucker?" the deputy asked. "Sure is a hot one today, ain't it?"

"Deputy, it's nice to see you," she said with a friendly smile. "It surely is. But then, most every day's been a hot one since I arrived in Texas."

"Well, we could hardly tell you it was this hot or else you might notta come," he joked, good naturedly patting her arm. "Jess sure is excited about school a'startin'."

"Her and me both," Hope replied. "I saw her on the playground the other day. She's gotten tall this summer."

"Taller and smarter. She's been readin' every book she can get her hands on, thanks to you, Miss Tucker."

"Oh, Jessica is a natural born scholar," Hope replied, praising one of her best little students. "She's going to go far."

"Bless you, Miss Tucker," Deputy Forester replied with a genuine smile. "You sure are a gift to us! You take care now."

"Thank you, Deputy Forester," Hope said, turning to wave goodbye to him. "Be safe." She hurried on up the last few steps, a smile on her face. It was always nice to run into parents who were excited about what their students were learning.

Inside, she saw Mr. Garner's friendly face behind the counter and waited for him to finish up with Mrs. Stamine who said hello but wasn't nearly as friendly as she'd once been, before Hope's run in over the slates that had never come. She stepped up to the window next and greeted Mr. Garner and then asked if Mr. Stewart had a quick moment.

"I'll go see," he said with a smile before disappearing. When he came back, Mr. Stewart was on his heels.

"Miss Tucker, nice to see you." She wasn't sure if he meant it or not. "I've been meaning to have a word with you."

A lump rose in Hope's throat as she wondered what it might be he wanted to discuss. Had she done something wrong? "It's nice to see you as well, Mr. Stewart. I just wanted to stop by to ask you about the construction I noticed behind the schoolhouse."

"Yes, that's precisely what I've meant to speak to you about. Has Mrs. Howard mentioned it at all?"

"No, she hasn't," Hope replied, thinking it was odd that Nita hadn't said anything if she knew about it, but then, maybe she had been waiting for Mr. Stewart. "What is it exactly?"

"Why, it's your house," he said with his arms spread open, showing just how generous he was. "I've arranged for it to be built. Hopefully, it will be done by the time fall weather arrives, and you can move in so that you won't have to walk so far in inclement conditions."

Hope wasn't sure what to say, especially since she was under the impression that Mr. Stewart hadn't actually arranged for any of it. The idea that he would do so right after she'd heard Mr. Canton and Mr. Jones discussing giving him credit for something seemed like too big of a coincidence. But she could hardly say that. "Why, thank you, Mr. Stewart. I do appreciate it."

"Of course. It's just a small token of my appreciation for all you've done for the children of McKinney. We are lucky to have such a talented schoolteacher. All of the parents seem so happy with what you've accomplished, despite the playground."

She kept her smile glued to her face, ignoring his backhanded compliment. "I am looking forward to school resuming in a few weeks' time, and I'm certain we'll get even more accomplished now that we have an entire school year to spend together."

"Indeed," Mr. Stewart said, his smile widening, and Hope realized that he'd thought she meant him and her—not her and the students.

Deciding it didn't matter, she turned to go. "Thank you again, Mr. Stewart."

"Have a good evening, Miss Tucker." He waved and disappeared, and Hope waved goodbye to Mr. Garner wondering if this would affect the election at all. She decided she'd have to trust Mr. Canton to know what he was doing and headed back to the Howard house, curious to see what Nita might say when Hope told her she knew about the cabin.

When she came to within a block of the house, she realized that Nicholas's wagon was out front and her stomach lurched into her throat. It had been difficult for the pair of them to avoid each other these past few months since he'd told her how he felt, and when they were in the same room, everything was awkward. Hope missed his friendship, the discussions they used to have. He was one of the few intellects she'd encountered since her arrival, so there weren't any other options for discussing serious matters. It wasn't as if she could talk about the French invasion of Russia with Brady.

Doc was seated across from his mother in the parlor when she opened the front door and immediately got up, as if he had to leave the room because Hope was there. "I'm sorry—I didn't mean to intrude," she said, finding a smile. "Please, Doc, don't go on my account. I just wanted to ask Mrs. Howard a quick question, and then I'll head upstairs out of your way."

Before Nicholas could answer, Nita said, "We were actually just talking about somethin' that involves you, Hope. Your cabin is goin' up next to the school. Did you know that?"

"I did," Hope admitted. "I just walked past there and went to speak to Mr. Stewart." She left out the part about him wanting to know if Nita had already told her. "He said he hopes it's finished before the fall weather comes in."

"It likely will be," Nita said. There was something about her tone that made Hope think there was more to the story than what she was saying. "You do know that Stewart is takin' credit for somethin' he ain't done, right? I mean, I hope you didn't thank him too heartily."

Hope looked from Nita to Doc, who was nodding, and she realized they knew more than she did. "I got the impression he may have been withholding information from me." She didn't know how to mention what she'd overheard, so she kept it to herself.

"We were just sayin' we think this whole thing is a little suspicious, Hope, and you need to be careful." Doc looked more concerned than Hope could've ever imagined was necessary, and she felt her stomach tighten with worry.

"What do you mean?"

"Well, we don't know anythin' for sure," Nita said, seeming to try to calm her son. "But... Mr. Canton and Mr. Jones said they come into a donation to get the house built and they'd be willin' to let Mr. Stewart take the credit so long as the school board approved the structure," Nita explained.

"All right...." Hope wasn't sure where this was going.

"Bein' as I'm the secretary, I got a look at the plans. They's complicated, Hope. It ain't yer run of the mill little cabin doodled on a sheet a'paper fer just anyone to build. This here sketch come from a real architect."

Hope suddenly realized where the conversation was going. "And why is that a problem?" she asked, already knowing the answer.

"So long as Mr. Canton and Mr. Stewart stand as intermediaries, I don't suppose it is. And we don't know where the money come from fer sure. But...."

"You need to be careful, Hope," Nicholas said again, stepping forward, the look in his eyes saying even more than his words. "If he's got his sights set on you...."

"Nicholas, don't scare her," Nita reprimanded.

"Well, Mama, you know what Brady said, about that barn raisin'."

Hope's neck was starting to ache a little from swiveling back and forth. "What are you talking about?" she asked, not that she didn't already have an idea.

Nita sighed loudly. "We think maybe this money come from Judah Lawless. Maybe he's tryin' to get his hooks in ya, make you think he's a good feller because he's designed yer house. Maybe he'll even have a hand in the buildin'. He ain't what he appears, Hope. We know Brady's warned you. I've warned ya myself."

"We just want you to be careful, Hope. Brady said he saw the two of you speaking to each other at the barn raisin', and he didn't like—what it looked like."

Hope scoffed, unable to believe her ears. "What it looked like was someone helping me carry two heavy buckets of water to the men working on the barn—and that's all. If Brady imagines he saw something else, then he is sorely mistaken. I can't even think of the last time I spoke to Judah Lawless!" That last part was certainly a lie, and maybe all of it was. She knew exactly when she'd last spoken to Judah. But then, there really hadn't been anything between them in the conversation Doc had mentioned. Implying that there had been would mean Judah might have feelings for her, and he'd made his position clear that night in the woods. Hopefully, no one knew about that conversation. That one would be more difficult to dismiss.

"All we's sayin' is to be careful," Nita said dismissively. "Could be

Mr. Lawless has put Mr. Canton up to runnin' for school board so he can change your contract. Maybe he's got eyes fer ya."

"Or maybe he is just looking out for the best interest of his niece and nephew."

"Like he was with the playground equipment?" Doc asked, rubbing the toe of his boot into the floor.

Hope stared at him for a moment, her forehead crinkling. How did he know that? She wasn't sure if she should deny knowing where the playground equipment had come from or just let it be. Seeing the look on his face, she decided it was useless to argue anymore about something that didn't matter. Whether or not she was interested in Judah made no difference since she knew full well he didn't care about her like that. "I appreciate the warning," Hope said, taking a deep breath, "and I'll bear it in mind."

"Don't trust him, Hope," Nicholas said, not for the first time.

Hope nodded, managed a smile, and said, "If y'all will excuse me, I'm tired from bein' outside in the hot sun." She headed for the stairs, thinking it really didn't matter how much trust she put in Mr. Lawless. He'd made his position clear, and chasing after him wasn't going to do either one of them any good. The Howards were wasting their time being afraid of a romance that would never even have the chance to bloom.

Her comment about being tired was an understatement. Hope sank down on her bed, wishing there were some sort of breeze in her room, but even with the window open, the white curtains hardly stirred. She could've fallen asleep if it weren't so unbearably warm.

Instead she lay there, staring at the ceiling, wondering how long it might take for her house to be done. Would Judah build it himself? Would his friends from church help? Or had Mr. Stewart found someone else to do the work and just let Judah foot the bill? Surely, he hadn't paid for it all himself. She rolled over onto her side and tucked her hand beneath her cheek. He sure must love Ginny and George a lot to go to so much trouble, she thought. It was hard to imagine someone capable of that kind of love could ever be accused of the kind of hate Nicholas and Nita thought he must've felt for his previous wives. Maybe Hope didn't know him as well as she would've liked to, but there was no way in the world someone who would build a schoolteacher he had only spoken to a handful of times her own little cottage could possibly be a cold blooded killer. It was just too bad everyone else in the town was too blind to see the truth.

Hope rolled over again so she was facing the wall. There had to be some way to make the rest of the town see they were villainizing a good person. She had no idea what it might be, but if she could do anything at all to make it tolerable for Judah and his family to live in McKinney, she wanted to help. Maybe, if she looked hard enough, she'd find a way. For now, she decided it was best to keep Mr. Stewart's secret, at least until the house was built and maybe until the election was over. Mr. Canton had to have something in mind for keeping it a secret, and she wasn't about to do anything to interfere. In the meantime, she'd do anything she could to help Mr. Canton win the election not because she secretly hoped he'd change her contract but because he was the best man for the job, and Hope was tired of seeing good men lose.

CHAPTER TWENTY

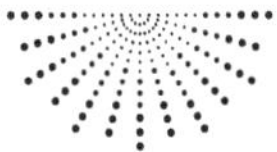

The infernal heat of summer eventually began to morph into a singe instead of a sizzle, and then the rains came, and Hope trudge through the mud and muck to get to the schoolhouse each day with her dress tucked into her boots, or if she was lucky, Mr. Howard would wake early enough to give her a ride on those days when she was likely to be swept into a sewer drain. The children lamented indoor recess, and the teacher did, too, and then around the last few weeks of September, there was another shift and the rain petered out, though it was still often warmer than the weather Hope was used to this time of year further north.

Each day, she inspected the progress on the little cabin from a distance, not wanting to get too close since it wasn't finished yet, and she had the idea in her mind that if she touched it, the building might crumple and disappear like the vision it was. Though the size itself wasn't remarkable, the way in which it was being put together, the craftmanship, as well as the materials themselves, were such high quality, it was no wonder it seemed to be taking longer than expected.

She had an idea that the slow rate of progress might actually have something to do with the school board election in the next month as well, but there was no one for her to voice her suspicions to, so she kept her mouth closed.

Not every morning revealed a change, but several times a week, she'd come in to see something had been done overnight, and the most progress could be marked of a Monday morning when she hadn't seen the structure in a few days. She felt certain by the beginning of October it was nearly complete, and she began to allow herself to think about the possibility of living there, uninhibited by her current hosts or their opinions about what she should or should not do and who she should or should not speak to.

It didn't make much difference anyway since she hadn't seen Judah in months. If he came to pick up the children, he kept a fair distance, and she'd only catch a glimpse of his hat or maybe his profile. He never seemed to turn to see if she was watching, nor did he ever make any effort to accidentally bump into her as he had those few times on the square. Hope pretended not to mind and tried not to think about him, but she was lying to herself; the burning feeling deep down within her heart told her she longed to see him again regardless of what anyone else said, particularly Judah himself.

In early October, she'd finally written a letter home asking for advice. She tried to keep her mood nonchalant, only inquiring of her parents about what they had done when they'd been away from each other for so long. Of course, she knew that predicament was quite different. Her parents wanted to be together and simply couldn't be because of the war. In her case, there was no catastrophe to get through that would eventually result in the two of them being together. Even if Hope's contract wasn't in the way, Judah still didn't want to be with her.

There was a slight chill in the air one morning when Hope finished styling her hair and headed downstairs, ready to grab her lunch and a biscuit to eat on the way to class. She wanted to get to school ahead of time to write some math problems on the board for her primary students. Their addition was starting to come along, and now that they were used to using their slates, she'd be able to get them started and then move to her older students.

Mrs. Howard was in the kitchen bustling around, preparing breakfast for her husband, and Hope didn't want to disturb her. Though they were still friendly, there'd been a strain between herself and the entire family originating with Nicholas's revelation about his feelings for her, and it was growing to be more of a chasm after Judah commissioned the cabin. Now, they would speak and be polite, but Hope wanted her freedom, and she was afraid she'd just about outstayed her welcome.

"Hope, good mornin'," Nita said with a smile. "I ran into Mr. Stewart yesterday. He says he's havin' a hard time findin' folks who'll put in the vote for him. He wanted me to ask you—would you mind speakin' to some of the parents when they come to get their children after school? Maybe even walk home with few of them and have that conversation?"

Hope stared at Nita wide-eyed, not having expected such a request. She'd been making signs and helping Mr. Canton for months, and now Mr. Stewart wanted her to support him? "Oh, I don't know if I'd be comfortable with that," she said, tossing her lunch together quickly. "I think I should try to remain as neutral as possible."

"Well, that's just the thing, darlin'. He knows you been helpin' out Mr. Canton in secret. I think everyone knows that. He's not too happy about it, and as you know, he's still your boss."

Hope froze, apple in hand and turned to look at Mrs. Howard. "What are you saying, Nita?"

"I'm sayin' I wouldn't give 'im no excuse to start lookin' for another teacher. Election day's not that far off. Who knows what he might do between now and then? He seems to think it might be a better idea to find someone who ain't so... how did he put it? Demanding. Listen, honey, I ain't tryin' to tell you what to do, but he asked me to speak to you, so I told 'im I would. And I'd just be careful, that's all. Don't be seen speakin' to no one who could get you in any trouble, you hear?"

She knew exactly what Nita was getting at then. Hope let out a sigh and thought of a compromise. "I will speak to the parents about the election," she said with as pleasant of a smile as she could force onto her face. She didn't need to elaborate any further than that.

"All righty then, darlin'. You have a good day." Nita turned back to the frying pan and Hope bid her farewell before starting for the front door. "Oh! I almost forgot!"

Turning back around, Hope saw Nita digging in her apron for something. "Ye gotta letter yesterday. I was in the post office, and Twinny handed it over to me."

"Oh. Thank you." Hope smiled and took it, wishing Nita wouldn't pick up her mail at all, or if she did, she'd put it on her dresser, as they'd discussed a few times before, but there was no reason to point that out now that—hopefully—her days in the Howard home were numbered. She took a look at it and saw the letter was from her father, and instantly Hope felt better about the entire universe. She slipped the letter into her own pocket, thinking she'd have to find time to read it later, maybe at recess.

Hope tried to put Mr. Stewart and his ridiculous request out of her mind as she made the walk to the schoolhouse. When she arrived, she slid the letter from her father into her desk drawer and went about writing the math problems on the board. Soon, the students began to arrive, chattering about how much fun they'd have at recess now that everything had dried out. By mid-day, Hope was distracted by an argument two of the older girls had had and she didn't find time to read her letter. That afternoon, she'd walked home with Sally and Hank to see if their mother knew how their father might intend to vote in the election and wasn't too surprised to hear that Mr. Canton was their favorite candidate. Hope said Mr. Stewart had been doing a fine job but understood why Mr. Canton might make a fine president and left it at that.

It wasn't until she was in her bed, the lanterns off all over the house, trying to find a wink of sleep, that she realized she'd left her father's letter in her desk drawer and hadn't even opened it. Hope let out a sigh and turned over, thinking she could just get it in the morning. But that question she'd asked, the one about how her parents managed to make it through when they had to be apart, was burning inside of her again such that she finally just decided to go get it.

The entire idea was ridiculous—almost as silly as the story she'd heard of her mother taking off to Springfield to try to find out whether or not Hope's daddy had been wounded at the Battle of Wilson's

Creek. Except, this wasn't a matter of life and death, and it wasn't going to fix anything that was wrong. But as she quietly slipped on a gown and her boots, pulled her hair back and tried to determine whether or not the moon was bright enough to light her path and if she should actually take the revolver her daddy had packed for her, Hope knew what she was really looking for, and it wasn't in the desk drawer.

Thoughts of the saloon and the rowdy bunch she could potentially encounter even though she wasn't going anywhere near the square or the red light district were convincing enough to make her slip the revolver into her pocket. She wished she had a proper holster, but it would have to do. Luckily, she knew how to use it. She'd just have to be careful not to put herself into a situation where she might have to threaten to use it.

Many months' worth of practice on the floorboards had taught her where to place her feet so that the hallway didn't announce her presence. Likewise, she was able to make it down the stairs and out the front door. Once she was standing on the front porch, she inhaled the crisp October air, surprised she'd actually made it out without getting caught or changing her mind.

This was likely a violation of her contract all by itself. Sneaking off in the night unaccompanied would probably be reason enough for Mr. Stewart to let her go, if he should find out about it. And the schoolhouse was just a few lots over from his own house. She assumed he'd be asleep this time of night since it was almost midnight, and she had decided not to take a lantern, so hopefully she wouldn't draw attention to herself. But it was Friday night, and there was a chance people might be up later than usual. She'd just have to take her time and be quiet so as not to alarm any of the folks whose houses she'd have to pass by.

The moonlight was bright, and it wasn't hard at all for her to navigate across the yard and out to the street. She'd made this walk so many times, it was second nature to her now. Her mind wandered a little as she went. The entire town seemed different washed in shades of gray. Were her students all asleep? She hoped so. Tucked in warm in their beds, happy thoughts and dreams dancing through their minds. None of them hungry or feeling unwanted or unloved, she hoped.

She thought of her family back home. Her sister was planning a spring wedding, and Hope would have to find a way to attend. She couldn't miss Faith's big day. Her mother was likely asleep now, though it wouldn't be too big of a stretch to picture her still sitting by the lantern working on her embroidery. Her daddy was in bed, no doubt, but probably not asleep. He'd be worrying about her, about the rest of the family. That's just what he did.

As Hope approached the schoolyard, she heard the soft sound of hammering back behind the schoolhouse itself and saw the faint glow of two or three lanterns. She realized then that she'd been right—even if she didn't want to admit that this is why she'd come. Hopefully, he was here, and this wasn't just a group of his friends from church put to work by an architect too busy or too cautious to do the job himself.

Hope slipped inside the school first to grab the letter so she'd at least have that out of the way should she be distracted later. The thunk of the door behind her as she went out the back entrance caused a pause in the hammering and a soft whinny from the horse still tied to the wagon on the other side of the cabin. She wondered if anyone else had ever come out this late at night to see what was going on, but then the fact that no one had demanded work stop or that Judah Lawless be banned from working on public property made her think no one who lived within earshot cared or had noticed.

He stepped between the two-by-fours that comprised the wall closest to the school. The other three sides were done, though the windows needed framing and installation, and she remembered from earlier there was some interior work to be done, like trim and all of that fancy stuff she'd never imagined having in a house of her own—not that she'd own it, but it would feel like home once she had a chance to move into it. In the dim light it was hard to see his face, but she knew it was him by his walk, and she imagined he likely knew her, too, though he was probably confused. Still, she kept walking, almost as if she were in a dream. For a moment, she pondered that notion and thought she might awake and find herself back in her too-small bed at the Howards' place.

But she wasn't there—she was standing in the schoolyard at midnight, staring into forbidden blue eyes, praying this didn't end up being the biggest mistake she'd ever made but also knowing she was too involved now to care.

"What are you doin' here, Miss Tucker?" Judah asked in a harsh whisper. "Are you sleepwalking?"

"Something like that," Hope replied, stifling a giggle. "I forgot a letter from my daddy in my desk, and I come to fetch it."

"You walked all the way down here in the middle of the night for a letter? Must be important." He adjusted his hat on his head and smiled at her like he only half believed her.

Hope pulled the letter out of her pocket. "It is. I asked him a few important questions, and I really want his opinion. It could've waited, but, I figure as long as I've got his pistol in my pocket, I'll be okay."

"I'll take that as fair warning." That easy smile she'd noticed all those months ago slid into place across his handsome face, and Hope felt the flapping of butterfly wings in her stomach.

"Have you been doin' all of this on your own?" she asked, gesturing toward the structure.

"For the most part. Some of the frame the boys from church helped me with, but yeah, most of it I've done. That's why it's so slow going. And it's hard to see this time of night. But I can't hardly come and work on it during the day."

"That's a shame," Hope muttered, but she didn't say more. "I've been watching the progress. You sure do fine work."

"Well, thank you," he said, looking down at the ground and wiping at his brow beneath his hat. "It'd be better if I could see what I was doing."

She laughed, a little louder than she meant to this time, and he put a finger over his lips to shush her. "Sorry," Hope whispered. "It's your fault. You're the one that made me laugh."

He let her comment go, and a serious expression came over his face. For a moment, Hope felt as if he was taking her in. It was almost as if he'd missed her as much as she'd missed him. "I'm sure you oughtta be gettin' back, but do you wanna see it right quick? Get the official tour?"

"Yes, I'd love that," Hope replied, no longer caring about the possibility of getting herself into trouble.

"You have to watch yer step because there's boards and tools all over the place right now." He offered his arm, and Hope took it, trying not to dwell on the feel of his muscular bicep beneath her hand. She walked along with him to the opening that would be the front door, once it was hung.

"This is the front room, obviously. I wanted you to have plenty of room for a table and lots of light." She noticed there were two windows and lots of space for a desk as well as some comfortable chairs near the fireplace. "There's still some work to be done on the chimney. I have a friend who's a mason, and I want him to come out and check everything before we call it finished."

"It looks amazing," Hope said, not sure what else to say.

"Watch your step here." There was a gap in the flooring and then a few wooden planks lying across the floor as they went into the next room. "This is the kitchen. Same thing here with the fireplace."

"So I'll have two?" she asked, surprised she'd even have one as nice as the fireplace in the living room, let alone two. She hadn't noticed that there were actually two when she'd looked at the structure from afar.

"Well, I figure you don't wanna be cookin' in your living room," he said. "The wash basin will have a pump."

"That's wonderful." The kitchen seemed to be a decent size for a single woman.

He led her back through to the hallway running parallel to the kitchen space. "And there's two bedrooms, in case you have guests. I thought your folks might come visit you. This room's a little bigger than the other."

Hope followed him inside, careful of the flooring again. "What's this doorway?" she asked, gesturing at a hole in the wall.

"Closet," he replied. "There'll be another one in the guest room."

She never expected to have closets either. "Those will come in handy, especially if my folks send down more of my belongings." The idea of having all of her books here and the rest of her clothing was appealing.

Judah took her back to the hallway and showed her the other small bedroom before he took her into a little space at the back of the house. "And this is the washroom."

"Washroom?" Hope repeated.

"Yep. There'll be a pump and a drain." He pointed at a hole in the floor with his boot. "I wish I could get you a fancy toilet, but I thought Mr. Stewart would raise an eyebrow at that since he don't even have one."

Hope was speechless. She looked around, and finally said, "You mean I'll have a room just for bathing? With its own pump?"

"Sure. I mean, you'll still have to heat it up, but it beats lugging buckets in from the well or the kitchen, don't you think?"

She noticed another, smaller fireplace near the place where he'd indicated the pump would be. "I don't even know what to say. This is more like a palace than the little cabin I had in mind."

"I like to think of it as an educator's cottage," he replied with a smile. She could tell he appreciated the compliments.

"Well, I really don't know how to thank you," Hope began, turning around and taking it all in again without letting go of his arm.

"You don't need to thank me, Hope. If I can get it done before the end of October, you'll be able to move in before it gets too cold. Then you won't have to walk in the inclement weather. I'm sorry it wasn't finished before the rain hit. I really have been doin' my best to get it done."

"Don't apologize." Hope insisted, turning to face him. "You've done amazing work. And... did you pay for all of this?"

Judah looked uncomfortable and released her arm, though he didn't travel too far. "Let's just say I contributed."

"Judah—"

"It was the least I could do."

His stare was heavy, and Hope took a deep breath, not sure what that meant but figuring he wouldn't elaborate no matter how hard she probed. She exhaled slowly, and then took a step backward. "Well, I do appreciate it, all of it, more than you can ever know."

"You are very welcome, Miss Tucker. What you've done for these kids, for this community... anyone who can't appreciate that deserves to be run out of town."

Realizing she was standing in the cramped quarters of the washroom, Hope decided she needed some fresh air. Carefully, she stepped back through the hallway. Judah followed, and she could sense his hands behind her, ready to catch her should she misstep. She managed to wind her way through the unfinished timbers so that she was behind the house and that's when she realized there was a smaller structure here. "What's this?"

"Oh, I figured you'd wanna get a trap at some point. You'd need a place to keep it. And the pony."

Her head was shaking back and forth as she took it in. "I can't believe.... Well, but I guess I should. You really have thought of everything." Hope glanced down and noticed she'd fit on the edge of the floor between two of the support beams, so she sank down and took a seat, taking it all in.

Judah looked hesitant to join her and leaned into the timber where his hand had been resting. "You probably oughtta head back home before they realize you're gone."

"Home. Interesting word," Hope muttered, her hand automatically feeling for the pocket where she'd slipped the letter from her daddy.

"I know what you mean." Reluctantly, he stepped off of the structure, and then sat down a few beams over from her.

"Why do you stay?" she asked, hoping her question wasn't too personal. "Just because of the children?"

"Mostly," he replied, staring at the ground, his fingers interlaced as he leaned on his knees. "That and I ain't got nowhere to go."

She turned and looked at him, noticing how the moonlight played across his serene blue eyes. "Can't go back to Kansas?"

"I could," he said quickly, sitting up. "They didn't run me outta town or nothin'. Just ain't nothin' there for me 'cept a buncha bad memories."

She caught his eyes and immediately began to shake her head. Having come this far, she decided she had nothing to lose. If kissing him in the woods hadn't already revealed her true feelings, what more could she possibly do? "I just don't understand it. At all. I look at you, and I see this fine, intelligent man who would do anything for his family, for his community. Educated and refined. And they look at you and they see—something else. How is that even possible?"

"Hope..."

"Truly, Judah, I don't get it. I have been wracking my brain for months, trying to determine how anyone could possibly think you're capable of the heinous acts Brady and the others say you committed. I don't think you could ever even harm a fly."

He scoffed then, and she tipped her head to the side, waiting. "I would never harm a fly," he said in that quiet, teasing lilt. "Whenever I encounter any winged creatures, I do my best to capture them and take them out to the forest where I let them go. Often with a cube of sugar for their trouble."

Hope covered her mouth to dull her laughter but couldn't hide it all together. She dropped her eyes and stared at a scuff mark on her boots barely visible in the moonlight. "All right. Maybe a fly. But certainly never anyone you cared about." She looked back at him then, but he wasn't looking at her. He was staring off into the distance. Hope took a deep breath and finally said it. "I don't believe there's any way in this world you killed your wives."

The words hung between them for so long, Hope expected to see them take form and tumble to the ground, landing with a thud on the packed earth. He swallowed hard enough for her to hear it, see his Adam's apple bob up and down, and she held her breath, waiting for him to tell her she was right, that it never happened, that the town was full of fools and vigilantes.

"You're wrong, Hope."

Slowly, he turned his head to look at her, and Hope felt all the blood rush out of her face. It didn't seem remotely possible, and she prayed he'd tell her more because the person she was looking at was not a murderer. Despite his words, she just couldn't accept it.

He shifted so he was looking back at the structure that would be a small barn in a few days with a little more work, and Hope realized he wasn't going to say more on his own. But she hadn't come out in the middle of the night to leave on that note. "What do you mean?"

Judah sighed heavily, like he was extinguishing a fire with his breath. "I mean, I didn't kill Sylvia. That was... a terrible accident. But... my first wife, Isabella, yeah." He took his hat off, ran his hand through his caramel hair, and placed it back on his head before he turned and looked her in the eyes. "I killed her."

The words floated on the surface of Hope's mind for several moments, unable to sink in. She just couldn't accept them, not in and of themselves anyway. He looked as if he was done speaking, refocusing out on the horizon somewhere.

She shifted her position, the revolver knocking against her thigh as she did so. Hope couldn't imagine ever pointing a gun at someone she loved and pulling the trigger. She couldn't imagine Judah killing someone he loved either; even with that admission, she realized there was something she was missing. There had to be.

"Why?"

The question came out so quietly that when he didn't react, she thought for a moment he hadn't heard her. She was considering asking again, even though the logical part of her brain that didn't play into the hand of emotion was warning her to let it go. She continued to stare at his profile, willing him to answer her, letting the question form and reform on her tongue without emission several times before he finally began to speak.

"My pa was sixty-two years old when he married my ma. She was a little bitty thing, only eighteen at the time. But she seemed happy enough with him. He'd been a fur trapper all over the West before he headed back to civilization for a while, met my ma and decided it was time to have a few kids, try his hand at bein' domesticated." He turned and looked at her briefly, and though Hope wondered where in the world this story was going, she kept her mouth shut and listened.

"We moved to the Wyoming Territory when I was two or three. Civilization didn't quite take to Pa the way he hoped it would. So we settled on the edge of the world, just us and bears and wolves and other critters liable to eat us if they took a notion.

"But there were other folks out there, dangerous ones. My pa had been around 'em enough in his earlier days to know how to keep 'em happy, keep us safe. He knew all the rules of the tribes and how to get along, and many of them recognized him as a fair and honest white man, so they left our family alone." He slipped his hat up a little, looked at her for a moment, and then returned his focus to the inanimate structure in front of him.

Judah sighed. "When I was ten, a family built a little sod structure about five miles from us. We probably wouldn't have ever even knowed they were there if we didn't see the smoke from their fireplace one cold mornin'. Pa rode over and checked it out. I went with 'im. Family only spoke French, a language my pa spoke a version of thanks to all the Cassian trappers he'd met in his former life. My pa tried to warn 'em that there was a ton of Indians in those parts, and he'd decided to put his little dwellin' on the fringes of one of their sacred grounds. The Frenchman, feller by the name of Pierre Boudreaux, didn't listen to Pa, though. He had about a dozen kids, oldest of which was just a little older than me. I noticed Isabella right from that very first visit, but she didn't say nothin' and I just gawked at her."

Hope thought she saw a flicker of a smile on his face, and for a moment, she found herself jealous of his deceased wife. But she still kept her mouth closed for fear he'd finish with his story prematurely.

"It was about two years later when Mr. Boudreaux decided to start farmin' on the sacred grounds. That did not go over well. One mornin' we got up and saw a bunch a smoke in the air, and since it was summer, that didn't make no sense. Pa wouldn't let me go with 'im. He rode over, and sure enough, that entire family was massacred, their house on fire. Pa never would tell me what he saw, but I overheard 'im tellin' Ma one night, and the thought of it was enough to make me wretch. So, Isabella had been the only one to survive. She'd managed to hide somehow underneath her mama's body, and they'd missed her. She was outside or else the fire'd a got her. Obviously, she lived." He turned to look at Hope again. "But she wa'nt really alive."

"What do you mean?" Hope asked, her voice still a whisper.

He sighed again. "Isabella lost her mind the night her family died. And I don't think no one could blame her. She hardly spoke any English, and it was hard for us to understand what she did say, but it was mostly about what she'd seen done to her family. She'd scream in the middle of the night, run outta the house. My ma did her best to take care of the poor creature, but Isabella was a fragile little angelic thing who was so lost in the tragedy that'd struck her family, there weren't no gettin' her back.

"I should'a knowed that. But I wouldn't accept it. I did everything I could to try to reach her, to try to let her know I loved her, that I'd take care of her. When she was fifteen, and I was seventeen, I finished buildin' us a little cabin behind my folks' place and asked her to marry me. I don't know if she even knew what she was sayin' at that point, but she agreed. So we were married, but not in the biblical sense. If I even tried to kiss her hand, she'd start screamin' like I was tryin' to kill her."

While she wondered why he'd seen fit to include that information, Hope was glad to know it for some reason. She realized it was none of her business, and still it made the rest of the story somehow more manageable.

"One afternoon, Pa and I were out in the field. Isabella was gloomier than usual that mornin'. She hadn't eaten much at all for the last few days, and I was worried about her. I'd asked Caroline and Ma to check on her when they had a chance, and they told me later they'd gone over a few times during the day, and she seemed like her usual self. But about the time Pa and I were gonna call it a day, I heard the sound of a pistol firin' and knew immediately what she'd done."

A whimper escaped Hope's lips, and she covered her mouth as he turned to look at her. She was confused, but waited for him to explain; imagining that poor girl taking her own life after such a horrible tragedy struck her family was devastating.

"We ran in and found her on the floor by the table, one of my six shooters in her hand. Only she hadn't done a very good job." Judah let out a mournful sigh. "I'll spare you the details, Hope, but it wasn't pretty at all. And she was still alive and in God awful pain. There wasn't gonna be no saving her, so there was only one thing to do." Hope felt tears slipping down her cheeks as she anticipated what he would say next. "Pa said he'd do it, but I knew it had to be me. I was the one who'd promise to keep her safe, and I'd failed. I couldn't get to where she'd been, to try to find her, and bring her home again. And in her suffering, she'd decided she wanted to be with her family once more. Endin' that pain for her was the only way I could make things right."

Judah stopped and gazed up at the sky, and Hope imagined he was thinking of her up there, looking down at them now. She imagined Isabella was grateful he'd given her mercy instead of trying to fix something that could never be unbroken.

She wiped at her cheeks, letting the story set in, before she said quietly, "You didn't kill her, Judah. That's not murder. What you did was an act of love, an act of kindness to end something she couldn't do herself."

"Whatever you wanna call it, Hope, I still shot my wife in the head, and that's somethin' I have to live with every day of my life." He was looking at her now, and his eyes were heavy with the weight of the past.

There wasn't anything she could say to take the pain of the past away from him, and she felt like he'd done enough storytelling for one night. Asking to hear about Sylvia seemed foolish and selfish, so she didn't. "Thank you for letting me know what happened. I'm glad you did. I wish everyone could know."

"No one else needs to know."

There was a finality about the statement that told her she needed to keep his business to herself. Hope nodded. "Still, I appreciate it. I'm sure it's not an easy thing to speak about."

"I haven't told that story to anyone else except Sylvia."

She was shocked but tried to hide her surprise. Obviously, Paul must know, too, which meant Sylvia or Caroline must've told him. "You can trust me not to repeat it."

"I know."

Despite her surprise that he would so readily trust someone he'd hardly spoken to, Hope nodded. "I wasn't wrong though," she reminded him. "You didn't murder her."

"But I did kill her."

"I wouldn't call it that."

"Don't matter what you call it, Hope. She's gone just the same."

No argument came to mind, so she kept her mouth shut, wishing there was something she could do to ease his pain, but she knew in her heart there was nothing. She wondered what it had been about Sylvia that had made him try to find love again. She must've been a remarkable woman, and Hope wished she could hear her story, too, but it was getting late, and she wasn't going to press him.

She didn't have to. "We moved to Manhattan a few years later. Caroline fell in with Sylvia right away. She was a perty girl with shocking red hair and a feisty way about her. When I finished up with my studies, Paul came to work for me, and we got to be good friends. At the time, I was still under the impression I might be happy someday. I'd married Isabella so young, I didn't realize what life had in the cards for me yet.

"I didn't pursue Sylvia, though." He chuckled a little bit, and Hope smiled, glad he at least had a few fond memories to share. "She chased me like a fox in the hen house—only in this case I guess it was the rooster she was after. Eventually, I gave in, and we started courtin'. Sylvia was the complete opposite of Isabella—full of life, a friend to everyone. Always busy doin' whatever she could for anyone and everyone."

"She sounds like a lovely woman." Once again, Hope found herself slightly jealous and had to argue with herself about how ridiculous that was considering the circumstances.

"We had a neighbor lady who was near a hundred years old, and she insisted on takin' care of her own animals even though both Syl and I volunteered to do it for her. There was this dang nail in that barn that constantly slipped out of the wall, and yet she insisted on hangin' her lantern there, even though I told her a thousand times not to. I even put a nice hook in for it and everything. I'd pull the nail out, and next time me or Syl would go over there, she'd a put it back in. I didn't understand it at the time, but Syl said, 'That's just the way Mrs. Wilson is,' so we left it."

Hope could see where the story was going, and her stomach turned over. She swallowed hard and waited for him to finish.

"Well, one morning, I'd gone to work, and once again, there was a cloud of smoke on the horizon that alerted me there was somethin' not right. Paul and I both ran over there as fast as we could. Syl'd gotten there first." His voice trailed off a little, and Hope realized he probably had never told anyone this story before. "She'd gone in to try to help. But...."

"She didn't make it out?"

He shook his head. "Paul was furious. I ain't never seen anyone so angry in my whole life. He couldn't understand why I'd let her do somethin' like that. And I was so beside myself at losin' Syl, I couldn't even begin to explain to him that I'd done everything I could think of to try to keep Mrs. Wilson from settin' the barn on fire with that damn lantern." He shook his head a few times and wiped at his eyes. Hope remembered what Caroline had said on their way to the barn raisin'. It hadn't even been four years since Sylvia had passed away. "He ain't ever forgive me for that, and I guess that's okay because I ain't ever forgive myself either."

Hope inhaled through her nose, held it for a second, and then let it go slowly. She wished she had some words of wisdom, something to say to make him feel better about his past, but there was nothing that could be said that she hadn't already said before. Finally, she decided if she couldn't say anything profound, she could at least say something heartfelt. "I'm so sorry, Judah. No one should ever have to go through what you've been through. It's just awful...."

He was quiet for a long time, and she assumed he was trying to get himself together. She couldn't blame him for being emotional about the deaths of two wives. She'd never lost anyone close to her, but even the thought of losing someone she loved left her stomach in knots and a sense of dread in her heart.

The moon had moved several degrees in its path across the sky while they'd been sitting there, and Hope knew she needed to get back. Something told her, once she got up, it would be weeks, maybe months again before she had the opportunity to speak to him, so she was reluctant to go. Knowing about his past didn't change a thing about how she felt. In fact, in many ways, it made her care even more for him. While she could certainly understand why he'd said he'd never marry again, Hope couldn't help but think there might be a glimmer of a chance he had feelings for her. After all, he'd shared his most intimate secrets with her. Cordia always said, "Where there's a Will, there's a way, and if you have Faith, you can always have Hope."

Not for the first time in her life did Hope think her mother had named her correctly.

"I should be heading back to the Howards'," Hope said quietly, though she made no move to stand.

Judah jumped a little, rubbing his hands on his pants like he'd forgotten she was there. "Oh, yeah. I reckon you should. But it's awful dark, Hope. You sure you don't want me to give you a ride?"

"No, thank you," she said, finally standing. She turned to face him, and he pulled himself up off the floor so that they were toe to toe. "If anyone sees... we'll both have consequences."

"I suppose yer right. The last thing I wanna do, Hope, is get you in any sort of trouble on my account. That's why I've been avoiding doin' any of this work in the day time, any time people might see it and start jumping to conclusions."

"I wouldn't care what anyone had to say, Judah, if it weren't for my contract. I hope you know that. It isn't you I don't want to be seen with, it's just that I can't be seen with any man at all." She thought he might bring up the Howards, but he didn't.

"It's for the best, Hope. Even if you didn't have that contract, you shouldn't be seen with me."

"Judah, you haven't done anything wrong." She took a step forward, and her hand came up of its own accord, though she stopped short of touching him. Her hand hesitated for a moment before she dropped it back to her side.

He didn't step back, but he didn't move any closer either. "Hope, I meant what I said before. Now that you know the truth, you should understand that I could never even consider courtin' anyone again—especially not someone like you. You deserve a man who can make you happy, someone who can keep you safe. Someone who can provide a good life for you, and I can't do none of those things. So... I ain't sayin' I think you're sweet on me or anythin' like that, Miss Tucker, but if you ever start to have any of those notions in yer head, you just go ahead and send 'em right on out, you hear? Because nothin' good can come of it."

A flare of anger boiled up inside of her, and Hope took a step backward. She wasn't sure if she was mad that he was insinuating she might have feelings for him—which she obviously did—or if she was mad that he was denying her, even though she hadn't even professed anything to him. "Judah, you sound utterly ridiculous," she said, trying to keep the sharpness out of her voice. "First of all, I don't need anyone to tell me how I should or shouldn't feel, and secondly, the idea that you should never find a woman you love again because of the horrible tragedies that have afflicted you in the past is just... horse hockey."

He bit back a chuckle and put his hands up between them. "Now, Miss Tucker, don't you go usin' unchristian language."

"Do you think that's funny? That anything I said was remotely humorous?"

"No, Miss Tucker, I don't. I just... sometimes if you don't laugh, you'll cry."

She remembered a similar remark from back when she'd gone to the barn raising with Caroline, though she couldn't quote it at the moment. "Listen, Judah, I'm not going to stand here and defend myself when I've nothing to defend."

"Good."

She growled at him, and he leaned back. Hope took a deep breath, trying to decide whether she should insult him and tell him not to flatter himself into thinking she had feelings for him or yell at him for being such an imbecile that he wasn't even willing to give her a chance. Neither of those options were viable, however, since her contract wouldn't allow her to pursue any sort of relationship with him should she be so inclined. And obviously, she was either sweet on him or she had a habit of kissing strangers in the woods; she wasn't sure which one was worse.

So Hope said nothing, only turned around and headed for the Howards' place, thinking maybe it was a good thing she wouldn't see Judah again for weeks or months or maybe years if she was lucky. Maybe by then, she'd know what to do about the obnoxious fact that she was falling in love with him.

The idea had her stopping in her tracks. She'd only taken ten or fifteen steps. She swiveled back around to look at him and wasn't surprised at all to see him watching her, his hands folded across his chiseled chest she shouldn't be able to envision shirtless, though she could just the same, that playful, amused expression on his face. "You're infuriating."

"You're intoxicating."

She huffed again. "Now, why would you go and say something like that right after what you just told me?"

"What's that now?"

Hope muttered a word under her breath she'd only heard her father say once when he'd accidentally hit his thumb with a hammer. She turned around again, and this time, she was certain she would not turn back to face him.

Judah caught her by the arm and spun her around, pulling her close to his chest. They were in the shadows, away from the lantern light, and the moon was almost completely obscured by clouds. Anger pressed her to struggle against him, but desire overcame her compulsion, and when he tipped his head and brought his mouth down to cover hers, Hope slipped her hand around the back of his neck and pulled him in. His lips were warm and tasted of salt and sweat, and the scent of cedar from the planks and his own perspiration filled her senses as his hands encircled her waist.

It was over too soon, and when he released her, it was harsh; a chasm of at least a foot was suddenly between them, leaving her cold and alone. "I'm sorry, Hope. I should not have done that."

She didn't know what to say. Of course, he should have—and he should continue to do so whenever he wanted for the rest of their lives. But she couldn't say that. She couldn't say anything at all. And as Judah slowly backed away, toward the house he was building for her, Hope watched for only a second and then turned to walk back to her room, the feel of Judah Lawless still on her lips and the idea that there was still a possibility she could have him in her heart.

CHAPTER TWENTY-ONE

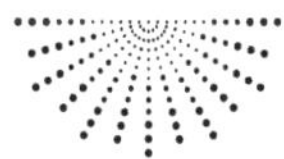

Weeks went by, and Hope saw absolutely no sign of Judah. The little cabin continued to come together, so she knew he was working, and by the end of October, Mr. Stewart announced the place was ready to move into. Hope was glad for it, especially since her relationship with the Howards continued to disintegrate, but when she took her few items and hung them in the closet Judah had made for her, she felt more alone than she had in a very long time.

Her father's letter had some good advice in it, though she wasn't sure how in the world she could apply it. He'd basically told her what she knew to be true. If she truly thought a person was worth fighting for, then she owed herself a well-fought effort. Anything short of that would leave her an old woman with many unanswered questions.

Despite the good advice, it probably wasn't worth the risk of going after the correspondence in the middle of the night if the result had been anything other than the conversation she'd had with Judah. And the kiss. But now, it was just another painful memory of a man she couldn't even see, let alone be with. And with the election looming, it seemed as if Mr. Stewart taking credit for her house had won him a lot of votes; there was a good chance her contract wouldn't be changing anytime soon.

Maybe it's for the better that way, she thought to herself one Friday afternoon while the students played outside during lunch. She watched them from the porch, making sure everyone played nicely. That was hardly an issue anymore. They'd all come so far and did such a nice job of treating each other like one big family, even the Pembrokes. Hope had gotten a letter from Mr. Cartwright asking her if she'd consider coming back to Lamar to stay when she came up for her sister's wedding since Lola could no longer teach, and they were having a hard time finding anyone with the sort of skills Hope had, but Hope had turned him down. For better or worse, this was the path she'd chosen, and she was determined to stick it out for at least the next few years. After that, maybe she'd think about trying to find a man and settling down, though she had a hard time imagining anyone would come along and sweep her off of her feet now that she had an idea what it felt like to be so truly infatuated with someone that he kept her up at night and kept her mind wandering in the middle of the day.

Thinking of Judah brought her eyes over to Ginny. She was still Hope's best student by far, and Hope was so proud of everything the young girl had accomplished. She was sitting beneath a large maple tree, among the fallen red and orange leaves, reading a book to Sally. Both of them looked enthralled, and it made Hope's heart happy to see them so enthusiastic about whatever book it was spread on Ginny's lap. She decided to go over and see what the book was.

The girls were so engrossed they didn't even notice her until their teacher had sunk down beside them. "What are you reading?"

"Oh, Miss Tucker! You frightened me!" Ginny laughed. "It's *Alice in Wonderland*. Have you read it?"

"Yes, I have," Hope replied, giggling with the girls. "It's one of my favorites."

"We're just at the part where the Mad Hatter is having a tea party," Sally replied. "Do you think I'll be able to read it on my own someday?"

"I do," Hope said with a nod of her head. "And soon. Why don't you read me a little, Ginny?"

Ginny obliged, reading aloud in her most entertaining voice, even changing the pitch and tone for each character. Hope could see why Sally liked to listen so much, and after a few minutes, there was a crowd of other students sitting around, even some of the boys.

Hope was so caught up in the story, she accidentally let recess go long. When she realized her mistake, she hurried the children inside and got them started on their math, glad it was a Friday afternoon and she could use a long week of hard work as an excuse for a little extra fun. The rest of the day seemed to fly by, and soon enough she'd sent all of the children out for the weekend and went about tidying up the schoolhouse, glad she'd only have a few yards to walk to reach her own residence.

She was sweeping the floor when she noticed Ginny's book underneath one of the desks. She thought the girl must've dropped it. Her eyes immediately went to the window, but of course, their wagon was long gone. There was a chance she might come back for it that evening, but somehow Hope doubted her mother would be willing to come all the way back into town just for a book, even if it was one that Ginny loved. She felt sorry for the girl that she wouldn't have it to enjoy over the weekend. With a sigh, Hope placed it on the corner of her desk, thinking maybe someone would come and get it during the night.

It was a silly thought, really, and as she sat in a comfortable chair she'd bought herself, looking out the window at the schoolhouse until late into the night, pretending to be embroidering but really keeping an eye out in case Ginny told her uncle of her lost book, and he decided to come and get it, Hope felt foolish. It was half past midnight before she got her wits about her and hauled herself off to bed, thinking about how desperate and ridiculous she would've seemed if there were anyone else in the world who knew what she'd been doing. For once in her life, having no one else around seemed to have paid off, however, and as she pressed herself to sleep, she determined being utterly alone wasn't always as horrendous as others made it out to be.

In the morning, she utilized her indoor washroom, dressed in one of her more cheerful gowns, had a bit of breakfast, and then headed back over to the school to find that the book was still sitting on her desk. It crossed her mind that Caroline might come into town to pick it up, and it would've made perfect sense for her to simply leave it there since the school was always unlocked. However, by noontime, when the book still hadn't moved, Hope decided the neighborly thing to do would be to drop by the Pembroke house and leave the book. It didn't matter much that five miles' distance didn't quite make one a neighbor.

With all of the money she'd saved up living with the Howards, Hope had purchased a small pony trap and a little dappled mare to pull it. The barn Judah had built her was the perfect size for both, and Hope loved having a companion of sorts to talk to on days when there were no children around and she had no reason to go into town. Now, she hitched Whinny up to the cart, tucked Ginny's book under her leg so it wouldn't fly off the seat, and headed out in the direction Caroline had taken her when she'd gone to the barn raising so many months ago.

The weather was perfect. Hope had wrapped a shawl around her shoulders and worn a hat that covered her ears, but it was just a bit crisp and not at all cold. As she rode along, part of her hoped she'd run into Caroline on the way into town so she could just hand the book off and not have to worry about seeing Judah. Or maybe he'd be out in the field with Paul or off at a neighbor's house building something, now that her house was finished. There were lots of reasons to think she might not see Judah at all—and lots of reasons to hope she might.

She did pray no one saw her headed out of town. Most Saturday mornings were busy with wagons coming and going, heading to the market or to the square to get supplies, so there were other buggies on the road, but she didn't recognize any of the faces headed to town and hoped none of them recognized her either. She had an explanation for what she was doing, but that didn't mean people wouldn't speculate. If there was one thing she'd learned about the Texans she'd taken up with, these folks sure did like to make assumptions.

The stories of Judah's two wives had haunted her ever since he'd revealed the truth to her, and Hope had even had a few bad dreams where she came across a burnt out cabin in the woods with lots of children's bodies scattered across the yard or a woman's corpse on the dining room floor. She was glad to know the truth, but at the same time, her imagination was so vivid, those sorts of stories always stayed with her longer than they should've. It was hard to think about how much more difficult the entire situation must be for poor Judah. She thought if she were him, she'd be a hermit, off somewhere away from civilization, avoiding everyone and rude to those who stumbled across her path. But he was pleasant almost all of the time, and she remembered marveling at how polite he'd been even to those who were rude to him. It was a testament to his character, she thought.

As Hope drew nearer to the place where she thought she should turn, she slowed the pony down a bit and looked around. She'd tried to etch a sketch of the road into her mind at the time in case she ever needed to find Ginny and George's house. She was fairly certain she had the right junction when she noticed an apple tree with long, twisted branches off a little ways into an otherwise well-tended farm field. She decided to give it a try and turned the corner, hopeful she'd be able to find her way back to this main thoroughfare if she found out she had been mistaken.

Thinking back, she recalled Caroline had said their house was about two miles down the road, so she tried to keep track of about how far she'd gone. Sure enough, she saw a house up on the left in the distance and knew for certain it had to be the Pembroke place. Brady had mentioned how fancy it was, and Caroline had even said something about her brother building her the house of her dreams. The large two-story structure with a wide porch and intricate gingerbread looked slightly out of place on the open, rolling farmland. This had to be it.

She pulled into the drive and wound her way back to the house, which sat a short distance off of the road. Stately trees stood on all sides, and she could tell Judah had been careful about where he placed the structure, which didn't surprise her in the least. The barn was a fair distance behind the house, and in one of the trees, she noticed something curious but didn't have too much of a chance to figure out what she was looking at since she could feel eyes on her the moment she brought the cart to a stop.

Hopping down, Hope grabbed the book and secured Whinny to the hitching post, thinking there was no reason to go to too much trouble since she would only be a moment. With a deep breath, she made her way up the walkway to the porch and gave a slight rap on the door, certain it would open directly.

When Judah pulled the door open, Hope muttered, "Crud," under her breath and then felt a crimson fill her cheeks. He looked every bit as enticing as he always did and part of her wanted to run back to the pony cart before she did something idiotic—again.

"Nice to see you, too, Miss Tucker," he laughed, having discerned her comment, no doubt.

Hope shook her head, unable to control the smile that played at her lips. "It is nice to see you, Mr. Lawless. You see, that's the problem, now isn't it?"

He snickered at her again but didn't comment. "What brings you out here?"

"I don't suppose Ginny's around is she?" She wanted to peer past him into the foyer but stopped herself.

"I'm afraid not," he replied, leaning on the doorjamb. "She went into town with her mama and George."

"Of course she did." Hope sighed, thinking she should've left well-enough alone. "Was she looking for this?" She held up the book.

"Amongst other things," he nodded. "You come all the way out here to bring her a book?"

"Yes, I did." Hope realized they both knew that wasn't the truth in its entirety, but she could hardly say otherwise. She handed the book to him. "Would you mind seeing that she gets it? I know she wanted to read it this weekend." Her fingers grazed his as he took the book, and she fought any acknowledgement of the pulses that sent a wave of shivers up the length of her arm and down her spine.

"I'll make sure she gets it, Miss Tucker."

"Thank you." Hope cleared her throat, and realizing there was nothing else to say, she took a step backward. She couldn't quite seem to get her eyes to follow her, though, and they stayed locked on his face. Without his hat on, it was even easier to see how handsome he was, and she thought about how unfair life had been to him, and how unfair it was being to her presently.

"You headed home then?"

Was there something to that question or just a general inquiry? "Is there somewhere else I should be headed?" she asked, not sure what he was getting at but hoping he was thinking along the same lines as she was—that it was a crying shame for her to have come all this way and just turn around and leave again. But then, she was an uninvited guest, after all, and it seemed as if Paul wasn't in the house either, so she would be alone with a single male, a strict violation of her contract, which was still in place. And she hadn't forgotten Mr. Stewart was looking for reasons to get rid of her, particularly if he was reelected.

"No, I guess not. It's a lovely day, isn't it? Do you have plans?"

Hope couldn't help but giggle. What sort of plans could she possibly have? "No, I do not. Except for with a similar bound volume that's waiting for me at home." For a moment, she imagined what she might be doing if she were back in Missouri with all of her friends and family. Maybe apple picking or working in the yard with her daddy. A pang of longing hit her, but she brushed it aside.

"You should get out more. There's some young ladies at your church about your age. You could socialize with them."

"I guess I could," she replied. "Celia is nice enough."

He laughed, and she realized he thought she was joking. "I suppose so," he said with a shrug. "What about Anna?"

It was Hope's turn to laugh. "I don't think she's too fond of me." She had hardly spoken to Anna since the barn raising. "I'm fine, Mr. Lawless, I assure you. I have plenty of friends. In my books."

His smile widened. "You do know those folks ain't real don't you?"

"They seem real enough to me." She took another step backward, thinking now was as good a time as ever to flee. She already felt ridiculous for having come, and now that her social life had been thoroughly scrutinized, she saw no reason to hang around.

"Hope, you wanna see somethin' straight outta *The Swiss Family Robinson*?"

She remembered noticing something in one of the trees behind his house when she'd pulled in and thought it must've been a treehouse.

Of course, she wanted to see it. The idea that anyone would know she was out here alone with him crossed her mind, but the chances were slim someone would come by and notice her pony so far off the road, not to mention they'd have no way of knowing she wasn't visiting Caroline, unless of course, they also happened to see the woman in town near the same time, which was a stretch. So she found herself saying, "That does sound interesting."

He smiled at her and stepped out onto the porch closing the door behind him. She followed him down the steps and around to the back of the house, neither of them saying a word. Hope folded her hands in front of her and kept her eyes on the ground, hoping she didn't regret putting herself in another situation where she'd be close to him for a bit and then torn away from him for an eternity.

"There it is," he said, and Hope lifted her eyes to see a sprawling oak tree with a huge treehouse built high above her head. It seemed massive to her, almost as big as her little cabin, and it had to be high enough to rival the second story windows of the house to her back.

At first, she didn't know what to say, so she just gasped in wonder. Finally she managed, "This is amazing, Judah. Did you build this yourself?"

"I sure did," he said, and she could tell by the beam of his smile that he was proud of himself, though she imagined the house behind her, which he had also built, was likely more difficult than the simple structure above her. "It's a pretty nice little place. You can even see the top of the courthouse from up there."

"You can?" It was hard to imagine, but then the courthouse was huge. "Is it for the children?"

"Oh, no. This is where I live—weather permitting. I mean, if it's too cold or rainy, I have a room in the house, but most of the time, this is where I'm at when I ain't workin'."

Hope pulled her eyes away from the treehouse for a moment to stare at him, trying to determine if he was serious. She could tell that he was. While it seemed strange, she imagined it had something to do with Paul not being too fond of Judah after his sister's death. She decided not to ask. "Well, it surely is a spectacle."

He returned his attention to the house for a moment before he looked back at her. "I'd invite you up to see the view, but the climb's a little difficult. If I'd made it too easy, George'd be up there all the time. I let him and Ginny visit, but only when I'm around to give 'em a hand. I'd hate for one of 'em to get hurt."

Hope looked at the base of the tree and saw several planks hammered into the side at wide intervals and realized that's what he was talking about. Rather than a ladder or even a rope, one had to climb the rungs. The first one was probably waist high on her and would be difficult for the children to access. She thought she could manage, and she was curious to see the view, though it did enter her mind that technically she'd be going into a single gentleman's house without a chaperone. Still, what were the chances anyone would find out?

"I'd like to see the view, if that might be possible," she said, looking him in the eye. It wasn't the boldest action she'd ever taken where he was concerned, but it did still seem a little out of character for her.

"I'd be happy to show it to you, Hope. But... do you think you can manage gettin' up and down? Up's not nearly as tricky as down, and yer gown is awful long."

Hope glanced down, trying to remember what she was wearing. She'd put on one of her better weekend dresses. It had a full, dark blue skirt and a matching top. She was wearing her regular boots underneath, though. "I think I can manage."

Judah looked back up at the treehouse and then at her, and she thought he was going to tell her no for a moment. It was awfully high, and she certainly wasn't dressed for the occasion, but eventually, he said, "All right. But you'll have to be careful, Hope. I don't want nothin' to happen to you."

Hope scoffed, thinking that was the understatement of the year. He'd all but said he couldn't be around her because he seemed to be under the impression his mere existence was dangerous to women. "I'm sure I'll be all right."

She approached the tree, and he walked along with her. Once she made it to the rungs, she inspected them for a moment and then looked up to see there was no door, only a bit of a step from the last rung into the house itself. It didn't look too difficult if she could get her foot up onto the first rung. But coming down would be trickier.

"I can give you a boost, if you'd like," Judah offered.

Even standing right next to him made her breath catch in her throat, and she couldn't imagine having his hands on her again, not after the last time when he'd kissed her in the moonlight. "Let me try," she said, not looking into his eyes.

He stood back a bit, and Hope grabbed hold of a higher rung before attempting to swing her foot up to the lowest one. She couldn't quite manage; it was just out of reach due to the way her skirt gathered. She put her boot back down and tried with the other leg but still couldn't get there.

Judah cleared his throat, and she turned her head to look at him. A smile broke across his handsome face. "Fine," she said, narrowing her eyes at him.

A chuckle escaped his lips as his hands came around her waist, and Hope let out a little gasp, not realizing his intentions. He lifted her right off of the ground high enough that she was easily able to place her foot on the first board. "You got it?" he asked, not yet letting her go.

"Yes," was all she could manage considering how unusual, yet enticing, it felt to have both of his hands around her. He'd picked her up like she weighed no more than a small child, and when he released her, she hated how suddenly cold she felt.

After she found the first footing, the rest of the climb was easy enough. She tried not to think about the fact that he was right behind her and was either staring right at her bottom or potentially up her skirt. Thank goodness she'd worn her nice knickers. When she got to the top, she pushed down on the floor of the treehouse and raised her trunk up enough that she could sit on the floor and scoot out of the way, leaving room for Judah to finish his ascent. He took a large step right into the room, like it was nothing at all, and moved across the space to a wide window.

Hope needed to catch her breath. It wasn't any more vigorous an activity than walking to school or climbing a flight of stairs, but her heart had been beating rapidly the entire time, and being close enough to Judah that she could smell that woodsy scent of his had emptied her lungs even without the trials of getting to the treehouse.

She turned and took in the room. There was another window across the way. Both of them had red curtains that caught the breeze. A small bed sat beneath the far window with a little table next to it, and nearer the center of the room was a cabinet. She thought it must be odd to keep one's clothes outside and wondered if it served some other purpose or was just there to make it seem more like home. In front of the other window, where Judah was standing, pushed back in the corner, was a rocking chair. All of the furniture looked to be handmade, and she imagined he'd done it himself. So much for not being a carpenter.

"Do you need helping getting up?" he asked after giving her a moment to compose herself.

"I'm fine," she assured him, reaching up to grab hold of one of the tree branches to pull herself to her feet. A glance at the opening reminded her she'd have to be careful when it was time to go back down. Reaching the first step would be a strain, and she wouldn't be able to see the rung below her because of her skirt.

A glimpse out the window made all of that slip right out of her mind. It truly was a magnificent view, different than just looking out a window in a house. The tree branches and leaves, already turning red and orange, framed the window so that she felt as if she were looking at a finely crafted painting. The fields were golden in the sun, and the sky was a brilliant blue, almost the same shade as Judah's eyes. Off in the distance, she could see the top of the courthouse, as he'd mentioned, and she thought about how magnificent it was to see God's creations mingled with the sight of progress.

"It's something else, isn't it?" he asked, grinning at her.

"It's... amazing," she replied. "How long did it take you to put together?"

"Not long. Not half as much time as it took me to build your house." He laughed, and Hope did, too. She realized he could've gotten her place built a lot more quickly if he'd been able to work on it during the day time.

She wanted to say more, but couldn't think of anything else to say.

They hadn't had too many conversations, but the last one was so deep, she wanted to avoid those topics if possible. It was a fine line, wanting to get to know him better weighed with the understanding that there could be no reason behind it.

"Tell me about your folks, Hope."

She looked over at him, surprised at the question. It made no sense to her that he'd ask about her family when he'd made his position clear, and yet, it was a topic she spoke easily about. "My daddy grew up on a farm. His folks died of tuberculosis when he was young, and he lost his brother to marauders right before the Battle of Carthage. So he enlisted. Took his sister to stay at his aunt's place, and that's where he met my mama. She wrote to him during the war, and they fell in love and got married as soon as he come back. Unfortunately, his sister died of TB on the same night as Quantrill raided our hometown of Lamar. My mama defended her parents' house that night, and my granddad got shot. He never did fully recover. Anyhow, my folks moved back out to the farm for a while, and that's where my little sister, Faith, and I were born. When I was about ten, we moved back to Lamar, and now Daddy works at the bank, Mama takes care of my grandparents, and Faith is a seamstress. She's gettin' married soon. That's about it, I guess."

She'd summed her whole life up into a paragraph, and none of it sounded nearly as exiting or as tragic as his story had been. She could tell him more—about Jaris and Carey Adams and how her mama shot at the raiders, but those details were reserved for people she'd have in her life forever, and she still wasn't sure Judah was letting her into his.

"From the sound of it, I'd say yer a lot like yer mama." He smiled at her, like he was fond of her parents already, and Hope raised an eyebrow. "After all, you were packin' heat the other night."

He said it like it hadn't been nearly a month since the last time she'd seen him, but she let that go. "Well, I wasn't sure if any of those men from the saloons might be headed home at the same time I was," she said with a shrug, her eyes oscillating from the gorgeous view out the window to the gorgeous man a few feet away from her.

"What made you decide to come here?" he asked, adjusting so that he was leaning against the window and looking at her.

"I assume you mean to McKinney and not your abode in the clouds?" He laughed and nodded, and she chuckled at her own joke. "I wanted an adventure, I guess. My friend Lola is Mrs. Howard's niece. She told me about the position, and it sounded like the sort of journey I'd always longed for. It isn't that I didn't like my life in Lamar or enjoy the school I was teaching at. I was under the impression that if I came to a more remote part of the country, I'd have a better chance at helping children that might not otherwise have an opportunity to learn."

"I would say you've done that," he replied, a serious look on his face for once. "Caroline says every time she goes into town she hears some parent or grandparent talking about everything their kids is learnin' from you. I guess this probably isn't the wild frontier you may have had in mind growin' up, but it's reasonably unsettled, untamed."

She had to agree with that. "And inhospitable," she muttered under her breath.

"Not to you."

"Doesn't really matter how they accept me if they can't treat everyone with the same respect. You haven't broken any laws, and yet they insist you're a criminal."

"Hope, I'd really rather not talk about all that, if it's just the same to you. I unburdened myself on you the other night, and I thank you for being a good listener, but for the most part, I try to keep all of that out of my thoughts. It ain't no way to go around in this world, thinkin' on those you've failed."

She remembered having the same thoughts only a few moments ago—that she'd rather not talk about it, and she couldn't blame him. "I'm sorry," she replied, placing her elbows on the window and resting her head on her hand. "I can't blame you there."

He turned around and moved over slightly so that his arm was near enough to hers that she could feel warmth radiating from him. "You think you'll stay?"

"In this treehouse? Maybe—if I can't get down."

The sound of his laughter rang off of the trees, filling the breeze and stirring the leaves. "I'll getcha down," he assured her. "I meant, do you think you'll stay in McKinney? If Stewart gets reelected, things'll continue to be tough on you."

"He may very well fire me," she said, the idea making her stomach churn.

"I don't think he can get away with that, not without cause anyway, and I ain't plannin' on tellin' anyone I brought you up here. So unless one of them blackbirds up there is kin to the school board president, I think yer all right."

Hope glanced up at the branches outside of the window and thought that if Mr. Stewart had a minion, it would likely be a crow. "He'll still be the superintendent of schools, even if he doesn't win the school board election," Hope reminded him. "Which won't mean much, I suppose, but nevertheless, he'll still be my boss."

"Mr. Canton won't let the school board fire you if he wins."

"And if he doesn't, well, who knows what'll happen."

"The parents will protect you." Judah seemed sure of himself. "So long as they don't have any reason to think you're doing anythin' that ain't fit."

She looked him in the eye then, thinking she'd done plenty recently that they might think wasn't fit. Even if she hadn't done anything untoward, she had broken her contract on several occasions—knowingly and with malice aforethought. The idea made her think she should probably leave before she was discovered.

But then Judah placed his hand on top of hers, and Hope forgot she was a schoolteacher at all, and for a moment, she was Hope Frieda Tucker, just a girl, who happened to think Judah Lawless was the kindest, most generous, intelligent, handsomest man she'd ever met.

"I know I've been awful unfair to you," he said quietly, looking out the window instead of at her. "And I can't pretend to think it's all right. But... Hope, I must confess I ain't never met anyone like you before." He turned and looked at her then, and she stared into his blue eyes, not knowing what to say.

He turned back and started to pull his hand away, but she flicked her wrist in time to catch it, and he stopped, letting her intertwine her slender fingers through his rough ones. "I don't understand why you think you have to continue to punish yourself for something you didn't do."

"It's not that," he said, still not turning to look at her. "It's not that I think I deserve to be alone the rest of my life, Hope. It's just...." He was looking at her now, and she could tell by the glistening in his eyes that it was difficult for him to say what he was about to tell her. "I'm afraid."

"Afraid of what?" she asked, each word measured.

He drew in a deep breath, still holding her gaze. "Afraid... it'll happen again. Afraid that anyone I love is gonna end up gone. Hope, if anything should ever happen to you...."

"Nothin' is gonna happen to me, Judah. I live ten feet from where I work. I never go anywhere except the library. The worst thing that could happen is one of the swings could hit me in the stomach or a child could drop his lunch pail on my toe!" He broke into a smile and began to laugh at the ridiculousness of her statement, and she laughed along with him, reminding herself about what he'd said—if you don't laugh you'll cry.

His face went serious again. "I ain't willin' to take the chance, Hope. But if I were... it would be with you. That is, assumin' you don't kiss every feller who follows you into the woods."

"So far my record is one for one," she said, tweaking an eyebrow at him. He smiled and reached up, brushing a curl behind her ear, and she felt the finality of his words settle into her chest. She wasn't sure what might be worse--knowing he could never love her so she'd have to spend the rest of her life wishing he could, or knowing that he did love her, and she'd still be without him.

"Listen, Hope, I think I'll probably head back to Kansas soon. Paul's not comfortable with me here, and I think McKinney can move on and find someone else to talk about. There really ain't no reason for me to stay 'cept the children, and they're probably better off without me, too."

"Do you think so?" she asked, increasing her grip on his hand as if he might be leaving right that moment.

He leaned back against the window, drawing little circles on the back of her hand with his thumb. "I do. It's likely for the best.

Everyone in town knows Doc Howard's sweet on you. He's a good man, Hope. The kind that'll keep you safe, won't let nothin' happen to you."

She could feel tears filling her eyes, and she knew what her mama would say—she didn't love Doc Howard. But that would beg the question of who did she love, and something told her right now was not the time to confess how she was truly feeling about the man standing in front of her, the one tearing her heart out and tossing it out the window. He'd leave—she knew he was strong enough to do that. How, she didn't quite understand, but then, he'd been through enough in his life that he had to have built many layers of protection around his own heart, and for the moment, she was slightly jealous of that armor, even if she didn't envy him the way it'd been formed.

"Don't cry over me, Hope. I ain't worth it."

She nodded and used her free hand to swipe away at the solitary tear that fell down her cheek. He was wrong—he was worth it. But she would find a way to keep her tears in check until she was in the solace of her own home, the one he'd built for her.

"When do you think you'll go?"

"Soon," he replied quickly. "There's a town springin' up not far from Manhattan on the rail line. They need people who can throw buildin's up quickly but soundly. Buddy of mine sent me a telegram a couple of weeks ago."

Hope took that in, her head bobbing up and down. "Do the children know yet?"

"Not exactly, but I've been tellin' 'em for a while it won't be much longer. I don't think George understands, but Ginny's mature enough to handle it, I think. She'll write me letters."

"I'm sure she'd enjoy that aspect of it, but I know how fond they both are of you."

"Counting Caroline then, I guess that's four people who might miss me a little. Those numbers are in my favor."

"There are other people who will miss you. The people from your church. Mr. Canton. Paul will, too, even though he might not admit it. Judah, just because the people in town are mostly fools doesn't mean there aren't some who can see the good in you."

"Ah, Hope, if everyone was as kind-hearted and optimistic as you are, this world would be a better place." He glanced down at her hand where he held it fast in his, and she thought he might let it go, but he didn't. "Will you do me one little favor before you leave?"

She pulled her eyes away from their hands and met his eyes, her breath catching as she wondered what he might ask. She couldn't help but nod, though. Whatever it was, she would do it. He wouldn't ask too much of her, she was certain of that.

"Will you dance with me? I know it's forbidden, and I heard you turn down every poor bastard who asked you at the barn raisin', but I don't think anyone'll see us up here, and I figure one little dance never hurt anyone."

Hope stared at him for a moment, thinking how wrong he might be. A little dance could hurt her, very much. But it could also turn into a precious memory, the kind that would linger for years after he was gone, and she was still trying to put herself back together.

"I'd love to dance with you, Judah. But there isn't any music."

He stood up off of the window sill, pulling her over toward the center of the room where there was plenty of space, and put his hand on her hip. "You leave that to me."

His feet began to move, and she fell into step with him even before he began to sing. It was soft and low, close to her ear, and his voice was a sweet tenor, clear and true like none she'd ever heard before. He knew every word of the song her daddy used to sing her mama, and as the words rang through the air, Hope couldn't keep the tears out of her eyes. She rested her head on his shoulder and tried to hold in the memory of the way he felt, his scent, his breath on her neck, thinking it all seemed like a dream, and soon enough she'd awake in her bed, and none of it would've been real.

I'll twine 'mid the ringlets of my raven black hair
The lilies so pale and the roses so fair
The myrtle so bright with an emeral hue
And the pale aronatus with eyes of bright blue.

I'll sing and I'll dance, my laugh shall be gay
I'll cease this wild weeping, drive sorrow away.
Tho' my heart is now breaking, he never shall know
That his name made me tremble and my pale cheeks to glow.

I'll think of him never, I'll be wildly gay
I'll charm ev'ry heart, and the crowd I will sway.
I'll live yet to see him regret the dark hour
When he won, then neglected, the frail wildwood flower.

He told me he loved me, and promis'd to love
Trough ill and misfortune, all others above
Another has won him; ah, misery to tell
He left me in silence, no word of farewell.

He taught me to love him, he call'd me his flower
That blossom'd for him all the brighter each hour
But I woke from my dreaming, my idol was clay
My visions of love have all faded away.

WITH THE LAST REFRAIN, Judah stopped, his hand moving from her waist, and as Hope looked up to meet his eyes, his palm caressed her cheek. Her hand flew up to meet it, to hold it there, to hold him there. Through her tears, she could see he was just as pained as she was, and the idea that none of this made any sense rushed to her head. How could he possibly think of leaving, of deserting her when it was obvious he was in love with her, too? Rather than give into the kiss she was certain he was about to press to her lips, she said, "I... can't do this, Judah. I just... can't. If you wanna go, I know I can't talk you out of it. But...." She saw his eyebrows knit together and realized she probably wasn't making any sense. Hope pulled away from him. "I should go."

"Hope, wait," he said, taking a step toward her, but he was confused, and she was a flurry of skirts as she took off for the only exit, thinking she would sort everything out better once she was on solid ground again, once she was out of the reach of those penetrating blue eyes.

She was already through the doorway, searching for the first rung with her boot when she realized he was warning her to be careful. He was right to caution her, she realized. She was distracted and moving too quickly for her own good, but she felt the first rung with her boot, and then the next, and the next, and with each successful step, she picked up speed and confidence, until she reached for another board about halfway down the tree, and it wasn't there. And it wasn't anywhere. Before she realized what was happening, Hope was falling. The last thing she saw before she hit the ground was Judah's eyes wide with fear as he screamed her name—right before everything went black.

CHAPTER TWENTY-TWO

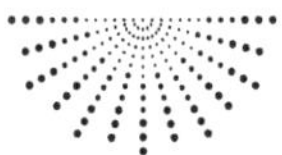

Something was wrong. Before Hope even opened her eyes, she was very aware that there was a pain in her head beyond anything she'd ever felt before, and as her eyes cracked open, and sunlight penetrated her pupils, she squinted against the sharp, pulsating pain that filled her entire skull.

Closing her eyes again, she let out a soft groan and moved her hand to her head. She couldn't remember much of anything, nor could she place where she should be. It seemed like she was in her own room, in her own cabin, but that didn't quite seem right.

"Hope? Are you awake?"

The voice also didn't match her last recollection. It sounded like her mother, and then her father, calling her name, and rushing to her side. Knowing she'd have to open her eyes again to find out for sure, she braced herself and then slowly opened one eye and then the other.

The forms were fuzzy at first, especially since she was peering at them through her long eyelashes. But she would know her mama and daddy anywhere, and when she heard her mother gasp and say, "Thank you, sweet Jesus," another wave of confusion washed over her. Clearly, something had happened, but for the life of her, Hope couldn't figure out what it might be.

"Don't try to move, now," her father insisted, hovering over her. "You've had an awful blow to the head."

"I'll go fetch Doc Howard." The sound of Mr. Canton's voice across the room and then the scurry of footsteps was a fleeting thought before she returned her full attention to her parents.

"What... what happened?" Hope asked, her voice just a croak. "How are you here?"

Her mother sat down beside her on the edge of the bed. "We were sort of hoping you could tell us that first part, Hope. You've had an awful head injury, honey, and no one seems to know what happened. Mrs. Howard sent a telegram near a week ago, urging us to come at once."

"A week ago?" Hope attempted to shoot up in bed but couldn't, and her mother's steady hands would've prevented it even if she'd had the strength. Still, the movement sent another pain through her head, this one even sharper than the last.

"Yes, honey. You've been laid up for almost a week without moving much at all or opening your eyes. Here, have some water." Cordia carefully lifted a glass to her daughter's lips, and Hope drank as much as she could without moving her head too much. The water helped, but she still felt woozy, and every time she moved her head at all, it felt like a railroad tie was being hammered through her skull.

"Do you remember anything at all about where you were or what you were doing?" her mother asked, setting the glass aside.

Hope tried to remember the last thing she'd done before she woke up in bed, but everything was sort of hazy. She could recall finding Ginny's book right after school let out on Friday and wondering if the girl would come and get it, but after that, she couldn't think of anything at all. "I... don't know. How did Mrs. Howard know I'd been injured?"

Her parents exchanged glances, and Hope recognized the expressions on both of their faces. They knew more than they were letting on. Will spoke next, his words measured. "Hope, darling, does the name Judah Lawless mean anything to you?"

All of the oxygen left her lungs as Hope shot up in the bed. Her mother reached out and placed a hand on each shoulder. "Calm down,

Hope, now. Be careful. The doctor said you had an awful bad crack in your skull."

The movement was rewarded with a blinding ache that left her dazed, and Hope inhaled deeply several times before she dared to open her eyes again. When she did, she could see her parents were frightfully concerned for her. "I'm sorry."

"Don't be sorry, honey, just be cautious. We don't wanna go makin' it worse now," her mother insisted.

"Right." She took another deep breath. "Why did you ask about Judah?"

"You do know him, then?" Will asked, taking a step closer to the bed and folding his arms, his lips drawn in a tight line.

"I know him. His niece and nephew are students in my class. We've been sort of... friends, I guess you could say." She examined their faces for a moment. "What does Judah have to do with my head?" She searched back through her memories, but as far as she could tell, the last time she'd seen Judah had been the night he'd told her what had happened to his wives, nearly a month ago.

"He was the one that brought you in to Doc Howard, Hope," Cordia explained. "He said you'd been out at his place, taking a book to his niece, and you fell. That's all he'd say."

Hope did her best to try to reconcile what her mother had just told her with her last memories. It did make sense that she might've decided to take the book out to Ginny. She knew her best student would want to read it over the weekend, and it was possible something had happened while she was there, but what she couldn't make sense of is why Judah wouldn't say more. "Did he say how I fell? What I hit my head on?"

"No," Will said quickly, shaking his head in aggravation. "He wouldn't say anything else at all, and according to Mrs. Howard, when the sheriff come, he wouldn't say a word to the lawman. The only thing the sheriff had to go on was what he'd told the doctor."

Alarmed, Hope attempted to lean in slightly, but she still couldn't move her head without it hurting, though it seemed to be dulling slightly now that she was upright and had learned to expect it a little more. "What do you mean the sheriff came?" she asked, each word measured.

Her parents looked at each other again before her mother said, "Hope, would that man have any reason to try to hurt you? Mrs. Howard says he's a murderer, and it's a wonder you're alive at all."

"What?" Hope exclaimed. She would've come out of the bed if her mother hadn't held her down. Her head was no longer a concern, despite the fact that everything went black for a few seconds before her mother got her re-settled.

"None of that, now Hope." Her father's hands were on her, too, and Hope settled back against the headboard, taking more deep breaths. "I take it you either didn't know that or disagree with the assessment."

"No, I do know." Hope tried to shake her head to clear it and realized that was a bad idea. She raised her hand to the side of her head and felt a thick bandage there. With a huff, she closed her eyes tightly, hoping to find a way to explain herself and calm down at the same time. "What I mean to say is, I know what other people think about Mr. Lawless, but it isn't true. He's not a murderer, Daddy, and he'd never do anything to hurt me. Whatever happened, it had to have been an accident."

"You seem very sure of yourself, darlin'," Cordia said, not letting go of her daughter. "And Mr. Canton seemed surprised as well. He's been here most of every day since you were injured, and he said more than once he wished Judah'd say somethin' to someone, because he didn't think he'd hurt you either. But everyone else...."

"Everyone else is wrong." She had no doubt in her mind that whatever had happened, Judah had not purposely hurt her. She'd be willing to bet everything she had on it. "Where is Judah?"

"He's up at the courthouse, in the jail," her father said, his voice slightly sympathetic but still skeptical. "I tried to talk to him a few days ago, but he wouldn't say anything to me either except for that he was so sorry you were hurt, and he'd take full responsibility. I asked him how you'd gotten hurt, and he wouldn't say. Hope, are you sure you don't recall anything?"

She took a deep breath and closed her eyes, trying to imagine herself with Judah. Had she been inside of his house or outside? Had she stayed to speak to him, or had she left right away? She took it no one else was home or else Ginny or George would've said something about what happened. Try as she might, nothing came to mind. "No, I can't remember anything past finding Ginny's book Friday afternoon."

Cordia let out a sigh and looked at Will, and Hope felt tears coming to her eyes, thinking of Judah, down at the jail. He had to be beside himself, no matter what happened. He was innocent of any crime, she was sure of it. But for the life of her, she couldn't figure out why he wouldn't explain what had transpired. Not that it mattered; they would still accuse him of trying to hurt her. None of it made any sense at all. If he'd been trying to kill her, why would he bring her to the doctor?

Before they could further discuss the situation, she heard her front door open and the sound of hurried footsteps. "Hope, oh thank God!" Nicholas exclaimed, flying in the door. "Why are you sitting up? You should be reclining."

"Doc, I'm fine. Or I will be," she insisted, wanting to ask him to tell her everything he knew, but he already had his medical bag open and was taking her mother's place, pulling Hope's eyes wide open and staring into them.

"How do you feel? Does your head still hurt?"

"Yes, but I'm fine."

He shook his head, clearly not convinced and not liking whatever he'd seen in her eyes. "Look over there. Now back over here. Okay. Up, down." Hope did as she was told. "I believe you still have fluid on your brain, Miss Hope. Your skull was fractured. It'll take it a few months to completely heal. Until then, you need to be in bed."

"In bed? For months? Surely you can't be serious, Nicholas. I'm fine. It just hurts a little." She wasn't being completely honest, of course. Her head hurt almost as badly now as it had when she first woke up, especially since he'd let so much light into her eyes. But she needed to get out of bed and get to the jail to see what was happening with Judah. She certainly didn't trust Sheriff Roan to handle anything judiciously.

"Hope, you just need to rest. Anna's been teachin' school and doin' a good job. The sheriff is handlin' the situation with that scoundrel Lawless. I'm sure the sheriff'll wanna talk to you now that you're awake. But you just need to rest."

"Scoundrel?" Hope repeated. "Nicholas, does it make any sense at all that a person would crack me over the head and then rush me five miles to try to save my life? What kind of an imbecile would do something like that?"

He blanched slightly, but then shrugged and said, "I don't know, Hope, but that's what happened. I've been tellin' you all along to stay away from him. No one said he was a smart murderer."

"That's absolutely ridiculous," Hope said, wanting to shake her head but afraid to do so. "Why in the world did you call the sheriff?"

"What would you have me do? A known murderer brings in a woman bleeding from the head and won't tell me nothin' except for she was out at his place droppin' off a book and fell. He wouldn't even say what ya hit yer head on. I had no choice, Hope."

She narrowed her eyes at him, thinking he most certainly had a choice. "He's not a known murderer, Nicholas. He didn't kill either one of those women."

"How do you know that?" he asked, folding his arms.

"I have the newspaper clippings that say exactly how Sylvia Pembroke Lawless died." It was the first time that Mr. Canton had spoken since returning with the doctor, and Hope turned her head a little too quickly to look at him, having forgotten he was in the room.

"You do?" Cordia asked for all of them, her eyebrows knitting in confusion.

"Course I do," Mr. Canton nodded. "After all, if I was gonna trust my library and part of my funds for buildin' this house to a man, I needed to know a little bit about him. I didn't say nothin' to Judah about it, but I sent for 'em just the same."

"Does it say that she died in a barn fire at a neighbor's place?" Hope asked, certain Mr. Canton could confirm what Judah had told her.

"It does. Says the elderly neighbor set her barn a-blazin' and Mrs. Lawless come over to try to help. By the time Mr. Lawless arrived on the scene, there was nothin' anyone could do. He rushed in and tried to save both of 'em, but they was already gone."

Hope turned her eyes to Nicholas. He looked down for a moment, mulling it over. "That doesn't necessarily mean anythin'."

"It does. You know it does. And he didn't kill his first wife either. Paul's just mad because his sister passed away, and he's tryin' to blame someone. And y'all were foolhardy enough to take what he said in a drunkin' rage and spread it all over town."

"I didn't spread nothin'," Nicholas protested.

"Well, you didn't do anything to stop it. Dr. Howard, thank you for everything you've done to help me when I was injured, but I assure you, I'll be just fine. My mama's here now, and she's a trained nurse. I don't think I'll be needing your services anymore."

"Hope, come on," Nicholas said, shaking his head. "You can't be serious."

"I believe my daughter asked you to leave, Dr. Howard." Will wasn't messing around, and the doctor was smart enough to know better than to irritate an already angry father.

With a deep breath, Nicholas gathered up his belongings, pulling himself to his feet. "You're gonna regret this someday, Hope, you should know that."

"Don't make this somethin' it isn't, Nicholas."

He scoffed, stopping at the foot of the bed. "Ain't it, though, Hope? You think I'm blind? You think Brady didn't come back from that barn raisin' and tell me the two of you was makin' eyes at one another? I should've turned you in to Mr. Stewart right then. They'll string him up; they're already down there, you know? I'll be there to pronounce him when it's all over."

Hope stared after the doctor with her mouth hanging open, unable to believe someone she'd counted as a friend for all of these months would say something so horribly ugly. Once he'd slammed the front door, her mother moved back to where she'd been sitting earlier. "Don't mind him, honey. Jealousy will make a person say some awful things. He'll regret that later."

It took Hope a few more moments to regain her composure. "But he's right, isn't he, Mr. Canton? They very well might try to string Judah up."

Mr. Canton scratched his balding head. "The sheriff's been waitin' on Judge Donald Peppers to arrive from out on the circuit before he does anything, but I have it on good authority that Roan's already said if the judge don't see fit to go to trial, Roan might accidentally leave a few doors unlocked."

Hope's breath caught in her throat. She couldn't believe what she was hearing. She knew the townsfolk weren't fond of Judah, but the fact that they might actually try to lynch him for hurting her was absolutely unthinkable.

"Of course, they was all thinkin' you might expire at any moment. Now that they see you're okay, and you can vouch for the fact that you don't hold any ill-will toward Judah, maybe they'll disperse."

"Maybe," Hope said, thinking it might be possible she could convince them. But she knew there weren't a lot of people in the area who hadn't already decided Judah was a murderer. Convincing them not to take up vigilante justice might be impossible.

"Mrs. Howard wanted me to let her know when you was awake, but now I'm thinkin' I'll hold off on that," Mr. Canton continued.

"Can you think of any reason in the world why Judah wouldn't tell us what happened?" Cordia asked, patting Hope on the leg.

"Yes," she said, placing her hand over the top of her mother's. "I'm certain he was trying to protect me."

"Protect you from what?" Will asked, the concern growing on his face again.

"From Mr. Stewart, the superintendent and school board president."

"And bank president," Canton added, his tone showing his disdain.

"Sounds like he runs the town," Hope's father muttered.

"Why would you need protecting from him?" Cordia's expression also showed her alarm.

"Because he's been wanting to let me go for a few months now, since he found out I was trying to help Mr. Canton win the school board presidency. And if Mr. Stewart had evidence I had been unchaperoned with a single male, like Nicholas was just sayin', then he could force me out for breach of contract."

"I see," Cordia replied, pursing her lips together. "Have you been spending time with Mr. Lawless?"

"Not exactly," Hope said. "I mean, not on purpose anyway. I did see him at the barn raisin' but we didn't even dance together. And then I came out here one night before the house was finished to get a letter I'd left in my drawer, and he was workin' on the cabin. We talked for a few minutes. That's when he told me what happened to his first two wives. So... nothin' for Mr. Stewart to start a scandal over." She wasn't about to admit to her folks in front of Mr. Canton that she'd kissed Judah that night in the woods or that he'd kissed her outside of this very house. And despite the fact that she knew for certain she hadn't danced with Judah that night at the barn raising, for some reason, she had a distinct memory of twirling around in his arms, though she couldn't place it. Flashes invaded her mind's eye--of his smile, her hand in his, pressing her cheek to his shoulder, but she couldn't put it all together. She wondered if it had anything at all with what had happened the day she'd been injured.

"Maybe if I go back to the courthouse and talk to him, tell him yer awake, he'll let us know what happened, especially if he knows that yer willin' to own up to speakin' with him a few times in private. You are, aren't you?" her daddy asked.

"Yes, of course I am. I'd do anything to get him out of jail." Her father nodded, a look of pride on his face. To Hope, there was no question. Even if she never taught again, she'd tell the world every last detail of every conversation she'd ever had with Judah if it got him out of jail.

"Well, I suppose I should head back up there."

"No, Daddy, wait," Hope insisted. "I wanna go with you."

"Hope, honey, you can't do that," Cordia insisted, smoothing back her hair on the side of her head opposite her wound. "You've had a horrible head injury. You have to stay in bed."

Hope stared into her mother's eyes, tipping her head only slightly. "Now, I know the Cordia Pike Tucker who drove to Springfield by herself to check on her beloved didn't just say that to me."

Her father chuckled, and her mother's eyes widened. "I wasn't alone. Frieda was with me."

"And I won't be alone either. My folks'll be with me. But you know you're wastin' your breath tellin' me to stay here."

"I think that settles that," Will said, and Cordia let go a sigh of acceptance. "I'll go hitch up the horses."

"And I'll go find those newspaper articles for Sheriff Roan," Mr. Canton said.

"Best hold on to those and wait for the judge," Hope advised. "You give 'em to Roan and they're liable to disappear.

"Good point," Mr. Canton replied, slowing his pace.

"And Mr. Canton?" He stopped and turned to look at Hope. "Thank you so much—for everything."

"My pleasure, dear. You are by far the finest teacher I've ever known, and one of the best people. I'm so glad you're feeling better." He smiled at her and then continued on his way, and Hope said a little prayer thanking God for such an intelligent, kind-hearted man to be on their side.

"Well, I guess we need to get you dressed," Cordia muttered, standing. "I must say, though, I think this is a bad idea."

"That's all right, Mama. Bad ideas are generally worth it when they serve a higher purpose."

Cordia stopped halfway to the closet and turned to look at her daughter. "And what purpose would that be, honey?"

"I love him, Mama." The words flowed from her mouth as the gospel truth, and she'd never been more sure of anything in her entire life.

"Ain't no purpose higher than that," Cordia assured her with a nod before she turned back to the closet to find something for Hope to wear. Hope agreed with the sentiment, though it did cross her mind that there was a distinct possibility Judah did not feel the same way about her. But if that was the case, she'd have to deal with that later. For now, her sole objective was to get him released from jail. Any repercussions would have to be faced another time.

CHAPTER TWENTY-THREE

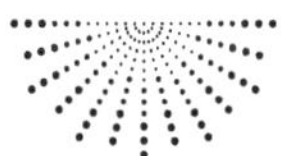

There was a crowd outside of the courthouse, and as soon as Hope saw it, her stomach lurched up into her throat. It might've only been twenty or thirty people, but she knew why they were there. The handful of lawmen keeping them at bay was only mildly reassuring as her father found a place to hitch the wagon and then came around to carefully lift her out of the seat. Her head was still aching, but her mother had given her some medicine, and it was helping. If it didn't make her sleepy or groggy until after she figured out what their next step needed to be, and until after she'd hopefully had a chance to speak to Judah, then she wouldn't regret taking it.

If the people in the crowd noticed her, their dispositions didn't change any, and Hope thought it was just as well until after she'd had a chance to speak to Judah. The last thing she needed was a rush of deputies trying to keep her away from his cell.

The courthouse was just as imposing on the inside as it was on the outside. Luckily, Will had been there earlier in the week and knew exactly where to go. He took Hope by the hand and led her past offices and other official looking rooms to a side hall that led to the jail.

Hope had never actually been inside of a jail before, though there was a small one in Lamar she'd been past a few times. Once again, she found her stomach in knots. She prayed she'd have a chance to talk to Judah. Maybe he would tell her what happened or at least say something to jog her memory.

Inside, there was a desk across from a few cells. Hope's eyes immediately flew across the faces of the occupants, but Judah wasn't one of them. There were just a few men who looked like they'd probably gotten picked up on public intoxication charges the night before. One of them had a bloodied lip. She steered clear of them and followed her father across the room, her hand still tight in his, to the desk.

"Why, if it isn't Miss Tucker! Thank the good Lord!" Deputy Forester shouted, leaping up from his seat. "We sure have been worried about you, young lady."

"Deputy Forester, it is so nice to see you," Hope said, smiling in return. "Thank you for your prayers. They must've worked. I'm feeling much better now."

"I'm so glad to hear that. My daughter Jess will be glad to know her teacher's all right. Have you seen the sheriff? He'll wanna know right away."

"Sure is good to see you," another deputy, one Hope knew from church, by the name of Cal Huckley said with a smile that displayed he was missing a front tooth.

"Thank you, Deputy Huckley," Hope said, smiling at him in turn. "No, I haven't seen the sheriff yet, but I'm looking forward to explaining things to him. You see, deputies, this has all been a mistake. Mr. Lawless didn't do anything to me. It was an accident."

"An accident?" Forester repeated, looking across the room to Huckley who was just walking over. "You don't say?"

"Yes, that's right. Mr. Lawless would never hurt anyone. All of those stories about his past are false. Mr. Canton has documentation to prove he didn't hurt his wife in Manhattan, Kansas, and he's on his way to get it right now."

"Well, if that don't beat all," Huckley said, slapping his leg. "I told the sheriff that rock was too big to bash anyone over the head with."

"I thought the same," Forester commented.

Hope took that in and nodded, even though she wasn't quite sure what they were talking about. Her parents exchanged glances but didn't say anything. Hope realized the deputies likely never met her mother and did a quick introduction of both of her parents before asking, "Did the two of you go out to the Pembroke place and have a look around?"

"I did," Forester nodded. "Along with the sheriff and several other deputies. Huckley stayed here to man the place."

"Sure was hard, too. Soon as folks heard, they wanted to lynch 'im right away." Huckley shook his head, and Hope fought the bile rising in her throat.

"I thank you for keeping them from doing that," Hope said with a nod. "What in the world made the sheriff think that Mr. Lawless could lift such a heavy rock and hit me in the head with it before I could get away?" She hoped they would say something to give her a clue as to what they were speaking of.

"Well, I don't rightly know. I told 'im, it looked to me like Mr. Lawless was right. That rock sure did have blood on it, but it was buried in the ground so deep, and it didn't look disturbed. Looked to me like what Mr. Lawless said to Doc Howard was the God's honest truth, that ye jest fell." Forester scratched his chin as he thought it over.

"Course it would've helped if Mr. Lawless would've said somethin', anything, to the sheriff, but he ain't said a word to no one 'cept his sister and your pa since we brought 'im in. And all he said to them was that he was sorry, which didn't help much," Huckley added.

"Now, tell us what did happen," Forester insisted. "You went out there to return a book and fell and hit yer head on that rock? But what was you doin' in the back yard?"

"In the back yard?" Hope repeated, thinking as hard as she could. Why would she have gone into the back yard? "You know, Deputy Forester, it is all a little hazy, but I think there was something I wanted to see back there." She had no idea what it might've been, but if the barn was there, maybe an animal. Or maybe she'd had to go around back to find someone? Was it possible no one came to the door?

"I betcha a day's wages it was that giant treehouse," Huckley said, removing his hat and running a hand through greasy dark hair. "Sounds like that was somethin' else."

"That's exactly what I was wondering when I noticed it," Forester agreed. "I come back and told Huckley all about it. Largest treehouse I ever did see."

"Treehouse?" Hope repeated as her mind flooded with images. She could see it, too, and the more she thought about it, the more she realized exactly what had happened. It all hit her like a wave, and if her father's arm hadn't been around her shoulders, she might've buckled in half right there in the jailhouse. "Yes, that's exactly what it was!" She knew she couldn't tell them precisely what had happened because it wasn't their business, and she didn't want to disclose any personal details. A memory of Judah's arms around her, his soft voice in her ear as they swayed back and forth across the treehouse floor invaded her thoughts, and she had to close her eyes for a moment.

"Are you all right, Hope?" her mother asked, her hand on Hope's arm.

"I'm fine, Mama. But they're right. I saw the treehouse from the road as I was pullin' in, and I asked Mr. Lawless if I could go up and see the view. I hadn't ever seen anythin' like it before either. He let me go up, against his better judgment, and when I was comin' back down, I didn't wait on him like he tried to tell me. And I fell." There was no need to tell them she was running away from Judah before he had a chance to further damage her heart or that it had been his idea for her to go up in the treehouse to begin with.

"Well, I'll be," Deputy Forester said. "Why didn't he just say that?"

"Maybe he did," Hope replied. "I know he told Doc Howard I fell, though I'm not certain if he said where from. But, I'm not sure if you folks realize this or not, but Doc Howard's been sweet on me since the day I stepped foot in this town, and outta jealousy, he tried to make it seem like more. I suppose Mr. Lawless didn't say nothin' about me bein' up there in the treehouse with just him because it would be a violation of my teaching contract to be alone with a single man, even though nothin' happened."

"That does make sense," Hockley agreed, adjusting his pants by running his thumb behind his belt. "And Mr. Stewart and Sheriff Roan are good friends. I bet Mr. Lawless was afraid Stewart'd let you go."

"I'm certain he would," Hope agreed. "But I'm more worried about Mr. Lawless at the moment. Seeing him locked up for something he didn't do just isn't right. I'm willing to risk my position to see him set free."

"Miss Tucker, yer the best schoolteacher we could've ever hoped for. Jess just loves you. She's cried over you every night since this happened. If Mr. Stewart tried to let you go, he'd have a lot of angry parents on his hands." Forester shook his head as he spoke, and his eyes let Hope know he meant each word.

"I appreciate that, Deputy Forester. I am eager to see all of my students again and let them know I'm all right. But I'll need the both of you to help me convince Sheriff Roan to let Mr. Lawless go."

"We heard Judge Peppers should be here shortly 'bout an hour ago. Maybe when he hears what you have to say, he'll set Lawless free. Judge Peppers is a fair man by all accounts." Huckley offered a small smile, and Hope felt slightly better, hoping he was right.

"That's good to hear." She looked at her father, who nodded reassuringly, and let out a deep breath. Turning back to Forester, she asked, "Did you say Mrs. Pembroke had been in to see her brother? Do you know where she is now?"

"Well, I don't know for sure, but I heard she was at home with the children while she sent her husband to try to track down a lawyer from Fort Worth. They didn't think no one from around here would be able to do a fair job. Course, that was a couple of days ago, and I'd a thunk he'd be back by now."

"We'll make sure he has a good lawyer if he needs one, Hope," Will said, his voice low, and she knew if it was necessary, her daddy would do whatever needed to be done to get one. He'd know the law well enough to get by, she assumed, because of his dealings with the bank. She thought it was slightly ironic that her father, the bank president from home, might be squaring off with Mr. Stewart, the bank president here in McKinney, but it was just a testimony to the kind of power that office incurred—and how, when a corrupt man took office, everything could go awry.

"Them poor kids is probably beside themselves," Hockley muttered.

Hope couldn't bear to think of poor Ginny and George. Caroline was probably upset that she couldn't be there with Judah, but then, she'd have no one to leave her children with. Who knows what the crazy townsfolk might try to do?

"Deputies, would it be at all possible for me to speak to Mr. Lawless for just a few moments? I'm certain he must be worried about me, and he likely won't believe I'm all right unless he sees me for himself."

The two deputies exchanged glances. "Well, Miss Tucker, we're under strict direction from the sheriff not to let nobody down there...."

"Down there?" Hope repeated. "Where is he?"

"He's in solitary, in the basement," Forester replied with a gulp. Hope looked at her father and realized he'd known this all along, but she couldn't blame him for not mentioning it. The news would just upset her.

"Please, Deputy Forester. I'll only be a few minutes." She didn't want to set a time limit because she realized once she saw Judah, it would be difficult to pull herself away, but she wanted to assure them that they wouldn't get caught. At least, she hoped not. She needed the cooperation of these two men who seemed to think she'd remembered what happened from the beginning. Doc could attest to a different story, but he'd have no way of knowing she hadn't remembered until the deputies had mentioned the treehouse.

Once again, the men looked at each other before Forester finally said, "All right. But just for a minute." Hockley nodded in agreement, and Forester reached into a drawer in the desk and took out a keyring that looked to be for special purposes. He picked up a lantern off of a shelf and lit it, and Hope pulled away from her parents.

"Are you sure you want to go alone?" Cordia asked in a steely whisper.

"I'm sure, Mama. I'll be fine." There were things she needed to say to Judah that didn't require an audience.

Forester unlocked a door near the other cells, holding it open for her, and Hope stepped through, though she waited for the man to squeeze past her in order to illuminate the walkway. The staircase wound down into the basement, and Hope felt like she was headed toward a dungeon.

It wasn't far, though, and eventually, she found herself in a musty hallway. There was another door with a lantern lit next to it, and through bars in a window in the top of the door she could see another lantern inside, though it seemed to be the only light. Forester unlocked the second door and said quietly, "You won't have much time."

"Thank you," Hope replied with a nod, wishing she'd remember not to move her head, and she stepped through the door into near darkness, holding her breath and bracing herself for what was to come.

CHAPTER TWENTY-FOUR

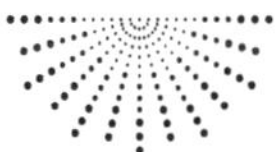

There were no windows in the basement cell, and the light from the lantern cast long shadows along the floor and up the far wall. Judah was standing with his back to her and didn't even turn around when she stopped in front of the small cage where they'd been holding him for nearly a week.

It was inhumane to say the least. His room contained a mat on the floor, a tattered blanket, and a bucket. Hope thought if she laid down on the floor inside the cell, she could likely touch all four walls at once. And he'd suffered all of this on account of her.

She didn't want to startle him, but since he hadn't moved at all since she'd entered, and she'd been standing there for several seconds, she finally decided to just say something. Maybe once he realized it was her, he'd come back to reality. "Judah?"

His head flinched, and his shoulders straightened, as if he couldn't believe his ears. When he turned to face her, it was slow, cautious, but as soon as his eyes fell on her face and he saw that he wasn't hearing things, and she really was standing before him, he made the few steps it took to reach her in a hurry. "Hope?" He reached through the bars and gently touched her face on the side away from the bandage. "Is it really you? Oh, my God! Hope, I thought you were gone!" His other hand was around her waist, and he pulled her as close as he could until she was pressed up to the bars, being careful of her injury all the while.

Tears cascaded down her cheeks as a laugh mingled with a sob and escaped her lips. "It's me," she assured him. A look of relief washed over him, and his blue eyes filled with tears as his hands swept over her, brushing back her hair and caressing her cheek. "I'm alive."

"Thank God," he said again. "I thought for sure...."

He didn't finish the sentence, and she was glad because she knew he'd thought if she died it was his fault. She reached through the bars then and snaked her hand around his waist, wanting to touch him as much as he needed to feel that she was real. He pressed his lips to her forehead, and Hope slid her hand up to the back of his neck. Without a second thought, his mouth found hers, and Hope cursed the bars that separated them. Despite the inconvenience, she relished the taste of him, his scent, the fact that his arms were around her again. Her tears mingled with his as he continued to kiss her and it wasn't until his hand grazed her bandage that he finally pulled back. "How are you?" he asked, not moving away at all but looking into her eyes.

"I'm all right," she said even though all of the movement had sparked a fresh ache in her head. "Doc says my skull is fractured, but it'll heal."

"Thank the good Lord for that. I thought you were gonna die, Hope. Your head was bleedin' so much, and you wouldn't open your eyes."

"I know. Thank you for taking me to the doctor. If you hadn't, I probably wouldn't have made it." She ran her hand down the front of his shirt, seeing that there were bloodstains on it and thinking how savage it was that they hadn't even allowed his sister to bring him fresh clothes. "But none of that matters now. We just need to get you out of here."

Judah dropped his eyes. "I'm not sure that's possible at this point, Hope. They've been trying to lynch me for days. Sheriff Roan would love to set up the gallows himself."

"Well, Judge Peppers is on the way, and I'm not gonna let that happen. Look, those folks're mad because they think you did this on purpose, but once I tell them the truth, that I fell of my own accord, they'll disband, I'm sure of it. Besides, Mr. Canton has newspaper clippings that show you didn't harm Sylvia either. They're wanting to make you into something you ain't, and I'm not gonna let 'em."

"Well, I see they have messed with the wrong schoolteacher," he mused, and Hope felt fire coming into her cheeks for a different reason altogether. "I am so very sorry that this even happened, Hope. It was my fault, whether it was an accident or not. I never should've let you go down by yourself."

"It wasn't your fault at all!" Hope shot back. "I should've listened to you and waited. I was the idiot who thought climbing down a tree in a long skirt was a good idea."

"You wouldn't have rushed off if I hadn't been acting like a fool," he reminded her.

Hope hadn't had the chance to think about exactly why she was rushing away from him, but his words brought the scene back to her now. He'd danced with her, sang the song her father used to sing to her and her mother, "I'll Twine 'Mid the Ringlets," and then she thought he was going to kiss her. She'd taken off because she was confused and didn't want to get hurt again. In a way, perhaps he was right, but that didn't make the fall his fault—it was an accident. "I think you need to stop blamin' yourself for everything that happens to the people you love. You seem to be of the opinion that you're cursed or something, Judah, and that just ain't the case. You've had a lot of horrible things happen to people that you care about, but what happened to me wasn't an act of God or a punishment. It wasn't the devil stickin' his hand in where it don't belong. It was me rushing off in a tizzy and gettin' my feet tangled up, and that's all. If you're about to tell me that we can't be together because somethin' bad might happen to me, then you best think again."

His eyes widened, and he leaned back slightly to take her in, though his hands never left where they'd come to rest on her waist. "Exactly what are you sayin' Hope Tucker?"

"I'm sayin' we're meant to be together, and you need to stop runnin' from it." The courage was flowing through her blood vessels now, and she continued to speak as if he was the one she'd come there to convince a travesty had been committed and not the judge or the sheriff. "You can't kiss me one moment and then tell me you're leavin' the next, Judah Lawless. I won't stand for it."

He stared at her for a long moment before a crooked grin spread across his face. "I'm not sure exactly what happened when you hit yer head, Hope, but this is different. I think I like it."

"Good. Because you're gonna have to put up with me for a while, Judah Lawless. Because I love you. And you love me. And don't you dare deny it."

"You what now?" he asked, his eyes growing even larger. He tipped his head forward as if he hadn't heard right the first time.

Hope took a deep breath and grabbed ahold of the bars in front of her with both hands. "I said I love you. You already knew that. And you love me, too. I can tell it by the way you look at me, so don't be saying that you don't."

His smile broadened again, and he slowly began to nod his head. "All right. I won't."

Inhaling through her nose, Hope tried not to think about what she'd just said as all of the gumption seemed to flow right out of her, and she realized her hands were shaking. "You won't... what?"

"I won't deny it. I love you, Hope Tucker."

She swallowed hard, glad to finally hear the words. "I know." Her voice had a quiver to it she hoped he didn't pick up on. "I just said that."

"But I kinda like the sound of it. Can you say your part again?"

"What? When I threatened you a moment ago--or the other part?" she asked, beginning to smile back at him as the nerves left her.

"No, the other part."

She cleared her throat. "Oh. That part. I said... I love you, Judah. I do. And there's nothin' you can do to stop me."

"Good. I'm tired of fighting it. I figure if you can survive falling out of a tree, then maybe my curse is broken."

"Or maybe there isn't a curse at all, and you've just been unfortunate in the past. But all of that's behind you now."

He nodded, and she slowly ran her hand down the front of his shirt again, realizing they were almost out of time. "What about the school?" he asked resting his forehead against the bars in front of them. "If we tell them the truth, Stewart'll fire you on the spot."

"I know. I don't care. I mean... I do, but you're more important. If we tell everyone that Mr. Canton commissioned my house, and I ask the folks to vote for him, they will. But you were leaving."

"I was," he agreed, his voice almost a whisper now.

"And I think that's probably for the best. I think... even if everyone believes our story, this isn't the place for you. They're all brainwashed against you."

"You could come with me," he said, looking her in the eyes. "After a proper ceremony, of course."

Hope's heart caught for a moment as she thought about what he was saying. "What do you mean?" she asked, completely unprepared for the possibility he was presenting to her now.

"Nothin'," he said, though she saw a flicker of mischief in his eyes. "Is yer Pa still around?"

Hope could put two and two together and replied, "He's upstairs with my mama."

"That's good to know. Let's just take things one step at a time for now, all right? I still gotta get out of this hellhole before we can talk about a future together, but Hope, you're right. I'm tired of trying to run away from you. I ain't never met anyone like you in my whole life, and I've been sitting here for nearly a week thinking I'd killed you, too. I didn't tell them what happened mostly because I didn't care to live anymore. I figured a world without you in it was no place for me either, so I was just gonna let the good Lord set things in motion as He saw fit. Now, with you standing in front of me, I know for sure, wherever I go, I need you with me. I do love you, Hope, more than I've ever loved anyone. And I promise, from now on, I'll keep you safe until my dying breath."

Hope couldn't think of a single word to say, so she leaned forward and pressed her lips to his through the bars and hoped he'd understand that everything he'd said was encompassed in her kiss. This was a love worth fighting for, and even if she had to convince the entire world of his innocence, she'd find a way because there was no doubt in her mind, she was meant to be with Judah for the rest of her life.

The rattle of keys caught her attention, and Hope pulled away, though she was fairly sure Deputy Forester had heard most of their conversation. He had a sheepish grin on his face as he said, "Miss Tucker, I'm afraid we should head upstairs now."

"All right, Deputy." With one last look at Judah she said, "I'll get you out of here. Soon. I promise."

"I believe you." He didn't tell her again that he loved her, but he didn't need to because Hope could see it in his eyes.

CHAPTER TWENTY-FIVE

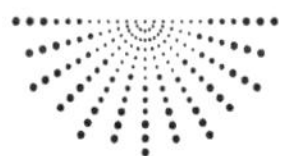

Hope sat on a wooden bench in a small office off of the main courtroom. Her head ached and she had a crick in her neck, but she'd rather be sitting in here waiting on Judge Peppers than standing outside. Confronting the angry crowd had been terrifying, but as soon as they saw it was her, they'd all stopped shouting, and an eerie silence had fallen over them. Hope had spoken her mind, though she was afraid her voice hadn't traveled to the back of the throng. She'd told them all Judah hadn't done anything, that she'd fallen, just like he'd said. She went on to say he hadn't killed either of his wives either, and they had proof, though she didn't elaborate, and before long, the crowd dispersed, most of them shouting that they were glad she was okay. She might've taken the opportunity to tell them that they should all vote for Mr. Canton, too, but she decided that might be a bit too much. She was left standing with her parents and about ten deputies who suddenly found themselves without much to do.

One of them walked her inside of the courthouse and told her to wait there, and as soon as Judge Peppers arrived, he'd let the magistrate know she was waiting. He didn't seem too concerned that someone would have to relay to Sheriff Roan, who was at the saloon, running things of course, not drinking, that the schoolteacher had awoken and spoiled all of his plans for a lynching.

And so she waited, leaning her head on her daddy's shoulder. Neither of her parents had asked her much of anything when she came back upstairs, only if she was okay, and she assured them she was. Under normal circumstances, Judah's words would've brought a smile to her face, but until he was free, she was too filled with worry to be overjoyed.

The sound of the door opening startled her, and Hope shot up. While she was glad to see Caroline's familiar face, along with Mr. Canton, she was disappointed it wasn't the judge. Still, Judah's sister closed the gap between them quickly, and if it wasn't for Cordia's arm keeping her down in her seat, Hope would've jumped up to hug her.

"Hope, thank the good Lord you're all right! I was so relieved when Mr. Canton showed up to give me the news. How are you?"

"I'm all right," Hope assured her. "I'm glad to see you. How are the children?"

"They're better now that they know you're gonna make it. I took 'em over to Melissa's and then rode in with Mr. Canton. Paul ain't back yet." She made a face that let her know she didn't quite trust her husband, which Hope thought was a shame, but it did seem like he should've been back a long time ago if he was only going to Fort Worth. It wasn't that far. "Have you seen Judah?"

Hope lowered her voice. There was a deputy over by the door, and it wasn't one of the ones who'd let her into the basement. She wasn't sure whether or not he could be trusted. "I have. He's relieved, but I shouldn't say more." She made a small gesture toward the deputy, and Caroline caught on.

"I have the newspaper clippings," Mr. Canton assured her. "I think it'll be enough to persuade the judge that Mr. Lawless doesn't make a habit of hurtin' young women."

"I have every report back home," Caroline said, her face bleak. "I kept 'em all. So, if he needs any more proof...."

Hope felt relieved. She had visions of Sheriff Roan or Mr. Stewart bursting in and ripping the articles to shreds, though she thought that seemed ridiculous even for them. She couldn't even imagine what Mr. Stewart would be doing in the courtroom.

"You may as well have a seat," she said, gesturing to the other side of her daddy. "They say the judge should be here soon."

Caroline let out a deep breath and did as was suggested. Hope could see her fingernails were chewed to the nub and couldn't blame her. Judah's sister had deep, blue bags under her eyes, and her hair was sticking out every which way like she'd just tried to scoop it into a bun before she ran out of the house, and it hadn't quite stayed where she'd put it.

Silence overcame them again, and Hope was about to doze off when she heard more footsteps. This time, the heaviness of them let her know the people coming were male, and she opened her eyes to see a tall, older man in a cowboy hat walk in, followed by Sheriff Roan and Mr. Stewart.

"Well, Miss Tucker!" Mr. Stewart said, his smile seeming more than a little forced. "I'd heard you'd recovered. It's nice to see it's true."

"Yes, I'm just fine, Mr. Stewart," Hope replied, managing to stand up with the help of her parents. "Thank you for your concern. I assure you, this can all be explained easily enough, and then, I think you'll all see why Mr. Lawless is completely innocent."

"Miss Tucker, that man tried to murder you," Sheriff Roan chimed in before anyone else could speak.

"No, he didn't," Hope protested, trying to keep her voice steady. "Not at all."

"If y'all don't mind, I would like to hear what Miss Tucker has to say, but first, I'm gonna have a seat at this desk over here." Judge Peppers was at least a head taller than all of the other men, and no one even thought of disagreeing with him. He ambled over to the desk in front of where Hope and her family had been waiting and had a seat, giving a loud sigh. Hope imagined it'd been a long journey for him.

No one said anything at all for several minutes, and Hope debated whether or not she should sit back down or rush over and be heard. Her parents looked at a loss as well, and just when she was about to resume her position on the bench, Judge Peppers said, "Now, I have heard Sheriff Roan's version of what has transpired, Miss Tucker, but I would like to hear from you. And only from you. Everyone else, have a seat. Miss Tucker, are you able to stand or shall I have them bring you a chair."

"I am able to stand, thank you," she replied, but Mr. Canton was already out the door, and a moment later, he returned with a wooden chair for her which he placed in front of the desk. Hope sat down, even though she thought she might be more comfortable standing. She took a deep breath, not sure if she should begin or wait for the judge to ask her a question.

"Now, before you speak, keep in mind, this is sorta like a hearing in that you need to tell me the whole truth of the matter, Miss Tucker. You wouldn't lie under oath, so don't tell me any untruths now, you hear?"

"Yes, Your Honor," Hope replied, trying to sound sure of herself. "I understand."

"Very good. Now, why don't you tell me exactly what you remember."

"Well, Friday afternoon—that is, I suppose that would be last Friday now—I was cleaning up my classroom, and I noticed a book on the floor. When I saw that it belonged to one of my students who loves to read, I decided I'd take it to her the next day. So Saturday morning, around ten, I believe, I took the book and rode out to her house in my pony trap."

Hope tried to ignore the fact that Mr. Stewart and the others were even in the room. She'd tell as much of the story as necessary without revealing too much. "When I got to the Pembroke house, I noticed a treehouse in the back yard and thought it looked intriguing. It was larger than any other treehouse I've ever seen." She cleared her throat, hoping he couldn't tell she'd embellished slightly there. "When I went to the door, no one was home except for Mr. Lawless. He and I have spoken to each other on a few occasions, and he is always polite and kind. I handed him the book and mentioned the treehouse. He seemed reluctant to show it to me, but he did just the same. We climbed up the treehouse, and I looked at the spectacular view. He warned me a few times to let him go down first, but I realized I may be considered in violation of my teaching contract because, technically, I suppose Mr. Lawless is a single man, though he is in fact a widower. At any rate, when I realized the situation, I took off down the boards hammered into the side of the tree as steps. I thought the first step would be the hardest, and with each one, my confidence grew. Mr. Lawless shouted at me to be careful, but I thought for sure I could manage. Then, I remember, my foot slipped, and the next thing I knew, I woke up back in my bed, and nearly a week had gone by." Hope took a deep breath, glad to have that over with.

The judge listened to each word. "When you awoke, Miss Tucker, did you immediately recall all of that?"

"Oh, no, not at first," she admitted. "I'd had such a horrible blow to my head, it took me about an hour for it all to come back. At first, all I recalled was finding the book, and then I remembered taking it out to Ginny Pembroke. Eventually, the rest of the details came back to me."

"I see," Judge Peppers said. His hands were steepled in front of his face, and Hope couldn't get a read on him, no matter how hard she tried. After a few moments, he let out a long breath and said, "Sheriff Roan?"

The sheriff jumped to attention and came over. "Yes, Yer Honor?"

"Will you kindly explain to me why in the world you thought it was necessary for me to travel halfway across the county for this situation? Clearly, what transpired was nothin' more than an accident, and you was ready to let the crowd lynch a man for simply helpin' a girl to the doctor."

"But Yer Honor," Roan protested, "This man ain't just any man. He was involved in the deaths of two former wives. While Miss Tucker might think she recalls what happened, my men found a large rock out in the yard, and we're certain he used it to bash her head in."

"Where is this rock?" the judge asked, though he looked annoyed more than anything else.

"I'll go fetch it from the other room right now." Roan jumped to attention and scurried off, and Peppers shook his head, his eyes following the stout man out the door.

"Your Honor, if I may," Hope said quietly, "Mr. Canton has newspaper clippings that will clearly show that Mr. Lawless was not involved in the death of his second wife, and his sister can attest to the fact that he didn't kill his first wife either. This is nothin' more than a witch hunt, Sir."

Judge Peppers didn't seem to have a doubt in his mind, but he turned to look at the bench. "Which of you is Canton?"

"I am, Your Honor." The slight man lifted a finger.

"Well, let me see."

Mr. Canton pulled the clippings from the breast pocket of his jacket as he came across the room. He laid them on the desk and stood with his hands folded in front of him. Peppers only glanced at them, made a small humming noise, and then handed them back. "Thank you. You can be seated."

As Mr. Canton took his seat, Judge Peppers looked at Caroline. "You the sister?"

"Yes, Sir."

"Your brother ever kill anyone?"

"No, Your Honor," Caroline replied without hesitation. Hope was glad she didn't feel inclined to tell the specific truth about Isabella.

Before Judge Peppers could say more, the door came open, and Roan came in, lugging the large rock. "Here it is, Your Honor."

Peppers raised a hand to his forehead and began to shake his head. "You want me to believe a man picked that boulder up off of the ground and hit this young lady in the head with it?"

"Well, yes, Your Honor. See, there's blood all over it." He set the rock down on the desk with a thunk, and Hope was shocked to see just how much of her blood covered the top of it.

"Get it out of here," Peppers replied with a sigh.

"But, Your Honor... surely you can't think that we've overreacted. We have a young lady with a head injury, one the doctor thought would never awake, a suspect who wouldn't say nothin' with a history of involvement in nefarious activities."

"What you have is an unfortunate accident, Sheriff Roan," Peppers said, pulling himself to his feet. "And a town that wants a lynching! Why he didn't say anythin' I don't know. Maybe he was tryin' to protect her virtue. But I don't have enough information to take this young man to trial. So... take your boulder there, and release him into the custody of his sister, you hear me, Roan? And the next time you wanna interrupt my regular circuit for some ridiculous made up crime, you best think twice about it!"

Roan was clearly agitated, but he didn't argue. He took the rock and headed for the door, attempting to balance it on his hip and nearly dropping it. Hope let go a loud sigh of relief, but she knew this wasn't quite over yet. Roan had to actually unlock the cell.

Judge Peppers turned back to Hope. "I am sorry you were injured, miss, but it looks like you'll be all right now. Best of luck to you."

"Thank you so much, Your Honor," Hope replied, reaching for the hand that he offered, hoping he realized she meant for more than his good wishes.

He tipped his hat at her mother and Caroline before walking out the door, and Hope stood with tears in her eyes thankful for the victory. The rest of the room erupted in hugs and cheers, except for Mr. Stewart who was left fuming.

"Do you think they'll actually let him out without a fight?" Hope asked as her mother wrapped her arms around her.

"I sure hope so," Caroline replied. "The children will be so happy to see him."

"Miss Tucker, I hate to interrupt your jubilation, but you do realize you have broken your teaching contract, don't you?" Mr. Stewart asked, stepping into Hope's line of sight.

"I suppose by the strict letter of the contract that's true, Mr. Stewart, but I'm not sure it matters much. You may go ahead and begin your search for another schoolteacher."

"What's that, Hope?" Caroline asked, and Hope looked from one surprised face to the next.

"Yes, that's right. I won't be staying in McKinney. As much as I love my students, and as much as I appreciate all that you've done for me in particular, Mr. Canton, I can't stay in a town that would treat Mr. Lawless so unfairly. So... I'll be leaving soon enough."

"Where will you go?" Mr. Canton asked, clearly disappointed, though he seemed to understand.

"I'm not rightly sure," Hope admitted. "But wherever it is, it'll be someplace where a person is free to enjoy the present, dream of the future, and not have to suffer from the ghosts of their pasts." Caroline had tears in her eyes as she wrapped her arms around Hope, both hopeful the nightmare would finally be over soon.

Mr. Stewart walked off in a huff, and Hope had the feeling he wouldn't be the last angry person she saw that day, but none of it mattered so long as Judah had his freedom. The rest of them followed behind, Hope praying the whole time that there wouldn't be any difficulty getting Judah out of the prison cell.

When they arrived at the jail, she was shocked to see Deputy Forester coming up from the basement with Judah behind him. Forgetting all about her aching head, Hope ran to Judah, and he opened his arms wide for her, embracing her tightly as tears misted both of their eyes. "You did it, Hope," he whispered, kissing her temple on her uninjured side.

"All I did was tell the truth," she replied, looking him in the eye. Then, lowering her voice slightly, she added, "Well, mostly."

"I was a fool for ever trying to run away from you, Hope. I promise, it'll never happen again."

"I'm holding you to that, Judah Lawless," Hope replied with a twinkle in her eye. He leaned down and found her lips with his, and she was certain life might not always be easy, but they would find a way together no matter the circumstances. After all, her mother had named her Hope for a reason, and as long as she had that, everything else would come in good time.

EPILOGUE

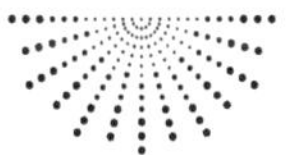

"Now class, repeat your sums as they are written on the board," Mrs. Hope Lawless instructed as she stood in front of her class of twenty-five students. The students answered in unison, and she smiled proudly at them as they read off the addition problems in loud, clear voices.

It had been almost a year since she and Judah had married and moved to Morganville, Kansas, and while it hadn't been easy for either one of them to say goodbye to the children, it had been for the better. Now that he was gone, the Pembrokes had been welcomed back into the community, and Anna had taken over as the schoolteacher. Ginny wrote Hope once a week, and she was still excelling at her lessons because Anna was an exceptional teacher—though Ginny insisted not as good as Miss Tucker.

Anna had sent an invitation to Hope asking her to attend her wedding to Brady, but Hope hadn't taken her up on the offer. Since Mr. Canton had won the school board president election, Anna was allowed to marry and keep her position. Of course, Mr. Stewart had remained superintendent of schools, which was contentious for everyone, but he seemed to accept Anna Wilcox Howard much better than he ever had Hope, and from all accounts, the school was doing quite well. As for the Howards, Nita had written to Hope, and they were on friendly terms again now, but if she went the rest of her life without seeing Doc or Brady again, that would be fine with Hope.

The house Judah built for Hope in Morganville was far larger and more elaborate than anything she'd ever dreamt of, but then, she hoped one day they'd fill it with children, and then it would make sense for it to be so big she had to holler at him from the kitchen if he was in the front of the house. He was busy putting up all sorts of buildings around their thriving town without a worry at all about what rumors might be spread about him. Folks here knew nothing of his past, but Hope had a feeling even if they did, there wouldn't be any speculation of fault on his part without Paul and his need to lay blame where none was due. She prayed for Paul Pembroke every night, hoping he'd find some solace in his sister's memory and leave his bitterness behind.

It had been difficult saying goodbye to her parents again, but they were much closer now than they were when she was in Texas, and she'd traveled back home for her sister's wedding and planned to go back at Christmastime. Maybe by then she'd have some news to tell her folks, and they'd be a step closer toward filling that large house.

Her students finished with their arithmetic just as it was time for dismissal. "All right, class. That's all for today. Please make sure to practice your reading tonight, and if I've assigned you mathematics homework, please make sure you do that as well. I shall see you on Monday!"

Her students all rose from their seats and went about gathering their belongings, the older ones helping the younger ones into their coats as it was a chilly fall day. Hope waited for the last one to go and then began to straighten up her classroom, feeling blessed to have such wonderful students to teach.

She'd just finished sweeping the floor and gathering up her books and lunch pail when a familiar sound caught her attention, and she couldn't help but smile. A beautiful melody sailed in through the autumn air, and she began to sing along as he hummed. "I'll twine 'mid the ringlets of my raven black hair...."

"Good afternoon, Mrs. Lawless," Judah said, pausing his song as he stepped through the door.

Despite being his wife for over a year now, he still took her breath away, and the twinkle in his blue eyes let her know he still felt the same. "Good afternoon, Mr. Lawless. How is the construction site today?"

"Busy as ever. But I am done for the day, and ready to take you home for the weekend. I thought maybe we could do some apple picking tomorrow, maybe go for a horseback ride...." He moved closer to her, and Hope left her items on her desk and went to meet him.

"That sounds lovely. So long as I'm with you."

"Well, I had planned on accompanying you, if you don't mind."

"No, I don't mind at all," Hope replied as his arms wrapped around her. His breath was warm on her face, and she bit her lip, eager to have his mouth on hers.

"Good, 'cause you can't get rid of me now, Mrs. Lawless, no matter how hard you try."

"Good, 'cause I ain't tryin' to, " she replied, and Judah brought his lips down to hers, taking every last trace of her breath. She wrapped her arms around his neck, leaning into him. When he finally released her, they both smiled, thankful just to be together.

Judah began to sing again, twirling her around the front of the classroom, occasionally bumping into the students' desks, and Hope laughed, singing along in her high soprano. Following her dreams of adventure in the frontier hadn't been easy, but they'd led her here, and as her beloved spun her around in his strong arms, Hope was certain there was nowhere else in the world she'd rather be.

A NOTE FROM THE AUTHOR

Hi there!

I just wanted to say thank you so much for reading *Cordia's Hope: A Story of Love on the Frontier.* I hope that you enjoyed reading more about the Pike/Tucker family. *Cordia's Will: A Civil War Story of Love and Loss* was the first novel I ever started writing (though I finished *Deck of Cards* before I completed *Cordia's Will*) so it was a lot of fun to come back to these characters I've known for so many years. I'm debating about whether or not to continue this series. Perhaps a book about Faith Tucker is in order? If you have an opinion, please let me know in an email to authoridjohnson@gmail.com or leave your thoughts in a quick review where you purchased this book. Reviews are always appreciated!

If you like historical romance, please check out my other work, such as the Ghosts of Southampton series which revolves around a couple falling in love during the *Titanic* disaster. I also write Paranormal Romance, Contemporary Christian Romance, and dabble in a few other genres.

You can download several of my books for free just for signing up for my newsletter. *Leaving Ginny* and *Saving Cadence* are based on longer works, but you can also read *Transformation, So You Think Your Sister's a Vampire?* and *Melody's Christmas* by clicking the lengths.

Thanks again for choosing my book!

ALSO BY ID JOHNSON

Stand Alone Titles

Deck of Cards

(steamy romance)

The Doll Maker's Daughter at Christmas

(clean romance/historical)

Beneath the Inconstant Moon

(literary fiction/historical psychological thriller)

Pretty Little Monster

(young adult/suspense)

The Journey to Normal: Our Family's Life with Autism (*nonfiction*)

Forever Love series

(clean romance/historical)

Cordia's Will: A Civil War Story of Love and Loss

Cordia's Hope: A Story of Love on the Frontier

The Clandestine Saga series

(paranormal romance)

Transformation

Resurrection

Repercussion

Absolution

Illumination

Destruction

Annihilation

Obliteration

A Vampire Hunter's Tale (based on The Clandestine Saga)

(paranormal/alternate history)

Aaron

Jamie

Elliott

The Chronicles of Cassidy (based on The Clandestine Saga)

(young adult paranormal)

So You Think Your Sister's a Vampire Hunter?

Who Wants to Be a Vampire Hunter?

How Not to Be a Vampire Hunter

My Life As a Teenage Vampire Hunter

Vampire Hunting Isn't for Morons

Vampires Bite and Other Life Lessons

Ghosts of Southampton series

(historical romance)

Prelude

Titanic

Residuum

Heartwarming Holidays Sweet Romance series

(Christian/clean romance)

Melody's Christmas

Christmas Cocoa

Winter Woods

Waiting On Love

Shamrock Hearts

A Blossoming Spring Romance

Firecracker!

Falling in Love

Thankful for You

Melody's Christmas Wedding

The New Year's Date

Reaper's Hollow

(paranormal/urban fantasy)

Ruin's Lot

Ruin's Promise

Ruin's Legacy

Collections

Ghosts of Southampton Books 0-2

Reaper's Hollow Books 1-3

The Clandestine Saga Books 1-3

For updates, visit www.authoridjohnson.blogspot.com

Follow on Twitter @authoridjohnson

Find me on Facebook at www.facebook.com/IDJohnsonAuthor

Instagram: @authoridjohnson

Amazon: ID Johnson

Follow me on Bookbub: https://www.bookbub.com/authors/id-johnson